T0106031

Also by Justin Gustainis

The Hades Project
Black Magic Woman

EVIL WAYS

A MORRIS AND CHASTAIN
SUPERNATURAL INVESTIGATION

JUSTIN GUSTAINIS

SOLARIS

First published 2009 by Solaris
an imprint of Rebellion Publishing Ltd,
Riverside House, Osney Mead,
Oxford, OX1 0ES, UK

www.solarisbooks.com

ISBN: 978-1-84416-765-4

10 9 8 7 6 5 4 3 2 1

A CIP catalogue record for this book is available from the
British Library.

Designed & typeset by Rebellion Publishing
Printed in the US

In Memory of
Pat Grogan

Ursus Major has an extra star now,
that the scientists can't explain.

Sleep well, bear.

*"The children are far from safety; they shall
be crushed at the gate without a rescuer."*
Job 5:4

*"He said to me in a dreadful voice that I had
indeed
escaped his clutches, but he would capture me,
still."*
St. Teresa of Avila

*"How long, O Lord, how long will the wicked
triumph?"*
Psalms 94:3

PROLOGUE

The Middle East
April, 2003

Baghdad, Iraq
April 9th

The Americans were at the edge of the city, and in another day—two at the most—they would occupy it completely. Sporadic automatic weapons fire in the distance indicated that some remnants of Saddam's army (the fanatical Republican Guards, probably) were still either brave or foolish enough to offer resistance. The rest of Saddam's forces had either fled or made an abrupt return to civilian life, leaving their military careers in the dust, along with their uniforms. Most of the city's police had followed their example, reasoning correctly that trigger-happy Americans might not make fine distinctions between one kind of Iraqi uniform and another.

For the next few days, until the Americans established complete control, chaos would rule the city. The looting had already begun, and there was no one to stop it.

It was the day the five men had been waiting for.

They made their way through the narrow side streets and alleys of the Al-Salhiya district, at least fifty feet between them to avoid the attention that a

9

group walking together might draw. Each wore the dishdasha robe and checkered kaffiyeh headscarf common to lower middle-class Iraqis. Their garments were neither too clean nor too dirty. Their beards were neither too long nor too short. Every one of them could speak near-perfect Arabic with an authentic-sounding Iraqi accent. The weapons and tools they carried were mostly hidden under their clothing, although two of the men had the canvas carry-alls that many in Baghdad used the way Western college students use backpacks.

Their winding course finally brought them to the mouth of an alley directly across the street from the great, fortress-like building that houses the Iraqi National Museum. The ornate front doors were open wide, and through them, in both directions, poured a stream of men. Some appeared to be alone; others made up groups of three or four. Those entering the building were mostly empty-handed, but those leaving never were. Their arms were full with bowls, cups, swords, statuettes, and other artifacts from ancient Mesopotamian history.

The five men, out of sight within the alley, silently watched the looting for several minutes.

Finally, the team leader spoke, his voice just loud enough to be heard by the other four. Even so, he spoke Arabic. There was no reason to break character, and, in any case, this was not a good place to be overheard speaking English. "This is as good a time as we are likely to see," he said. "No one will notice us entering with that mob, and"—he glanced up, noting the position of the sun—"darkness will hide us when we are ready to leave. Questions?" The team leader's name was Miles Hawkins, although all of the identification he carried said he was Mohammed al-Sayeed, a carpenter from Rumallah.

Ten seconds passed in silence. "All right," Hawkins said, in Arabic. "Let's go." If he was tense, his voice failed to show it.

They crossed the wide street quickly, making no effort now to disguise the fact that they were together. They drew little attention as they passed through the doorway and went up a short flight of broad stairs into the museum proper. Hawkins turned left without hesitation, and the others followed. They could hear alarms going off throughout the building as various priceless treasures, some thousands of years old, were ripped from their supposedly secure exhibits.

The men passed quickly through two of the exhibit halls. In the third, they slipped through a side entrance into a hallway, which took them to an inconspicuous metal door that was marked, in Arabic, "Private. No admittance."

Hawkins looked at one of the men, a tall Russian whose name was Alex Scrodin. Scrodin immediately stepped forward, producing a stick of putty-like substance from under his robe. He began to break off chunks of it, which he then carefully molded to the door's three hinges, as well as the lock itself. Then he reached under his robe for the detonators.

The others didn't bother to watch Scrodin as he worked. Instead, their eyes moved restlessly around the corridor, searching. They didn't care about surveillance cameras, since there was almost certainly nobody manning the control center that such a camera would feed. Alarms didn't concern them, either. One more alarm amid the cacophony rising throughout the building would make no difference. The men were on the lookout for something more proactive that might have been put in place to protect a door this important—something lethal. But they saw nothing to give them cause for worry.

Three minutes later, Scrodin gave a small grunt, and backed away from the door. He was now holding a device about the size and shape of a garage door opener. He nodded at Hawkins, who made a sharp clicking sound with his tongue. Immediately, all the men began to move back the way they had come, down to the end of the corridor and around the corner.

Hawkins said, in Arabic, "Masks." Each man quickly donned a small, light, state-of-the-art gas mask that was said to be proof against any poison gas, nerve agent, or biowar aerosol known to science. Hawkins found himself hoping that the Iraqis hadn't concocted a deadly gas that modern science *hadn't* heard about.

The men dropped to the floor and lay flat, covering their ears. Scrodin looked toward Hawkins and, receiving a nod, placed his thumb on one of the electronic device's buttons, took in a breath, and pressed it.

The explosion was achingly loud in that confined space, but the damage it caused was focused and controlled, just as the men had intended. The heavy metal door, ripped free of its latch and hinges, lay flat on the corridor's floor, smoking slightly.

Beyond, the empty doorway yawned at them, a great black rectangle with no light showing behind it. The men were prepared for that, and had brought small but powerful flashlights. They got to their feet, plaster dust from the ceiling trickling down their robes to fall unnoticed on the floor. The gas masks stayed on.

At Hawkins's signal, they rapidly made their way, single-file, down the corridor and through the doorway, into the darkness and whatever awaited them there.

Two hours later, all of them were dead. Except one.

Istanbul, Turkey
April 11th

"He'll be here by six," Pardee said. "His train pulled in about five minutes ago, and I've been scrying him ever since. He wasn't followed as he left the station."

"Satisfactory," Walter Grobius said. It was the highest praise he ever gave. He was sitting on the suite's king-size bed, back against the headboard, and hadn't looked up from his laptop. Pardee wondered whether the old man was buying England, or merely selling France.

Pardee went over to one of the big windows and looked down. The penthouse of the Hotel Sultanhan afforded an excellent view of Istanbul's insane rush hour traffic, for what that was worth. "We could have picked him up when he crossed the border from Iraq two days ago," he said mildly. He was tall, and very thin—but there was nothing about him that looked frail.

Pardee was the only living person allowed to question Grobius's decisions, even obliquely.

"But then you couldn't have watched his progress

with your magic, to make sure that no one was interested in him." His voice had the rasp of a longtime smoker, although the old man had never touched tobacco in his life. "Plenty of people would love to get their hands on the Book, you know that. And it's only a matter of time before word gets out that it's been... liberated."

Pardee allowed himself a quick smile. "Yes, that should cause quite a stir, in certain circles."

"They can stir themselves into a frenzy, for all I care, once the thing is in my possession and secure."

Grobius put his laptop aside and looked up for the first time since Pardee had entered. The clear, sharp blue eyes were a startling contrast to his seamed, weathered face. "Besides, we have friends in Istanbul, in case there's trouble."

"People you've bought, you mean." There was no criticism implied. Not even Pardee would have dared go that far.

"What other kind of friend is there?" The old man's voice contained no irony—just a statement of cold fact. "Now, suppose you call room service and conjure us up some dinner. But first, hand me my medication. It's time for another dose."

Miles Hawkins, a battered old valise next to him, sat on a park bench, apparently at ease. He had chosen this bench with care—it was directly across Piyerloti Caddesi from the front entrance of the Hotel Sultanhan. Although looking toward the hotel, Hawkins was less interested in the former Ottoman palace's elegant marble façade than he was in the traffic around him, both pedestrian and motorized.

It was only one and a half kilometers from the train station to Istanbul's best hotel, and Hawkins had walked it, despite the heat. He'd wanted to stretch his legs after the long train trip—and, more importantly, wanted to see if he'd picked up any ticks. That would have been impossible to do in a taxi, especially in the rush hour traffic.

Hawkins had spent a number of years with MI6, Britain's Secret Intelligence Service, and "ticks" was the term by which Her Majesty's spooks referred to opposition surveillance. Now, after using every reflective surface he'd passed to unobtrusively check behind him, then spending ten minutes in the park vetting everything that moved, Hawkins was virtually certain that nobody was interested in him. The old man had insisted that he arrive clean, but Hawkins would have made sure, anyway. It was simply good tradecraft, even though that trade had changed considerably since his cloak and dagger days.

Without appearing to do so, Hawkins was watching the traffic patterns on Piyerloti, which had three lanes running each way. When he finally saw that a gap was about to develop, he rose in one smooth motion, grabbed the valise, and sprinted across the street. He'd cut it fine—as it was, a taxi nearly nailed him from one direction, and a blue Mercedes sedan from the other—but that was all right. If Hawkins barely made it, then someone on his tail would not make it at all. As he approached the hotel's big glass doors, Hawkins used their reflection to check behind him one last time. No one had tried to follow him from the park. He was clean.

Two minutes later, Hawkins stepped out of

the express elevator into the elegant foyer of the penthouse, and was immediately confronted by two large men in suits, Turks by the look of them. Hawkins stood still, spread his arms a little, and waited for the men to pat him down, which they did with a clinical thoroughness that paid no regard whatever to their subject's personal dignity. Hawkins bore this stoically—he had been there before, many times—but then one of them tried to take the valise from him.

Hawkins pulled it back roughly. "Uh-uh, mate. No way. This stays with me. Ask your boss, he'll tell you."

But the security man, who may or may not have understood English, was persistent. He reached for the valise again, while his companion moved in and grabbed Hawkins's other arm.

Eighteen seconds later, the door to the penthouse opened to reveal a tall, wiry man with a shaved head and black goatee. "I thought I heard a commotion," he said, taking in the carnage.

"Mister Pardee," Hawkins said with a nod, straightening his tie. The two security men lay strewn about the floor, not moving, one of them bleeding copiously from the mouth. "I'm sorry about that, but these gorillas—"

"It doesn't matter," Pardee said, and opened the door wide. "Come in, please." He didn't spare the security men a second glance.

Pardee brought Hawkins into the suite's master bedroom, where Grobius was again sitting up in the bed, pecking away on his computer. The shadows under the old man's eyes looked a little darker than nine months earlier, when Hawkins had last seen him.

"The prodigal is returned," Pardee said.

Grobius nodded. "But not, it would appear, empty-handed."

Hawkins hefted the valise slightly. "No, not at all. I've got what you want."

Grobius closed the laptop and set it aside. His hands trembled a little. They had not trembled nine months ago.

"And where are your colleagues, who took part in this adventure with you?"

Hawkins gestured toward one of the windows with his head. "Out there. Waiting for me to come out. And they know what to do, if I don't."

"Very wise of you, I'm sure," Grobius said. Pardee was standing a little behind Hawkins, so only Grobius saw the smile that briefly crossed the wizard's face.

Grobius pointed at the valise and said to Hawkins, "Show me."

Hawkins placed the valise on the bed, produced a key, and unlocked it. Then he carefully lifted out a bundle made of some ornately decorated cloth. "This tapestry, here, was in the same vault as the book," he said. "I needed something to wrap the thing in, so I figured this would do. I suppose it's valuable, considering where they were keeping it." With exaggerated care, Hawkins placed the bundle on the bed near Grobius's feet. "You can have it—no extra charge."

"How very kind." Grobius might have been thanking him for passing the salt at dinner. His eyes never left the bundle on the bed.

Hawkins finished unwrapping the tapestry, let it fall open, then stepped back.

Resting on the cloth was a thick volume bound in old, cracked leather. On the cover, faded but still legible, were several esoteric symbols and a few words in Arabic.

Pardee stepped forward and bent over the book. He studied the symbols on the cover carefully, and ran his long, thin fingers gently over them, several times. Then, with great care, he opened the book and carefully studied several pages apparently selected at random. Finally, he slowly closed the volume and looked up at Grobius.

"Oh, yes," he said, in the voice a man might use after fantastic sex. "It's genuine. Exactly what we wanted."

Grobius nodded. "Very well." Hawkins thought this was the first time he had heard genuine emotion coming from the old man. Grobius was staring at the book, and continued to do so until Hawkins finally felt obliged to cough gently.

Grobius blinked a couple of times, then looked up. "Well, I expect you'll be wanting your money."

"Yes, sir." Hawkins managed to keep most of the eagerness out of his voice.

Grobius reached for his laptop again and began working the keyboard. Less than a minute later, he pressed "Enter," watched the screen a moment longer, then shut the computer down.

"Duly transferred to your account in Barbados," he said to Hawkins. "Ten million dollars."

Hawkins reached into a pocket and pulled out his Blackberry. "You won't mind if I just confirm that, sir."

"You'd be a fool if you didn't."

It took less than thirty seconds with the device to

bring a wide grin to Hawkins's tanned face. "Very good, Mister Grobius. A pleasure doing business with you, sir."

"That works out to two million for each of you, assuming you're dividing it equally."

"Yes, sir."

"Is that what you're doing—dividing it equally?"

Hawkins looked at the old man. "No offense, Mister Grobius, but what do you care?"

"I care because it annoys me when people lie to me. And when they do, I want to know why."

Hawkins stated to speak, but the old man's hand slashed through the air like a blade, cutting him off.

"Spare me your protestations," Grobius said. "You've been under surveillance ever since you left Baghdad. You left alone, and you've been on your own ever since. I knew your little threat was empty as soon as you made it. The other men on your team are not lurking outside, ready to take revenge if something untoward should happen to you in here. So, *where are they?*"

Hawkins stared at Grobius for several seconds, wondering if it was worth trying to keep the bluff going. But then he sighed and said, "I wonder if I might trouble you for a drink of water."

At a nod from Grobius, Pardee glided off to the suite's kitchen. "Sit down," Grobius said, his tone less angry. Hawkins stepped over to a nearby armchair and sat down gingerly, as if he was expecting the thing to grow teeth and bite him.

Pardee returned and handed Hawkins a plastic bottle of Evian water. Hawkins cracked the top and took a long swig.

"I must apologize for deceiving you," he said to

Grobius. "I figured as long as you got what you wanted, the specifics of getting it didn't matter to you. And I don't much want to talk about what happened back in Baghdad."

"But you will," Grobius said. It was not a question.

"Yeah, all right." He twirled the bottle in his fingers for a moment. "It was in the museum that it all went to shit. We'd followed the blueprint you'd given us—worked a treat, too. Everything was just where it was supposed to be—including the door leading to the vaults underneath the building. We blew the door, no problem. Went down the stairs to the first vault and kept right on going past it. Same for the second. You'd said the book was in the third vault, so that's where we headed.

"Scrodin, the explosives bloke, blew the combination lock. Took more juice, that did, than the one upstairs, but he got it done. Then we pried the vault open."

Hawkins took another long draw from the bottle of water. Then he sat there a moment longer, as if hoping that someone would interrupt him. No one did.

"Way I figure it, they had some kind of state-of-the art nerve agent *inside the vault*, all ready to go. Saddam probably had his boffins make it up special. One of those 'weapons of mass destruction' that wanker Bush is always goin' on about. The stuff must have been under pressure, because it dispersed into the hall pretty damn quick once we'd got the vault door open."

"How do you know that?" Pardee asked him. "Nerve gas would surely have been invisible to the naked eye."

"I know that, because it killed every man on the team in the next ten seconds, before we even had time to get into the bloody vault."

"And you alone survived to tell the tale," Grobius said. He might have been discussing pork belly futures. "Why is that?"

"Because I kept my gas mask on, that's why. We'd all put them on upstairs, in case there was something wired to the hallway door. Nothing. It was stuffy underground, and the other guys took their masks off so they could breathe better. Hell, the only reason mine was still on was, I was so busy thinking out the next move that I forgot about it."

"Did you attempt to render assistance to your fallen comrades?" Grobius asked.

"Waste of time. The gas killed them in a few seconds. Nasty stuff, nerve gas, and works pretty damn quick. And I know dead men when I see 'em."

"No doubt," Grobius said. "So then…"

"So then I went into the vault, found your fuckin' book, wrapped it in that pretty tapestry there, and got the hell out. Sir."

Grobius nodded. "What about the bodies of the others?"

"What about 'em? I had the book, and that was the objective. I wasn't about to carry corpses out with me, even if I was able to, which I wasn't."

"That raises a security issue," Grobius said.

"No, it doesn't. Look, we were all dressed as locals, with first-class forged ID, along with a few other bits for credibility—letters from somebody's mother, an address book written in Arabic, stuff like that. Sure, their prints are on file someplace, most likely. The Iraqis might eventually get positive IDs from Interpol, if they push it. Or the Yanks, who I guess are in charge now. But so what? Job's done, mission accomplished, and all that. A whole lot of stuff got lifted from that museum. Nobody's going to get upset about some old book."

Grobius gave a grudging nod. "Possibly."

Hawkins scratched his unshaven chin. "You know, I read Arabic pretty well. Wouldn't have been much good for you on this job if I didn't."

Grobius just looked at him.

"I took a quick look through that little volume there, just to be sure I had the right one. The script's old, not the sort of Arabic they use nowadays. I couldn't make sense of most of what I saw. But the cover says it's the *Book of Shadows* by some bloke called Abdul Alhazred."

"Did you have some point you wished to make?" Grobius asked softly.

"Nah, it's just that that name rang kind of a bell, when I first saw it. Wasn't this Alhazred the one that wrote the *Necronomicon?*

"The *Necronomicon* is a myth," Pardee said. His right hand had found its way into his pocket. "Product of the fevered imagination of that pulp writer, Lovecraft. It never existed, nor did its putative author, this Alhazred. That's not an uncommon Arab name, you know."

Hawkins shrugged. "If you say so. But I've heard people talk about that *Necronomicon* sometimes, as if it was real."

"People talk about Atlantis, too, I understand," Pardee said with a tiny smile. "And Excalibur, as well as the Holy Grail. They aren't real, either."

"Yeah, you got a point there."

"There have been fakes of this *Necronomicon* over the years. But Mister Grobius doesn't purchase fakes, nor works written by *fictional* characters."

"Sure, no offense," Hawkins said. "Just asking."

"None taken, I'm sure," Pardee said. "Well, if that's everything... He looked toward Grobius, received a nod. "I'll just see you to the door, Mister Hawkins."

"Enjoy your money," Grobius said, in a voice that was expressionless as his face.

Pardee returned a few minutes later. "One of the Turkish guards is dead," he said. "They tried to take the case away from Mister Hawkins on his arrival, and he objected. Most efficiently, I may say."

"Make sure that the Turk's family gets enough money to keep them quiet." Grobius looked at the book resting at the foot of his bed. "I was beginning to think we would never get our hands on this."

"Those stories our people planted about weapons of mass destruction did the trick, as I predicted. Bush was just looking for an excuse. He should be grateful to us for providing one."

"I doubt he'll write us a thank-you note," the old man said, then looked up at Pardee. "And speaking of excuses..."

"Hawkins was lying, of course. I could see the deception rising from him like smoke. He killed the others, probably as soon as he was sure he'd found the book."

"Ruthless bastard," Grobius said, with what may have been a touch of admiration. "Greedy, too. Still, he's saved us a certain amount of trouble."

Pardee nodded. "He's left himself as the only loose end."

"Wait until he's well away from here to snip it off."

"Of course. I'll go see him tonight."

"Good. Now, have someone notify O'Rourke that I want the plane ready to fly out tomorrow morning at seven," Grobius said. "We're going home. There's a great deal to do."

Miles Hawkins got to bed a little after 2:00am. He'd found a room in a medium-priced hotel within sight of the Blue Mosque. Hawkins might be officially a wealthy man now, but the money was stuck in his Barbados account until morning. Tomorrow he could go to a bank, arrange a wire transfer of a half million or so, and then start spending it. Get a decent hotel room, for starters. Maybe even in that palace where Grobius and his trained cobra, Pardee, were staying. Then Hawkins remembered the security man he'd killed, and thought maybe another hotel would be a wiser choice.

He'd had enough wiggle room left on his Amex card to pay for this place, and enough ready cash to afford a bottle of good champagne and a medium-priced whore, who'd left half an hour ago. Well, at least the booze had been worth the price.

Hawkins downed the last mouthful of the champagne straight from the bottle, went into the tiny bathroom to take a piss, then crawled into the creaking bed. He hoped he wouldn't be sharing it with any of the local insect life, which was one reason he had chosen this place and not something more down-market. In the Middle East, the cheaper the hotel, the bigger the bugs.

Even though he was still charged up from the recent experience of becoming a multi-millionaire, fatigue, combined with the alcohol, soon prevailed. Hawkins fell into a deep sleep, and found that Pardee was waiting for him.

Hawkins was back in the vault under the Iraqi National Museum. He had just killed Scrodin, the last member of the team. Hawkins's pistol was effectively silenced, so the other three had died in the hallway without a lot of noise. They were all still half-deaf from the explosion that had blown the vault's door, anyway. The three in the hall had been easy to dispatch from behind, one quick shot each to the back of the head.

Scrodin had actually seemed surprised when he'd looked up from the glass case containing the book, to find Hawkins's pistol pointed at the middle of his forehead. But the surprise lasted only a second, and then Scrodin was sprawled on the floor, dead like the others.

So far, the dream was an accurate reflection of what had really happened. But then, as Hawkins was using the stolen tapestry to wrap around the Book of Shadows, *he heard a familiar voice say from the vault entrance, "Most efficiently done. My congratulations." Hawkins's head snapped up, and he saw that Grobius's man Pardee was standing in the doorway, grinning like the Cheshire Cat. In his dream, Hawkins was so dumbfounded that he never even tried to raise the gun.*

"You're quite the cold-blooded bastard, aren't you?" Pardee said conversationally as he approached Hawkins. "Quite the credit to Her Majesty's Secret Service. After four murders in as many minutes, I'll

wager your hand isn't even shaking."

Pardee was standing right in front of Hawkins now, and in his eyes Hawkins could see something that made him want to scream.

"Neither is mine. See?" Pardee held up his right hand, which was as steady as a boulder. But then, instead of lowering it, he plunged it straight into Hawkins's chest. Through the skin, the sternum, the fifth and sixth ribs, all the way to the heart. Yet there was no rent in Hawkins's flesh, no blood gushing from what should have been a terrible wound.

Pardee smiled, the way a shark seems to, just before it bites your leg off. *"Give my regards to your friends,"* he said. *"I'm sure they'll be eager to see you."* Then he squeezed—hard.

The hotel maid discovered Hawkins's body in the morning. Getting no response to her knocking, she'd let herself in to do the work she was paid for. Seeing Hawkins in the bed, she'd at first assumed he was asleep, and started to withdraw quietly. Then she'd gotten a look at his face.

The medical examiner's verdict, rendered two days later, was "death from cardiac arrest." Doctor Kerim hesitated briefly before signing the form that would officially close the book on this dead Briton's life. Clearly, the man's heart had stopped beating while he lay asleep. Equally obvious, there was no sign of external trauma to suggest that death had been anything other than natural.

And yet Doctor Kerim was troubled, a little. The man had been comparatively young, and very fit. What's more, his arteries had been almost clear of the cholesterol deposits that are usually associated with heart attacks. And the doctor had seen, over the years, many others who had died in their sleep. Their faces were usually blank, untroubled, as if death had come during the night and courteously declined even to wake them. Nothing in Dr. Kerim's experience allowed him to explain the expression of terror that had been stamped on the man's face when he'd been brought in.

Well, such mysteries were not Dr. Kerim's business to solve. He signed the death certificate, dropped the clipboard onto the corpse's chest, and rang for his assistant. It was time to forget about this death, and move on to the next.

I

GENESIS

Chapter 1

Quincey Morris stood alone in the shadows of a decaying eucalyptus tree and wondered if this was the night he was going to die.

Morris was not by nature a pessimist. Indeed, he had an innate faith in the ultimate power of good over evil. But thinking morbid thoughts before beginning a difficult job was his way of guarding against complacency, which was as dangerous to someone in Morris's line of work as it would be to a lion tamer or trapeze artist—with the same fatal results likely to follow.

Except in Morris's case, death might not be the end of it.

The house he was watching from 200 feet away was built in the Spanish Mission style that Morris always thought of as Southern California Tacky. The property was surrounded by a high concrete wall that would have done any movie star's home proud. But the man who lived there now was no movie star.

Bet he could be if he wanted to, Morris thought.

Horror movies, maybe. Jason and Freddie, watch out, 'cause the real thing's in town, now, y'all.

Morris had researched the subject, as he always did before carrying out one of these specialized home invasions. He knew that Lucas Fortner was an occultist of mid-level skill and above-average malevolence. He was said to have spent a year in Budapest, studying black magic under the infamous Janos Skorzeny. A year with Skorzeny made Fortner dangerous. Five years would have made him too deadly to mess around with.

In the moonlight, Morris could just make out the jagged bits of glass that had been set into the top of the stone wall. He knew that the glass was coated with viper venom (Black Mamba, supposedly) that was reapplied weekly—more often, during the rainy season—to keep its potency up.

Morris checked his watch and saw that it was just after 4:00am. Time to go. There were still two hours of darkness left to skulk in, but midnight was long enough past so that some of the Powers guarding Fortner's place would be at less than their full strength.

Morris would not have approached that house at midnight for all the gold in a rapper's teeth.

He patted his pockets to assure himself that all his gear was where it should be, then started across the street. He did not cross in a straight line, but angled to the left—a path that would take him to the property of Fortner's neighbor, a producer at DreamWorks Studios with absolutely no connection to the occult. Morris had checked. He always checked. He was a professional.

The producer's grounds were of interest to Morris

for a couple of reasons. One was that the exterior wall was considerably shorter than Fortner's, and free of broken glass, venom-coated or otherwise. The other reason involved an ancient oak tree on the property—the one that rose up tall and stately a mere ten feet from the wall separating the producer's grounds from Fortner's, with several of its branches overhanging Fortner's property.

Morris scaled the producer's wall with little difficulty, swung his legs over the top, and dropped lightly to the ground on the other side. He stood crouched among the plantings and flowers, all his senses alert. There were supposed to be no guard dogs on the property, and no human security either, but you never know these things for sure until you're on the scene. Morris spent the next two minutes absolutely still. He saw no movement except the flowers and shrubbery swaying in the gentle breeze, heard only the drone of crickets and cicadas, smelled nothing except for mimosa and sweet jasmine. Then he straightened slowly and began to make his careful way across the grounds.

As he approached the oak tree, Morris took from his pocket a gemstone, about the size and shape of an almond, that his witch friend Libby Chastain had given him. He stopped, held the stone in his open palm, and waited.

If Fortner had decided to hedge his bets by placing some kind of protective spell on his neighbor's trees, that gemstone would glow bright red.

The stone retained its pale blue color. The tree had not been ensorcelled.

Morris slipped on a pair of thin leather gloves to protect his hands, then began to shimmy up the trunk of the great oak. After ten feet or so, he was able to reach the lowest branches, which made his ascent easier. He continued climbing until he reached a branch that seemed thick enough to bear his weight. He crawled out about half its length, then hung from it with both hands, listening hard for the telltale *crack* that would betray weakness in the limb. But it held him without complaint.

This was important. The second worst thing that could happen tonight was for the branch to give way while Morris was on his way onto Fortner's property.

The worst thing would be for that branch to break while Morris was trying to get *out*.

Sitting on the branch now, with his back carefully braced against the trunk, Morris uncoiled from around his waist a twenty-foot length of rope. It was the kind of line that mountain climbers use, except that Morris's had been dyed jet black.

He crawled slowly along the branch, pausing every few seconds to listen for any sign that the thing was going to give under his weight.

Now he was just over the wall that stood between the producer's grounds and Fortner's. The deadly shards of broken glass grinned at him in the moonlight.

Three feet further, and Morris carefully tied one end of his rope around the branch, using the knots that he had practiced a hundred times while blindfolded.

From between the leaves, Morris could see Fortner's house, a sprawling, two-story structure. No lights burned in the windows, which was unsurprising. Fortner was away in San Francisco for three days, having left that very afternoon. Morris had watched him board the plane, and waited for it to take off, just in case. The man lived alone, which meant there should be no human presence in the house tonight.

Which did not mean, of course, that the place was unguarded.

Morris stayed on the branch for the next ten minutes, watching Fortner's house and grounds. Finally he decided that whatever might be protecting the property, he wasn't going to learn about it from the safety of the producer's tree.

Morris lowered the rope to the ground inside Fortner's wall. He twitched it a few times, to see if anything below would react to the movement. Nothing.

Wrapping his legs around the rope, Morris used his gloved hands to control the speed of his descent. A few seconds later, he was on the ground, watching and listening before moving on.

Morris was halfway to the house when he picked up movement out of the corner of his eye.

He froze, then slowly turned his head to get a better look. Whatever was out there, it was keeping to the shadows. And it was *big*.

Morris thought about some pictures he had seen in *People* or someplace about movie stars and their exotic taste in pets. One well-known actor had a leopard, shipped all the way from Africa. Another, who had played Tarzan in several films, was photographed next to the cage containing his pride and joy—a Bengal tiger. Some states had laws about that sort of thing—but not, apparently, California.

If members of the Hollywood crowd could get any

of the great predator cats, then presumably Fortner could, too.

The creature moved again, revealing a hint of black fur in the moonlight. A black panther? Fortner would probably enjoy the symbolism of such a sentry. And the damn thing would be dangerous, too. All leopards were formidable, whatever their color. And once they had tasted human flesh…

No, not a panther. It was closer now, and Morris could see that this thing had a short tail, its fur long and shaggy-looking. And it didn't move with a cat's fluid grace. Instead, it had the bouncing muscularity of a—dog?

That was all right. Morris could deal with dogs.

Hell of a big pooch, though, if that's what it was. It looked to be the size of a bull calf.

Then he saw the eyes. They were looking right at him, and they were glowing like hellfire.

Morris looked away instantly. Now he knew what he was dealing with.

Fortner had his grounds guarded by a Black Dog.

Those eyes were the creature's principal weapons. Some of the legends Morris had read claimed that locking eyes with a Black Dog would freeze you in place instantly, a helpless, living statue until dawn. Other accounts said that its gaze could strike a man blind, or speechless, or drive him instantly insane.

But you have to stare into its eyes for any of those things to happen. All the stories were in agreement on that. And after all, who wouldn't gape at such a horrific apparition?

Morris wouldn't, for one.

He closed his eyes tightly, then reached into the side pocket of his jacket, moving as if he were under water. Black Dogs usually relied on their basilisk gaze for both attack and defense, but Morris didn't want any sudden action of his to give this one an excuse to start acting like a real canine and tear his throat out.

He finally found what he wanted in his pocket. Morris removed the object carefully, then slowly went down on one knee. To make this work, he would need to be on the same level as the dog.

Morris could hear it now, drawing closer. He made himself wait, eyes still shut. He was only going to get one chance to make this work.

Now the thing was growling at him, softly, from a few yards away. It was preparing to attack.

In one smooth motion, Morris brought the small hand mirror up in front of his face, the reflective surface facing toward the Black Dog.

The creature's attention would be drawn by the movement, and it was probably looking at Morris's face now anyway, trying to work its mojo on him and wondering why he wasn't screaming, or running away, or doing whatever its victims usually did.

But now the dog's magical gaze was being turned back on itself by the mirror.

The growling stopped suddenly, as if cut off by a switch. There was a brief whimper, then—nothing.

Morris made himself wait for the length of ten breaths, then risked a look.

The dog was frozen in a crouch, as if it had been preparing to spring. The red and yellow light was gone from its eyes, and it made no sound as Morris stood and put the mirror away.

The Black Dog was now no more dangerous than any other lawn statue—at least until dawn.

He could have destroyed the thing, now that it was helpless, but that would have been petty. He was a professional, not some teenage vandal.

And anyway, if Morris were not out of there by sunrise, he would have bigger problems than Poochie to worry about.

A minute later, he was searching the house's exterior for the best way in. He had studied the original architect's plans, as well as photos taken from a distance with a telephoto lens. But Morris had a finely developed sense for these things that no image on paper could ever replace.

After a quick but cautious circuit of the place, he decided on the front door. Fortner might well expect any intruder to use a window or one of the auxiliary doors, and would thus concentrate more of his protective energies toward those access points.

Unless, of course, that's what Fortner figured I'd think, in which case the front door is going to have all the heavy artillery trained on it. Which means I'll be blued, screwed, and tattooed.

Morris shook his head impatiently at his own dithering. You could make yourself crazy trying to second-guess someone like Fortner. Sometimes you had to go with your instincts, and Morris's were telling him that the front door was the best bet.

He checked the front steps for traps or tricks, and found none. Then he spent the better part of a minute regarding the door with affection and good will. It might not matter, but he wanted there to be a good karmic relationship between himself and the door before he touched it. It pays never to take inanimate objects for granted.

As doors go, it was nothing special, considering the

ostentatious grandeur of the house. No glass in it, of course. Morris was never that lucky. Solid wood, walnut maybe, carved into a series of panels. The knob was plain brass, and the lock was complicated-looking and intimidating—or it would be, to anyone with less experience than Quincey Morris.

He produced the almond-shaped gem again, and passed it slowly over the doorframe, the door itself, and the lock. The stone did not glow red, which meant no magic was being used to protect the door.

Morris scratched his chin reflectively.

Did Fortner leave the door deliberately unguarded, so as to lull the unsuspecting intruder?

He just might, the bastard. You get through the door without breaking a sweat, then stroll inside humming to yourself, only to have an anvil dropped on your stupid head.

Or maybe…

Morris brought out a pencil flashlight and moved its narrow beam around the doorframe, very slowly.

And there it was—the faint bulge under the paint.

Just because Fortner had sorcery at his disposal didn't mean he had to forgo more mundane protections. And now Morris had spotted the wire for the alarm system.

You open the door, you interrupt the circuit, and all hell breaks loose. Morris didn't know whether the alarm would set off a klaxon horn, ring up the nearest police station, or trigger one of Fortner's nastier occult surprises. And he wasn't interested in finding out.

With a sharp knife Morris gouged into the doorframe about a foot above the knob, exposing the blue wire that he knew he would find there. Then, with a pair of insulated pliers, he clipped the wire, disabling the alarm.

The lock itself was relatively easy. Morris didn't even need the magically charged lock picks that Libby had made for him.

He turned the knob and, standing well off to one side of the entranceway, gently pushed the door open.

The darkness and silence within seemed to mock him.

He shined his light inside, revealing the long hallway that the blueprints said would be there. Several pieces of furniture were visible along the walls on either side—brittle-looking antiques in what appeared to be French Provincial. Fortner was said to be a connoisseur.

Spanish Mission architecture with French Provincial furniture. Some connoisseur.

Morris was three-quarters along the hallway when he felt a floorboard give imperceptibly under his foot. This was followed an instant later by the sound of wood moving against wood overhead.

Morris dropped at once to one knee, a posture that would allow him to run, dodge, or roll as needed. Then something flashed above his head from left to right, something long and black and sinuous that appeared to be suspended somehow from the ceiling. It struck the wall with a soft thud and rebounded, swinging back to the left.

When the dangling, wriggling shape bounced off the opposite wall, Morris was ready. He shot out a gloved hand, trying to grasp it a few inches from the end, just behind where the head would be, if his guess was right. Quincey Morris hated snakes.

Black Mamba venom on the glass shards outside. Bastard Fortner has to get it from somewhere. The Black Mamba, deadliest snake in Africa, maybe in the whole world. Jesus Christ, better not miss—

It was made of rubber.

Morris had held on to a few real snakes in his time, very reluctantly. The feel of a live reptile struggling against your grip, fighting to get free so that it can kill you, is something you don't forget. This thing he was holding now was utterly inert. It was not alive, nor had it ever been.

He stood, and examined his prize in the flashlight's narrow beam.

The black rubber snake, about three feet long, was suspended by a cord from a square hole that had opened in the ceiling. The floorboard must have been the trigger for the mechanism that would drop the toy reptile. Gravity and the length of the cord would send it swinging at eye level for a standing man of average height. The thing would be practically right in your face.

And what the hell was the point of that?

The rubber snake would certainly startle an intruder—God knows it had startled the shit out of Morris—but it wouldn't stop one. Nobody who had gotten this far would be likely to run away screaming just because of a toy on a string.

There had to be something more.

All right, you're creeping down this hallway like a good little burglar, you trip the mechanism, the rubber snake drops down and damn near scares you to death—then what do you do?

Your anger and residual adrenalin might cause you

41

to yank the cord in frustration, intending to tear it loose and toss the snake as far as you can throw it.

Morris sent his flashlight beam up toward the opening in the ceiling where the cord was attached. He couldn't see what the cord was tied to up there, but he thought there was a good chance that pulling hard on that length of twine might have very unpleasant consequences.

Note to self: leave the damn cord alone.

But what if you weren't the kind of person to let your temper get the better of you? What would Fortner have in store for you then?

If you didn't have Morris's presence of mind to drop down at the sound of the ceiling trap opening… then the next thing you'd know would be that there was a damn snake right in front of your face. Instinct would be to do—what?

Dodge aside, either left or right.

There was furniture here, on both sides of the narrow hall—an antique writing desk on the left, and opposite, some kind of occasional table.

So you dodge aside, right into the furniture. And then what happens?

Morris took from a pocket a thin metal tube about six inches long. Then he grasped one end and pulled, and the tube stretched to a length of four feet, which is what car radio antennas are supposed to do. Morris wasn't interested in receiving any radio signals, but he'd thought the device might have other uses.

Standing as far away as the extended aerial would allow him, Morris held one end and used the other to gently tap the side of the writing desk.

Nothing.

Morris frowned in the semi-darkness, then drew the aerial back and tapped a little harder.

Still *nada*.

He was probably just being paranoid. But he needed to know for sure, in case he had to come back this way in a hurry. It probably wouldn't hurt to give the writing desk another, slightly more forceful *tap*—and ten razor-sharp blades slid out of hidden recesses in the desk, glinting in the thin beam of Morris's pencil flash.

Morris went over for a closer look. The blades were only four inches long, but they gleamed wetly in the light, each one having been coated with some viscous liquid.

Trying to avoid the fake snake, you blunder into the furniture and get a shot of real snake venom for your trouble. Well, they said Fortner had a complicated mind.

Of course, there was no way to predict whether the unsuspecting intruder would dodge to the left or right. Which meant...

Morris gave the occasional table on the opposite wall a medium-hard rap with his aerial, and was utterly unamazed to see a similar set of blades spring out from their hiding places in the innocent-looking antique.

Note to self: don't bump into the furniture, podner. It just ain't healthy.

He continued down the hallway slowly, carefully, ready to react if another floorboard should move under his weight. But none did.

The hall formed a junction with a perpendicular corridor, and Morris knew enough to turn right, just as he knew the second room on the left was the one he wanted.

Fortner's workroom, where all the fun took place.

The door to the chamber where Fortner performed his black magic rituals was open, and for about three-tenths of a second Morris was relieved about having one less lock to deal with. Then common sense reasserted itself.

This was the most important room in the house. It didn't matter if Fortner had a million bucks in cash and the Koh-i-noor diamond stashed in his bedroom—this was the place that really mattered to him.

Why wasn't this room locked up tighter than Donald Trump's piggy bank?

Fortner may have been running late when he left. After all, he'd had a plane to catch. Maybe the man just forgot.

He puts snake venom on his walls, conjures up a Black Dog to guard the grounds, booby traps the hallway, then goes off and forgets to lock up the room that's the main reason for it all?

A small smile appeared on Morris's thin face. *Not too likely, I reckon.*

Morris produced the almond-shaped gem yet a third time. As soon as he held it within a foot of the doorway, the stone began to glow red as a stoplight—and for Morris, the message was the same: *stop right there, if you know what's good for you.* The doorway had a spell on it.

Morris used his aerial to probe the floorboards in front of Fortner's workroom. They were all completely solid. He carefully checked both the floor and the ceiling for the telltale edges of a trap door or deadfall. Nothing.

Standing off to one side, he gingerly broke the plane of the doorway with the aerial's tip. No reaction. He waved the aerial around the doorway—slowly at first, then faster.

Zippo.

Could be the stone was responding to the general aura of black magic attached to the room, rather than to the entrance itself. Sure, that's probably it.

Morris was about to walk through the doorway when a thought occurred to him.

He took a step back and brought out a small pocketknife. Pushing one sleeve back, he jabbed his forearm with the tip of the blade—just enough to produce a few drops of blood.

He smeared the blood over the rounded tip of the aerial, then slowly extended it toward the doorway again.

The instant the bloody tip crossed the threshold, there was a blur of movement in the doorway, a sharp *crack*, and the aerial was almost torn from Morris's grip by the force of a blow that left his fingers tingling.

He withdrew the aerial and examined it in the beam of his flashlight. The metal tip had been sheared completely off, as cleanly as if cut by pliers.

Morris looked at the doorframe. A steel blade, about three inches wide and running the entire height of the doorway, was now imbedded in the right side of the frame.

He wondered if Fortner was thorough enough to cover his bets both ways. Morris drew a few more drops of blood from his arm and repeated the intrusion.

This time, a blade concealed in the bottom of the doorframe flashed upward, too fast for the eye to see, and buried itself in the top of the structure. Another two inches was gone from the end of the aerial.

Morris felt his testicles retract involuntarily. If he had been stepping over the threshold at the moment that thing was set off…

Morris tried a third time. No reaction. He brought out the almond-shaped stone. No color change now.

He walked carefully into Fortner's workroom, alert for any other protections the man might have installed, whether occult or mundane. His flashlight revealed the large pentagram drawn on the floor with squat unlit candles at each of the five points, the magical swords and rods in a rack on the wall, the tapestries covered with occult symbols. No surprises there.

The large sink against one wall was a bit unusual, in Morris's experience. He shined his light in there, saw nothing except a lot of brown stains coating the porcelain. *Fortner should get himself some scouring powder, or something.*

There was a large worktable set against the wall opposite from the sink, covered with books and papers. Several tiers of shelves, bearing an assortment of jars, bottles, and vials, occupied the wall above it. Morris decided to start his search with the table.

Luck was with him. It only took a few minutes to find the large envelope with "Carteret" scrawled on the front. Inside were several smaller envelopes. One was labeled "hair," another "fingernail clippings," another "handwriting," and still another read "photos"—everything you'd need to cast a devastating black spell on somebody. Somebody like Morris's client. Well, Roy Carteret need have no more worries. Fortner would not be using these ingredients to work any hocus-pocus on him.

Morris had been holding the pencil flashlight between his teeth so as to leave both hands free as he riffled through the items on the table. But now he straightened up, which meant the flashlight clenched in his jaws was pointing straight ahead, at the lowest row of shelves.

Morris was busy thinking about his way out, and wasn't interested in whatever else Fortner might keep in his little sanctum, since he wasn't being paid to mess with it. He turned away and was taking his first step toward the door when what he had just seen finally registered on his conscious mind.

He turned back slowly, hoping that he had been mistaken. He directed the flashlight beam once again toward the lowest shelf, and the row of jars that rested on it.

He had not been mistaken.

Each jar contained a heart, floating in some kind of clear liquid.

Morris knew enough anatomy to realize that he was not looking at the hearts of pigs, or calves, or some other animal.

They were human hearts.

And they were small, each of them. Far too small to have come from adults.

They were the hearts of children.

Morris had been in Los Angeles for just over a week, casing the house and grounds and keeping an eye on Fortner's movements. Local TV news, as well as the *L.A. Times*, had featured several stories about the children who had gone missing over the last few months, with no clues to suggest what might have become of them. The police were said to be "following several promising leads," which Morris had recognized for the bullshit that it was.

The most recent disappearance had been reported a week ago, shortly after Morris had arrived in town. The *Times* said that this was the eighth case in the last five months.

There were eight identical jars on Fortner's shelf.

Morris knew that the practice of black magic sometimes involved the use of human body parts, and that some of the more arcane rituals specifically called for the organs of children. He had recently met a South African cop back East who'd been on the trail of a black magician who was murdering kids for their organs.

Morris didn't know what Fortner had in mind, but it must be something really nasty to require this kind of raw material, and in such a quantity.

Not my business, no sir. I've got what I came for. All I need to worry about is getting out of here in one piece, giving this stuff to Carteret, and collecting my money.

He directed the flashlight beam slowly around the room, taking in the tools of the black magician's trade—the grimoires, scrolls, pacts, magical ingredients, and various arcane devices.

It must have taken Fortner years to get all this stuff together. Decades, more likely.

The tools, Morris knew, had been made by Fortner himself. A magician's equipment must be attuned to him, and to him alone. It was a long, laborious process.

The flashlight revealed more mundane materials, too. Some of the shelves contained jars of ordinary chemicals, like magnesium, phosphorus, and sulfuric acid. There were large bottles of alcohol, used in some purification rituals. Morris even spied a box of Blue Angel wooden matches, presumably for lighting the candles, alcohol lamps, and incense burners.

I'm wasting time. Whatever Fortner is up to, it's no business of mine. I'm a professional. Get in, get the goods, and get out again. That's what I'm damn well paid for.

Morris supposed he could inform the police about Fortner. After all, they were eager for information about the child abductions.

Oh, sure. Absolutely. *"Excuse me, officer, but I was burglarizin' this fella's house the other night, and I came upon something you might be interested in. Oh, and did I mention that he's a practitioner of black magic, who's been stealing the kids to use their hearts in his wicked rituals?"*

He'd be lucky if they only laughed at him. A spell in jail or in the local loony bin would be more likely. And an anonymous call would most likely just be filed in the "nut" drawer.

No, there was nothing he could do about Fortner or his little projects. "Let sleeping dogs lie" was good advice, especially when the dog in question was a black magician who did not stint at murder.

It was a professional's attitude, and Morris was, above all else, a professional.

He sent the flashlight beam around the room one last time. *Ain't none of my damn business, anyway.*

Ten minutes later, Morris was shimmying up the rope that he had tied to the producer's tree. He had encountered no further interference on his way out of Fortner's house, or across the grounds.

He reached the branch to which he had secured the rope, grasped it, and quickly hoisted himself up into the tree. Then he unknotted the rope, drew it up, and wound it back around his waist.

Before starting his descent into the producer's property, Morris spared a final glance toward Fortner's house, where the flames were just now becoming visible in the windows, flickering like the eyes of a madman.

Morris nodded, once. Then he turned away and began his careful climb down the tree. He wanted to be well away before any fire trucks showed up.

Morris was a professional. But that was not the only thing he was.

It was just after dawn when Quincey Morris got back to his room at the Beverly Wilshire, and found that the FBI was waiting for him.

Chapter 2

Libby Chastain, white witch *extraordinaire*, was naked, wet, and horny.

The first two conditions were due to the fact that she was in the shower. The third stemmed from her break-up, a week ago, with her lover, Nancy Randall.

"I don't see why you won't do a threeway with me and Mike," Nancy had kept saying. "I mean, you told me you like guys, and I *know* you like girls. Come on, Libby, have some *fun*." Mike was Nancy's former boyfriend, and Libby had begun to suspect that he wasn't as "former" as she'd supposed.

"Being bi doesn't make me a skank, Nancy," Libby had told her. "Threeways, fourways, moreways—as one of my favorite TV characters used to say, *Homey don't play dat*."

But Nancy wouldn't leave it alone. Finally, Libby'd had enough, and told Nancy to pack her stuff and leave. *Just as well. She probably wouldn't have quit until she had us as the main attraction in one of those Tijuana sex shows—just me, Nancy, two dwarves, and a burro.*

Libby didn't regret her decision, but a week of celibacy was starting to take its toll on her ability to concentrate. Consequently, she was giving serious thought to using the shower massage gadget for a purpose its manufacturers had never intended. *Then again, maybe they did.*

She was reaching for the nozzle when she heard, very faintly, a sound made by the people who had come to kill her.

She didn't know for certain that they had lethal intent, but the magical wards on her condo's door and windows would have stopped an everyday crack addict or rapist, as well as raising one hell of a ruckus. The fact that Libby had heard nothing meant that whoever was out there had sufficient magical know-how to overcome her protections—and in near-silence, besides. People with that kind of skill don't just stop by to borrow a cup of sugar.

It might be coincidence that they had caught Libby at her most vulnerable, but she doubted it. She sensed a malign intelligence behind this invasion, and its agents were probably going to take her life in the next few seconds unless she found something to do about it *right now*.

All the rooms of the condo were charged with magical energy; some of this was deliberate on Libby's part, and the rest simply stemmed from the fact that she lived and practiced magic there. As a result, she could work some basic spells in her home without the equipment and materials that she would need to make them viable elsewhere. Libby quickly whispered the words of a simple levitation spell, and a few moments later found herself floating gently upward until her body was stopped by the high ceiling, her naked back pressed lightly against the textured paint. That would buy a few seconds when the killers came for her, but no more.

Libby darted her gaze around the room, seeking something, *anything*, that could be used in her defense. But she found no inspiration in the towels, shampoo, cosmetics, and other paraphernalia that occupy a modern woman's bathroom. Libby found herself shivering, even though the water in the shower had been running warm verging on hot when she'd left it a few moments ago.

Water.

Libby heard someone try the bathroom door quietly, only to find that it was locked. Most people don't bother to lock their bathroom doors when home alone, but Libby had gotten into the habit during the seven months that Nancy had stayed with her. If the bathroom door was left unlocked while Libby showered, she could usually count on a naked Nancy slipping in there with her, in hopes of starting something. It had been fun and exciting the first few times, but Libby usually took a shower in order to get clean, not to be groped by a sex maniac, even a friendly one.

The locked door gave Libby enough time to chant, softly but very fast, a conjuration spell that she hadn't used in years. She hoped that she still remembered it correctly, and apparently she did, because in the stream of the shower below her, a shape began to appear. The shape was female in form but smaller than a human woman, and it appeared to be made of water. The creature spread its liquid hands and looked upward toward Libby. *Why have you called me?* a mellifluous female voice said, inside Libby's mind. *Do you want to play a game?*

Water sprites, like most of the fey, are gentle, playful creatures.

Unless they are attacked.

The bathroom door burst open in response to a hefty kick, and two men stumbled in, each holding some kind of automatic weapon with a sound-suppressed barrel. Amped up with adrenaline and the urge to kill, the men opened up at the first human-looking form they saw. Their bullets passed harmlessly through the water sprite and buried themselves in the tile of Libby's bathroom.

Which is not to say that no harm was done.

After firing one long burst apiece, the men stood gaping at the translucent fairy that was occupying the shower stall. But they did not stand there long.

With a screech of rage that only Libby Chastain could hear, the water sprite flung itself at the two hit men. But the watery form did not soak them. Instead it quickly divided in two, each half forming a long thin stream—that instantly shot up each man's nose.

The streams went on and on, drawing substance from Libby's still-running shower. The men staggered back into Libby's living room, dropping their weapons as each desperately tried to draw a breath that contained air, and not water.

Libby allowed herself to drift slowly down from the ceiling. Once her feet were solidly on the floor, she grabbed a bath towel and began quickly to dry herself. But she did not turn the shower off.

Although white magic cannot be used to harm

people, it does not prevent evil people from, essentially, harming themselves. Libby did not think that her practitioner's oath required her to save people who had just tried to kill her. In any case, if she tried to interfere with the water sprite's vengeance, it might well turn on *her*. Libby had no desire to share the fate of the two killers who were now, she was sure, in the process of drowning while on dry land.

She was not looking forward to seeing what would be lying on her living room floor, but Libby knew she would have to go out there sooner or later, and sooner would be better.

She had telephone calls to make.

The man from the FBI was a compact, wiry-looking black man who had placed one of the room's easy chairs so that it faced the doorway. He sat there as Morris came in, both hands conspicuously in sight, one of them holding open the small leather case that contained his badge and ID card.

Morris stood in the doorway, very still, then took a slow step into the room, and let the door swing shut behind him. He glanced over his shoulder to see if anyone was standing behind the door. He thought those kinds of adolescent shenanigans might still be in the FBI's playbook, but the man with the badge seemed to be alone.

He stood up and took a couple of steps toward Morris, still holding out the ID folder, as if he thought Morris would want to examine it. "Special Agent Fenton, FBI," he said. "Although I guess you figured out that last part already."

Morris was still holding his room's card key. Now

he put it back in his pocket, his movements slow and careful. Some of these guys were always waiting for an excuse to show off one of the fancy moves they'd learned at Quantico—or worse, demonstrate just how fast they were on the draw. Morris had no desire to have his liver ventilated by a 9mm slug because some Fed overreacted to an innocuous movement.

"To what do I owe the pleasure, Agent Fenton?" Morris said evenly.

"Answering that one is gonna take us a while. Maybe we should both sit down."

Morris didn't move immediately. "Am I under arrest?"

"No, you're not," Fenton said, sitting down again "Yet."

Morris looked at him for a moment longer, then moved to sit down himself. There was another armchair in the room, but he chose the side of the king-size bed. In the unlikely event that things got physical, Morris figured he could get off the bed and into action a lot faster than someone sunk into a big, overstuffed chair.

"You know," Morris said, "I do have an office in Austin. No secretary, but there's an answering service that makes appointments, and they're pretty reliable. All you had to do was call."

"I'm aware of that," Fenton said. "Thing is, this can't wait, and I had no way of knowing when you'd be coming back. I mean, you have to go see Carteret first, don't you? Or were you just planning on a phone call to let him know that the job was done?"

Despite himself, Morris blinked a couple of times. "I'd sure be interested in knowing how you got a warrant to tap my phone," he said. "Or did you just decide that I was a terrorist, and skip the warrant entirely, probable cause be damned?"

Fenton gave him a satisfied-looking smile. "We didn't tap your phone, as a matter of fact," he said. "But we *were* able to get a warrant to look at some records. Your phone calls, both sent and received, for instance. And your bank records, which showed a recent wire transfer to your account from one James Tiberius Carteret. Southwest Airlines confirmed your booking of a flight to Los Angeles shortly thereafter. I was interested to see that you bought a one-way ticket. Didn't quite know when you were coming home, did you?"

"Maybe I was hoping to meet some honey over on Rodeo Drive," Morris said. "Hook up with her and spend a week at her place in Palm Springs, playing house the way the rich folks do. You ever think of that?"

Fenton ignored the sarcasm. "You were under surveillance from the moment you deplaned in L.A., of course. We noticed your intense interest in a certain residence on Mulholland Drive—which is currently the subject of a three-alarm fire, I understand."

"That right?" Morris said. There was no expression in either his face or voice.

"Yep. It's quite a conflagration, they tell me. Just a second." Fenton produced a complicated-looking phone, opened it, and began to use his thumbs on the keyboard. Then he waited about half a minute, looked at the screen again, and put the thing away. "Don't worry, looks like they've got it contained. It won't spread to the rest of the neighborhood, most likely."

"I'm sure that's good news for a number of people."

"It surely is. 'Course, arson isn't a federal crime, unless you burn down some federal property, and Mister Fortner's place certainly doesn't qualify. Interesting fella, that Fortner. Did you know he spent a year with Skorzeny, back in the Eighties?"

There was silence in the room then, broken only by the distant sounds of rush hour traffic nine floors below. It went on for a while, until Morris broke it.

"You're an interesting sort of FBI agent," he said. "Did you say you were with the L.A. field office?"

"No, I didn't, because I'm not. I'm with the Behavioral Science Unit at Quantico."

Morris nodded, as if this didn't surprise him. "Behavioral Science. Well, now. I used to know somebody, worked for your outfit years ago, fella name of Will Graham."

"Before my time," Fenton said.

"Uh-huh, I expect it was. So what does Behavioral Science want with me? I'm not a serial killer, and I don't chase them down, either."

"I know the first part of that's true, but I'm not too sure about the second."

"Not sure I follow you, podner."

"What I mean is, you've been involved from time to time with people who were suspected of a variety of crimes, including serial murder."

"I don't associate with criminals, Agent Fenton. Given the choice, I don't associate with FBI agents, either."

"Just as well I didn't give you a choice, then." Fenton stood up, but not like he was in any hurry about it. "You mind if I take my jacket off? I've had

60

it on all night, and I'd like to feel the full benefit of the air conditioning in here."

"Be my guest."

Fenton slowly removed the jacket of a gray suit that, Morris estimated, must have cost him the better part of a month's salary. Once the suit coat was off, Morris could see Fenton's sidearm—some kind of plastic automatic, like a Glock or Sig Sauer, worn in a holster just behind the right hip. Morris wondered if Fenton was displaying the hardware for intimidation purposes, but decided that guys from Behavioral Science were a little more subtle than that. At least, he hoped they were.

Fenton placed his carefully folded jacket on top of the room's writing desk and sat back down.

"I didn't mean to suggest that you hung around with serial killers, Morris. But you've had dealings with a few, I know that for certain. There was Edmund Zaleznik, for instance. Remember him? St. Louis?"

Morris replied with a noncommittal grunt.

"Zaleznik, way I understand it, was supposed to be some kind of a wizard. Hired himself out to the St. Louis mob, as sort of a collection agent. He wouldn't actually do the collecting himself, of course. But if one of the local loan sharks, or maybe a bookie, had a guy who owed a lot of money and refused to pay, they'd give the poor bastard one more chance, while mentioning that something *real* bad was going to happen if he didn't come up with the cash in, say, forty-eight hours. And if he still didn't pay, then something bad *would* happen. Something nasty, painful, and fatal. Sometimes it would involve the whole family. That was Zaleznik's job, to make it happen. That makes him a serial killer, in my book."

Morris had sat up a little straighter. "A wizard, you say."

"Yeah, not first-class or anything. But certainly capable of working basic black magic. Enough to harm quite a number of people. Until somebody sent you after him."

"I wouldn't have thought the word 'wizard' gets used a lot, down there in Quantico," Morris said slowly. "Not a real scientific term, like *psychopath*, or *paranoid schizophrenic*."

Fenton sat there looking at him for a bit, before finally saying, "How's that friend of yours, Libby Chastain?"

It was Morris's turn to sit and stare. Then he said, "Libby's fine—or she was last week, when we spoke on the phone. Do you two know each other?"

"No, not personally. But we have a mutual friend: Garth Van Dreenan."

"The South African cop."

"That's the guy."

"Works for the Occult Crimes Unit over there."

"Yep. You know him?"

"We met once, a while back. Seemed like a nice enough fella." Morris snapped his fingers. "Fenton. I thought that name rang a bell. You and Garth were working those child murders, the ones where the poor kids' organs were removed while they were still alive."

"Yeah, that was our case."

"I was kind of busy at the time, but I heard later that you solved it, the two of you."

"Solved?" Fenton suddenly looked tired. "Well,

there was a resolution, anyway. Maybe even some justice, I don't know."

"What the hell *are* you, Fenton? And don't keep saying 'Behavioral Science.' Guys from Quantico don't use words like 'wizard' and 'black magic.' Not with a straight face, they don't." Morris shook his head impatiently. "Who are you really with? The damn X-Files?"

"The X-Files Unit does not exist, and has never existed," Fenton said, as if quoting somebody. "It is a myth, perpetrated by rumor and popular culture. The Federal Bureau of Investigation investigates crimes against the United States committed by living, breathing people, and does not acknowledge the existence of the so-called *paranormal*."

"Okay, I gotcha," Morris told him. "Now, what's the real story?"

Fenton ran a hand over his face. "Look, Morris, until fairly recently, I was a normal FBI agent—well, as normal as Behavioral Science gets. There are people in the Bureau, you know, who figure that, to investigate and apprehend psychopaths, you've got to be a little nutty yourself."

"Yeah, I've heard that one," Morris said. "All that 'gaze into the abyss' stuff, right?"

"'He who fights monsters must take care that he does not himself become a monster. For when you look deeply into the abyss, the abyss is also looking into you.' Old Fred Nietzsche, damn his soul."

"I can see you've given this some thought."

"Hell, yeah. Therapy and everything. And, you know, I never thought I'd find myself quoting that racist bastard George Wallace, but he did say one thing once that I kinda like: 'I got me a piece of paper says I'm not crazy—what've you got?'"

"Okay, you're not crazy," Morris said. "Duly stipulated."

"Well, last year they assigned me to work this series of child murders. The signature was pretty distinct, and as soon as the perp appeared to have crossed state lines, the Bureau was sent in. Or, more precisely, I was, since my partner had retired and I was working solo for a while."

Morris nodded. "Prepubescent kids, abducted, murdered outdoors near water, organs removed before death. Garth told me about it, that time I met him."

"Okay, so you know there were definitely ritualistic elements to the crimes. I was doing my job as best I could, liaising with local law, working up a profile, all that. But then the newspapers got hold of it. You can imagine the stories."

"Hell, I even remember one of them: 'Cannibal Killer Strikes Again.'"

"Fuck, yeah. Even though there was no evidence that any of the organs were consumed by the perp. But that kind of crap got people excited, especially in the states were the kids had been killed. So they started bugging their reps in Congress, which means pressure on the Bureau."

"Pressure on Behavioral Science, you mean."

"You got it. So my boss had this bright idea of calling in a 'consultant' from overseas."

"And that was Garth. All the way from South Africa."

"And over my objections. I'd never even heard of this Occult Crimes Unit, and didn't see what good a fucking consultant was going to do the investigation, anyway. But my boss wanted to be seen doing something above and beyond the usual investigative routine, and maybe shut the damn politicians up for a while."

"Uh-huh. And you're telling me all this why, exactly?"

"Because during the course of that investigation, I saw some stuff that shook my assumptions about the way the world is, about what kind of shit really goes on, sometimes."

"Black magic, you mean," Morris said.

"Yeah, and the other kind, too—white magic, the kind your girlfriend practices."

"Libby's not my girlfriend. We work together, that's all."

"Whatever. Thing is, that case changed the way I look at the world. And when it was over, I took a chance, a big one. Wrote up a confidential, 'Eyes Only' report for my boss, and told what *really* happened. It was pretty different from the official report I'd already turned in."

"I can imagine," Morris said. "Is Jack Crawford still in charge over there?"

"Nah, he died a few years ago. Heart attack. I work for Sue Whitlavich now."

"Really? I've heard of her. Read her book on serial killers when it first came out. Seems like a real smart lady."

"Like a whip. And a good thing, too. All those brains means she's more open-minded than a lot of people at the Bureau, even some in Behavioral Science. So, she read my confidential report, called me in, and we had a long talk."

"And the fact that you've still got your shield

means that she didn't decide you were crazy."

"It means more than that, Morris. It means whenever the Bureau stumbles across something real hinky, they give it to Behavioral Sci. And Sue usually gives it to me. And she doesn't ask too many questions, long as I get results."

"Sounds like we're finally getting to the heart of the matter," Morris said. "So you're here, in L.A., and in my room, and you're in a big hurry, because…"

"Because somebody's killing kids again. Only this time, it's worse."

Gunther Krause slipped into the abandoned house through the back door a few minutes before sunrise. There were stories that the undead could take the form of mist that could be directed anywhere they wished to go. If that were true, Krause had yet to figure out how to manage it, which was a pity. It would have made his existence much easier.

Still, he had little cause for complaint. He had been using this place as his daylight refuge for two months now, and it had served him very well. The structure had been condemned as unsafe, so no one came here, even stupidly adventurous children.

Krause would not have minded a visit from some children—but only after dark, when he was able to receive them properly.

As he made his way through the decrepit living room, Krause glanced down at his shirtfront. *Damn, bloodstains again. And I thought I was being so careful tonight. Well, looks like a new shirt for Gunther. Maybe I'll take it from my next meal, before I open him up to feed.*

Krause was four paces from the basement door

when he suddenly realized he was lying on the floor. A moment later, the pain hit him—a searing, merciless agony at the base of his spine that only one thing could have caused. *Silver*.

He heard them then, the sounds of boot heels crossing the uneven wooden floor. A few seconds later, the owner of the boots came into view. Krause didn't really need to breathe anymore, but he gasped, nonetheless. He had in an instant taken in the black hair, the pallor, the scar along an otherwise beautiful, if hard, face. The woman's shirt and pants were black, to match the boots. In one hand she held the still smoking, silenced .25 automatic that she had used to fire a silver bullet into his spine.

Through teeth clenched tight in pain, Krause managed, "They say you don't... exist. A legend... a myth, no more."

The woman let a tiny smile appear on her face. "And now you know better," she said, in a beautiful soprano voice that sounded like angels singing. "Pity you won't get the chance to spread the word."

"Who... who sent you?"

"The family of your second victim. The second in this town, anyway. You didn't disguise your work quite as well as you thought. They figured out that it was one of you leeches who killed him."

Her boots tapped out another slow rhythm on the floorboards as she walked over to the nearby window. Miraculously, its shade was still intact. She moved it aside a few inches and glanced outside. "Sun's almost up," she said, conversationally, and walked back to where the wounded vampire lay.

"What are you... waiting for?" Krause moaned. "Finish it."

"In due time," she said. "Which will be very soon, now."

"Just… because your first shot… missed…"

She laughed with what sounded like genuine amusement. "Missed? Oh, dear gracious me, no. That bullet went exactly where I wanted it."

"Why maim… not kill?"

"Because I wanted to spend a few minutes having this little chat with you, Gunther. You don't mind if I call you Gunther, do you?"

A few minutes later, she sauntered back to the window and peered out again. "Ah, sunrise!" she said. "Looks like it should be a beautiful day."

She turned back toward Gunther Krause again, and for a moment there was something in her face that would have frightened half the demons in hell. Then she reached down slowly and grasped the bottom of the window shade.

"Any last words?" she asked pleasantly.

"Fuck you… you twisted fucking… cunt."

Hannah Widmark, known in some circles as Widowmaker, smiled broadly. "Well, those will serve, I suppose."

She yanked the bottom of the shade down hard, then released it.

She stood there for a full minute longer, watching impassively and listening to the screams.

Then she left, her boots crunching as they walked over the gray ashes that lay strewn across the floor in the shape of a man.

Chapter 3

Howdy, this is Quincey Morris. Sorry I can't talk to you right now, but I'm off battling the forces of darkness. Or maybe I'm just taking a nap. In any case, leave a message after the beep, and I'll get back to you just as soon as I can, podner.

Libby Chastain sighed. Quincey was laying the Texan on pretty thick for someone who had graduated, with honors, from Princeton, but he had said once that some of his clients seemed to expect it. When the "beep" sounded in her ear she said, "Quincey, it's Libby. I've got a problem, a bad one. Call me as soon as you can, will you?"

Libby pocketed her phone and frowned at the two corpses that lay sprawled on her living room carpet. She was not looking forward to this next part. *Well, might as well get it over with. They're not going to get any less dead if I stand around and wait.*

She knelt down next to the nearest of the two corpses, and began methodically to go through his pockets.

Ten minutes later, she was looking at the small pile of objects that she'd recovered. There was no ID on either man, which confirmed what Libby had already suspected: these two were professional killers. Along with a few personal belongings was the wand that had been tucked into a boot worn by one of her would-be assassins.

Libby had seen this kind before, the magical equivalent of a cadmium battery. It had been charged with a limited amount of magical power, which would fade with use. Anyone with some intelligence and a little aptitude could use it, properly instructed. With one of these, you could perform a wide range of mid-level spells without putting in the years of study and practice that went into becoming a practitioner of the Art. Libby hated the things, looking upon them the way a true marksman views laser gun sights: they conveyed skills that the user hadn't earned, and didn't deserve.

Someone had charged this wand, and taught one of the men how it could be employed to disable the magical defenses protecting Libby's condo. The set of lock picks she'd found in the other man's pockets showed how the pair had overcome her more mundane protections.

But who had sent them? To her knowledge, she had no serious enemies among the magical community. The last witch to try to harm Libby had been Christine Abernathy, and Libby was quite certain that Christine would not be troubling anyone this side of hell ever again.

Until she discovered who was behind this, Libby was in serious danger. In warfare, whether mundane or magical, the aggressor usually has the advantage.

Libby could not count on the next team of killers that came for her to be as careless as these two jerks had been.

Well, first things first: she had two corpses to get rid of, and she'd better get started before decomposition set in. Once the smell of rotting flesh gets in your fabrics, even magic can be hard pressed to get it out again.

She hoped Quincey would call back soon.

"More kids are being killed for their organs?" Morris asked.

"Yeah." Fenton spoke as if the word had put a bad taste in his mouth. "Started about two months ago, near as we can figure. Same M.O. as before, more or less."

"Not much chance it's the same perp from last time, is there?"

Fenton shook his head. "None at all. Cecelia Mbwato was identified after the fact as the killer. She'd been operating with the assistance of a guy named, believe it or not, Snake Perkins. And both of them are as dead as two people can be."

Morris thought about what he'd found in Fortner's magic workroom. "Well, it seems I may have some good news for you," he said. He told Fenton about the jars he'd found, each containing what was almost certainly the heart of a child. "Looks like Fortner's your killer, and how's *that* for coincidence?" he said to Fenton. "You may need some specialized help when you go in to serve the arrest warrant. Even though a lot of his tools have gone up in smoke, Fortner's still powerful, which makes him dangerous. I can give you a few names of people with the right skills, if you want."

Fenton stood up and walked slowly over to one of the windows, where he peered out at the start of rush hour without much apparent interest. After a little while he turned back to the room. "That's good to know," he said, "but I've got a couple of problems with that."

"Such as?" This was not the reaction that Morris had been expecting.

"Well, there's that warrant you mentioned, for one. To get one, we've got to show the judge probable cause that something hinky's been going on in Fortner's place. "What do I say—*Your honor, I have reliable information gained from Mister Quincey Morris when he was burglarizing the place*?"

"There are ways around that, Fenton, and you know it. You could get an 'anonymous tip.' Or a 'confidential informant' could have given you the information. There's all kinds of things you can tell the damn judge."

"Yeah, and most judges recognize them for the bullshit tactics they are. But all right. Say we get a warrant to go poking around the burned-out ruins of Fortner's place. Maybe I even have you draw us a map, so that we can get to this workroom you're talking about without too much fuss. What do you figure we'd find there?"

"You'll find evidence that he's been killing children for their hearts."

"What evidence, specifically? You were in there— you oughta know."

Morris shook his head irritably. "For Christ's sake, Fenton, I told you already. You'd find those jars containing the hearts, one in each."

Fenton was looking at him, and Morris suddenly

realized he had missed something, but he didn't know what.

"Morris, did you happen to pick up any of those jars, maybe for a closer look?"

"Yeah, I did, as a matter of fact. But if you're worried about fingerprints—"

"That's not what I'm getting at. You said the hearts were floating in a clear liquid. Any idea what that was?"

"Sure—it was alcohol. You could smell it, even with the jars closed. Not surprising, a lot of labs..." Morris's voice trailed off and then he said, "Oh, fuck."

Fenton nodded, but not as if he was taking any pleasure in Morris's discomfiture. "The fire would have set the alcohol in those jars to burning, and that stuff gives you a hot flame, as you may know. My guess is all we'd find would be some scratched glass and a bunch of cinders. The lab people might be able to establish that it had once been human tissue, but that's about it. Identifying what kind of tissue—not real likely. And as for DNA—forget it. All we'd get for our trouble would be proof that Fortner had some kind of human tissue in his basement. Maybe he was doing research, and bought the stuff from a medical supply house. We'd never be able to prove otherwise. Thanks to you and your little box of matches."

Morris swore without raising his voice, and some of the colorful Texas imagery made Fenton blink. Finally, the FBI man held up a hand, palm out like a traffic cop.

"Hold up," he said to Morris. "Look, we're not gonna just let this go. I believe that you saw what you told me you saw in Fortner's place. Now that we know what he's been involved in, we'll start looking into his background, associates, all that. There's a chance we'll find a lead, something we can follow all the way to an indictment. And we'll be watching the bastard, twenty-four seven. He goes out hunting again, we'll catch him in the act, and stop him before he can hurt another kid."

There was a long silence before Morris said, "Then why are we talking?"

"Because it's not just Fortner. It can't be. Nine days ago, two kids disappeared—one in Omaha, the other one from some little town in Pennsylvania, Exeter or something. Their bodies were found the next morning, organs removed the same way as the others."

"I see," Morris said.

"Two abductions, two murders, same day. Something like fifteen hundred miles apart. And, by the way, we have some pretty good evidence that your buddy Fortner was in L.A. during that time."

Fenton leaned forward. "It's happening all over the country, Morris. Kids being taken, cut open, organs removed, then dumped someplace."

"Dumped near water?"

"In some cases, yeah. But water's not a common factor, the way it was with the five killings we had last year. It doesn't look like *muti* magic this time. But something is going on, something real bad."

"You're probably right, but I'll ask my question again: why are we talking?"

"Because I want you to stop it."

*   *   *

Pardee entered his master's study to find Grobius staring moodily out the immense picture window. "It's snowing again," the old man said, as if it were Pardee's fault. Grobius had been failing at an increased rate the last year or so, despite his doctors' best efforts and Pardee's magic.

"It does that, this time of year." Pardee was careful not to sound sarcastic. "You wanted isolation, and that usually means an area with severe weather, of one sort or another. There is a reason why isolated areas are isolated, after all."

"Well, it better not snow on the thirtieth. Some of them will be coming in by air, you said, and I don't know what effect bad weather will have on their ability to navigate. And I don't want it spoiling the ritual, either, by blocking the moon."

"I understand, of course. And I can assure you that it will not snow on Walpurgis Night. Not here, at any rate."

"And you know that how? Been consulting your crystal ball again?"

Pardee, like most professionals, did not appreciate badinage on the subject of his work. But he was careful to keep any irritation out of his voice when he said, "I have never used such a device, nor has any genuine practitioner of the Art. Such baubles are the toys of Gypsy con artists, nothing more."

"Then on what basis are you predicting that it won't snow?"

"I am not predicting it will not snow. I am guaranteeing it."

"You can do that, can you? Control the weather?"

Pardee nodded slowly. "Within a limited area, and only for relatively brief periods of time. But I can certainly hold the elements in check long enough for our project to succeed."

"That's reassuring," Grobius said. "Hanging on this long, not to mention all the work and money that have gone into it. And the lives. If it were all for nothing, just because of some fucking low pressure area... When are these precise conditions—the moon and so on—going to occur again?"

"I'd have to look it up," Pardee said. "But I think it's safe to say that it won't be within a reasonable time frame."

"Meaning there's no way I could live long enough, even with your magic and the wonders of modern science." The old man made a disgusted sound. "I suppose I'd be lucky to last until April of *next* year."

"That's quite possibly true. Which is why I intend to succeed the first time. I know how much this matters to you."

"Yes, it does. But why does it matter to *you*? Is it just the money?"

"The money's important, of course." Pardee said. "I enjoy the things money can buy, as much as anyone. But this is also the chance to do something that has never been done before. Oh, in the movies and cheap fiction, it happens all the time. But in reality, it has never been possible. Those who have tried have either simply failed, or both failed and died. Until now, that is. Quite a momentous occasion, or, rather, it will be."

"Pity is has to remain a secret. You could be named to the Wizards' Hall of Fame, or some such."

"I suspect it would be more like the Hall of Infamy. But that's all right. I have no concerns that my name will be forgotten."

"By those who matter, you mean," Grobius said.

"Exactly. Those who really matter will know."

Andrea McKinnon struggled to balance her heavy briefcase and two thick files of legal depositions while fitting her key into the lock of her front door. She finally managed, without spilling her work all over the front porch. She stepped inside, and kicked the door shut behind her.

She could have used magic either to get the door open, or to transport the paperwork from her trunk, or both. But she didn't like to use her power in public unless absolutely necessary. It tended to upset people, most of whom still thought that there was only one kind of witchcraft—the evil kind. Andrea supposed that she could have been doing more to educate the public about white witchcraft, but Lawrence, Kansas was smack dab in the middle of the Bible Belt, and the last thing she needed was a bunch of crazed fundamentalists howling outside her house at all hours.

Even worse, one of them might try to kill her, interpreting the scriptural admonition "Thou shalt not suffer a witch to live" in an all too literal fashion. It had happened in Oklahoma, a few years ago. One of her Sisters in the Goddess had been "outed" as a witch by the local paper, and soon a nutcase, off his medication and hopped up with the need to do something wonderful for Jesus, had thrown a pail of gasoline on her and then tried to set it alight. Fortunately for all concerned, the plastic disposable lighter the nutcase had flicked into flame and tossed toward the gasoline-soaked woman had gone out as soon as it was thrown, which such devices are designed to do.

Shrugging out of her raincoat, Andrea shook her head at the idea of it. Jesus of Nazareth had been, by all reliable accounts, a man of love and peace. The antics some of his followers got up to must sadden him greatly, even now.

She was measuring Maxwell House into her coffee maker when she heard the sounds coming from her living room.

A burglar? In this neighborhood?

Well, anything was possible. Meth had caught on among certain elements of the Lawrence underclass, and the resulting small army of addicts was gradually spreading, even into the suburbs, seeking money or anything that could be turned into ready cash.

But the wards on the house should have kept them out. As soon as they tried to get in, they should have felt an overpowering desire to go someplace else.

Worry about that later. For now, deal with the threat, whatever it was.

From a drawer next to the cutlery she removed the wand she kept there for emergencies, which this clearly seemed to be. It had been charged with a general-purpose spell that would give Andrea a wide variety of options, once she knew what she was dealing with.

Although she could not harm people with it, magic did allow her to protect herself, and a variety of non-lethal responses were possible. She could, for instance, freeze the intruder in place for the time it would take the police to arrive. But before calling

911, better be sure that this wasn't another squirrel that had gotten in to wreak havoc.

Andrea McKinnon walked softly to the doorway that led to her living room. The sounds were coming from her right, so she turned that way immediately on entering.

A man was going through her desk, presumably looking for money or valuables. He was tall and heavyset, and wore glasses.

"Hold it right there!" She was uttering the first words that would allow her to launch the freezing-in-place spell when the other man stepped up behind her and looped the wire garrote around her neck.

There was no prolonged struggle, like something out of one of the *Godfather* movies. Unlike the cord garrotes employed by fictional Mafia assassins, piano wire is quick, if messy, and the killer had chosen it precisely for that reason. He wanted the witch to have no chance to work some hocus-pocus on him, or his partner. Wire doesn't just constrict the victim's flesh—it *cuts*.

The killer was strong and skillful. Within four seconds, the piano wire had sliced through Andrea's throat to sever her windpipe, as well as both her carotid artery and jugular vein.

As soon as the blood began to spurt, the killer, whose name was Kittridge, released his grip on the garrote's handles and let the woman, already unconscious, fall forward to the floor. Within a couple of minutes she would die—either from choking or bleeding out, and Kittridge didn't care which.

The other man, who had a youngish face and prematurely white hair, stepped out from behind the desk and approached the still form, careful to avoid the spreading pool of blood. His name was Winter.

"Nice work," he said to Kittridge. "She didn't call the cops, did she?"

"Nope, didn't use the phone at all. Guess she thought her little stick, here"—he nudged the fallen wand with the tip of one expensive shoe—"was all the help she needed."

"Well, the bitch guessed wrong, didn't she? But we better clear out of here, anyway. Where's the next one?"

"New York. Pardee texted me a few minutes ago. O'Neill and his partner haven't reported in. Chastain must have got the best of them, somehow, so she's our problem now."

Winter snorted. "Should have sent us in the first place. O'Neill's a pussy."

"Well, he's probably a dead one. Or, if not, he will be, once Pardee gets hold of him. Come on, let's go."

As it happened, they were closing the kitchen door behind them precisely at the moment that Andrea McKinnon's heart stopped beating.

Chapter 4

Morris looked at Fenton and said, "I think you've got me confused with somebody else. Batman, maybe. Or James Bond. Somebody like that."

Fenton shook his head, just once. "No, I'm not confused about anything, Morris. I know who you are, and I know what you do. I just want you to do it on the Bureau's behalf. We'll pay your standard rate, which is pretty damn high for a ghostbuster, if you ask me."

"I don't believe I did. Ask, that is. But I am curious how you'd explain to the accountants back in the Hoover Building why you've got a 'ghostbuster' on the payroll."

"There's a budget for hiring consultants. As long as my boss is cool with it, I don't have to be real specific when I file the paperwork."

"And *is* she cool with it, your boss?"

"Yeah, as a matter of fact, she is. Sue's pretty open-minded for somebody with a Ph.D. from the University of Chicago."

"Maybe that means she's also good at handling

disappointment. I hope so, because I'm about to hand her some."

"You don't want the job."

"You got that right, podner. I absolutely do not want this job."

"Why not? It's the kind of thing you do all the time, isn't it?"

"No, it's the kind of thing I *used* to do, when I was young and stupid. I'm older now, and at least a little smarter. Or so I like to think."

Morris leaned forward. "Look, Fenton, from what you've told me, you've got several black sorcerers, in different parts of the country, killing kids for their hearts."

"Not just the hearts. In some cases, other organs were taken, as well."

"All right. The point is that these organs, properly used, are going to give the witches who took them a great deal of power. Hell, that's why they're *doing* it."

Fenton spread his hands a little. "See? That kind of insight is exactly the reason I want you for this case."

"And it's also the reason that I want nothing to do with it. You've got these people who have taken the Left-Hand Path, and you don't know how many of 'em there are, or who they are, or even where they are. What we *do* know is that they're willing to kill to get what they want, and that most likely they've acquired a hell of a lot of power, or will, soon."

"What's that mean—*will, soon*?"

"The organs themselves aren't powerful. They have to be used. They're like potential energy, in physics. You need a particular kind of ritual, or a series of them, to turn that potential into kinetic energy. And, considering the kind of people involved, we are talking about energy of the very worst kind."

"How bad?"

"Can't say, without more information. But bad; trust me. And dangerous. Look, Fenton, Libby and I spent part of last year on the trail of a black witch who was involved in some pretty nasty goings-on. She found out that we were looking for her, and tried to kill us. And damn near succeeded."

Morris shook his head slowly, like the bank officer does when turning you down for a small business loan. "You wanna play Wyatt Earp and face these folks down at some supernatural OK Corral, you go right ahead, and I sincerely wish you good fortune. But I'm not Doc Holliday, and I'm not goin' with you."

"Uh-huh." Fenton straightened his tie, which did not need straightening. "Well, we've established that you're neither Batman, James Bond, nor Doc Holliday. So just who the hell *are* you, Morris?"

"Just a guy with a dangerous, nasty job, who doesn't want to make it any more dangerous and nasty than it has to be."

Morris stood up. "Feel free to keep my name in your Rolodex. If something a bit less insane comes up sometime, give me a call and I'll see if I can help out. But not this time."

Fenton was still in his chair, and seemed in no hurry to go anywhere. "Well, I admire your honesty. I do. It's a quality in pretty short supply in Washington. Now let me—"

Fenton's cell phone rang. He pulled it from a pocket, checked the display, then said. "Sorry, I've got to take this."

He pushed a button and held the phone to his ear. "Yeah. No, I'm still in his room, but I'm almost done. Come on up, if you want. Room 942. Okay."

Fenton put the phone away and said to Morris, "That was my partner. I figured you might as well meet her, since we're going to be doing business together."

In the voice of someone starting to lose his patience, Morris said, "I thought I made it clear—"

"You did," Fenton said. "Now *I'm* going to make something clear, and you might as well sit down to hear it."

Morris didn't move. After a few seconds, Fenton said softly, "I said sit... the... fuck... down."

Morris looked at him. Mixing things up with Agent Fenton wasn't going to get him anything except arrested for assaulting a Federal officer. He slowly lowered himself back onto the edge of the bed.

"Thanks," Fenton said, sounding like he actually meant it. "Here's why you're going to work for the Bureau on this investigation, Morris. Not because you went all vigilante and burned down the best evidence we almost had tying anybody to these murders. Not because you're basically a decent guy who doesn't want any more kids to get cut open. Not because I'm authorized to double your usual fee, and I just did. But because you don't want somebody putting a quiet word in Fortner's ear, when he gets back, that you're the guy who burned his *hacienda* to the ground a few hours ago."

"You've got no proof of that."

"Fortner won't care."

After a few seconds, Morris said, softly, "No, I don't reckon he will."

"It's like you said yourself, just because his tools are gone doesn't mean he's not dangerous. You want to spend the next couple of years looking over your shoulder? That assumes Fortner doesn't come for you sooner, of course."

The look that Morris turned on Fenton was one of pure hatred, but his voice was mild when he said, "I don't suppose calling you eight different kinds of motherfucker would change anything, would it?"

"Nope," Fenton said. "But you go ahead, if it'll make you feel better."

Morris was considering doing just that when the knock sounded on his door.

He looked at Fenton. "You want to get that, or shall I?"

Fenton shrugged. "It's your room."

Morris went to the door and opened it. The woman standing in the hall had auburn hair, an upturned nose, and freckles, and she looked for all the world like a female leprechaun in a business suit—an effect that was spoiled when she flashed her credentials and said, "Special Agent Colleen O'Donnell, FBI. You would be Mister Morris?"

"The very same." Morris stepped back to allow her entrance. After closing the door, he looked at the woman more closely. "Sorry, but have we maybe met before? There's something... familiar about you."

She gave him a second, more careful look before saying, "I don't think so, Mister Morris," then turned to confer with her partner. Morris was watching her curiously, when suddenly it hit him. It wasn't Colleen O'Donnell herself who was familiar; it was the aura surrounding her. Morris had been trained to sensitivity in such things, and the vibe that the female agent gave off was the same one that Morris had sensed many times when in the company of Libby Chastain.

Fenton's partner was a white witch.

Morris closed the door on the two FBI agents, after making a reluctant promise to stay in touch. He hadn't said anything about recognizing Special Agent O'Donnell as a member of what Libby Chastain called The Sisterhood. Fenton hadn't given any indication that he knew, and if he didn't know, it wasn't Morris's business to tell him. Still, having a white witch as a partner would have its advantages, as Morris himself had reason to know.

His exertions of the night before had left him sweaty and a bit grimy. Morris needed a shower. Besides, he often did some of his best thinking under warm water.

A few minutes later, Morris was reaching for the shower tap when a female voice behind him said, "Hello, Quincey."

He spun around, arms moving into the defensive posture that his sensei had taught him was best when you did not know the exact nature of the threat you were facing.

Libby Chastain was standing in the doorway of the bathroom.

Except it wasn't Libby, not quite. Morris found that he could see through her translucent form to the bedroom beyond. Morris put his arms down. He knew what Libby was doing; he had seen this manifestation before.

"This must be pretty important if you're using spirit transference to find me, Libby." He reached for a nearby bath towel. "Uh, you mind if I…"

"Not at all, please do." Libby's image smiled a little. "I'm sorry to show up at an, um, inopportune moment. This seems to be a day for having showers interrupted."

"What's wrong?" Morris finished tucking the towel around his waist.

"Some people tried to kill me a few hours ago. At home."

"My God! Are you, I mean, is your body…"

"I'm all right, apart from being frightened half to death." Libby briefly described the attack upon her, and what she had done about it.

"What about the bodies?" Morris asked. "You can't leave them there indefinitely, and the NYPD might not buy your explanation of events."

"Already gone. I worked a discorporation spell, then transported them to the East River, where they were materialized again. Now when water is found in their lungs, it won't seem surprising."

"If the bad guys, whoever they are, could break in once, they can do it again," Morris said. "You've got to get out of there, Libby."

"I already have. I checked into a hotel a little while ago. My *corpus* is lying on the bed while we talk. The door is triple-locked and warded, as well. It should be safe enough."

Morris ran a hand through his hair. "You know, you could have called, Libby. Saved yourself a lot of time and effort."

"I did, twice, and got your voicemail each time. I assume you haven't checked your messages for a while."

"No, sorry. It's been kind of a busy morning for

me, too." Morris told her about the Fortner job, and his subsequent visit from the FBI.

Libby's expression, already sober, took on a grim cast. "Children. Again."

"Yeah, and this time it's some kind of coordinated effort. That, or somebody has figured out how to be in two places, physically, at the same time. I never heard of any magic, black or white, being able to accomplish that."

"Nor have I. It's probably impossible, even for an expert practitioner. I assume you're not interested in a technical explanation of why that's so."

"Maybe another time." Morris frowned. "Libby, something just occurred to me—if you checked into a hotel, you had to use a credit card, didn't you? Unless you're in one of those places near Times Square that rents by the hour, cash only."

"No, I didn't think I could blend in effectively in a no-tell hotel. It's not that trying to pass as a hooker would bother me, it's looking like a *cheap* hooker that I find demeaning."

"So you used a credit card. They can find you that way, Libby. Won't even need magic to do it—just the skills of a good private detective."

"Not to worry. I was able to... persuade the young man at the registration desk that there was no need to run my credit card imprint until I check out. It's against company policy, of course, but he found himself willing to make an exception, just this once."

"All right, so you're probably okay for a while. But if there's a black magician involved, they'll find you, in time. You can't stay there indefinitely."

"I know. Moving from hotel to hotel will buy

some time, but it doesn't solve the basic problem. I need to know who's doing this, Quincey—and *why*. Although if I can determine the first, the second may well explain itself. But I'm not equipped to do this on my own. I need an investigator."

"You're probably right. But, like I told you, the FBI's got me in a vice, and they're squeezing pretty hard. Otherwise, I'd be on the next plane to NYC. Wait—have you considered our old buddy, Barry Love? This sounds like something that'd be right up his alley, or down his mean street, or whatever the expression is."

"I've already called him, and his answering service says he's out of the country, date of return unknown."

"Must be tracking down 'the weird shit' a long way from home. Damn it." Morris gave his reflection in the bathroom mirror a good, hard look. "All right, fuck the goddamn FBI. I'll be there tomorrow and we can—"

"No, Quincey, I don't want you taking that kind of chance just because you're helping me. Somebody like this Fortner could be a dangerous enemy."

"Yeah, tell me about it. I was in the guy's house, remember? But there's no way I'm letting you—"

"I've been thinking about that while we've been talking. Why don't I join you, in L.A. or wherever you're going next? It might get me out of range of whoever's after me, and even if it doesn't, I'd feel better with you to watch my back. Assuming you're willing to put yourself in jeopardy."

Morris grinned at her, or rather her manifestation. "Libby, for you I'd even put myself in *Wheel of Fortune*."

"Always the smartass. Anyway, I might be able to help you out with your case, so it's a win-win, seems to me."

"Yeah, me, too. Be just like old times. And once we get this business settled for Fenton, we can start actively finding out who's got it in for you, and then do something about it. Speaking of Fenton, I almost forgot to tell you: I met his partner, and she's one of your Sisters."

"Really? That's very interesting."

"Her name's Colleen O'Donnell, Irish as a pint of Guinness. Do you know her?"

"Name doesn't ring a bell, but then, we're not all acquainted, Quincey."

"Good point. I don't think Fenton knows, by the way."

"Hmmm. It may be that she doesn't trust him, yet. How long have they been partners, did he say?"

"No, but your buddy Van Dreenan didn't mention her when we met him last year, did he? Seemed like he was acting as Fenton's partner at the time."

"Yes, of course. Well, I expect she'll let him know when the time is right. Unless circumstances force her hand."

"And on a job like this, I wouldn't be surprised if they do. They're following the trail using the Bureau's resources, while I work what Fenton calls 'the occult side of the street.'"

"Well, maybe we'll all meet in the middle, and find out what the heck is going on."

"Could be that we will," Morris said. "Could just be."

Fenton and O'Donnell were stuck in traffic on Wilshire Boulevard.

Colleen shut off the engine. "May as well save some gas," she said. "Otherwise, the Director might have to request a supplemental budget appropriation just to get us back to the office."

"Buy oil stock. I do." Fenton said. After a moment, he asked, "Any news?"

"Some crime scene photos came in from Arkansas, where they found that kid on Tuesday. Or what was left of him." She moved her mouth around, as if tasting something sour. "I filed it with the other cases. They expect forensics results by the end of the week, and I can file those, too, for all the fucking good it will do."

"Maybe Morris can turn something up that remotely resembles a lead."

"Is this guy any good, Dale? I would have thought he was just some hustler, like that 'Ghost Whisperer' clown."

"No, whatever else he is, he's no hustler," Fenton said. "He's been linked to some pretty strange shit, over the years. Seems to have a knack for it. And he's got this partner, or whatever she is, some woman named Libby Chastain. She claims to be a white witch."

Colleen may have paused a little longer than necessary before she said, "Do tell. You've met her?"

"No, but that South African cop I worked with last year—Van Dreenan—he knows her. She's got some interesting… talents."

"You know, you never say much about that case," Colleen said. "Even though it sounds like it has a direct bearing on our current one."

"My report's on file," Fenton said, sounding irritated. "You can read it, if you haven't already."

"Oh, I have. And fascinating reading it makes, too. But it's got a lot of interesting... gaps."

"Cecelia Mbwato, a black female, age unknown, and Snake Perkins, a white male, age thirty-six, were engaged in a series of murders and ante-mortem mutilations of male and female children," he said rapidly, as if reciting by rote. "They removed certain of their victims' bodily organs, which were then preserved using African herbs, to be used in some alleged magical ritual."

"Yeah, all right, if you say so. But we're gonna have to talk about some of those gaps sooner or later. Seems to me—"

When she fell silent, Fenton turned and looked at her. "What?"

Colleen O'Donnell's eyes were vacant, as if the mind behind them was elsewhere. Finally, she asked, "What did you say about African herbs?"

"Lab examined some of the organs the suspects had with them. They were in some kind of a case that was thrown clear in the crash that killed them. Mbwato, at least we assume it was her, had used some weird mixture of herbs and stuff from Africa to preserve the poor kids' organs until they could do... whatever... with them."

"The organs *have* to be preserved, don't they? Rotting body parts are no good for any kind of black magic ritual."

"How the hell do you know that?"

"I've been reading up on it," she said. "Thing is, I remember something odd from one of the lab reports, about a substance that was found on one of the bodies."

Fenton was still looking at her, but now his face contained a trace of something that had not appeared there in quite some time, and it looked like hope. "Well, what are you waiting for?" he said. "Get us the fuck outta here!"

"Fuckin' A," she said, and reached down to turn on the siren.

Chapter 5

"Will a check be all right?" the woman asked, a little nervously. "I wasn't expecting you tonight, or I would have had cash on hand. I know it's what you prefer."

"Cash is more convenient, but I'll take your check, Mrs. Younger," Hannah Widmark said. "It's my fault, not calling ahead."

As always, Hannah wore black, from the rolled neck of her sweater to the steel-reinforced tips of her boots. No trace of makeup covered the long scar that traversed the left side of her face, from ear to chin.

Mrs. Younger tore a check free and presented it. "Here you are," she said. "That's right, isn't it? I wouldn't want to cheat you out of any of your fee."

Hannah glanced at the check before slipping it into a pocket. "It's fine, Mrs. Younger, don't worry." Something like a smile appeared, very briefly, on the marred but still beautiful face. "Nobody ever cheats me."

At the door to her apartment, Mrs. Younger hesitated. "There's something I need to ask you before you go," she said.

"What is it?"

"That… creature that killed Robert…"

"The vampire."

"Yes, the vampire. Did he… suffer before he died?"

"Suffer?" Hannah pursed her lips for a second, before saying, "Yes, Mrs. Younger, he suffered a great deal."

An expression appeared on the older woman's face that would have done credit to an Apache maiden of 150 years ago, about to skin a prisoner alive. "Good," she said fiercely. "Good!"

In the elevator, Hannah found herself in the company of a heavyset man in his late thirties. He wore too much cologne and appeared a little drunk.

Looking over at Hannah, he said, "Nice outfit, honey. What are you, some kind of dominatrix?"

"No." Her voice held no inflection. She did not look at him.

"So what's with the get-up, then? You a commando? That it? Or do you just *go* commando?" He seemed to think this was the funniest thing in the world. Hannah ignored him, until he made a very bad mistake.

"Hey listen," he said, and put a hand on her shoulder.

When the elevator door opened at the lobby a few seconds later, it revealed a middle-aged couple with a small dog on a leash.

Hannah slipped past them with a polite, "Excuse me."

But instead of entering the elevator, the two

of them stood and gaped at the man who was slumped in one corner, moaning softly.

"My God, what happened to him?" the husband asked.

"He fell down and broke his arm," Hannah said over her shoulder. Then she walked onward and out, into the dark.

Libby Chastain, now back in her own body, sat down at the hotel room's desk and opened her laptop.

Not all of Libby's communications involved out-of-body experiences.

She glanced at her watch and made a quick calculation. Garth Van Dreenan, of the South African Occult Crimes Unit, should be at work now. He didn't like to take personal phone calls while on the job, but had no objection to digital communication. She opened up her Yahoo Instant Messenger, selected a name from her long buddy list, and clicked to open a dialogue box.

Libbywitch: Hi, Garth. Are you there?

After ten or fifteen seconds, she received a response.

Occultcop: Elizabeth! How nice to hear from you.

Libbywitch: How've you been?

Occultcop: Surprisingly good. I have met someone. A woman, I mean.

Libbywitch: Cool! Are the two of you dating?

Occultcop: That is not the term we use here, but I would say that we are seeing each other.

Libbywitch: I'm glad for you. You deserve someone to love you, & vice versa.

Occultcop: Thank you. But you never get in touch

simply for social reasons, Elizabeth. So, now that the pleasantries have been exchanged, perhaps you should tell me what is really concerning you.

Libbywitch: You see right through me. And you're not the first one today.

Occultcop: ??

Libbywitch: Sorry, never mind. I guess I was just postponing an unpleasant subject.

Occultcop: It will likely not become more pleasant with the passage of time.

Libbywitch: You're quite right. Quincey's been dragged into something, and I'm trying to help. Garth, someone is killing kids again. And taking their organs. While still alive.

Occultcop: Jesus Gott.

Libbywitch: And it gets worse. There appears to be more than one killer.

Occultcop: Well, we know that the late Cecelia Mbwato and Mister Snake Perkins—may they both be burning in hell as we speak—worked as a team to commit their butchery. So this is not, unfortunately, unprecedented.

Libbywitch: Yes, but that's not what I meant. It seems that there are different killers, operating in various parts of the country at the same time. Or so the FBI thinks.

Occultcop: But the modus operandi is the same?

Libbywitch: As far as I know, yes.

Occultcop: When did the killings start?

Libbywitch: Quincey says about two months ago.

The line was silent for over a minute.

Libbywitch: Garth? Are you still there?

Occultcop: Yes. Sorry. Thinking.

Libbywitch: Anything useful emerge?

Occultcop: Perhaps. But I must ask you to indulge me in what an ancient philosopher would call dialectic.

Libbywitch: All right, Socrates, fire away.

Occultcop: Very well. We have a series of murders. For what purpose were they committed?

Libbywitch: You know the answer as well as I do: to take some of the victims' organs.

Occultcop: Ante mortem, correct?

Libbywitch: Yes, the poor kids were still alive, according to the autopsy reports.

Occultcop: And why would a person or persons do this? What would be the purpose to be served by these barbarous acts?

Libbywitch: For use in a black magic ritual. The organs of children are very powerful talismans among those who follow the Left-Hand Path.

Occultcop: How many organs, in all, have been taken?

Libbywitch: I don't know. I suppose I'd have to see all the autopsy reports and add up the numbers. Quincey said that he had personally seen a series of jars containing eight hearts. What does the total matter, anyway?

Occultcop: Bear with me, if you will. So we have multiple murders, committed by multiple perpetrators, all acting in concert, or so it would seem.

Libbywitch: Yes, it looks that way.

Occultcop: Why would any group of people want that many powerful objects?

Libbywitch: To put together some kind of spell or ritual, and one requiring that much magical power is most likely going to involve something very big, and very nasty.

Occultcop: Such as what?

Libbywitch: I can't begin to imagine. The mind boggles.

Occultcop: Very well, put that aside for now. There is also the matter of timing.

Libbywitch: What about it?

Occultcop: This coordinated effort began, you said, two months ago.

Libbywitch: Yes, that's when the FBI started getting reports of bodies being found.

Occultcop: And the killings continue still, ja?

Libbywitch: I think Quincey said the FBI told him the most recent victim discovered was last week.

Occultcop: If these murders had the same starting point, is it not reasonable to posit the same end point, as well?

Libbywitch: Come again?

Occultcop: When people work together, it means they have a common goal. Eventually, they expect to reach it.

Libbywitch: And since they started together, more or less, their goal represents a shared time, place, and purpose.

Occultcop: Very good, Elizabeth, Socrates, as well as Plato, would be proud of you. Time, place, and purpose. And if you can determine one of those…

Libbywitch: It might lead us to the other two.

Occultcop: Exactly. So it seems to me that you must decide which of those three threads shows the most promise, and proceed to unravel it. Perhaps the whole garment will thus be revealed. But there is one more consideration, Elizabeth.

Libbywitch: What?

Occultcop: You had best, I think, do it quickly.

*   *   *

The FBI's Los Angeles field office had assigned their visitors from Quantico a temporary office that was, surprisingly, both spacious and well lit. As soon as she came through the door, Special Agent Colleen O'Donnell made a beeline for the desk where her laptop waited.

"Should have brought this with me," she said to Fenton as the computer booted up, "but I didn't figure I had diddly-squat to show you, so there was no point. Okay, here we go."

She had opened up the case file concerning the murder of Eric Benteen, aged eleven. She quickly scrolled down to the autopsy report.

"Bingo! I was right. Here—check this out."

Fenton looked over her shoulder, as she used the cursor to indicate the place she was interested in.

"Carbonic acid?" he muttered. "What the hell's that?"

"Having spent two dreary years as a Chem major in college, I believe I can answer that question, Special Agent," she said brightly, and swiveled her chair to face him. "Carbonic acid, that is, H_2CO_3, is the residue left when CO_2 in solid form degrades to assume its normal gaseous state."

Fenton looked at her. "Okay, Colleen, you've had your fun. You're brilliant, duly stipulated. Now will you fucking speak English?"

"If you insist, Dale. Carbonic acid, which was found in the vic's body cavity, is not a natural product of human biochemistry. Rather, it's what you get when dry ice melts."

"Dry ice." Fenton was stroking his chin.

"Uh-huh. When you started talking about how Cecelia what's-her-name was preserving the organs she took with magic African herbs, or something, it got me thinking that these killers have to preserve the organs, too—at least, until they use them in whatever obscene ritual they perform."

Fenton nodded slowly. "They're using dry ice to preserve the organs, right from where they're harvested at the scene."

"Well, we don't know if all of them are doing it. I'll have to go back and check all the autopsy protocols to find out. But it sure looks like *this* motherfucker is using it."

"What would the good nuns say, if they could hear your mouth now, Colleen?"

"With any luck, they'd all have heart attacks and die on the spot. Well, except for Sister Mary Alan, who was almost human. But we digress."

"Yeah, all right." Fenton tilted his chair back to study the ceiling. "Dry ice is pretty hard to make at home, isn't it?"

"Damn near impossible. You need temperatures that the average kitchen's freezer can't begin to approach. You also need some kind of pressurized tank, and you can't get those at Wal-Mart, last I heard."

"So, somebody needs a source of dry ice. Who'd make that? Or maybe have on hand a supply that they got someplace else?"

"Let's find out," she said, and turned back to the computer.

Less than five minutes later, Colleen had created a new file, and started cutting and pasting information into it. "It's used to keep frozen stuff cold during transport, when you don't have a refrigerated truck available. Ice cream and frozen food, mostly. And here's one I didn't know about—dry ice blasting."

Fenton was reading over her shoulder again. "Cleaning residue from heavy equipment. Dry ice pellets fired under pressure takes the gunk right out. Huh."

"Yeah, the things you learn in this job. Next time I play Trivial Pursuit, I'm gonna kick ass."

Fenton sat down again and waited, as patiently as he could, while Colleen worked the computer.

"Hey, looks like we caught a break," she said. "I just checked back where this poor kid's body was found. I was afraid that he was one of the vics from Chicago, or one of the other big urban areas. Take us forever to track down dry ice users there."

"I take it such was not the case," Fenton said.

"Nope. Body was found in the Adirondack Mountains, upstate New York. And there's only one town of any size for like"—she squinted at the computer screen again—"thirty, forty miles in any direction."

"What town?"

"Some hole in the wall called Plattsburgh."

Walter Grobius's Idaho compound was probably large enough to apply for statehood. If human beings lived there, it might even have succeeded. Apart from the great house that stood, more or less, in the center, the place was largely open ground, some of it overgrown and wild, surrounded by a concrete wall that would have done credit to the federal prison system.

It had amused Grobius to include a mansard

roof, complete with a widow's walk, in the house's design. It is the defining characteristic of virtually every haunted house ever depicted in popular culture. He and Pardee stood there now, watching the groups of workmen as they scurried about the property. The snow of a few days earlier had melted, and a gentle breeze ruffled the coats the two men wore.

"I trust everything will be ready in time," Grobius said.

"It must be, therefore it will," Pardee told him.

"I would be tempted to remark upon your infernal confidence, but puns are a form of humor, and this is a matter for which humor is inappropriate."

"Humor yes, but not wit. Wit is appreciated in many places, even some that might surprise you."

"Really? Even... there? Well, that would explain your own variety, which is often insufferable."

Pardee smiled without displaying any teeth. "And yet you continue to suffer it."

"But not for much longer. I won't be requiring your services after the thirtieth. You can take your money and go."

"Truly 'a consummation devoutly to be wished,' as Marlowe might put it."

Grobius frowned. "What are you talking about? That's Shakespeare, from *Hamlet*."

"True, Shakespeare got the credit, but it was Christopher Marlowe who wrote it," Pardee said. "But, at least, Marlowe *is* recognized as the author of another worthy piece of drama—*Dr. Faustus*."

Grobius looked at him sharply, as if waiting for Pardee to say more on that subject. When he didn't, the old man returned to watching the work below.

"I've been thinking about the security problem those men represent."

Pardee understood immediately. "There is no need to kill the workmen once they are finished. That many deaths would bring unwanted attention, at a very inauspicious time for us. In any case, it is quite unnecessary. They have been told that they are digging a series of barbeque pits, for a very large party that is planned for the end of the month."

"And the altar?"

"A special table for the guest of honor."

Grobius's smile was a few degrees below that of the wind-driven air. "I see. And is this charade of yours working?"

"Completely. The workers have accepted it without question. They are largely indifferent, in any case. They think mostly of their wages, sports, beer, their families and what they invariably refer to as 'pussy.'"

"And you know this, how?"

"I have eavesdropped on some of their lunchtime conversations. From a distance of course. And I've read the thoughts of a few of them. They suspect nothing."

"Good." After a brief pause, Grobius quoted, "'A special table for the guest of honor.'" He shook his head. "Now I know what you meant about wit."

Pardee sketched a bow. "I do my humble best."

"And let us hope that the guest of honor shows up, after all the trouble we're going through."

"He will. I am sure of it."

"And he'll keep the bargain I will offer?"

"Most certainly. He always keeps his bargains, as long as the other party acts in, pardon the expression, good faith."

"Well, you can vouch for that, should it be necessary."

"I can," Pardee said softly. "I can, indeed."

EXODUS

Chapter 6

As one of America's busiest airports, O'Hare International is well equipped to meet the weary traveler's every need. It has, for instance, six different bars, of various sizes and decors, in which the voyager can drown his or her sorrows while hoping that a delayed flight to Kansas City or Pasadena won't be cancelled altogether. Quincey Morris had chosen a watering hole in the international terminal, the one without any "No Smoking" signs.

He had been nursing a bourbon and water for almost twenty minutes when a man slipped into the empty chair beside him, immediately pulling a box of Dunhill cigarettes from the pocket of his wrinkled, but elegant, sport coat. "Hello, Quincey, mate. How's tricks?"

Morris signaled for the bartender. "Not too bad, John. Yourself?"

John Wesley Hester had a thin, square-jawed face that was saved from starkness by his emerald-green eyes; they gazed out at the world with an air of innocence that utterly belied his twenty-odd years' experience as a criminologist specializing in the occult. He held a chair at one of the elite Cambridge colleges, but preferred to spend most of his time, as he put it, "in the field." The revenue from several popular forensics textbooks he'd written allowed Hester to indulge his tastes in fine clothing and cheap women.

As the barman approached, Morris's visitor said, "I'm having Scotch, if you're buying. The good stuff. The beer in this bloody country's a disgrace, always has been."

"At least we serve it cold," Morris said mildly.

"My point, exactly," Hester said. He ordered Chivas Regal, straight up, then lit up a Dunhill.

"I appreciate you meeting me at such short notice," Morris said.

"No problem at all, mate. I'm on my way back to the UK, anyway. Might as well pass through Chicago as anyplace else."

"Where you coming from?"

"Washington. The state, that is."

"Seattle?"

"Nah. Some people were having a bit of bother in the North Woods. Pretty country up that way."

Morris nodded. "I'd heard there was some trouble around those parts, recently. Dead cattle, even a couple of dead people. The papers were being cautious, for once, but it sounded like werewolf activity to me."

"Which is exactly what it was," Hester said. "You won't be hearin' of any more, most likely." A glass of Chivas was placed in front of him, and he hoisted it in Morris's direction. "Cheers."

Morris lifted his own glass in return. "Cheers."

He noticed that the tip of Hester's left pinky was missing, truncated at the first joint by a small mass of fresh-looking scar tissue. He wondered how Hester had lost the fingertip, and whether it had been cut off—or bitten.

After a sip of his scotch, Hester said, "So, all right, Quincey. What's on your mind?"

"Someone's killing pre-adolescent children. Abducting them and removing vital organs—while the kids are still alive. It reeks of black magic, John."

"That it does. Fuck." Hester squinted through a haze of cigarette smoke. "Thought that wicked business was all settled last year, when that bitch Cecelia Mbwato started her all-expense-paid tour of hell."

"You knew her?"

"We crossed paths a couple of times. Nasty bit of work. Ugly as sin, too. You're not tellin' me she's been resurrected, somehow?"

"There's no evidence that she has. For one thing, it looks like that more than one person's involved. There's been abductions taking place at more or less the same time, hundreds of miles apart."

"Bugger." Hester stubbed out his cigarette in a nearby ashtray and immediately lit another. "Who's your client, then?"

Morris made a face. "The FBI."

"Get on! Quincey Morris, working for the Feds?" Hester laughed briefly. "Did they give you a badge, an' all?"

"No, I wasn't exactly recruited," Morris said. "It's more like blackmail"

"Blackmail? What've they got, pictures of you and

some cute little heifer gettin' a bit frisky? I've heard about you cowboys."

"Go shag your mother, John. No, they found out some stuff about my last job. Passed on to the wrong party, it could cause me no end of trouble. Maybe even the lethal kind."

"Well, that sucks, don't it? How's it going, so far—turn up anything?"

"Not much. I'm still trying to pick up a lead. I figure, something like this, it can't stay secret forever. So I'm asking around, talking to people who might've heard something I can use. Like your own self."

Hester shook his head slowly. "Haven't picked up a thing, sorry. Although…" He drained his glass and signaled for a refill. "I don't know if this has got anything to do with your business, but I did hear that a curator at the National Museum over in Baghdad has figured out that the *Book of Shadows* is missing. They haven't a clue about how it was lifted, or by who, or even when."

"The one supposed to've been written by the mad Arab, what's-his-name, Alhazred? I thought that was bullshit, just like the *Necronomicon*."

"Don't be too sure about that one either, mate. But I *know* the fuckin' *Book of Shadows* is real—I saw it with me own eyes, years ago. They were keepin' it under real tight lock and key, in a vault under the museum. A bloke I knew who worked there, he owed me a favor. So I had him give me a tour of the stuff that the tourists never see. Just as well Saddam never heard about that little episode, or my mate would've been in for a trip to the acid baths, most like. Jealous of his secrets, Saddam was."

"Okay, let's say that the book's real, and that

somebody's ripped it off. What's that got to do with my problem?"

"Don't be thick, Quincey. You know what kind of stuff's supposed to be in that bloody thing. Imagine an adept of the Left-Hand Path with that book, along with all the magical power gained from those nasty kiddie sacrifices you've been talking about."

Morris looked at him, then reached for his own glass and drained it in one gulp. "Something pretty damn scary, most like."

"You got that right." Hester shrugged, wrinkling his thousand-dollar sport coat even further, if that were possible. "Course, that don't mean the two things are connected, at all. We got no reason to believe they are."

"I know," Morris said. "But, still..."

"Yeah," Hester said, and took another drag off his cigarette. "But bloody still."

The two men were silent for a bit until Hester said, "You didn't come out to Chicago just to chat me up, did you? I'd have stopped off in Austin, if you asked me to."

"No, I'm meeting Libby Chastain. She's due in on a flight from New York in a couple of hours."

"Ah, the fair Libby. How's she doing, then?"

"Not bad, except when people are trying to kill her."

"Christ, what the hell for?"

Morris sketched the details, as he knew them, of the attempt on Libby's life.

Hester shook his head. "And she's got no idea who's trying to snuff her? Not even a guess?"

"She says no. We're going to try to sort it out, as soon as I get this thing for the FBI finished. She's going to help me out on that, and I'll watch her back in the meantime."

"So, why Chicago?"

"I want to look up a guy I know who lives here. He's in the business, too, and we're hoping that maybe he's heard something."

"You can't just ring him up, and ask him?"

"This guy doesn't do too well around machinery. It tends to malfunction."

"Right, okay, I know who you mean, now. Chicago's resident wizard."

"The very same. And if we come up empty with him, there's a couple of other fellas in town I can talk to. They don't much like telephones, either."

Hester nodded, frowning. "If I didn't have a couple of mates who need me in the Big Smoke, right quick and real bad, I'd stick around and help you with this mess."

"I know you would, podner, and I appreciate that."

"Next round's mine," John said, reaching for his wallet. "Besides, I need a full glass, to make a toast I have in mind."

After Hester ordered another round, Morris said, "You know, I've always wondered how you fit in among the dons of Cambridge, talking like, uh…"

"A diehard product of the workin' class?" Hester smiled at Morris with half his mouth, then said, in a posh accent that Prince Charles might have envied, "In point of fact, I do possess the ability to speak in a manner more befitting my station, on those occasions when I so choose." The smile became a grin. "I just don't bloody well choose to," he said. "Irritates the pompous bastards of academe no end, that does."

When the drinks came, John raised his glass with curiously delicate, nicotine-stained fingers. "Here's to luck, mate," he said solemnly. "'Cause you're gonna bloody well need some."

Sandra Jenkins was in a pissy mood as she opened the door to her apartment. She'd started her damn period, and had a pounding headache, besides. And when she'd dropped her car off at the garage on the way to work this morning, the idiot behind the service counter had assured her that the cracked wheel bearing that had been causing so much trouble would be fixed by 4:30pm, with the oil and filter changed, to boot. After work, she'd cadged a ride to the garage with one of her co-workers, who'd offered to wait while Sandy made sure that her car was ready.

"No, it's fine, you go ahead," Sandy had told the woman. "They've had it all day, and they promised me it would be all set. Thanks for the lift!"

And of course Mister "It'll-be-ready-today-I-promise-lady" had said, with no trace of embarrassment or contrition, that the replacement wheel bearing had turned out, *mirabile dictu*, to be neither in stock nor available locally, but would almost certainly arrive tomorrow in plenty of time to be installed by the end of the workday. Probably.

Sandy had been trained, patiently and well, never to lose her temper. For a woman adept in witchcraft, even of the benevolent variety, maintaining emotional control was essential, lest something both unfortunate and embarrassing take place. As she'd called for a cab, Sandy had found herself wishing that there was a spell that could induce machinery to fix itself. She'd have to bring it up at the next meeting of the Circle, to see if her Sisters had any ideas.

But some clouds actually do have silver linings. The increased adrenaline flow that accompanied her bad mood had made Sandy's reactions just a hair faster than they might otherwise have been. So when she walked into her apartment and saw the man rising from his seat on her sofa, a man she had never seen before and had certainly never invited inside, her response was a tad quicker then it would normally be. She was moving even before the man behind her, who had been hidden by the open door, snaked his arm around her throat.

As a kid, Sandy had been enamored of a short-lived TV series entitled, improbably, *T.H.E. Cat*. The titular character, a former cat burglar turned professional bodyguard, used to wear a dirk concealed up his sleeve. When he was threatened, moving his arm a certain way would cause the weapon to drop into his hand, usually ruining some bad guy's day.

All of that had long been forgotten, until Sandy had come upon a re-run of the show on TV Land a couple of months ago. Although she did not find T. Hewitt Edward Cat quite as cool as she'd remembered (and the plot, truth be told, seemed pretty lame), she still thought the trick with the knife was a good one. She'd wondered if it could be duplicated with a magic wand.

It could. With a slim, pressure-sensitive sheath worn on her right forearm, Sandy was able, by flexing some muscles just the right way, to cause the wand to fall free and into her hand. True, she had dropped it the first twenty or thirty times she'd tried, but had eventually become quite proficient. All she had lacked was somebody to impress with her new skill.

Until now.

In the instant she had seen the intruder, Sandy had known he was an enemy. And if he had been skilled enough to get past the wards protecting her home, he was dangerous. The magically charged wand was dropping into Sandy's hand, even as the other man tightened his grip around her neck.

You can't work a spell if you can't speak, but Sandy was able to gain a few seconds' grace by the distinctly non-magical technique of stomping on the attacker's instep with the heel of her right shoe. The man grunted, and his grip around her throat loosened, just a little. That was all the edge that Sandy needed.

Using the tip of her wand to trace three invisible symbols in the air, she muttered, very quickly, the words of a spell designed to reverse negative energy. The anger and malevolence of her two attackers was suddenly directed back at them in the form of a sudden, debilitating pain. Sandy's spellcraft instructor had explained, years ago, that the pain was purely psychosomatic. White magic did not allow the deliberate harming of another, but it did permit, under some circumstances, *convincing* someone that he was being harmed.

Sandy stepped clear of the man behind her just as he collapsed to the floor, moaning. A moment later, his companion across the room did the same.

She then carefully laid down a freezing spell, which would hold each man motionless until the police could arrive. As soon as the two were immobilized, Sandy relieved their perception of pain, even though part of her did so reluctantly.

She called 911 to report the attack, and was assured that officers would respond posthaste. Putting the phone away, Sandy considered using a truth spell to find out who the men were, and why they had wished her harm. But in order for them to tell her, they would have to be unfrozen, and that could be dangerous. Better to let the police handle the interrogation, and try to kibitz the information from them later.

As Sandy looked at the two supine forms on her rug, she considered that she would have to credit herself with greater martial arts skills than she actually possessed when explaining to the police what had happened. But if need be, she could give the officers a little magical "push" that would encourage them to accept her story, an account that would be far more credible than "I stopped them with my little magic wand, officer" would ever be.

Sandy gave vent to a long, weary sigh. She'd been having a bad enough day before she got home, and now this. On the other hand, she could, right this second, be at the mercy of these two thugs, so things could have been worse. Besides, her headache was gone. As she heard the sound of a siren, distant but growing nearer, she prepared to lift the freezing spell, timing it to work just as the police walked through the door.

A smile finally passed over her face as she said aloud, "Beat *that*, Mister Cat."

*　　*　　*

If Plattsburgh, New York were much farther north, it would be in Canada. A pleasant little town of about 50,000, it is nestled along the shore of Lake Champlain, with Vermont visible on the other side. There are companies in Plattsburgh that use dry ice, but there are not many of them.

The foreman at Beauvais Plastics had just finished explaining to Agents Fenton and O'Donnell what they had already learned at the first three industrial firms they had visited. "So, the pellets come out this nozzle here, under high pressure, and then you clean whatever you pointin' it at. Works damn well, too."

"The dry ice isn't made until just before you're set to clean something with your machine here," Fenton said.

"Yessir, that's the way she works. No point in making up a bunch of dry ice just so it can sit in the tank. Hell, it could even explode, once the stuff starts to vaporize. This here tank is airtight, ya see? No place for the pressure to go."

"So, if someone came in asking to buy say, a couple of pounds of dry ice…" Colleen said.

Earl Trombley opened a fresh stick of Nicorette gum and popped it in his mouth before answering. "Well, I'd say a couple things. One is that I'm not authorized to sell dry ice to nobody, and I'm sure as hell not gonna give it away, neither. Number two is, even if I said okay to number one, if I pointed this here nozzle into some container, like an ice chest or whatever, the pressure'd slam the damn cooler half way across the room. Can't do it."

"I take it that nobody's asked you to try," Colleen said.

"Nope, not once. I'd remember."

Fenton and Colleen thanked Trombley and turned to leave.

"Hell, if somebody came in here lookin' for dry ice," Trombley said, "I'd send 'em to Price Chopper, or maybe Hannaford's."

They turned around again. Colleen, who was closer, said, "Excuse me?"

"You know, one of the supermarkets. They got those big displays, with the fresh seafood. Gotta keep that stuff cold, you know. Fish goes bad, everybody in the store's gonna know it pretty quick, eh?"

"And they use dry ice for that, to keep the fish fresh." That was Fenton.

"Yep. My cousin Marty, he works over at Hannaford's. Says the stuff comes in on the refrigerated truck, every week, along with the frozen food. I dunno know where they pick it up, some warehouse, I guess."

They thanked Trombley again, this time with a little more enthusiasm.

As they walked out to their car, Fenton asked, "How many supermarkets they got in this burg?"

Colleen produced her iPhone and started tapping things on the screen. After a few seconds, she said, "Um, four. But two of them look like discount places—probably no fresh fish displays there."

"That leaves Hannaford's and, what was the other one?"

"Price Chopper." She consulted her little screen again, like an oracle poring over entrails. "Looks

120

like they're only about a quarter-mile apart. Both are near that mall we passed coming in."

"Well, then let's go shopping."

"You know," Colleen said as she turned the ignition key, "I think that's the first time I've ever heard a man say that."

As Libby'd told Morris, she had used a slight magical influence on the desk clerk who had checked her into the Holiday Inn, persuading him not to run her credit card number through the system until she was ready to check out. But even Libby could not control the way that data networks work—and fail to work.

She had a flight to Chicago to catch, and had allowed herself three hours to get to JFK, check in, and wait in the usual long line for security screening. Since her flight left at 1:15pm, she was standing at the Holiday Inn's front desk a little after 10:00am, packed and ready to go.

The same young man who had checked her in yesterday was holding down the fort. His nametag read "Walter." When Libby handed him her room pass card and said she was departing, he smiled, said, "Of course, Ms. Chastain," and began to work his own brand of magic on the computer keyboard. After a few seconds, he stopped typing and frowned. "It looks like I didn't get your credit card imprint when you checked in."

Libby smiled at him. "Really? You must have forgotten, that's all. Things were pretty frantic around here yesterday, weren't they? You can run it now though—here you are." She handed over a gold Amex card and waited while Walter slid it through a scanner and then typed some more.

It only took half a minute or so for the American Express computer to tell the Holiday Inn's computer that Libby's card was legit. Walter typed a bit more, but then stopped and muttered, "Damn."

"Something wrong?" Libby wasn't worried about her credit card; she always paid on time and her credit score, the last time she'd checked, was approaching 700. But clearly, something was going on here.

Walter looked up at her apologetically. "The system just went down, Ms. Chastain. Your card was fine, nothing to worry about there. We should be up and running again in a few minutes."

"Well, since my card already went through, why don't I just get going and you can deal with the computer once it's feeling more cooperative."

"I'm sorry, Ms. Chastain, but we can't do it that way. I need you to sign both the hotel's statement and the American Express charge authorization, and I can't print those until the computer's working." He gave her a reassuring smile. "It does this, every once in a while. But the network never stays down for long. If you'd like to have a seat, I'll let you know as soon as we're ready to process your checkout. Or, if you prefer to wait in the hotel coffee shop, I can go find you as soon as we're all set here."

Libby gave him her best smile, and with just a little *push* said, "Are you sure you can't just let me leave now?"

Walter blinked a couple of times, but then said, "I'm sorry, Ms. Chastain, but I just can't do that. I could lose my job."

Damn. "All right, then, I'll just sit over there, near the plants." Even a little magic could not always overcome vested self-interest.

Walter was telling her the truth. She would have detected the deception if he had lied to cover up his own mistake. Still, she was starting to feel uneasy. Libby wasn't sure if her credit card number was stuck somewhere in the Holiday Inn's system, or whether it had already made its way into the American Express credit card database. If the latter, it could now be accessible to authorized parties, like credit bureaus. And maybe some unauthorized parties, as well.

Eighteen blocks away, in another hotel, a laptop computer that lay open on a bed gave a series of clearly audible beeps. That was what the two men who had come to kill Libby Chastain were waiting for.

Kittridge looked at the screen, then typed in a command. The information on the screen changed, and now it contained what he wanted. "She's just used her Amex at the Holiday Inn on West Forty-Fifth," he said. "Let's go."

Winter stood up, struggled into his sport coat, and picked up the briefcase that contained their essential equipment. The rest of the luggage could stay—there was no time to check out. If they had the chance to come back for their stuff later, fine. If not, that was okay, too; each had learned long ago not to bring anything on these trips that could not be easily replaced.

It took just over six minutes before Walter called over, "Ms. Chastain? The system's up again." As Libby rapidly approached the front desk, he gave her an apologetic smile and said, "We'll get you checked out in no time at all. Sorry for the inconvenience. In fact, I'm authorized to give you this coupon, good for twenty-five percent off the standard room rate at any of our nine hundred-plus hotels and resorts..."

The taxi bearing Winter and Kittridge came within sight of the Holiday Inn just as Libby was climbing into the back of another cab in front of the hotel. "Shit!" Kittridge said under his breath. He looked a question at his partner, who nodded agreement immediately. The two had worked together for a long time, and understood each other very well.

Kittridge leaned forward so the driver could hear him. "Listen, we've had a change in plans. You see that cab in front in the Holiday Inn, the one that's just pulling out? I want to see where it goes. Follow it. Not too close."

The driver, a Nigerian national who had been pushing a hack for eight years, looked back over his shoulder. "What? You make a joke? 'Follow that cab,' like on TV?"

Kittridge locked eyes with the man. "*Do I look like I'm joking?*"

The Nigerian blinked twice, and looked away. "No, sorry, sorry."

It was time for Winter to be Good Cop. He leaned forward and said, "Sure, no problem. We know it must sound a little weird. Look, we'll pay you double the meter, once this is done, okay? Make it worth your time."

The driver's eyebrows went up. "Double? The whole fare, including now?"

"You got it, pal," Winter said, and sat back. "Now do what the man said: follow that cab."

The driver managed to keep Libby Chastain's taxi in sight without having to ride on its bumper and draw undue attention. He was forced to run a couple of lights on the yellow to avoid losing his quarry, but he seemed immune to the angry blatts from other drivers. He was probably used to it.

The little caravan ended at JFK Airport. Libby got out in front of Terminal 4, paid her driver and carried her single bag inside, walking rapidly.

"Let us off at the same place," Kittridge said, then gave the driver the money he'd been promised. As the two killers walked into the terminal building, Winter said softly, "We can't do it in here."

"Too many people, too many cameras. But let's see where she's going. Once she gets on a plane, she's trapped until it lands, I don't care what kind of a witch she is. We'll find out where she's headed, and call Pardee."

"That means someone else'll get the job," Winter said. "Too bad. We could've used the dough."

Kittridge shrugged his big shoulders. "There's plenty of other jobs. Hell, he'll probably give us another one while I'm still on the phone with him."

"I hope so." Winter kept his voice low. "How many of these witch bitches is he after, anyway?"

"Far as I can tell—all of 'em."

Chapter 7

The head seafood guy at Price Chopper supermarket was named Guy Chavot, and he was only too happy to cooperate with the forces of Truth, Justice, and the American Way, which he seemed to think were embodied in the two FBI agents who sat with him in the employees' break room. Fenton and O'Donnell had each learned that FBI credentials gained respect from a civilian in direct proportion to said civilian's distance from Washington, D.C. Unfortunately, some civilians were so impressed, it made them talkative.

"Yeah, we sold some dry ice a while back. We normally get a call for it around Halloween, you know—throw some in a basin of water and it makes a spooky-looking fog. A lot of people like to use it at kids' parties, I guess. I sell the stuff at cost. Don't make any money, but it's good customer relations, and that always pays off in the long run. The district manager, Mister de Grandin, is always saying—"

"But you've had a more recent request," Colleen said. "Something that didn't involve Halloween."

"Uh, yeah, sure. Like I was sayin' before. About,

I don't know, three–four weeks ago, I sold some to Annie Levesque." He pronounced it *LeVeck*. "I think she bought, like, six-and-a-half pounds of the stuff. Well, we weigh it in kilos. Three kilos."

"Did she say what she wanted it for?" Fenton asked.

"Naw, and I didn't ask, neither. Annie's always been kind of a weird one."

Fenton and Colleen exchanged brief looks, then Fenton asked, "Weird in what way, exactly?"

"Aw, she's into all that occult stuff. Fortune telling, Tarot cards, love potions, all that kinda stuff. Must pay pretty well, though. She always seems to have enough money, and she ain't on welfare or food stamps or nothin'."

Colleen leaned forward in her chair a little. "Has she had any conflicts with people in town? Any disputes, incidents, maybe bad blood with someone?"

Chavot adjusted his glasses, although they did not appear to need adjusting. "Well, folks around here mostly give Annie a wide berth. She comes into town; nobody bothers her much. She buys stuff she needs, pays cash money, then goes back to that cabin of hers, out in Redford, someplace."

"People are afraid of this woman?" Colleen asked. "How come? Is she unpleasant, violent, unstable, what?"

Chavot waved a hand, as if clearing cigarette smoke away. "Aw, there's stories. I never paid 'em no mind. About how, years ago, some high school kids're supposed to have egged Annie's car. Ruins the finish, that does. You've gotta wash it off right away, otherwise it—"

"What about the high school kids?" Fenton said.

"She have them arrested?"

"Naw, something happened to 'em. Supposedly, within a week, all four kids took sick and died. Like I said, there's just stories. Nobody can name any of the kids if you press 'em about it."

Fenton glanced at Colleen again, before asking, "How long ago was this, supposedly?"

"I dunno. Like, ten years, or something. It's all bullshit, you know. Just stories people tell, like the ones about seeing Champy."

"Who? Champy? Champ of what?" Fenton seemed lost now.

"Ah, you know, the prehistoric sea monster that's supposed to live in Lake Champlain. Funny, though—the only folks that ever see him are drunks with no cameras, seems like. It's just a gag to sell T-shirts, stuff like that, to the summer tourists."

"Gotcha," Colleen said, and turned to Fenton. "Lots of lakes around the world have local legends about some kind of monster living there. Loch Ness is probably the best known, but there's gotta be a dozen of them." A smile briefly lit up her face. "All selling shirts to the tourists."

As they walked back to their rented car, Colleen said, "I guess you know that Annie Levesque scares the shit out of him, right?"

"Oh, yeah. Methinks he doth protest too much."

"A scholar, no less."

"Fuckin' A."

Once they were inside the car, Colleen said, "If there's time before we leave, I want to get one of those Champy T-shirts."

"Favorite niece or nephew?"

"Hell, no. For me. I think it'd be kinda cool to

wear it to the next meeting of my... circle." She let the sentence trail off, as if she regretted starting it, but Fenton didn't seem to notice.

"Circle?" he asked. "What the hell's that? Some kind of sewing circle?"

"Close. We're into craft." Her voice was casual. "Just a bunch of crafties, sitting around, talking about different aspects of craft. Scrapbooking, decoupage, stuff like that."

"Yeah? Doesn't sound like you, somehow. I'd have figured BMX racing, skydiving, something adventurous."

"Oh, I do adventurous stuff, too." She smiled, a little. "We all have more than one facet to our lives, Dale."

"Guess you're right." As Colleen started the engine, he said, "Next stop, we oughta check out the other supermarket, just in case somebody else has been buying up dry ice lately."

"Not too likely, is it?"

"Nope, but we gotta consider all possibilities, just like they taught us at Quantico. Then, I guess we're heading downtown, what there is of it."

"Police HQ, you mean."

"Yup. You know, you're pretty smart, for somebody with freckles."

Colleen made an unladylike snorting noise. "Smart enough to know that we better find out what happened to those high school kids."

"Think all that really went down, huh?"

"Fuckin' A."

Pardee's phone started playing "Tubular Bells," the theme from *The Exorcist*. In addition to a certain

130

amount of wit, Pardee also had a keen sense of irony.

"Yes?" Pardee could have communicated with his minions through magical means, but he did not wish to frighten them. At least, not yet.

"It's Kittridge, boss. One of Chastain's credit cards finally showed up online, but by the time we got there, she was in a cab. Took her out to JFK. We had no chance to close the deal."

"I very much hope you obtained her flight information." Pardee's voice contained no hit of menace whatever. It didn't have to.

"Sure, boss, sure. No prob. She's on United, Flight 441, nonstop to Chicago. Arrives three forty-five, local—or it's supposed to, anyway."

"Which airport—O'Hare or Midway?"

"O'Hare. The big one."

"You're not just guessing about that, are you? Because if you were to guess incorrectly…"

"No, boss, I checked it out, absolutely."

"Very well." Pardee thought for a moment. "I have another assignment for you."

"Great, glad to hear it."

"It's in New Jersey. A place called Avon, sometimes known as Avon-by-the-Sea. Do you know it?"

"Nah, but we'll find it, no prob. Winter's from Jersey, he probably knows where it is. If not, we'll score a map, someplace."

"All right. Your client is one Judith Maloney." He repeated the name, then provided an address, which he also said twice.

"Got it, boss."

"You didn't write any of that down, did you?"

"Hell, no. I'm no amateur."

"Then make sure you do not act like one when you get to New Jersey. Call me when you've made the sale."

Pardee terminated the call without any social amenities, then called a number with a Chicago area code. Libby Chastain was one fish he very much did not want to escape his net. Or the gaff to follow.

"Yeah?" It was a man's voice, businesslike and impersonal.

"You know who this is, Strom."

"Yeah. Yeah, I do." The voice took on a note of eagerness.

"I have more work for you."

Libby Chastain came out of the little tunnel that temporarily connected her plane with the terminal and saw Quincey Morris immediately. But before going to him, she made herself scan the other people who were waiting for disembarking passengers from her flight. It wasn't always possible to tell who wished you ill just by looking, but Libby's witch sense was finely tuned, and there was always the chance she'd pick up harmful intent in time to do something about it.

But no one seemed to be paying her any attention at all—apart from the tall, dark-haired man in the blue suit, his beard stubble noticeable even this early in the day. She went to him then, and they exchanged a brief hug.

"Quincey, it's so good to see you," she said softly.

"It's good to be seen, Libby. At least by you."

As they walked toward the main terminal building, Morris leaned closer and said, "By the way, I spent the last half hour checking out all the people in the immediate area of your gate. I don't have your infallible instincts, but I didn't see anybody who looked like trouble."

"That's good, she said. "I've had enough trouble for a while."

"Did you check a bag?"

"I had to. Some of my gear might raise a few eyebrows if I tried to take it through one of the security checkpoints, and I have no desire to have my name end up on some watch list."

"Or witch list."

"That, too. I just hope my suitcase didn't end up in Omaha, or someplace."

They entered the terminal and followed the signs to the luggage carousels. Neither of them noticed the man, holding an open copy of *Forbes* magazine, who was seated in a position where he could watch everyone who came out from that set of gates. Once he determined where the man and the woman were heading, Charlie Strom stood up and followed, pulling a phone/walkie-talkie from his jacket pocket.

Strom was a big man, and he walked aggressively, as if there were people determined to get in his way and he was equally determined that they weren't going to succeed. Apart from the walk, the only thing distinctive about him was his hair, which was white on the sides and dark on top. On someone twenty years younger, it might have been a fashion statement, but in Strom's case it was a genetic quirk that showed up in his family every other generation or so. Being conspicuous was a bad thing in his line of work, but some perverse pride kept him from dyeing it a uniform color. Most of the people who learned what he did for a living didn't usually get much time to ponder his appearance, anyway.

Strom held the device to his ear, his big paw covering it to muffle what might come through the earpiece, and pushed the "Talk" button.

"Lee." He made his rough voice as soft as he could.

Another voice, male and a little higher than Strom's, came back almost instantly. "Yeah."

"She's heading toward the baggage claim. And she's got some guy with her."

After a moment, the voice came back. "Cop?"

"Hard to say. He's too well-dressed for CPD. Could be federal, maybe."

"Shit."

"Yeah, I know."

"Well, you weren't gonna burn her in there, anyway. Too many eyes." Another pause. "What you gonna do?"

"If he's a Fed, he won't be alone. He'll have somebody in a car waiting. I'm gonna hang back, see where they go once they pick up her bag. Stay loose, kid."

"Gotcha, Charlie."

"And be ready to move—fast."

There is an elegant, expensive apartment building in Philadelphia's Main Line area. It boasts state-of-the-art security—and, unlike many such places, the boast is justified. This is why Hannah Widmark lives there. It is vital to her that her dwelling space, and its contents, be protected while she is away. When she is at home, of course, no extra protection is necessary.

In contrast to the building's ritzy façade, Hannah's

apartment is stark, even Spartan. Her bed is a mattress on the floor. Her desk, which is also where she takes her meals, is a card table, with a folding metal chair behind it. There is no television, radio, or any other form of entertainment to be found there.

Despite the general sparseness, there are two areas of the apartment where money has been spent generously. One is the large steel gun case, with its electronic lock that requires a nine-digit pass code to operate. This impregnable armoire contains firearms and ammunition, laser sights and illegal sound suppressors. It also holds a number of other objects and devices not immediately recognizable as weapons—but they are.

The other place in the apartment where Hannah has spent money is the combination exercise room and dojo. It contains one of the best exercise bikes made, a treadmill that might belong in an NFL locker room, and a Stairmaster. There is also a Bowflex machine and a selection of free weights.

In the middle of the room, hanging from the ceiling by a stout chain, is a full-size punching bag that would not look out of place in a gym where Mike Tyson used to train. Off to one side is a device shaped like the upper half of a man's torso, but made of ballistic-grade black ceramic. At various points on the dummy's chest, neck, and head are recessed lights, which wink on and off at random when the device is turned on. The idea is that someone wearing boxing gloves will try to hit the area marked by a light before it winks off and another one comes on. It operates at four speeds, and this one is set at the highest.

Hannah Widmark has broken three of them.

In the bare living room, Hannah sits cross-legged on the floor, cleaning and oiling the components of a stripped-down firearm, which she has laid out on a sheet of oilcloth. The parts comprise an M-40A3 rifle, the model that has been issued to Marine Corps snipers since 2003. It is not available for sale to the general public.

On the mantle opposite from where Hannah sits is a rare touch of domesticity: next to a small stuffed toy bear with a dirty face, there are two photos in polished wooden frames. One shows a man and woman side by side, arms around each other's waist. The other shows the same man and woman in a group shot with two children—a girl and a boy, who appear to be about six and eight years old, respectively. The woman in the photos bears a striking resemblance to Hannah Widmark, but she differs from the woman sitting on the floor in two significant ways: she does not have the long scar that runs along Hannah's left jaw line, and she is smiling.

The cell phone on the carpet next to Hannah rings. She opens it, glances at the display, then puts it to her ear and says, "Yes?" Pause. "Yes, I'm available." Another, longer pause. "Let's not discuss it on the phone. I'll be there tomorrow, and I'll meet you wherever you like, any public place. And bring a picture of her with you." Pause. "Yes, I understand that she's dead." Hannah's gaze shifts to the framed pictures across the room, and something passes across her hard face so fast it might never have been there at all. "Bring a picture anyway."

Chapter 8

"Annie Levesque, huh?" Detective Pierre "Pete" Premeaux looked across his desk at the two FBI agents and shook his head slowly. "Crazy Annie."

"Is that what people call her?" Colleen O'Donnell asked. "Crazy Annie?"

"Some do." Premeaux picked a Starbucks cup out of the clutter on his desk and drained what was left of the contents. "But not to her face."

Fenton nodded. "We'd heard that the locals are wary of her," he said. "We were wondering why."

Premeaux crumpled the cup, tossed it toward a wastebasket twenty feet away, and missed. "No disrespect intended, Agents, but why do you care?"

"She's beginning to look like a viable suspect in a couple of unsolved homicides," Colleen told him.

Premeaux stared at her. "Those two kids," he said flatly. "Wilson and Dufresne."

"You don't exactly sound surprised," Fenton said.

"No, I guess I'm not," Premeaux said. "The M.O., with the organs removed like that, had 'occultist' written all over it, but there was never evidence to connect any of it with Annie."

"And yet you thought of her," Colleen said. "What prompted you to do that?"

Premeaux tilted his chair back slowly. "There was something... weird... that went down around here, about ten years ago. I was new on the force then, and it wasn't my case, anyway. But everybody was talking about it, cops and civilians both. Made the papers, too—bits of it, anyway."

"We'd heard something about that," Colleen said. "We were hoping you could enlighten us as to the details."

Premeaux looked at her, then at Fenton, then back. "You know, it occurs to me that murder ain't a federal crime."

"You're right, it's not," Fenton said. "Usually."

"But it might be," Colleen said carefully, "if it were part of a larger conspiracy involving similar murders taking place in a variety of locations, and crossing state lines."

The detective's bushy eyebrows went up, then slowly came back down. "I'd been hearing some stuff about that, lately. Nothing official, you understand, just the grapevine." He shifted his weight and let his chair come level again. "Kids are being killed all over, aren't they? And their organs taken. While still alive."

"Officially, we're not allowed to confirm or deny that," Fenton said. "But, unofficially..." He let his voice trail off.

"If that information were to get into the media, even locally," Colleen said, "it would land us in some seriously deep shit with our boss."

"Yeah, I follow," Premeaux said. "You don't got to worry about that. Not with me." Then he swiveled his chair toward his computer's keyboard. "Let me take a quick look at the file. Don't want to get my facts wrong."

A few minutes later, he turned back to face them. "It was eleven years ago," he said. "I was close."

"Something about kids egging her car, wasn't it?" Colleen said.

"Yeah, and not just hers. These four junior high assholes decide it'd be fun to throw eggs at a bunch of parked cars. So, one Friday night, a little after dark, they stop at Price Chopper, buy four cartons of eggs, and head for the K-Mart, which is close by. The place is still open, there's quite a few cars parked in the lot, and so these morons let fly. All four cartons worth. Then they take off, most likely giggling like schoolgirls."

"Being an asshole comes easy at that age," Fenton said. "Adult level of testosterone meets kid-level judgment."

"Yeah, tell me about it," Premeaux said. "Lots of us do stupid shit at that age, but most of us don't deserve to die like those kids did."

"So, what happened, exactly?" Colleen asked.

"Well, as you probably figured out already, one of those cars that got egged was Annie's, that old Caddie she was driving back then. The responding officer took down the license numbers of the cars with egg on 'em, in case the owners wanted to press charges, later."

"Pressing charges assumes the perps are in custody," Fenton said. "If I can use the word 'perp' to refer to kiddy shit like this."

"Oh, they were in custody quick enough," Premeaux said. "One of them was ID'd by a neighbor, who was driving into the lot just as the kids were tear-assing out. She reported what she'd seen, once she heard about what had happened. The kid was brought in for questioning. I wasn't there, but I imagine they had a confession out of him in five minutes, and the names of the other kids in five more. Kids that age, they don't usually stand up too well to pressure."

Fenton smiled, a little. "Not exactly hardened criminals, huh?"

"Never been in trouble before, any of them. So, you can imagine how it went for them."

"Um, I'm guessing community service and a stern talking-to from the judge," Colleen said.

"Yeah, pretty much," Premeaux said. "I think their parents had to pay for a bunch of car washes, and those kids were probably grounded until they were, like, thirty." He stopped, and the levity was gone from his voice when he went on, "Or they would've been, if they'd lived that long."

"So how does Annie Levesque tie into this?" Colleen asked. "I mean, apart from the fact that her car was one of those that got egged."

"Here's where it starts to get weird," Premeaux said. "As part of their punishment, each kid was ordered by the judge to write a letter of apology to every one of the car owners involved. Me, I might've said one letter per person, and all four kids sign it. But the judge wanted to make it tough, I guess. So, each of those kids wrote a letter to Annie Levesque saying how sorry he was, just like they wrote to seventeen other people. Now, I figure the other seventeen read the letters, tossed 'em, and that was that. But the ones sent to Annie all came back, marked *Return to Sender*."

"Wrong address?" Fenton asked.

"Nope, it was her mailing address, all right, same one she's used for years and years. Now, some of this stuff I'm gonna tell you wasn't in the report, but it's things I heard at the time, from other cops, okay?"

Fenton shrugged. "Sure, fine."

"You'd assume that the post office had sent the letters back unopened. But when the kids, or their parents, opened the envelopes, there were a couple of things different. One was that each kid's signature had been cut off from the bottom of the letter."

"Oh, dear," Colleen said. Premeaux looked a question at her, but she shook her head.

"The other difference was something that had been added. Each envelope contained a white feather."

Fenton shifted in his chair, which drew Premeaux's attention. "That mean something to you?"

"Nothing important," Fenton said, but his face suggested otherwise. "It's just that a white feather is used as the symbol of a curse in some schools of *voudoun*."

The detective peered at him. "That right? And how'd you get to know about stuff like that?"

"I told you we work in Behavioral Science," Fenton said. "Some of the crimes we investigate have occult... aspects to them."

"Yeah, I bet they do," Premeaux said, then looked at Colleen. "And how about you, Agent O'Donnell? What was so interesting about the signatures being cut from the letters?"

"In order to curse someone in black magic, whether

141

voudoun or some other tradition, you usually need something from the intended victim. Hair, nail clippings, clothing. Or a signature."

Premeaux nodded slowly. "Working for that Behavioral Science Unit must be even more interesting than I'd have thought."

"It has its moments," Colleen said. "So, what happened to the four kids?"

"A few days later, they took sick. Real sick. All four of them. Terrible pain in their bellies. Parents probably thought appendicitis, and there were calls to 911, followed by some fast trips to the hospital, where the docs did every damn test they could think of. And they came up with zip. Zilch. *Nada*."

"The poor kids," Fenton said. "Hell, the poor parents."

"And to make things worse, none of the painkillers they tried at the hospital did any good. Hell, they were even giving those kids the drugs they use with terminal cancer patients. No effect at all. Two days later, the kids died." Premeaux glanced at his computer screen. "No, sorry, one lasted for three. Cause of death as listed as—"

"Let me guess," Fenton said quietly. "Either stroke, cardiac arrest, or they went into shock."

There was silence in the room, until Premeaux said, "And just how the fuck did you know that?"

"I didn't, but it wasn't hard to guess. I know more than I ever wanted to about death by torture," Fenton told him. "And, if there's no significant blood loss or damage to a major organ, most torture victims go out one of those three ways. It's the body's way of reacting to pain it can't stand anymore. For the lucky ones, it happens sooner, rather than later."

"I hope you won't take offense, Agent Fenton, if I tell you that's information I hope never to have to think about again."

"I don't blame you at all," Fenton said. "So, what killed those poor kids?"

"Two went into shock, one had a stroke, and the last one's heart just gave out."

The room was quiet again. Then Colleen O'Donnell said, "You know what we're going to have to do, don't you?"

"Pay a call on Annie Levesque," Premeaux said.

"And sooner," Fenton said, "rather than later."

Libby Chastain's suitcase was a big, battered square of Samsonite that had gone out of style when Ronald Reagan was president.

"Every time I travel with you," Morris said, "I keep hoping you've invested in some new luggage. The fashion these days is for soft bags, you know. Absorbs the bumps better."

"There's stuff in here that shouldn't be absorbing any bumps, at all," Libby said. "As you have reason to know."

"Smartass remark hereby withdrawn," he said, grabbing the thing off the baggage carousel. As they started toward the exit marked "Ground Transportation," Morris said, "You know, I've never asked why it doesn't offend your feminist principles for me to carry this beast for you."

"I look at it as exploiting the oppressor," she said, with a sweet smile.

Outside, as they waited their turn for a taxi, Libby asked, "So, where are we going to meet your friend, Harry?"

"There's a pub near his office where he likes to hang out. He said he'd be there most of today. At least, that what I *think* he said. When I called him, the connection was full of static, and then the line went dead entirely. Technology tends to flake out fast then Harry's using it. He said once that his magical aura, or something, is what does it."

Libby nodded pensively. "Yes, in his magical tradition, I can see how that would be a problem. Wizards of his type carry a lot of energy around them."

"Yeah they're not gentle souls, like you Wiccans."

"Ha!" Libby said, as a taxi pulled up in front of them. "Bring the bag, slave."

"That didn't sound very gentle."

Charlie was walking fast as he pressed the "send" button on the walkie-talkie. "Lee."

"Yo."

"They're in line for a cab. Pull up to the exit just behind the taxi stand. You know the one I mean?"

"Be there in three, big man."

It was more like two minutes later when the stolen Oldsmobile they were using pulled up to the curb in front of Charlie, who wasted no time scrambling into the passenger's seat.

"They're next in line for a cab. See them—the woman with the green top and the tall guy in the suit?"

"Yeah, I got 'em now." Lee was younger than Charlie, and skinnier. His hair was swept back in a pompadour that Elvis might have envied. He had on the Wayfarer sunglasses that he wore day and night, indoors and out. "I see what you mean about that guy," Lee said. "He's not local law, not with those threads."

"And if he was a Fed, he'd have a car, and another Fed to drive it."

"So what do we do, man?"

"Follow, wait for a good chance, then burn 'em."

"The guy, too?"

"He gets in the way, he gets in the way. Tough luck. You're not getting soft on me, are you?"

"Shit no, I was just thinkin' that nobody's payin' us for him. He'll be a freebie."

"Sometimes in this business, you gotta make sacrifices, Lee. Okay there they go. Stay close, but not too close, huh?"

"You got it."

Quincey Morris gave the driver an address in midtown, and sat back in his seat. "I hope Harry's still there," he said to Libby. "If not, we can try his office, which is just down the block."

"I hope he knows something about that... business you're looking into," she said, mindful of the driver, who might have big ears. "It'd be nice if we had somewhere to start."

"Harry knows a lot of people, and he's got his fingers in a lot of pies."

"Sounds unsanitary, but I know what you mean. How do you two know each other, anyway?"

"We'd each been hired separately to investigate what turned out to be two ends of the same case. We met in the middle, so to speak, and decided to cooperate. Worked out pretty well."

"Let's hope it does this time, too," she said.

"Maybe he'll even have some thoughts about who might have sent those two visitors I had the other day."

"Yeah, that is pretty damn odd. I won't insult you by asking if you've been thinking about who might have the motivation to send those fellas calling on you."

"I've been thinking about little else, and it's gotten me nowhere."

"Well, it makes sense to somebody, I reckon. Sooner or later, we'll find out who."

"Then pay a visit of our own."

"You can count on that." As he spoke, there was something in Morris's eyes that made Libby very glad she was not the person he was thinking about.

They were silent for a while, until Morris told the driver, "I think that it's coming up, on the other side of the street. Just let us off anywhere along here, will you?"

Throughout the journey, they had not once looked behind them.

"Cab's lettin' 'em off, Charlie."

"I got eyes. Slow down. We don't want to pass by until they're both on foot."

"This is what the ghetto boys call a 'drive-by,' ain't it? Never did one of those before."

"We was all cherry once, kid."

"You wanna use this thing, or me?"

"What thing?"

"This wand doohickey that Pardee give us. He said it would, like, overcome her magic for a little while, long enough for us to take her out."

"Fuck that, put it away," Charlie said. "A bullet in

146

the head is a bullet in the head—I don't care if she's a witch or the fuckin' Pope."

"Yeah, man, but Pardee said—"

"Fuck Pardee, too. He's got no respect, the way he talks to us, like we're fucking morons, or something. We'll show the bastard how to make a hit. Get your window all the way down."

From the holster under his arm, Charlie pulled a long-barreled .44 Magnum, and he could see that Lee had that rapid-firing Tech-9 of his ready. "Okay," he said tightly. "Let's drop the hammer."

She and Morris were standing at the curb, waiting for a break in the traffic, when Libby Chastain noticed the black Oldsmobile heading their way very fast, then heard the squeal of its brakes as it suddenly slowed. Inside were two men.

She snatched her suitcase from Quincey's hand, shouted "*Servate nos—iam!*" then released the handle just as the car pulled up opposite them.

The ensorcelled bag rose four feet into the air, broadside to the Oldsmobile. It moved with blinding speed to absorb the five fast shots from the driver, and when the boom of the other man's Magnum sounded, the suitcase was between that weapon and Libby, too. The driver fired three more times, with the same result, and two more magnum slugs fired from the back seat also buried themselves in the bag's side.

Meanwhile, Quincey Morris had hooked an arm around Libby's waist and yanked her behind the shelter of a parked car. Then he reached for his cell phone to call 911—for all the good that would do them now.

The driver could be heard yelling, "Shit, I told you!" as he pulled from between the seats a cloth bundle that parted to reveal a foot-long metal rod. The driver pointed the rod at Libby's bag and shouted "*Macabo*—no, uh, *Makibo!*"

Then the car exploded.

Libby knelt next to Charlie Strom who, his back broken, lay amidst the wreckage of the Oldsmobile. He was bleeding from several places, and the left side of his face and neck were horribly burned. He twisted and squirmed, like a snake that has been run over by a truck.

Using the first two fingers of her right hand, Libby began making some cryptic signs in the air. At the same time she spoke, very fast, in a language that has been dead for over 2,000 years.

Perhaps half a minute later, Strom stopped writhing on the asphalt and lay still. His good eye stared at Libby Chastain. From over her shoulder, she heard Quincey say, "This one's gone."

"I've been able to block your pain, but I can't heal you," she told Strom. "Your wounds are too extensive, and I don't have the right gear with me to even make an attempt. I'm sorry."

Charlie Strom's mouth moved, but no sound came out.

"Tell me who sent you," Libby said gently. "I need to know, so I can protect myself. Who hired you to kill me?"

The mangled lips moved again, but this time a strangled voice managed to say, "And if... I don't, I s'ppose you'll... turn the pain back... on."

Libby shook her head, although she wasn't sure

if Strom could see her. "No, the spell stays in place, regardless. But, please, tell me. I won't lie to you—you're fading fast. You might not even last until the ambulance gets here. Do something decent, as your last act on this Earth."

What was left of Charlie Strom's mouth split into something that might once have been a grin. "Lady," he croaked, "I haven't got the time." Then the grin was gone, forever.

REVELATIONS

Chapter 9

Redford, New York, is the kind of place for which they invented the word "boondocks." Twenty miles outside of Plattsburgh, it is a community of isolated houses, with lots of wild ground between them. It's the perfect locale for people who value their privacy.

Annie Levesque's driveway was an eighth of a mile long, unpaved, and sloped upward at an angle that must have played hell with efforts to get it plowed out in the wintertime. Having reached the top, Detective Pete Premeaux turned off the engine of the unmarked police car, and he and his two passengers sat looking at the place that Annie Levesque called home.

It was a smallish log house, a type common to that area. It looked mundane at first glance, but closer inspection revealed some things that were not quite right. All the windows were boarded up from the inside, although each appeared to have an unbroken glass pane in place. The smoke that came from Annie's chimney was the black, roiling kind that you associate with a working factory, not the placid white of wood smoke. On the end of the roof opposite the chimney, looking incongruous, was a satellite dish that looked to be in better repair than the rest of the house.

The carcass of a butchered deer hung from a hook on the porch, a pool of blood spread out from beneath it, about a million flies partaking of the buffet. Premeaux, Fenton, and Colleen O'Donnell got out of the car, and slowly approached the house. As they drew closer, they could see an intricate, circular symbol painted on the front door.

"I drove through Amish country in Ohio, once," Premeaux said. "That there looks kinda like one of the hex signs they all have on their barns."

"Not quite," Colleen said. "Those are designed to *repel* evil. This... well, this is something else."

Premeaux knocked on the heavy wooden door and it opened immediately, as if the woman had been standing behind it, waiting for them. Displaying his badge and ID card, he said, "Miss Levesque, I'm Detective Pete Premeaux from the Plattsburgh Police Department. These two folks are Special Agents from the FBI. We'd like to ask you a few questions."

She stared at him. "Questions? What kinda questions?"

"About a couple of cases we're investigating. It won't take long. Can we come in?"

More staring. Then she said, "No, I don' t'ink you can do dat. I come out."

She stepped out onto the porch and pulled the door shut behind her. "Now, what you want wit' me?" She had a pronounced French-Canadian accent, not uncommon so close to Quebec Province.

"Is there some reason why you don't want us to come inside, Ms. Levesque?" Fenton asked politely.

"This my house, my property. You got maybe a warrant, something like dat?"

Fenton shook his head.

"No? Den we talk out here. I like da fresh air, you know? Good for my heart."

Annie Levesque looked to be in her early fifties, and the years had not been kind to her. She was somewhere between plump and fat, and her skin had a yellowish cast to it that, in some parts of the world, would have suggested malaria. Limp brown hair hung down, just touching the old gray sweater she wore atop blue polyester stretch pants.

Annie Levesque's heavy face bore the sour expression of someone who knows that the world has proved a miserable place so far, and it isn't likely to get any better tomorrow.

"What you people want wit' me? I got work I gotta do."

"What's that symbol you have painted on your door, there, Ms. Levesque?" Colleen asked. "It's quite unusual."

Annie slowly turned her head and looked at Colleen as if seeing her for the first time. If so, what she saw didn't please her—her eyes widened briefly, before narrowing to slits that, if anything, made her look more unattractive than before. After slowly looking Colleen up and down, Annie said, "My cousin Hervé, he make the folk art. He asks can he make some on my door, I say sure. Says it bring good luck. Why not?"

"So, your cousin," Colleen said, "he didn't mention that it represents an ancient demonic curse,

155

calling the powers of hell down on anyone who might trespass?"

Annie's laugh, like everything else about her, was unpleasant. "Demons? Curse? You make crazy talk, lady." She turned back to Premeaux. "Dat why you come up here? Waste my time with crazy talk?"

"No, we didn't," the detective said. "We wanted to ask you about dry ice."

More of the stare—this time accompanied by the running of her tongue over thick lips. "Dry ice? I don't know nothing about no dry ice. You still makin' the crazy talk."

"The seafood manager at Price Chopper says otherwise, Ms. Levesque," Fenton told her. "He told us you've bought three kilos of dry ice from him in the past month or so."

Her eyebrows went up in an exaggerated show of comprehension that would have embarrassed a high school production of *Our Town*. "Oh, you mean da *hot* ice. Dat what we call it 'round here. Hot ice, 'cause it like burn when you touch it, eh? Yeah, I get some from the supermarket. So what?"

"So, we'd like to know what you use it for," Colleen said.

The grin she gave Colleen revealed that Annie Levesque's teeth had not received the attention of a dentist for quite some time. "I use it in one of dem old fashion' ice cream makers, like from da old days. You gotta get it real cold. Some folks use the reg'lar ice wit' rock salt, but da hot ice work better. More cold, eh?"

Colleen nodded as if this made perfect sense to her. "That must be a really old ice cream machine you have."

"Yeah, sure. It belong to my mother. Pretty old, I guess."

"You know, I'm very interested in antiques of that sort—old machinery, and so on. I'd love to see it!"

This time, the reptilian stare went on for the space of three or four breaths. "Is broke. I had to t'row it away, can't get parts no more. Sorry." She did not appear in the least contrite.

"What did you do with it?" Fenton asked. "I mean, how did you dispose of it?"

"I take to da landfill, wit' my other garbage, two, mebee t'ree weeks ago. Is in there someplace, you wanna go look." The ugly grin had made a reappearance.

"Probably not worth the trip," Fenton said. "But not everything around here is an antique, is it?" He glanced upward. "I couldn't help but notice the satellite dish on your roof. You watch much TV, Ms. Levesque?"

"Yeah, sure, I watch." The grin was gone now. "Not too much else out here to do, eh?"

"Do you ever watch any of those *CSI* shows? They're very popular, I hear."

"Yeah, I guess I watch dat sometime. So?"

"Well," Fenton said, "if you watch any of those shows, you've probably heard of DNA analysis. Every person's DNA is unique, did you know that?"

"You say so, I believe you. Look, I gotta get back—"

"And DNA can be extracted from almost anything on the human body." Fenton went on as if she had not spoken. "Blood, fingernails, urine. Even hair. Just a single strand of hair can identify the person it belonged to."

Premeaux had been watching Fenton closely, and now said, "The thing is, we're investigating a couple of murders where DNA evidence could prove very important," he said.

"Murdered? Who got murdered? I don't know about no murder."

"It was those children," Premeaux said. "Suzanne Wilson and Billy Dufresne. You must have heard about it."

She nodded slowly. "Oh, yeah, sure, I see somet'ing on da news. Terrible, eh? But what dat got to do wit' me?"

"This wasn't in the news reports, because we withheld it from the press," Premeaux said. "But those poor kids were cut open, and some of their bodily organs were taken—while they were still alive."

"*Mon Dieu*," Annie said. Then: "How you know they still alive when this happen?"

"The presence of free histamines in the blood," Fenton said. "You only find those levels when someone has died in great pain. The CSI people were able to determine that."

"And they discovered something else, too," Premeaux said. "Inside the body cavity of one of those poor kids, they found a hair. A human hair. And it did not come from the victim. They checked."

"Which means it can only have come from one place," Fenton said. "The head of the person who cut that child open."

"That's right," Premeaux said. "And since DNA can be extracted from a single hair, we now have a DNA profile of the person that hair belonged to.

All we need is something—or someone—to match it to."

"And that's the main reason why we're here, Ms. Levesque," Fenton said. "To ask you to voluntarily contribute a hair sample. We only need a couple of strands, and it won't hurt, I promise." His face grew hard. "Not nearly so much as those kids were hurt. Not even close."

Annie Levesque looked at him. "And what if I say, I don't wanna do dat? What den?"

"Then we'll come back with a court order, and take what we need," Fenton said. "Even if we have to place you in cuffs to do it."

Fenton was bluffing like mad, and he was glad that Premeaux had picked up on it and was playing along. There were no hair samples found in either victim, and even if there had been, they had no probable cause on which to base a warrant request. Fenton wanted to see what Annie Levesque would do, or say, when the pressure came on. He had a hunch it would be revealing.

Annie nodded slowly, as if nearly resigned to her fate. She sighed and said, "I wanna call my lawyer, see what he t'ink about this. You wait here." She turned back toward her front door.

Colleen O'Donnell had deliberately not taken part in the tag-team badgering of Annie Levesque. Instead, she was observing the woman carefully, waiting for the darkness that must surely be inside her to emerge.

She watched Annie Levesque reach her front door, then rest her hand on the curse symbol painted there, as if she were about to push the door open but had stopped to think about something. Colleen heard the woman start to speak, very softly and strained to focus her concentration. Finally, she was able to pick up a couple of words. They were neither English nor French. After a second or two. Colleen recognized the language.

It was ancient Chaldean.

That was when she grabbed Fenton's arm, backpedaled quickly, and shouted, "Get off the porch! *Now!*"

Premeaux was on the other side of Fenton, so Colleen was unable to reach him, as well. He seemed to have no notion of what was going on.

Which was why he did not immediately follow the two FBI agents as they tumbled off the porch to fall a couple of feet into the dirt.

Which was why he was still standing there, reaching for the pistol on his hip, when the windows in the house exploded outward, all at once.

Which was also why a razor-sharp shard of glass nine inches long was able to bury itself deep in his throat.

"Libby, come on!"

Libby Chastain looked up from the corpse of Charlie Strom, a dazed expression on her face.

"We've got to get out of here," Morris said. "Unless you want to spend the next four days in police custody, making up lies about what just happened."

There were sirens in the distance now, drawing closer.

"But where can we go?" she asked. "Police will be here any—"

"There." Morris pointed at the pub across the

street where they were supposed to meet Harry the Wizard. "We'll go there."

There were concrete steps leading down from the street into the pub. As Morris and Libby made their way inside, carrying their luggage, the few patrons at the tables looked up incuriously then went back to what they had been doing—eating, drinking, talking, or all three.

As they approached the bar, Libby said softly, "My Goddess, Quincey, what *is* this place?"

"Apart from the obvious, you mean?"

'Look at the layout—thirteen windows, thirteen pillars, thirteen tables."

Morris turned from signaling the bartender and scanned the room. "Hmm. Interesting decorating scheme."

"And the arrangement of those tables is designed to disrupt any magical energy that might be released in here."

"Yeah, Harry told me once that this place is sort of neutral territory for the city's occult crowd. No magic of any kind allowed on the premises. Kind of like Las Vegas used to be for the Mob."

Behind them, a polite voice said, "Help you folks?"

The bartender was a tall, lean man of indeterminate age; he might have been an old forty or a young sixty. He had a wise look, as if he had seen everything at least twice, and was incapable of being surprised by anything.

"For starters, I think we could use us a drink," Morris said. "Libby?"

Libby Chastain turned from her examination of the room and said, "Double vodka, straight up, please. Ice cold, if you've got it."

Morris said, "And I'll have a bourbon and branch water."

The bartender looked at him. "Sorry? What water?"

"I forgot, that's what they call it back home. Bourbon and soda, please. Double. And is there someplace we can put our luggage?"

"On any of the empty tables is fine," the bartender said and went to make their drinks.

A minute later, he set their libations down in front of them. "Looks like you folks had some trouble out there," he said, with a head gesture toward the street.

"Did you see it?" Morris asked.

"Saw enough."

"Then you know we were the victims. Or would-be victims, anyway."

"Yeah, that seemed pretty clear. It was also clear that this lady has one heck of an interesting taste in luggage."

The bartender extended his hand. "I'm Mac. I own the place."

Morris and Libby each shook hands, then Morris said, "We came in here for a couple of reasons. One was, we're expectin' to meet a fella here. As for the other reason—truth is, we really can't afford to be dragged into a big police investigation. It might give whoever sent those guys out there another crack at us."

Mac nodded. They had all heard the sirens draw closer and closer, and then stop. "They'll have detectives canvassing the area soon, asking if anybody saw anything. You figure anybody noticed you folks coming in here?"

162

Morris and Libby looked at each other. "I don't think so," Libby said. "There weren't a lot of people around, and I threw together a cloaking spell as we were crossing the street. Um, what I mean is—"

Mac gave her a smile. 'You don't need to explain, Miss Chastain. I know what a cloaking spell is. Heck, everybody in here would know, if you asked them."

Libby glanced back at the half-dozen customers. "Yes, I expect they would."

"Tell you what," Mac said. "Why don't you give me your bags, and I'll stash them in the back room. You might want to visit the restrooms, clean up a little before the detectives get here. Then you can sit down at a table, have another drink, maybe something to eat, and relax, just like you've been here for the past half hour. Which you have."

Libby glanced at the other patrons again. "But what about—"

"Nobody here saw anything, that happened in the street, Miss Chastain, and nobody noticed exactly when you folks came in. You can take my word on that."

Morris nodded. "Appreciate that," he said. "But I have to wonder why you're willing to lie to the law for a couple of perfect strangers."

"You're friends of Harry's, aren't you? He described you pretty good, Mister Morris, and said you'd have a lady with you."

"Where *is* Harry anyway?" Morris asked.

"He left, about an hour and a half ago. Asked me to give you this."

Mac produced a plain white envelope with "Quincey Morris" written on the front. Morris tore it open and quickly read the single sheet that was inside. "Damn!"

Libby said softly, "Uh, Quincey, you might want to avoid using words like that in here. You never know who, or what, you might conjure up by accident."

"Yeah, you're right. Sorry."

"I take it the news isn't too good."

"Not so's you'd notice, no. Harry had to leave—not just leave here, but leave town. He said some urgent business came up for the Council, whatever that is, and he had no choice but to go off and attend to it."

"Well… darn," Libby said, catching herself at the last moment.

Ten minutes later, after cleaning up as best they could with soap and hot water, Morris and Libby were seated at a corner table. Mac brought over fresh drinks and a bowl of pretzels. "Usually, customers serve themselves," he said. "But since you're guests and all, I thought I'd make an exception this—oh, look who's here."

Two hard-faced men in cheap sport coats and awful ties had just come in. They had thick necks, cheap haircuts, and an aggressive way of walking. Had they worn flashing neon signs around their necks that said "Cop," they might have been a little more obvious, but not much.

"Guess I better go talk to the guardians of public order," Mac said. "Excuse me."

"I reckon they'll get around to us sooner or later," Morris said.

"We'd better not try to leave until they do, then." Libby said. "Just call attention to ourselves."

Morris took a pull at his fresh drink and said, "By

the way, I will never, ever make fun of your suitcase again."

"Well, you know, I was thinking of getting some of that soft stuff that's in fashion these days. It absorbs the bumps better, they say, but it's not nearly so good as Samsonite when it comes to stopping bullets." For a white witch, the smile that Libby gave him looked positively wicked.

"Okay, okay. I give. Let me up," Morris said. "Sure is a terrific spell you've got on that thing, though. Come up with it yourself?"

"Not entirely. It's a variation on one that's usually used on more static objects—doors, windows, and so on. But, considering the kind of people I've been hanging around with, lately…" This time, her smile was gentler. "I thought it would be useful to have something handy that could offer protection in transit. And speaking of protection, now that we know your friend isn't here, what did you have in mind?"

"There are a couple of other people in town I'd like to talk to. They're plugged into the whisper stream, to varying degrees, and might have heard something. I want to get that done quickly, then get us the… heck… out of Dodge, Libby. The bad guys know you're here."

Libby nodded thoughtfully. "And if we stick around, I suppose it's only a matter of time before they try again."

"Yeah," Morris said. "And next time, you might not be carrying your luggage."

Chapter 10

Special Agent Colleen O'Donnell lay sprawled on her back in the dead grass and dirt of Annie Levesque's front yard. She and Fenton were covered with small pieces of glass, but they had been out of the direct line of impact when all the house's windows magically exploded, and had suffered only minor cuts.

Detective Premeaux, however, was bleeding from half a dozen places, most seriously at the base of his throat, where a long, jagged shard of glass protruded. Premeaux fell to his knees, one hand gripping the spear of glass as if trying to pull it out; before he could succeed, he collapsed onto the porch. Blood pulsed from his wound.

Colleen knew that Premeaux was dying, and she ached to go to him. But if she did not deal with Annie Levesque *right now*, there were soon going to be three dead cops out here, not just one.

Fenton appeared to be dazed. He had not been prepared for the backwards tumble off the porch, and had struck his head on the hard ground. Colleen reached over, touched his head gently, and uttered a phrase that would render him unconscious for a short while. She was probably going to do something in the next few moments that Fenton should not see, or, more importantly, interfere with.

Kicking her legs out in front of her, just as she had learned at Quantico, Colleen did a hip roll and came to her feet smoothly. Annie Levesque, who appeared a bit shaken by the ferocity of the explosion she had caused, was fumbling with the latch on her front door. If she got inside, Annie would have access to whatever black magic paraphernalia and potions she kept there; and for Colleen to follow, into a place charged with Annie's diabolical energy, would be suicidal.

In unknowing imitation of her sister witch Sandy Jenkins, Colleen kept a wand stashed up the sleeve of her blazer. Colleen's slim scabbard was not spring-loaded, but she could still pull the wand out fast when she needed it.

Like now.

A wand is a pre-charged instrument, like a battery in the mundane world. It can allow you to work some kinds of magic quickly, but only some, and its power fades with use.

Colleen pointed her wand at the door and uttered a quick spell to jam the latch in place. It wouldn't hold for long, not on Annie's own house, but it would prevent the bitch from getting inside for a few moments.

This confrontation would be over, one way or another, very quickly.

Annie Levesque realized what was going on and turned to face Colleen. Keeping one hand touching the arcane symbol on her front door, she used the other to point a chubby finger at Colleen and utter another phrase in ancient Chaldean. Colleen instantly felt the air around her become warm, then hot, then very, hot, and knew that Annie's spell was designed to cause her to burst into flames.

Colleen pointed her wand at herself and said the words that would dispel Annie's magic. A moment later, she felt the temperature start to drop and knew she had succeeded. But Annie had now turned back to the latch working magic to dispel Colleen's spell and get the door open.

Instead of freezing the latch again, Colleen aimed her wand at Annie's right hand, and said the words that would paralyze her fingers temporarily. After fumbling with the door a moment longer, Annie turned back to Colleen, who was ready this time for another fire spell. But instead, Annie waved her hand in a sweeping gesture that seemed to encompass her whole yard and shouted something in an arcane language, her whole body shaking with the power she was expending.

Colleen was concentrating on keeping the paralysis of Annie's fingers going while simultaneously trying to figure a way to bring this chess match to endgame. Annie was considerably older than Colleen, and had clearly been practicing the craft much longer. Colleen was younger and somewhat faster, but Annie was stronger—and on her home ground. In a protracted contest, Annie was going to prevail, which meant that Colleen, and then Fenton, would die here.

There was a ritual in the Sisterhood, rarely practiced, that involved the sacrifice of some of your own blood to temporarily increase your magical power. The potential benefits were great, as were the risks—but there was no way to bring that to bear here. Colleen was juggling too many things, as it was.

She had enough awareness left to hear the sound of the earth cracking in several places around the yard, and from the corner of her eye she could see a patch of ground open as something horrible crawled out from beneath it.

There were bodies buried in Annie's yard, probably victims of her magic in years past. Annie was now calling them forth, and it wasn't hard to predict what she would command them to do. Colleen could protect herself against these reanimated corpses, but at the expense of taking her attention, and power, away from Annie, who would then be able to get into her house and access all the power stored within. Checkmate.

The creature that Colleen could see in her peripheral vision was almost out of its grave now, and she assumed the others were making similar progress. In a few more seconds they would be on her. She would either fall victim to their attack, or to the one Annie would level at her as soon as she gained entrance to her house.

If Colleen could hurt Annie, the necromancy would stop instantly. But white magic cannot be used for that purpose.

But a white witch was not all she was.

Colleen O'Donnell was also an agent of the Federal Bureau of Investigation. The Bureau doesn't deal in magic, but it does instill in its agents another, more temporal kind of power.

Colleen transferred her wand from her dominant, right hand to the weaker left. She would not be able to hold Annie much longer, now. She could hear dragging footsteps as the revenants approached her from behind. An unpleasant leer grew on Annie's sallow, heavy face. It lasted for, perhaps, two seconds.

That was as long as it took Special Agent Colleen O'Donnell to draw the Glock 10mm from the holster on her right hip and fire two rounds into Annie Levesque's black heart.

Eleanor Robb had just sat down to watch *American Idol* when the telephone rang. She was tempted to let the answering machine take it, but something in her witch sense told her that this call was important. Wishing she had invested in a TiVo, Eleanor switched the set off and answered the phone.

"Eleanor, it's Rachel. Are you all right?"

"Sure, I am. Why wouldn't I be?"

"Because something's going on, something bad. I don't know what it is, but in the last seventy-two hours, two of the Sisterhood have been murdered."

"Goddess save us! Who?" Fear reached out an icy finger and touched Eleanor Robb's heart.

"Andrea McKinnon in Detroit, and Cindy Presler in Wilkes-Barre—that's in Pennsylvania."

"May their souls be at peace," Eleanor said. She tried to force herself to think rationally. "Are they sure it's murder?"

"No doubt whatever—and there's more. Sandra Jenkins sent me an email that two men tried to kill *her* in her apartment yesterday."

"Merciful mother! Were they using magic?"

"Sandy says no. But they must have used some to get past the wards she'd set up."

"Who *are* these people? Crazed witch-hunters, or something?"

"Sandy thinks they were hirelings. It wasn't possible for her to question them at the time, and they're now in the hands of the police. Sandy says she'll monitor the investigation, to see if these creeps tell the cops anything."

Eleanor stared at the wall opposite her, without really seeing it.

"Ellie?"

"Thinking. Just a sec."

Half a minute passed in silence, then: "Rachel, there are three things we need to do, and quickly."

"All right, I'm taking notes. Go on."

"We need to find out if any other Sisters have been victims of these... whoever they are."

"Which means getting in touch with all of them—to see who answers the phone, or responds to email, and who doesn't."

"Exactly. And in the process, we can do the second thing, which is to warn the others about what's happening, and urge them to be on guard."

"Gotcha. What's the third thing?"

"I'm still working on that one."

Two days later found Quincey and Libby back in Mac's pub, one of the few places in Chicago where they felt reasonably safe. It was lunchtime, and they were pleasantly surprised to find that the food was good; a lot of places that call themselves "pubs" focus on providing booze, with the cuisine something of an afterthought.

"I wish your reporter buddy had more specific information about that guy in Ohio," Libby said.

She sat with her back to the door, but knew that Quincey was vetting anyone who came in behind her.

He swallowed a bite of his tortilla and said, "Yeah, I hear you. Carl keeps his ear to the ground for goings-on in the occult world, but it's more of a sideline with him. Tony, his boss, doesn't approve of what he calls 'all this superstitious claptrap'—he keeps sending Carl off to cover flower shows, stuff like that."

"I've never heard of this guy he mentioned, Tristan Hardwick. Sounds like a character out of Jane Austen."

"I don't know him, either. But, hel—uh, heck, Libby, we can't keep track of all of 'em."

Libby speared a crouton with her fork. "What I don't get is why the police released him. If they had reason to believe he was involved in that poor kid's murder…"

Morris gave her a crooked smile. "You don't watch *Law and Order*, do you?"

"No—what does that matter?"

"It's just that if you did, you wouldn't be surprised by what happened. Cops make a bust, then the judge decides the key evidence against the guy's inadmissible. Maybe somebody forgot to get a search warrant, or something. But without that evidence, whatever it was, the D.A.'s got no case worth a damn. So the bastard walks."

'It still doesn't seem right."

"That just proves you're a better witch than you are a lawyer, Libby."

"Thanks for the compliment—both sides of it."

They ate in silence for a while. Then Libby

said, "Kent, Ohio. Isn't that where they had those shootings, at the university there?"

"Yeah, but that was a long time ago. I'm pretty sure they don't do that anymore."

"But it's still a college town, though."

"As far as I know, it is. So?"

"So that means they probably have some good bookstores. You know me and bookstores."

"Just so long as you don't go there alone," Morris said. "You never know who might be lurking among the do-it-yourself books. Speaking of which..." Morris hesitated. "We need to get us some help, Libby."

"Another investigator, you mean?"

"Uh-uh. You and me, we're about the best investigators I know, at least for this kind of stuff. I was thinking more along the lines of a bodyguard."

"Oh, come *on*, Quincey."

"What—you don't think we need somebody? If you weren't quick with the magic yesterday, you'd have been dead out there in the street, Libby. Probably both of us would be."

"But I *was* quick enough, that's what matters."

"But next time you might *not* be, or might not get any warning. That's what *really* matters."

Libby put her fork down, frowning. "So, what, we're supposed to have some gorilla with no neck and a .45 under his armpit following us around?"

"No, I had something a little different in mind." Morris cleared his throat. "Libby... look, I'm sorry, but it's the best choice under the circumstances. It really is." Morris looked past her and nodded his head, once.

Libby blinked, then her eyes widened. "Quincey, tell me you didn't—"

That was when Hannah Widmark slipped into the vacant chair next to her. "Hi, kids," she said, pleasantly. "How's ghostbusting?"

Charlotte Kenyon drove through the suburban streets as fast as the traffic and prudence would allow. The line at the grocery store she'd stopped at on the way home from work had been both long and slow. *Sort of like a good fuck,* she thought. *But not nearly so much fun.*

It had been quite a while since Charlotte had had a fuck—good, bad, or indifferent. As a working single mom she barely managed to juggle all the duties of both job and family and still manage to get (if she was lucky and none of the kids was sick) six hours of sleep a night. Doing the horizontal polka with somebody (even assuming a likely candidate were available) would require scheduling weeks in advance, just like a play date.

That's what Mom needs. A play date of her own, preferably with some hot guy who's hung like a horse.

Her driveway was coming up, so she pushed thoughts of sexual longing aside and began to focus on her present responsibilities. The first of her three kids should be home from school in about fifteen minutes. She could give Mark a glass of milk and a cookie, then ask him about his day while she began dinner preparations.

Household chores were actually somewhat easier for Charlotte when nobody was home, since she could use a little magic to move things along. Dishes might wash themselves, or dust could be commanded to fly off surfaces and into the trash bin.

Charlotte juggled two bags of groceries while unlocking the back door. She noticed her key slid into the lock more easily than usual, as if the lock had been oiled. *Sliding right in because it's so well lubricated. Get it out of the gutter, Charlotte.* She plopped the bags onto the kitchen table, scattering a number of toys in the process.

She had started taking the groceries out of the bags and putting them on the table, when she heard a floorboard creak behind her—a floorboard that should not have creaked, on its own.

Charlotte Kenyon picked up a can of peas to use as a missile, if necessary. She was about to pivot and face the threat, whatever it was, when the .22 slug entered her brain. She collapsed to the floor, dead before she even knew she'd been shot.

The man who had killed Charlotte was unscrewing the silencer from the barrel of his .22 pistol when the phone started ringing. He did not, quite, jump. "I oughta answer it," he said to his partner. "Say something like, 'Hi! Charlotte can't come to the phone right now. She's, like dead.'"

"Pardee would skin you alive, you do something like that," the other man said. "Come on, let's boogie."

The answering machine came on, and the dead woman's voice said, cheerfully, *Hi! You've reached Charlotte, Mark, Cheryl, and Sarah. Leave a message at the beep.* The two killers were heading for the door when another female voice said, "Charlotte, this is Rachel Harvey. You need to call me ASAP. At least three of the Sisters have had... accidents, bad ones. There may be more on the way. I don't want you to have one, too. Call me, okay?"

The man who had killed Charlotte looked at his partner. "That mean what I think it means?"

"Yeah, I bet it does. The bitches have figured it out. Pardee's gonna want to know about this."

"Then let's get the fuck out of here, so we can tell him."

Chapter 11

Colleen O'Donnell stared at the body of Annie Levesque, who lay in a pool of blood on her front porch. Colleen was shaking; she had never taken a life before, and all the training in the world cannot prepare you for that. The fact that she'd had no choice didn't make her feel any better about it. She uttered a quick invocation against panic, and found herself growing calmer almost immediately. Good—she had some fast thinking to do.

She looked at Fenton, who lay on the ground a few feet to her left. She could keep him unconscious a while longer, but eventually he would wake up, and demand an explanation. She'd better have a good one ready.

She shifted her gaze to the porch, where Premeaux lay. His eyes were open and staring, and the blood no longer pumped from the wound in his throat. The detective was dead.

Colleen considered her situation, which did not look promising. In the FBI, like every other law enforcement organization in this country, you have to justify the use of deadly force.

I fired my weapon at the suspect in self-defense. She had raised several of the dead and sent them towards me, with probable injurious intent. Further, I had reason to believe that her attempt to enter her house was equivalent to reaching for a weapon, since the dwelling contained, almost certainly, a number of implements of black magic, and the power to give them maximum strength. These, if employed by the suspect, would undoubtedly have resulted in the deaths of both myself and Agent Fenton.

Yeah, that would look great typed on Form 344-J, "Report of Agent Discharge of Firearm, Fatality Resulting." Colleen would lose her job, and would likely either stand trial for murder or end up committed to a hospital for the criminally insane. And people like Annie would still be out there, murdering kids.

Even though Colleen knew that the shooting was righteous, she could not tell the truth in justifying it. *Well, if the truth won't work, what kind of lie might do the trick?*

She looked around the crime scene—for that's what it was, now—seeking something that she could use in the fiction she would have to create. The revenants summoned by Annie Levesque had collapsed, with the death of their resurrector. Colleen would have to use a spell to return the remains to their graves before awakening Fenton. The bodies would have to be dug up officially later, so that they could be identified and returned to their families.

Her gaze passed over Fenton, who was covered with small glass fragments from the magic-induced

180

explosion, the body of Annie Levesque, even more repulsive in death than it had been in life, then the corpse of Detective Pete Premeaux, sport coat rucked back to reveal the pistol he wore in a belt holster, and the house itself, with its windows—

Premeaux's pistol. Premeaux, who had died minutes before Annie Levesque. Annie, lying dead, herself. Fenton, who'd seen nothing that had transpired since the explosion.

Colleen's thoughts raced. Once she had the story clear in her mind, she went over it again, more slowly, looking for weaknesses or inconsistencies. She could find none.

Kneeling over Premeaux's body, Colleen said a brief prayer that his spirit might find rest. Then, after pulling on the latex crime scene gloves she always had with her, she carefully pulled the detective's Colt Commander automatic from its holster. Colleen checked that there was a round in the chamber, then cocked the hammer.

Stepping carefully to avoid the blood pools, she went to the body of Annie Levesque, knelt down, and wrapped the black witch's dead right hand around the pistol, index finger on the trigger. Then she lifted the hand, until the pistol was pointed at the general area where Colleen had been lying after her tumble from the porch, and slowly pressed down on Annie's finger. The weapon fired, sending a round into the dirt of the yard. Colleen then let the hand drop, allowing the pistol to fall free.

After causing, by means yet unknown, the explosion that resulted in the death of Detective Pete Premeaux, suspect Annie Levesque approached the detective's body and removed his sidearm from its holster. She then pointed the weapon at me and fired once, missing me. Believing that the suspect intended to fire again, I drew my own weapon and returned fire. Suspect Annie Levesque was struck by two rounds from my weapon, leading to her subsequent death.

That was a story the FBI's Committee on Professional Responsibility would find credible, even though there was barely a word of truth in it. Colleen made herself say another prayer, this one for the soul of Annie Levesque—even though, as a practitioner of black magic, Annie was almost certainly damned. Then she looked toward her partner's supine form. It was time to get rid of these zombie corpses and bring Fenton back to the world.

Quincey Morris had never been married, but he nonetheless recognized the *We're going to talk about this later* look that Libby gave him. He was not expecting to enjoy that conversation, but was confident he had done the right thing by sending for the tall woman in black, who now sat opposite him.

Hannah Widmark had brought her drink with her from the table where she'd been waiting—something dark on the rocks. She set the glass down in front of her, and in that musical voice said, "It's about time, Quincey." Then she turned her head a little and, after the briefest of hesitations, nodded and said, "Hello Libby."

Libby returned the nod without smiling. "Hannah."

Hannah said, "So, I understand you guys need personal security against the Forces of Darkness."

She said the last phrase with no trace of irony.

"It's more for Libby," Morris said. "She's the one they're after."

"Doesn't matter. If you're in the line of fire, they'll take you down without a thought. These creatures aren't discriminating about their victims." Hannah's inflection didn't change, but there was something in her voice right then that made the little hairs stir on the back of Morris's neck.

"Be that as it may, we sure appreciate your help," Morris said.

"You don't have to appreciate it, Quincey." Hannah took a sip from her glass. "Just pay for it. As you know, I charge a lot. But then, I'm worth it." Once again, Hannah spoke as if irony had left the building.

"Seems to me that I should be the one paying," Libby said, with a glance at Morris. "After all, it's my life you're here to save, Hannah." Her teeth were clenched as she said the last part of that.

"Doesn't matter to me who pays, as long as somebody does," Hannah said.

"You and me, we'll talk about that later, Libby," Morris said. He looked at Hannah. "From here, we're headed to Kent, Ohio. That's in—"

"The northeast corner of the state, about twelve miles northwest of Akron," she said. "Have you booked your flight, yet?"

"No, I thought we ought to talk with you, first. But I'll buy us three tickets on the next flight out that way. Get us into Akron, maybe, or Cleveland."

Hannah shook her head. "No, just text me the flight info once you've got it." She reached into the heavy shoulder bag she had placed on the chair next to her and produced a plain black and white business card, which she gave to Morris. "I'll pay for my own ticket, and bill you."

"What does it matter whether you get your money now, or later?" Libby asked. She sounded more irritated than curious.

Hannah gave her a tiny smile. "It matters, because I don't want my name showing up in a computer linked to your names. It would be, if Quincey here paid for all three tickets with the same credit card. If the opposition—whoever they are—check the passenger manifest, I don't want them noticing my name. For the same reason, I won't be sitting near you."

"Pity, that," Libby said.

Hannah flicked a glance her way, then said to Morris. "If I go around with you, then I'm just part of the bull's-eye. But if I'm off at a distance, I can get a clear idea of the threat picture, and I'm in a better position to do something about it."

"Something lethal, you mean," Libby said.

Hannah shifted her gaze to the glass containing her drink. The ice cubes seemed to hold a fascination for her, because she did not look up as she said, "There's a story I heard once, it's kind of interesting. Out in the sticks somewhere, a woman is walking home in the late fall, when she comes upon this big rattlesnake. There's been a cold snap, kind of unusual for that time of year, and the rattler wasn't able to get back to his burrow, or whatever you call the place that snakes live. He's clearly freezing to death. Since this is a fable, the snake can talk. He says to the woman, 'Please help me. If I don't get inside someplace warm soon, I'll die.' The woman, who's no fool, says, 'But you're a rattlesnake. Your bite would mean death for me.' The snake says, 'I promise, if you help me, I'll never bite you, ever. I don't forget favors that others do for me.' So, being a compassionate sort, the woman gingerly picks up the snake and stuffs him down inside her coat to get warm. Then she starts walking again. Another ten minutes, and she's home. She starts a fire in the wood stove, and gently lays the snake down near it. After a half hour or so, the snake is doing much better, and thanks the woman for her kindness. She says, 'It's still too cold for you to go outside. I'm tired from that long walk home, and I thought I'd sit in my rocking chair next to the stove for a while. Would you like to curl up in my lap?' The snake says 'Sure, why not?' She picks him up, and as soon as she does, he twists in her grasp and bites her, right on the side of the neck. A little later, as she's lying on the floor, dying, she asks the snake. 'After all I did for you, why did you bite me?' And the snake says to her"—Hannah raised her head then, to look directly into Libby Chastain's eyes—"he says, '*You knew what I was, when you took me in.*'"

Then, after glancing back in the direction from which she'd come, Hannah said, "I'm going back to my table now. Puts me in a good position to watch you, the front entrance, and the door from the kitchen, all at the same time." She turned to lift her oversize bag from the adjoining chair, which caused one black sleeve to pull up a few inches.

Libby may have been making a belated effort to be pleasant when she looked at Hannah's wrist and said, "That tattoo you've got there, it looks new."

"It's a sigil against demons," Hannah said. "Got

the idea years ago, from a private eye I know in New York. Very useful protective devices. I have a number of them, all over my body." The tiny smile appeared again. "Ask Quincey—he's seen them all."

Hannah pushed her chair back. "Oh, that's right, Libby, I was forgetting—so have you," she said, then stood, and walked away.

Libby Chastain and Quincey Morris looked at each other without speaking, their expressions unreadable. Finally, as if by tacit mutual consent, they went back to eating their lunch.

Pardee closed his cell phone and put it down carefully, resisting the urge to smash it in a million pieces, either magically or through sheer brute force.

The room in Grobius's mansion that Pardee used as an office offered a good view of the grounds, where workmen were completing preparations for the Ceremony. Had they known the true nature of the enterprise in which they were engaged, they would likely all walk off the job immediately, never to return.

Pardee stared down at all the activity without really seeing it. His thoughts were elsewhere.

So the Wiccans now knew that they were being stalked and slain, like deer in a forest. They would be wary now, their pathetic white magic defenses in place.

And that cunt Chastain had escaped, *again*. The one whose life he wanted more than any of the others. Pardee shook his head in disgust. He would have said she had the luck of the devil, but he knew that particular force was on his own side.

He stood at the immense window for perhaps

fifteen minutes. Pardee's mind had been trained to allow him to think about several things at once, and by the end of that time he had made three decisions. He picked up his phone and began to implement them.

He sent a blast email to all his teams of assassins, ordering them to stand down: remain in place, continue surveillance of their targets, but let the white bitches live—for now.

Then he called one of Grobius's computer geeks and instructed the man to continue monitoring Libby Chastain's credit card activity, but now to broaden his focus to include the transactions of one Quincey Morris. The man described as accompanying Chastain could be no one else.

His third call was to Roderico Baca, who was a wizard of considerable power—although not, of course, in Pardee's class. He instructed Baca to make certain preparations, and to be ready to travel on very short notice.

When Pardee put the phone down this time, he was in considerably better humor. It might be that the remaining white bitches could be allowed to live. They would be cowering in their holes like frightened rabbits now, and would offer no interference to the Ceremony—which was, after all, the whole point of the murders.

But not Chastain. Pardee regarded being thwarted twice as a personal insult. In any case, he and Chastain had some unfinished business between them. Pardee planned to mark that particular account "Paid in Full" soon enough.

His mistake had been targeting Chastain with mundane hit men, equipped with a little magical power. But Baca was an adept of the black arts, and there would be no mistakes this time.

Pardee was so pleased with himself that he thought a little celebration was in order. He picked up his phone again. "Send Nancy and Chantelle in to me. Yes, now. And what's that new girl's name—Margaret?—send her in, as well."

A contented smile appeared on Pardee's lean face. A couple of hours' recreation, and then he would make his report to Grobius. The old man should be pleased—everything was going so *well*.

Chapter 12

"Yeah, local law's been out here for about an hour. State Police, County Sheriff's people, and some cop, works for the township, who I swear could have been the model for Barney Fife."

"You're not old enough to remember that show, Colleen."

"I'm old enough to watch cable TV at two in the morning. Hold on a sec—there's a plane flying over."

"I wondered what that noise was."

"Sue? Can you hear me now?"

"Yeah, you're fine. Go on."

"So, I spent about half an hour giving my statement. They're with Fenton now."

"You sure he's okay?"

"Seems fine. No signs of concussion. They're trying to talk him into a visit to the hospital, but he's resisting. Don't blame him for that—he wants to get inside that bitch's house, and so do I."

"Well, make the most of it, because I want you back here, tomorrow. Fenton can stay, but you've got a date with the Shooting Board."

"Oh, for the love of... do you know how long that's likely to take?"

"Nope, my crystal ball's in the shop, for an oil change. How's yours working?"

"You know what I mean, Sue. I'll have to write and file a report, then each of those guys has to get around to reading it, when it doesn't interfere with his golf date with some senator, then they've got to find a common empty slot in their schedules for a hearing... it's gonna take *weeks*."

"Yeah, you're probably right. But rules is rules, kiddo. They get all huffy and officious down here when you kill somebody."

"That shoot was fucking righteous, Sue."

"I'm not saying it wasn't. From what you've described, it sounds like you had no choice at all. And the Board may well agree. But we've gotta go though the procedure. You know the regs, same as I do."

"Uh-huh. Sue?"

"That's my name, don't wear it out."

"I need to ask for a favor."

"Why do I have the feeling I'm not gonna like this? Go on, ask."

"I need you to put off filing a report on this incident."

"Sure, you do. How could I expect anything else? And I should risk my career over this, because..."

"Annie Levesque wasn't in this alone."

"Whoa, kiddo. It hasn't been determined that she was 'in' anything, yet."

"She killed one cop, and tried to kill two more, Sue. You figure she did that because she didn't like Fenton's aftershave?"

"Um. Okay, say you've got a point there. Well, we already figured there was some kind of conspiracy going on. That's why the Bureau's involved, remember?"

"The clock's ticking, Sue."

"What's that supposed to mean?"

"The longer this goes on, the more kids are going to die."

"The investigation's not gonna stop just because you're cooling your heels down here in Quantico for a while. Fenton'll stay on it. Maybe I can find him another partner. Just for the interim. Maybe."

"Two 'maybes' means you can't really spare anybody, doesn't it?"

"Yeah. Yeah, fuck, it probably does. But Fenton's good, you know that."

"He's just one agent."

"Right. And if you were still there, it would be just two agents. You're good, too, kiddo. But you ain't no damn task force."

"I never claimed to be. But I'm... uniquely qualified for this investigation, Sue. It's very, very important that I be involved. Sue? You still there?"

"You're telling me this case is one of *those*."

"One of what?"

"*Woo-woo* stuff. Things that aren't supposed to happen, except they sometimes do."

"Yeah, I'm afraid so. It's one of those."

"Not to belabor the obvious, but—you're sure?"

"Yeah, I am. For reasons I don't want to go into right now, I am absolutely fucking positive."

"Sweet fucking Jesus on a goddamn bicycle."

"Don't blaspheme Sue. It's not becoming."

"Yeah, and fuck you, too Colleen. All right, listen."

"Yes?"

"Sometimes emails go astray in cyberspace, and nobody can explain why. Like, say, the email I send to the board members about your little incident. If it doesn't bounce back to me, I could reasonably assume they'd received it, but they might not even know it existed. Shit like that happens, sometimes."

"I know. I'm pretty sure it's all Bill Gates's fault."

"Probably. Anyway, that might work—for a while. But, here's the thing."

"What?"

"Your shooting, with attendant circumstances, is bound to make the local media. Hell, up there, it'll be a nine-day wonder. Biggest story since Farmer Brown's barn burned down."

"That's unkind—but, yeah, I expect you're right."

"If it stays local, that's not a problem. But if one of the wire services picks it up, it's sure to get into the *Post* or the *Times*. That happens, and the game is up, over, *finito*. Guys on the board will see it, and they're gonna start asking me why they have to hear about an agent-involved shooting, with fatality resulting, from the goddamn papers."

"Yeah, I understand. Well, I guess that's a chance we'll have to take. Assuming you're willing to take it with me. Sue? Hello?"

"You know, we've been having all kinds of trouble with the damn computer system down here, Colleen. I think this stuff was obsolete when Bill Clinton was still getting his dick sucked in the Oval Office. Files are getting misplaced; even the email is messed up. In fact, I think I better file a trouble report with IT.

They'll probably get around to it by Christmas. *Next* Christmas."

"Thanks, Sue, I appreciate this. I mean, a lot."

"Thank me by stopping these bastards from killing any more kids."

"That's just what I had in mind. Wait—looks like Fenton's done giving his statement. He's waving me over and pointing at Annie's house. I think they're letting us inside."

"Then go and get your ass in there, girl."

"Yes, *ma'am*."

Tristan Hardwick had lived in Northeast Ohio for all of his twenty-eight years, including the four he spent earning his degree in Accounting at Kent State University. He had first been exposed to the occult as an undergraduate, courtesy of a remarkable young woman named Anya Preston he'd happened to sit next to in his Comparative Religion class. Years later, he would wonder if their meeting was really as accidental as it had seemed at the time.

The two of them exchanged only a few words, but Hardwick made her laugh at some witticism about their professor, who was late to class, as usual. The prof's habitual tardiness allowed Hardwick and Anya to have a number of five-minute conversations in the weeks to follow. Hardwick eventually found the courage to ask her out (courage being called for because she was what guys in those days called a "fox," and he was what everybody in those days called a "nerd"). They went to the new Martin Scorsese movie the first time, then the next week to the Brown Derby for dinner, and gradually one thing led to another.

But in this instance, "one thing led to another" does not refer to sex—although, beginning with their third date, Anya Preston was banging him stupid on a regular basis. Rather, their association led her to introduce him to some friends who, like Anya, were interested in the occult—especially black magic.

That, in turn, led to Hardwick being invited to some "gatherings" of a coven in Cleveland. These occasions consisted of a half-assed satanic ritual cribbed from books, followed by group sex involving all those present. Tristan Hardwick thought he'd died and gone to heaven—failing to realize that he was, in fact, headed rapidly in the opposite direction.

It was through the Cleveland coven that Hardwick fell under the spell of Morgan Godfrey. Godfrey did not associate much with the Cleveland people, viewing them, quite rightly, as dilettantes more interested in the sex than in the rituals that preceded it. But there was some contact between them, and Tristan Hardwick's name came up, more than once.

Finally, Godfrey had issued an invitation, making clear that Hardwick was under no compulsion, and must attend of his own free will. That itself might have raised red flags for some, but not for Tristan Hardwick, who was, in effect, star-struck. People at the coven spoke of Morgan Godfrey in hushed tones, and Hardwick had come to understand that Godfrey was something that the coven members would never be: The Real Deal.

It was on a Friday night illuminated by the full moon that Tristan Hardwick made his way to the ritzy Cleveland suburb of Chagrin Falls, a name whose irony he came to appreciate only later.

Hardwick was not seen back in Kent until Monday, and he refused to speak of whatever he had seen, or done, at Morgan Godfrey's elegant home. He said nothing of the obscene rites, the blood sacrifice, the eating of human flesh, or the being who had been summoned to the gathering.

Hardwick never talked about what that being had offered him, and the price he had agreed, by most solemn oath, to pay. But if the phrase "changed man" has ever had true expression, it was in Tristan Hardwick. After that weekend, he became cold and remote, and stopped attending the coven's weekly ceremonies. He showed no more interest in sex with Anya Preston. His sense of humor, for which he was well known among his friends, disappeared entirely. In time, he moved into Morgan Godfrey's home as a permanent guest—permanent, that is, until Godfrey introduced him to a man known only as Pardee. After that, Tristan Hardwick belonged to Pardee, body and soul. In the years that followed, Hardwick had performed, faithfully and well, a number of unpleasant tasks on behalf of his master. Then the day came when Pardee sent him back to Kent, with instructions to wait, and watch, and prepare.

Six weeks ago, Hardwick had learned exactly what he had been preparing for. He was given a task, and he carried it out without flinching. But he was just a little careless, leaving some of his DNA behind at the scene of his butchery. However, the police had been over-zealous, neglecting to obtain a necessary search warrant, and once the judge had ruled the key evidence inadmissible and the D.A. had grudgingly released him, Tristan Hardwick thought his troubles were over. And so they were.

Until the night, two weeks later, when the knock came at his door.

Not unlike Caesar's Gaul, all American college towns are divided into three parts. There's the campus itself, usually a sprawling mass of concrete and brick (except in New England, where's it's usually wood, ivy, and rot), the jungle (where the students tend to reside and recreate), and the town (where the permanent residents live—usually as far away from the campus and the jungle as they can get).

Morris and Libby had to drive through part of Kent's jungle to get from the Shady Tree Motel to the part of town where Tristan Hardwick lived. Libby was navigating, Morris's laptop open in front of her.

"Two more blocks," she said, "then make a left, at that light up ahead. See it?"

"Got it." Morris drove the rental car slowly, to avoid hitting any of the students who were crossing Water Street whenever and wherever they wished, heedless of traffic.

"I'm sorry about the accommodations, Libby. I figured we could have done better than the Shady Tree."

"Ordinarily, we would have. According to the AAA website, there are several places in town that sound rather nice. But I see on Kent State's home page that this is some kind of big alumni weekend. Not surprising that all the good places are booked. Anyway, I'm not especially dainty. Each room at our place has a bed and a shower, and that's all I really need. If the bugs prove to be a problem, I'll put a warding spell around the bed—yours, too, if you want."

"I'll let you know, thanks. We'll just take a quick run past Hardwick's house, then go back to Roach Central. Maybe grab some sleep."

"I still don't understand what you're trying to accomplish with this... reconnaissance mission."

"Two things," Morris said. "One is to make sure he still lives there. Your witch sense will pick him up if he is, right?"

"It should, yes. That much evil would be hard to miss."

"The other thing is, I want to see if the place is under police surveillance."

"Why would it be? The case was thrown out, right?"

"Yeah, but cops really hate to lose—especially a case like this, with the murdered and mutilated kid. I wouldn't be surprised if they're keeping an eye on Hardwick, hoping that he'll try to do it again, so they can pounce. Hell, the cops might even be doing it off-duty, in their spare time. They got stung pretty bad on this case, Libby. Lots of bad press."

The Red Sea of students finally parted, and Morris had the car moving again—only to slam on his brakes a few moments later, as three young men, clearly intoxicated, crossed right in front of them. Morris tapped the horn, and one of the young men stopped, turned, and gave them the finger, before moving on.

"I don't suppose you could cast some kind of impromptu spell that would make that jerk's finger fall off," Morris said. "Or maybe his dick."

"No, sorry. White magic, remember? Can't hurt people with it, even those who deserve it. However…" She rolled her window down, watching the young men's progress, and waited. After three or four seconds, she stuck her head out, and in a voice that seemed to fill the street, yelled, "*Fuck you, you dickless fucking asshole!*"

The young man who had flipped them off was almost across the street by now. He turned to stare in amazement, but forgot to stop walking. He tripped over the curb and fell on his face, spilling the cup of beer he carried in the process.

Libby rolled the window back up as Morris accelerated. "There, see?" she said. "No magic involved. Well, hardly any. Just good timing. Feel better now?"

"Yes, considerably."

Libby turned in her seat to look back the way they had come.

"What?" Morris said. "He's not running after us, is he?"

Facing forward again, she said, "No. I was just looking to see if I could spot Hannah."

"You won't."

"Then how do we know she's really there?"

"She's there."

"You sound very certain, Quincey."

"I've worked with Hannah before."

"And done more than work, I gather."

"Pots and kettles, Libby."

"Ouch. Well, I deserved that, I suppose. Will it help if I say that I was quite drunk at the time?"

"There's nothing to help, Libby. What happened,

happened. With you and with me, both. Ancient history."

They had gone another block when Morris asked, "With you, did she do that thing with her tongue that—"

"This is it. Left here, Quincey. It should be, yes, fourth house on the right."

They continued down the street slowly, but not so slow as to be obvious to any watchers. Morris was looking for people sitting in parked cars within sight of Hardwick's house, while Libby closed her eyes and took slow, deep breaths, letting her finely trained witch sense hear and see and smell for her.

Libby sucked in her breath and sat up very straight. "Goddess, stay between us and all evil," she intoned softly.

"What? What's wrong, Libby?" Morris kept the car moving as he scanned the environment for some threat that Libby might have perceived. "What just happened?"

When she spoke, Libby's voice shook. "I was prepared to sense some dark power from that place, but not a great deal of it, really. After all, Hardwick isn't an adept, as far as we know."

Morris kept turning to look at her, giving just enough attention to the road to avoid crashing.

"Yeah, so?"

"Quincey, the power coming out of that house is far beyond anything someone like Hardwick should be generating. It's huge, and black, and malevolent."

Morris drove for three blocks without speaking, then said, "Well, I reckon one of us ought to say it, and it might as well be me: *what the fuck?*"

"I think," Libby said, sitting back, "that we have been misinformed."

In fact, they had not been misinformed. The strong vibes of black magic that Libby Chastain was sensing did not emanate from Tristan Hardwick. Rather, they came from the man who, ten minutes earlier, had knocked on Hardwick's door.

Chapter 13

Tristan Hardwick had recently had his lightweight wooden front door replaced with a stout metal one that contained a peephole. He'd realized that the family of his young victim, and the family's friends, might not be as willing as Judge Nathan to consider the matter closed. Hardwick didn't want to have anybody kicking his door down, nor did he want to open it to some vigilante one night, and receive a blast of buckshot in the chest for his trouble.

But the man Hardwick could see through the peephole did not appear to be carrying a weapon, and he looked nothing like the family of the late Tommy Doyle. If the visitor was a salesman, or worse, another reporter, Hardwick would get rid of him quickly.

Opening the door, Hardwick said, "Yes?" He thought his brusqueness might be intimidating to the man on his porch. In this he was mistaken.

"Señor Hardwick?"

"Yeah, that's me. What do you want?"

"My name is Roderico Baca. I have been sent to

you by a man we both know as 'Pardee.'"

After a few seconds' thought, Hardwick said, "All right," and stepped back to allow the man entry.

But his visitor remained standing at the threshold. "Are you inviting me inside?" he asked, formally.

"Yeah sure, whatever. Come in."

Only then did the man step into Hardwick's living room. Hardwick closed the door behind him and went over to where a couch, loveseat, and chair were arranged around a widescreen TV set. Standing in front of the couch, Hardwick made a gesture that encompassed the other two pieces of furniture.

"Please, sit down. Can I get you a drink?"

"Thank you, Señor, but no. Please, have one yourself, if you wish."

"Yeah, I think I will. Excuse me a minute."

From the kitchen, where he kept his booze, Hardwick could see that the man had settled upon the loveseat and sat down. *Strange-lookin' dude*. The man's coal-black hair hung down straight to rest on his shoulders. He wore what looked to Hardwick, an inveterate reader of *GQ*, like $2,000 worth of gray suit over his thin frame. The ensemble was completed by shiny black shoes, a tie that looked like it belonged in the Museum of Modern Art, and a shirt so white that it was almost hard to look at. Shirt and tie were separated by a gold collar pin, something Hardwick had heard of but never seen before, even in the pages of *Gentleman's Quarterly*. The face above it was composed and thoughtful-looking, the way monks often look in the movies.

Hardwick, bearing a double Scotch, took a seat on the couch. "So, mister—I'm sorry, I'm lousy with names, always have been."

His visitor did not seem put out. "Baca." he said, "Roderico Baca." He gave his first name the Spanish pronunciation, the first syllable sounding like "road" instead of "rod."

"Right, got it. So, what does Pardee want from me, Mister Baca? Does he have another… assignment?" Hardwick didn't know how much this guy knew, or how far Pardee trusted him.

"No, Señor. Pardee feels that you have done more than enough. You will not be asked to abduct and murder any more children."

Hardwick almost flinched. He had never used such blunt language in thinking about the job, either before, during, or after. He had thought of "sacrifices," "harvesting organs," "getting material for the ritual," but never the terms his visitor had just used.

Hardwick cleared his throat and said, "All right, fine. So, what brought you all the way out here to see me? I assume you were with Pardee in Idaho, and that's quite a trip."

Baca smiled without showing any teeth. "In fact, I was in Santa Fe, New Mexico, when I heard from Pardee. So I have, indeed, come a long way. But my main purpose was not to call upon you."

"Oh?"

"*Sí*. There are some other visitors to this fair city, Señor Hardwick. Unlike myself, they *did* journey here specifically to… converse with you."

"Me? Oh, you mean about the, um—"

"The abduction, mutilation, and murder of a small child, one Thomas Doyle. Exactly. These people came here from Chicago earlier today. When Pardee determined where they were going, he sent me here, to prepare a suitable welcome for them."

"You got here first? From New Mexico?" Hardwick was frowning. "What'd you do, charter a private plane?"

"Not precisely, Señor Hardwick. But I did provide my own transportation." This time, Baca did reveal his teeth, and Hardwick found himself fervently wishing that he might never see that particular smile again.

"Whatever," Hardwick said. "Well, if you're going to deal with these people—how many are we talking about?"

"Two, Señor. A man and a woman."

"Dangerous?"

Baca made a small dismissive gesture. "In their own way, perhaps. But they should pose no great difficulty for me."

"Okay, fine. So why are you here? Do you need some help?"

Baca's laughter seemed to contain much genuine amusement, mixed with a heavy dose of disdain. "No, Señor, but thank you," he said, when the laughter faded. "I will have to manage with my own humble abilities."

Hardwick, stung by the man's contempt, said, "Well, then, what did Pardee send some Latino sorcerer over here for? Just to bust my balls?"

Even to a journeyman of the black arts like Hardwick, the fury that came off Roderico Baca was like a live thing.

"*Latino*!" He practically spat the word. "I am not *Latino*, Señor. My blood has not been polluted by centuries of intermarriage with the savages indigenous to South America. No, Señor, no. My

204

family came to this country from Spain when I was seventeen years old. The Bacas can trace their ancestry back to King Philip the Second, one of the greatest rulers our nation has ever seen."

Hardwick caught movement in his peripheral vision, and turned his head in time to see the small bonsai tree behind the couch, which had been healthy and thriving a few minutes ago, wither and die before his eyes. He raised his hands from his lap, palms outward, like a man trying to stop an attacker—which is exactly what he was doing at that moment. "I meant no offense, I swear," he said. "It's just an expression, is all. Most people in this country who…" Hardwick searched desperately for a way to avoid saying "Latino" again, "speak Spanish as their native tongue have come here from South America. We Anglos rarely have the honor of meeting someone of pure Spanish blood."

After continuing the stare for a handful of heartbeats, Baca said, "Very well, Señor Hardwick. I accept your apology. I believe that you intended no insult."

"No, no, none at all," Hardwick said.

Baca nodded, as if suddenly bored with the subject. "As to the reason for my visit to you, Pardee has expressed concern that the individuals who have come to Kent today may, in time, be followed by others—persons whom I might not be present to deal with."

"Followed by others, who'll do what? Kill me?"

A Latinate shrug, which seemed to involve the man's entire body. "It is possible. But not, I think, on this occasion. I believe these two people hope to question you about what you have done—"

"*Allegedly* done. The evidence was thrown out, man."

A slight nod, the toothless smile again. "What you have *allegedly* done, and why, and for whom."

"Why? I mean if they're not cops, what the hell do they care?"

"That question remains unanswered for now, but Pardee nonetheless believes that these people may have interests that are inimical to his own."

"*Inimical*? What's that mean?"

Baca shook his head derisively. "And you, a college graduate. Of course, you did attend an American state university, so little should perhaps be expected. 'Inimical' in this instance means that these people may be Pardee's enemies. Apparently he knows one of them from an earlier encounter—a woman named Chastain, a so-called 'white witch.'"

"Doesn't matter who they are, man. I wouldn't say a fuckin' word about the Ceremony, or any of that stuff. Tell Pardee he can rely on me to keep my mouth shut."

Baca nodded solemnly, managing to convey both understanding and agreement in a few slight head movements. "I am sure that Pardee will accept your assurances."

"Of course, he will. He knows me. Now, if you don't—"

Baca went on as if the younger man had not spoken. "Or rather he would, if so very much were not at stake."

It took the space of three heartbeats for Tristan Hardwick to work out the implications of those words. He rose from the couch quickly. He may have been intending to attack Baca, or to run for the door, or even to get down on his knees and beg. Hardwick's purpose will never be known, because a wave of Baca's power instantly shoved him back to where he had been sitting. He gathered himself to try again, but Baca made a quick gesture with his left hand, and Hardwick found that he could not move. He was frozen in place, a helpless prisoner in his own body.

Baca rose slowly and began to remove the jacket of his expensive suit. "Pardee gave me a certain amount of discretion as to the precise means by which I might ensure your silence," he said, as if discussing whether it would rain tomorrow. He unbuttoned the cuffs of the white shirt and carefully folded each back three turns, to reveal wiry but strong-looking forearms. "At first, I was inclined to make this fairly quick, since I have other matters to attend to." Baca walked slowly toward the couch, and the younger man who would have screamed then, had he been able. "But that was before you called me *Latino*."

And then it began. Soon thereafter—very soon—it became unspeakable.

"They're giving us twenty minutes," Fenton said.

"Generous of them," Colleen muttered, scanning the big downstairs room of Annie Levesque's home.

Fenton, the latex evidence gloves he wore a stark contrast to his dark skin, was carefully opening drawers and giving the contents a quick look before closing them again. "We were lucky to get that," he told Colleen. "I told the Statie in charge that we have special training in these kinds of cases, and besides, if we found anything good, his guys could take credit for it with the media."

"Sometimes I think that's all these local guys think about," Colleen said, searching underneath the cushions of Annie Levesque's overstuffed sofa. "Who gets the fucking credit."

It took them eight and a half minutes to toss the single downstairs room and find absolutely nothing to indicate why Annie Levesque had been murdering children by extracting vital organs while they were still alive. They knew there was a central, malign intelligence directing this, there had to be. The abductions and murders were going on all over the country.

The two agents walked to the wooden stairs that led to the second floor. As they started up, Fenton said, "I also pointed out to Lieutenant McAsshole that we suspected Annie of connection to some terrorist organization, and I reminded him that those kinds of people often leave booby traps lying around their dwelling spaces. That seemed to make up his mind for him."

Colleen snorted. "That's us—cannon fodder for chickenshit cops everywhere."

The second floor contained the bathroom and two bedrooms, only one of which seemed to be in use for sleeping. Judging by the odor that permeated the bedroom, Annie Levesque hadn't changed her bedding in quite a while.

"I'll take this one," Fenton said to Colleen. "Why don't you get the room across the hall and the bathroom?"

Colleen looked at him, hand on one hip. "You're

not being *gallant* or anything, are you, just to spare me the smell?"

"*Gallant*? Me?" Fenton looked a little embarrassed. "Hell, one of us has gotta do it, and my sense of smell isn't that sharp, anyway. My wife's always complaining that I don't notice whenever she buys a new brand of perfume, or something. Your nose is real sensitive, though."

"How the hell do you know that?"

"Ah, come on, I've seen you smell stuff that nobody else in the room even noticed. Remember that time in Jacksonville—"

"All right, okay, never mind," she said, and turned toward the door. "As long as you weren't being *gallant*."

"Fuck, no."

The room across from Annie's bedroom was apparently used for storage, and it looked like there was ten years' worth of junk in there. Since Fenton wasn't present, Colleen used her witch sense to scan the room, searching for anything that might hint of black magic. Nothing. She did the same with the bathroom. *Nada.*

She met Fenton in the hall, just as he was leaving the bedroom. She looked a question at him, and he shook his head. "Not a damn thing, except that old Annie had an interesting vibrator collection, and some real odd tastes in porn."

"Do I want to know what those were?"

"Nah, keep your innocence for as long as you can." He made as if to step past her. "Excuse me."

"Where are you going?"

"Bathroom."

"But I just checked it. It's clean."

"I believe you. But, after breathing the air in that room for the last ten minutes, I need to wash my face."

Minutes later, as Fenton followed Colleen back down the stairs, he said, "Well, shit. I was hoping for some kind of a fucking lead, 'cause we sure could use one. But I guess it's okay to call in the locals, before they piss themselves with impatience."

He was almost to the door when Colleen said, "Wait."

Fenton stopped and turned back. "What?"

Colleen shook her head uncertainly. "I don't know, exactly. But there's *something*."

"That nose of yours again, huh?"

"Maybe. Or maybe I'm just psychic."

"Okay, we've still got a couple of minutes left. Go wild."

Colleen began to walk the unpolished wooden floor slowly. She wasn't sure what she was looking for, but she did know one thing: if Annie Levesque was a practitioner of the black arts, then she would have a special room in which to do her devil's work. It clearly wasn't upstairs, and you could see all of the main room here, just by turning in a circle.

Carefully, so as not to draw Fenton's attention, Colleen let her witch sense come to the fore. Almost immediately, she stopped and stared down at the wood beneath her feet. Then she dropped to one knee and began running her fingers over the floor's surface, as if feeling for something she had lost there. Then her fingers stopped. There it was: the barely visible line of a trap door leading into some kind of cellar.

Fenton, his back to her, was flipping through some magazines that had been left lying around, shaking each to see if anything would drop out. Colleen called her witch sense back, then, still on one knee, called, "Mulder? I've found something."

Fenton dropped the magazine and came over. "What'd you call me? Mulder?"

"Sorry," she said with a little smile. "I've wanted to say that, just once, ever since I joined the Bureau."

"Uh-huh, sure. Okay, Scully. What you got?"

Colleen had a heavy-duty folding knife in her shoulder bag, intended for use as a tool, not a weapon. It was as a tool that she employed it now, sliding the blade down into the thin crack in the floor. "I've got *this*, Special Agent, and I bet it leads to her workroom." Using the blade as a lever, she pried the trap door up a couple of inches, until she could get her fingers around the edge. Then she threw the hinged wooden door back all the way, sending it crashing onto the floor. The black square it revealed did not appear welcoming. Indeed, to Colleen it smelled like the deepest pit of hell.

"Okay, you might as well call in the Dudleys," she said to Fenton. "They can start on the rest of the place, but this baby down here—this is all ours."

The Shady Tree Motel, the only place where Morris and Libby had been able to find accommodation, was located a little way outside of Kent, on a bare patch of grass and asphalt surrounded on three sides by low hills and the trees that grew on them. Judging by the number of cars parked in front of the units when the two returned, business at the Shady Tree was not exactly booming.

They had requested adjoining rooms, with a connecting door between them. Management was happy to oblige but, as epitomized by desk clerk/ owner Ted Landry, was a little puzzled. Couples checking into the Shady Tree didn't usually bother with the charade of separate rooms. Not in this day and age—unless they were going to host one of those swingers' parties, something that had happened a couple of times before. Ted hoped that was the case again. He had managed an impromptu invitation to the last one, and had happy, erotic memories of what followed.

Libby Chastain and Quincey Morris, who were neither lovers nor swingers, could have shared a single room if accommodations were tight, and had done so on a few occasions in the past. They were comfortable with each other, and had a clear sense of their mutual boundaries. But, given the choice, they preferred the space and privacy of separate rooms.

Still, they enjoyed each other's company, most of the time. After leaving Tristan Hardwick's neighborhood, they had grabbed a quick dinner at a Friendly's restaurant before returning to the motel. Although Libby had the corner room, she had ended up next door in Morris's, leaving the connecting door open. Libby, shoes off, now lay on one side of the double bed, with Morris seated on the other, his back against the headboard. The room lights were off, the only illumination coming from the TV screen. The two of them gave little attention to the dumb horror movie that was playing, as they puzzled over the unusually strong black magic that Libby had detected coming from Hardwick's house.

"I don't get it," Morris said. "I spoke on the phone yesterday with a couple of people who know, or at least know about, this Hardwick fella. They both told me, independently, that he's a middleweight, at best. And one of them said that she was pretty sure Hardwick had been brought into the game by what's his name, Godfrey, in Cleveland."

"Morgan Godfrey," Libby murmured. "Now, there's a name to conjure with, you should pardon the expression."

"Yeah, I hear you. But it sure wasn't him you were sensing at Hardwick's place. That bastard's been dead for, let me think, three years, now."

"I'm not supposed to wish him damned and in hell, that's too much like a curse. So let's just say that I hope he didn't see heaven."

"That's a pretty safe bet," Morris said. "All right, so we're left with two possibilities—not counting the notion that your witch sense was somehow off, which I'm not inclined to consider very seriously."

"Nor I," Libby said. "It's never let me down before."

"So, either the intel we got on Hardwick was out of date, or just plain wrong..."

"Or Mister Hardwick was entertaining a visitor. Not the late Morgan Godfrey, but somebody at least as powerful, if not even more so."

"Somebody you couldn't handle, if push comes to shove?"

Libby gnawed her lower lip for a few moments before saying, "I don't know, Quincey. It's impossible to say. I guess it's like two gunfighters facing off in the Old West—they don't find out for certain who's the fastest, until one of them is lying dead in the street."

"I reckon I've got an ancestor or two who would've understood that metaphor pretty well," Morris said. "Maybe we'd be wise to avoid that particular showdown, if we can."

"Excellent idea, Tex. I haven't got anything to prove. But, we've still got a job to do."

"I know. Well, if our second scenario is the right one, and Hardwick had himself a visitor tonight, maybe whoever it was will be gone by tomorrow."

"Yes, the Goddess willing. So, you're thinking we cruise Hardwick's street again tomorrow, and see what kind of vibes I pick up."

"Yup. Then, depending on what you find, we decide whether we're going to move on Hardwick. And if we do, how."

Libby nodded, a trifle sleepily. "As plans go, there's this to say for it: I haven't got a better one."

The conversation eventually drifted into companionable silence. After a while, Libby dozed off. Morris saw that the horror movie on TV was over, and coming up next was *Once Upon a Time in the West*, one of his favorites. He decided he might as well just let Libby stay where she was, for now.

The room was quiet then, apart from the muted sounds of gunplay, macho dialogue, and the film's twangy soundtrack. A couple of hours later, Charles Bronson was just about to face off against Henry Fonda in the film's final showdown when Morris said, "*Libby*."

There was something in those two syllables that caused Libby Chastain's eyes to snap wide open. In a voice that did not sound sleepy at all, she asked, "What? What is it?"

"*Do you hear something?*"

Chapter 14

Roderico Baca stood on one of the hills overlooking the Shady Tree Motel and prepared to release hell—or a reasonable facsimile thereof. He had arrived a bit later than planned, having spent too much time enjoying himself with the late Tristan Hardwick. Thinking about that, he smiled to himself, wondering what the stupid police would make of what he had left behind.

But despite the delay, plenty of time remained for Baca to do his work. He knew that Chastain was down there—he could smell the bitch. He would assume, for now, that the man was with her. The two might even be fucking, right this minute. If so, they were about to gain a whole new understanding of *coitus interruptus*.

Baca had spent almost an hour in preparation, once he had set upon the method by which he would destroy Chastain and her companion. Several others might well join them, constituting what the U.S. military calls "collateral damage." Baca was not bothered in the slightest by this prospect.

He had chosen the spell he was using with great

care. Pardee had said he wanted Chastain's death to be nasty.

"Nasty" was one of the things that Roderico Baca did best.

He had drawn the necessary symbols in the earth, using a silver dagger he had made with his own hands. Then he mixed four of the key ingredients in proper proportion, all without the use of any kind of light. Baca had acquired the ability to see in the dark. That was appropriate, since, in a sense, it was where he lived.

Once the dry ingredients were mixed, to the accompaniment of the proper incantation, Baca was ready to add the final component. He reached into his leather bag and produced a small glass vial of baby's blood. The ancient spell specified that this ingredient be fresh—blood that is not refrigerated tends to congeal into an unworkable sludge very quickly.

Baca had made one stop on the way here from Hardwick's place. He knew the ingredient was fresh.

Although it is theoretically possible to perform black magic at any time, Baca much preferred the night for his work. Quite apart from the symbolism (and in magic of any kind, symbolism counts for much), it was known that the Dark Powers were stronger and more active after the light had fled. The darkness was also beneficial for a more pragmatic reason: some of the creatures that a black magician will call to do his bidding only come out at night.

Bats, for instance.

Despite their association with vampires in popular culture (which was a laugh, because, as Baca knew, vampires had no power to take the form of these creatures), bats are generally harmless to humans, the exception being the rabies virus that they sometimes carry. But rabies takes weeks to incubate before it kills, although its victims' final hours are very painful, indeed.

Disease aside, bats constitute no threat to people. They are generally small creatures, and most species eat nothing but insects or fruit. Even the fabled vampire bat, native to South America, will take less than a fluid ounce of blood from its host, whether animal or human.

But just because bats were harmless by nature didn't mean that they had to remain so.

Baca first sent out his power to call the bats to him, and from the skies for miles around, they came, by the thousands. Soon, they were flapping in the air above Baca in a great, circling cloud. He had them flying high above, lest the squeaking they use to navigate be heard on the ground and give warning of what was to come.

The Summoning was done. That was the easy part of the spell. Now for the Transformation. Baca spread his arms wide apart, summoning the power of the Dark Master he served, directing that power into the great mass of bats above him, causing the creatures to *transform*.

To *grow*—the bats began to double in size—some of them, to triple.

To *change*—even the largest of the bats had fangs less than a half-inch long. But no more. Under the command of Baca's magic, the bats' teeth grew, until they looked like parodies of Halloween decorations. The teeth were long now, and they were pointed, and they were very sharp.

217

Then, to *become savage*—bats have little capacity for emotion, but Baca's spell increased that capacity, then filled it with rage and the need to destroy. Any moment now, they would start fighting among themselves. But Baca had better quarry in mind.

Finally, he said a word of power five times and pointed at the motel room where Chastain and her boyfriend were staying. The bats could not see him point, of course; Baca's purpose was to focus the bats' energy and fury on one place.

And so he did.

Thousands of the devil bats dived, almost as one. Their goal was the building down below. Their need was to use their new, razor-sharp fangs to kill the warm-blooded creatures inside.

They descended on the Shady Tree Motel like a great, black tidal wave of death.

Small, powerful flashlights are standard equipment for FBI agents operating out in the field; Colleen and Fenton got good use from theirs as they made their way down a rickety ladder and into the underground chamber that had been Annie Levesque's workroom.

It smelled like old death down there.

The room appeared to be about half as large as the main floor above, which made it about thirty feet by twenty. Several wooden tables, both large and small, were placed about, and something that might have been an altar occupied most of one wall. Fenton noticed that there were thick, partly burned candles all over. Although not a smoker, he usually carried a small plastic lighter for emergencies. Approaching the nearest candle, he flicked the lighter into life, its small flame adding little to the illumination provided by the flashlights.

"*Don't do that.*" It was the first that Colleen had spoken since they'd arrived, and the small space seemed to magnify both her voice and its urgency.

"How come?" Fenton let the lighter go out. "It's not like we couldn't use some extra light in this shithole."

"No—this is *her* place, her special place, and you never can tell what... look, just don't light any of her candles, okay? I've got a bad feeling about it."

"Okay." Fenton put the lighter away. He had learned to trust Colleen's "feelings." He might make jokes about her being a half-ass psychic, but her intuition had saved their lives twice, in the eight months they'd been partners. Fenton wasn't so dumb as to reject out of hand things he couldn't explain—especially after some of the stuff he'd seen in the last year or so.

For Colleen, the room was pretty much what she would have expected. It was neater than Annie's living space upstairs; but then, what Annie had been doing down here probably mattered to her a lot more than watching TV or masturbating to kinky porn. The sheetrock walls were covered with cabalistic symbols, drawn in some kind of brown substance. Colleen didn't think it was anything made by Sherman-Williams or Glidden; she knew what color blood becomes when it dries. That, like everything else she could see, was pretty standard for practice of the black arts. Then her flashlight beam shone on one of the tables, and Colleen saw something that drew her closer. She played the light over the table's rough surface.

Fenton put down the book he'd been examining and came over. "Something?"

"You recognize the symbol." It wasn't a question.

"Sure, a pentagram. These occultists always have one, or several. Are you surprised?"

"Not by the thing itself, but the construction is interesting," Colleen said. "It's actually been carved into the table, rather than drawn on the surface, the way they usually do."

"Okay, sure, and that's important because..."

"In black magic, pentagrams like that are *used* for something, not just as decorations. So they have to be constructed very carefully. The length of the sides, the angles, auxiliary symbols, and so on, have to be exact. Get it wrong, and the results could be... unfortunate."

"Or so these people believe."

"Yes, of course, that's what I meant. So, if you carve the pentagram into wood, assuming you do it properly, you don't have to reinvent the wheel—or the star, in this case—every time you want to do a working."

Fenton looked at her oddly, although he was in shadow and Colleen couldn't see him. "All right," he said, "so this proves that Annie was punctilious, or obsessive, or paranoid, or maybe all three. Like I said before, are you surprised?"

"In a way. This technique is uncommon. In fact, I've only seen it once before. There was a woman in Massachusetts, Salem in fact, who had one of these carved in her workroom. This was last year, before you and I started working together. Abernathy, her name was. Christine Abernathy."

"Yeah, I remember hearing about that case from

somebody at Quantico. Didn't they find her dead, in that 'workroom' you were talking about? There was something weird about her death, but I forget what."

"*Weird* is a good word for it," Colleen told him. "The M.E. determined that she'd died of a massive infusion of snake venom. Made sense, since there were fang marks all over her."

"Nasty way to go."

"Yeah, but here's the weird part: no snakes were ever found on the premises, or any kind of cage where they might have been kept. And most of the venom that killed her wasn't from any of the poisonous snakes native to North America. She had *cobra venom* in her, Dale. Not to mention several other kinds that were never identified."

Fenton sent his flashlight beam to join Colleen's, which was focused on the pentagram. "So you think these two dead ladies are connected."

"That's what I'm starting to believe. The fact that both were black witches, okay, that could be coincidence. But carving a pentagram like this is an unusual technique. It suggests—no, make that *strongly suggests*—that they were trained by the same person."

"I think I've caught up with you, finally, "Fenton said. "If they were trained by the same person *then...*"

"It means they could both have been working for the same person *now.*"

"Fuck," Fenton said softly.

"Yeah," Colleen said. "*Fuck.*"

* * *

It was Sergio Leone who saved them.

If the Spaghetti Westerns he had made back in the 1960s weren't so damn good, Morris would have shooed Libby back to her own room hours earlier, and then gone to bed himself. The two of them would almost certainly have been sound asleep right this minute.

As it was, they were both wide awake, listening intently—to *something*. Eyes narrowed, Libby said, "It sounds almost like a big flock of—"

Then the world ended.

Or so it seemed, at first, when that great squeaking, flapping wave of devil bats hit the outside of the Shady Tree Motel. Baca had directed a good portion of them to attack the corner room, since that's where his witch sense detected Libby's scent. Morris, by the greatest good luck, happened to be looking through the connecting door toward Libby's room when both of her windows exploded under the assault of thousands of Baca's creations.

Quick reactions ran in Morris's family, and he was off the bed in an instant. With a kick that would have made his old sensei proud, he slammed the connecting door shut before the devil bats in Libby's room could come streaming through into his own.

Except for two of them.

The two monstrous creatures flew madly around the room for a few seconds, making high-pitched squeaking sounds. Then one launched itself right at Morris's face.

He was able to get a forearm up in time to save his eyes, and so the bat contented itself, for the moment, with savaging his arm with its unnaturally sharp fangs.

He tried to wrench it free, but the thing's claws were dug deeply into his arm, and Morris realized he could only rip the bat clear at the expense of his own flesh. Behind him, he could hear Libby screaming and he knew he had to do something *right now*. After a brief mental flash of the legendary British rocker Ozzy Osbourne, Morris did the only thing he could think of.

He brought his arm up to his face, and with one desperate snap of his teeth bit the damn thing's head off.

The bat's claws tightened around Morris' arm for a second, then released as the creature fell to the floor, blood spurting from the stump where its head had been. Morris spat the head out, trying not to vomit, and turned to see Libby crouched in a corner, screaming and swatting madly at the other bat, which was fluttering around her head, trying to get at her neck and face.

Morris was quick enough to pick flies out of the air, even in summer, when they were frisky. A bat was no problem at all. He snapped a hand out and grabbed the thing around its oversized, furry body, pivoted, and swung his arm down hard—in an arc that passed only a couple of inches away from the wooden back of the room's desk chair. Even Henry VIII's headsman could not have done a better, or quicker, job of decapitation.

Morris saw that the creatures were at the room's window now, so thick against the glass that the bright lights of the parking lot could not be seen beyond them. He could also hear them scratching and battering insanely at the other side of the connecting door that led to Libby's room.

Libby was still in the corner, covering her head with her hands, and sobbing. Morris wanted to go to her, but if he didn't do something about the window fast, they were going to have a lot more than two bats to worry about. In the distance, he could hear screams and yells as, he assumed, the bats paid calls on the motel's other guests.

Morris looked around the room desperately. There wasn't much to work with, since the Shady Tree did not go in for luxurious furnishings. Desk, chair, bureau, TV, bed…

Bed with… mattress.

Morris tore the bed linen away, then grabbed the queen-size mattress, and heaved it up and over, to jam as much as he could against the window. That would stop any bats that got though the glass—for a while. In the meantime, though, Morris was stuck bracing the damn thing. If he let go, it would fall away and their protection would go with it. He looked over his shoulder toward the far corner.

"Libby! *Libby*!"

She looked up at him slowly, her face white and tear-streaked.

"What can you work up? Come *on*, Libby, *magic*. You need to shore up the room, or drive off the fucking bats, or *something*!"

Libby shook her head slowly, like someone very drunk. "My gear… all in my room. Even my purse. Nothing… nothing here."

"There's gotta be *something*! Can't you improvise? I've seen you do it before. Jesus, I can't keep the fucking things out forever with this mattress. Come *on*, Libby!"

"I *hate* those things, Quincy, always have. Ever

since I was a little girl when some of them… goddamn fucking bats…" She began sobbing again.

Morris could hear glass breaking on the other side of the mattress.

"Libby! Libby!! What would your Sisters do, Libby? Would they be proud of you now Libby? Would they? *Would they?*"

For the first time since he had known her, Libby Chastain stared at him with loathing. That look hurt Morris worse than the bat's fangs had, but then he saw Libby Chastain wipe her hand across her face, sweep her hair out of her eyes, then start scanning the room. After a quick look around, she got to her feet and went into the bathroom. Morris had a moment's anxiety that she was going to break down again, but then she came back out, holding his toilet kit. She knelt, dumped the contents onto the floor, and started sifting through them—slowly at first, then more rapidly.

She looked up at Morris. "Have you got a lighter with you, matches, anything?"

"No, I don't, damn it—wait, on the bureau over there. Look in the ashtray."

The Shady Tree's management was still old fashioned enough to provide its guests with ashtrays and complimentary books of matches featuring the motel logo—old-fashioned, or they had an unusually large amount of fire insurance.

Libby dashed over to the bureau, found the cheap glass ashtray, and grabbed the two books of matches.

Morris could hear the bats tearing at the mattress from the other side. And this was a cheap mattress, which meant it was fairly thin.

"Your aftershave's got alcohol in it, and this deodorant…" Libby's voice was so soft, he could barely hear her over the noise from the bats. She quickly scanned the ingredient list on Morris's Mennen Speed Stick. "Aluminum hydroxide, close enough. All right."

Libby used Morris's toothpaste tube to draw an eight-inch circle on the rug, reciting the words of something that Morris couldn't hear as she did so. Then she poured the contents of his bottle of aftershave inside the circle, with more inaudible incantations.

Morris could hear some of the bats—they were inside the mattress, now.

Using her fingernails, Libby scraped small flakes of Morris's solid deodorant into the circle. Then, grasping one book of matches in the thumb and forefinger of both hands, she slowly raised it toward the ceiling, then lowered it, opened it, and placed it inside the circle.

Then she took the other book of matches, said a word three times, then lit one match, touched off the others with it, and dropped the blazing matchbook into the circle she had drawn. The other matches, and the alcohol-soaked section of carpet, caught fire immediately. A thin column of smoke began to rise. Libby spread her hands apart, closed her eyes, and began to chant something in what Morris suspected was ancient Aramaic.

And nothing happened.

The carpet smoldered within the circle, the matches and aftershave burned brightly for a few seconds before receding, and *nothing happened*.

After another ten or fifteen seconds of chanting,

Libby stopped and opened her eyes. The screeching, flapping, and clawing of the crazed bats continued unabated, and might even be louder now. She stared at the remnants of her failed spell. Then she looked up at Morris, a stricken expression on her face. "Fuck," she said.

Roderico Baca continued to pour his power into the mass of devil bats. Somehow, Chastain was alive—he could still sense her life force. Well, that would not last much longer. If need be, he could really exert himself, calling thousands more bats, to be transformed into winged nightmares that would do his bidding. Hundreds of thousands, could be summoned—millions, even. Roderico Baca had studied the black arts for many years, and knew their secrets well. His magic was powerful—certainly stronger than anything that Wiccan bitch below would be able to muster against him.

Baca was devoting most his concentration to sustaining the spell he had cast, and the rest in planning how to extend it. He was unable to give attention to anything else.

Such as someone who might be quietly coming up behind him.

The first indication Roderico Baca had that something was amiss was also the last thing he ever knew, as his consciousness exploded in a blood-red flash, bright as the sun, before being extinguished forever.

As she came closer, Hannah Widmark racked another round of triple-ought buckshot into the shotgun's firing chamber. But that was just habit—she knew that no follow-up shot would be necessary.

Most of Roderico Baca's head was splattered over the downslope of the hill where he had been standing as he looked upon his victims.

Hannah knew that a magical spell, whether of the black or the white variety, ceases with the death of its originator. She could see that the great mass of bats, which had virtually covered the Shady Tree Motel, was already rapidly dispersing. The creatures, back in their natural forms and inclinations, would be returning to the mundane little lives they had led before a black magician had made them instruments of terror and death.

Hannah stood looking down at the body of Roderico Baca. Suddenly, one steel-capped boot delivered a vicious kick that shattered three of Baca's ribs—not that he was in any condition to care.

The kick had turned the corpse over, onto its back, displaying what was left of Baca's face. Hannah stared into it, feeling whatever it was she felt on such occasions. Then she knelt and started going through his pockets.

IV

WISDOM

Chapter 15

In a U.S. Government warehouse outside Boston, Special Agent Colleen O'Donnell wrote her Federal ID number, FBI shield number, and signature at the bottom of the form she had just filled out, and handed it to one of the clerks working the front counter.

Then she walked over to the nearby waiting area and took the chair next to Fenton. "Shouldn't be too long." she said. "He's going to jump us over a few people in the queue."

"How'd you manage that?"

"Guess he must've liked my smile."

"Um. If I was to say something like 'Or maybe it was your tits,' that'd probably be sexual harassment wouldn't it?"

"Yeah, I guess. If I chose to treat it that way. And you know what a tight-ass I can be, sometimes."

"I better not say it, then."

"Just as well. You never can tell how people will react to stuff like that."

"Yeah."

After a minute or so, she said, "Anyway, I don't think they're that great."

"Huh?"

"My tits."

"Oh. Them."

Ten minutes later, the clerk called them over. "Okay," he said. "Looks like we've got two crates for subject Christine Abernathy. Says here, 'Clothing and household items.' Where you want 'em?"

Colleen and Fenton looked at each other. "Two crates," Fenton said. "Jeez."

She looked at the clerk, a middle-aged man with bifocals whose name tag read "Orville Lang," and said, "Is there an empty room around here, or maybe an office that nobody uses? We need to examine this stuff, and we'd prefer not to have to truck it someplace, then bring it back." She stared into the man's eyes, held them with her own, and *pushed*, just a little. "We'd really appreciate it."

Lang blinked a couple of times. "Uh, lemme check. Just a second."

"Wow," Fenton said softly. "Some smile."

Without turning to look at him, Colleen murmured, "No, I'm pretty sure it's my tits."

Lang returned and said, "Looks like Building Four's about half empty. Should give you lots of room, if you want it."

Colleen looked at Fenton with raised eyebrows, received a nod, and said to Lang, "That will do very nicely."

Half an hour later, Colleen and Fenton were in Building Four, a warehouse that was, as the clerk had promised, only about half-full with stored material. That meant there was enough open space left to play a regulation game of Arena Football.

They had the place to themselves—just them, a borrowed crowbar, and two wooden crates containing the worldly goods of the late Christine Abernathy.

"How come we've got this stuff, and not her family?" Fenton asked.

"There was no family that anybody could find," Colleen told him. "We looked pretty thoroughly, believe me. I realize we could've just left this stuff in the house, let the bank holding the mortgage worry about it. But, I don't know…"

"You had one of your feelings," Fenton said.

"Yeah, something like that," she said with a tiny smile.

"Well, looks like that intuition of yours was on the money, again." Fenton picked up the crowbar. "Might as well get started."

Like the main building where they had started, this warehouse had a long counter running across its front. That was where Colleen and Fenton piled Christine Abernathy's stuff as it came out of the crates.

Fenton started examining the clothing, checking each garment's pockets before putting it aside.

"This is a fuckin' long shot, to say the least," he said.

"Sure it is." Colleen did not look up from the pile of books and papers she was going through. "But, at the moment, what else've we got?"

"I think the answer to that would be *diddly-squat*," Fenton said.

"Fuckin' A."

They put in three hours, then broke for lunch at a

nearby Olive Garden restaurant, and went back to work at a little after 1:00pm.

It was 4:36pm, and Fenton was about to suggest calling it a day when he heard Colleen say, very distinctly, "Well, now."

"Got something?" He walked over to where she was still examining Abernathy's personal papers.

"Could be." Colleen was holding a spiral notebook that had been found in Christine Abernathy's workroom. Without looking up from the page she'd been reading, she said to Fenton, "Does the name 'Pardee' sound familiar to you?"

It was almost nine in the morning by the time Libby and Morris finished giving their statements, over and over, to the police—local, state, and even federal (as represented by an agent from the FBI's Akron field office, who wondered aloud if the bats were a new al-Qaeda terrorist weapon). In an unusual turn of events, the two of them didn't even have to lie to the cops—well, not very much, anyway. They did neglect to mention Libby's abortive attempt at impromptu magic, and, when asked about the scorch mark on his carpet, Morris said it had already been there when he'd checked in.

The police didn't push very hard. They had bigger problems to deal with—like figuring out what to say to the local citizenry, who were even now learning of the attack, courtesy of the gaggle of carefully coiffed TV journalists doing live remotes outside.

Very soon now, John Q. and Sally Public would be demanding to know why thousands of bats had descended in fury on the Shady Tree Motel, leaving behind the corpses of two elderly people staying in a room at the far end of the building. Mr. and Mrs. Robert McKittrick, seventy-two and seventy, respectively, had been found sprawled on the floor. Both had apparently bled out after being slashed and bitten a number of times that the Medical Examiner would only quantify as "more than a hundred" each. The McKittricks were the only fatalities, and the most serious injury among the survivors was the damage to Morris's left arm, which had already received medical attention. However, several other motel guests were found by paramedics to be showing recognizable symptoms of post-traumatic stress disorder.

Another puzzlement was why the bats had suddenly broken off their attack and flown away. No similar incidents had been reported anywhere else in North America during the night. That being the case, the authorities were prepared to tell the public, with apparent confidence, that the bat invasion had been some freak of nature, as yet unexplained, but unlikely to be repeated.

No one had yet suggested sending a team to look for evidence in the hills overlooking the motel. Eventually, someone would.

The Shady Tree had temporarily closed down by order of the police, so Morris and Libby went back to their rooms to pack. Morris had just finished latching his suitcase when he looked up and saw Libby Chastain standing in the connecting doorway. "Hey," he said, in a neutral tone.

"Hey," Libby answered. She did not sound neutral, but was instead giving a good demonstration of the DSM-IV's profile of "Depression (severe)." "Quincey, about what happened last night... I just don't know what to say."

Morris sat on the edge of the bed. He did not invite Libby to join him. "I was just coming into see you, to talk about that very subject," he said, harshly. "You really fucked up, didn't you, Libby?"

Libby stared at him, her mouth half-open.

"Jesus Christ, we could've both been *killed*. If those damn bats hadn't decided to call it a night for some reason, we'd both be at room temperature now. And all because of *you*."

"Quincey, that's not—"

"What the fuck happened, Libby? Did you forget how to do magic, all of a sudden? Or have you just lost your nerve?"

"Quincey, all my fucking gear was in *there*." She jerked a thumb back over her shoulder toward her room. "All of it. Along with a few thousand bats, as you might recall."

"So, now you can't improvise anymore, when our lives depend on it?"

"I *tried*, damn it! I used what was available, and I *tried*. I knew it was a fucking long shot. I didn't have the proper materials, and no tools at all—just toothpaste, deodorant, and your stupid aftershave, which by the way, went out of fashion somewhere around 1993. The odds were ten to one against, at least. But *I did what I could*, you ungrateful bastard!"

Morris looked at her thoughtfully, then nodded. "Yup."

"*Yup*? What the fuck is *that* supposed to mean?"

"It means," Morris said, in his normal, calm voice, "that I agree with every word you said, apart from the unkind remark about my aftershave. I just wanted to hear you say it. More important, I wanted you to hear *yourself* say it."

Libby looked totally out of her depth. "But... but, you were—"

"Everything you just said was true, Libby. Despite being scared shitless by the bats, which is a ridiculous phobia for a witch to have, if you ask me, and despite having nothing but crap to work magic with, you did the absolute best you could, Elizabeth Catherine Chastain." Morris's tone softened. "And I'm proud of you. Furthermore, if your Sisters knew, they would be, too."

Libby stared at him a little longer, then turned and stormed out of the room. As she left, Morris heard her say, loudly and distinctly, "MEN!"

Pardee closed the book he had been consulting, a 1584 version of the *Grimoirum Verum*. He dropped it onto the long, mahogany table in front of him, which was littered with old books, manuscripts, and scrolls in several languages. He began to pace the room slowly, occasionally looking out the huge window onto the grounds of Walter Grobius's estate, but not giving any attention to the work that was still going on down there in preparation for the Ceremony.

Then the pacing stopped. Pardee stood dead still; a smile sprouted on his face and quickly grew into a grin. It was time to go and see Grobius.

The old man sat at his enormous desk, nine brown prescription bottles lined up before him like soldiers at attention. They were joined by four oddly shaped containers whose contents were not the products of modern medical science. Grobius, a large bottle of Perrier open next to him, was systematically working his way through the collection, taking two pills from one container, four from another, and so on down the line.

Grobius did not look good today. His complexion had taken on a gray tint, and the flesh under his eyes looked unhealthy, even for someone his age. The old man's hands shook slightly as he made himself ingest the medicines.

He looked at Pardee and said sourly, "I'll need another treatment from your magic fingers sometime today. For all the good it's likely to do."

"It's kept you alive so far, along with the wonders of modern science and my own humble apothecary skills. Anyone else, if I may slightly flatter myself, would have succumbed years ago."

"Yes, I expect so." Grobius shook four green and white capsules from one of the bottles and gulped them down with a swig of the spring water. "But I'm glad it's almost over. We're on schedule?"

"Yes, essentially."

Grobius looked up at him, and there was sufficient intelligence and will left in the rheumy blue eyes to remind Pardee of how the old man had accumulated one of the world's great fortunes.

"Explain *essentially*," he said to Pardee.

The wizard lowered himself into one of the chairs that faced the desk.

"We want everything to go exactly right on the thirtieth," Pardee said. "This confluence of factors won't occur again for twelve years."

"Which I would be highly unlikely to see, yes. Tell me something I don't already know."

"I've been studying the ancient texts again, which,

oddly enough, caused me to remember the advice of Ulysses S. Grant."

"And that's relevant? Grant was hardly an exemplar for the office he held, as I recall."

"Grant was a mediocre president, true. But he had been a superb general. He claimed in his memoirs that the secret of his success was tilting as many factors as possible in his favor. Not just the big things, like choosing terrain and placing artillery, but the smallest details, as well. For instance, the day a battle was planned, Grant would not only make sure that his troops had been given breakfast, but that the food was a cut above the usual quality, to ensure that they would eat, and gain strength for the fight to come."

"I assume there's a point that you'll be getting to, in time."

"There is, indeed. I've been taking the same approach to the Ceremony that Grant took to his command. One might argue that the stakes are even higher, at least for you, than those Grant faced at the Battle of Shiloh. And the danger of failure is even greater, for some of us."

"I thought you said we had everything we needed. The grounds are almost ready. The black witches are preparing to join us, and the others, the white ones, are either dead or in hiding. You *said* all that, Pardee."

"I did, and I spoke truly. But I am a perfectionist— fortunately for you, if I may say."

"We'll see how fortunate I am, on the thirtieth."

"Indeed, we will," Pardee said quietly, and there was something in his voice that might have given Grobius concern, had the old man not been too sick to notice.

"So, what's the problem?" Grobius asked, reaching for more pills.

"The sacrifice, which I will offer at the climactic moment."

"You said we needed children. So I've had people find a dozen that nobody cares about, and made arrangements to have them brought here on the day."

"Thirteen. I wanted thirteen."

"I'll get you thirteen *hundred*, if it's what you need to get him here."

"I know. But I've been doing some additional research, and there may in fact be a sacrifice that he would find more pleasing."

"Along with the children, or as a substitute?"

"Oh, as a substitute, I think. No need to bloody the lily, to coin a phrase."

"So, what do you need, then?"

"A white witch. Someone who represents the antithesis of what we will be accomplishing that night."

"I suppose that makes a certain amount of sense. But I thought your idea was to kill them all, as a precaution."

"Not all of them, just enough to avoid any significant interference. And I believe that's been accomplished. But there's one in particular whom I would like to add to our program, as it were. Her death should please him immensely. And she has proved to be a thorn in my side of late, somehow managing to survive several attempts to eliminate her. I sent someone very skilled, very powerful, after the stupid assassins had failed twice. I don't yet know all the details, but she still lives, and the man I sent has disappeared. I must assume he's dead."

"I thought the white ones couldn't use their magic to kill."

"Not in most cases, but there are occasional odd exceptions. Besides, she's got a companion now, a man named Morris, whom I've heard of. He has made a nuisance of himself in the past."

"So you want this woman... what's her name?"

"Chastain. Elizabeth Chastain."

"You want her as some kind of ultimate sacrifice during the ceremony? You're not just doing this because she's pissed you off, are you?"

"No, I'm not. My research convinces me that her death, at the right point in the proceedings, will be a perfect capstone to the ritual. Granted, almost of any of these Wiccan cunts would do. So perhaps my choice of Chastain *is*... personal, but the desired effect will be achieved, nonetheless."

"All right, you're the expert. But if this Chastain has managed to avoid all your efforts to kill her, what makes you think it will be any easier to take her alive?"

"Because," Pardee said, "that is a task I intend to take on, myself."

For the second time in twelve hours, Morris made the turn onto the street where Tristan Hardwick lived. Glancing at Libby, he said, "You're sure you're up to this?"

"Yeah, I'm fine," Libby told him, sounding like she meant it. "Your little pep talk helped quite a bit, although for a few moments there you had me wishing that I *could* use black magic."

"Turn me into a toad, huh?"

"Oh, something *much* worse than that... Hey, what's all this?"

There were flashing red lights up ahead—lots of them. As they drew closer, Morris counted three police cars and an ambulance, all with their light bars going like mad.

They were parked in front of Tristan Hardwick's house.

Traffic was slowed to a crawl by all the curiosity seekers who had come out, in cars or on foot, in the hope of seeing something nasty. "Hardwick?" Morris asked. "Has to be, right?"

"Most likely," Libby said. "And here's a news flash for you: I'm getting almost nothing from the house now. Just the slightest trace of residual energy, which can last for days after somebody powerful leaves a place. But whoever it was that I was sensing out here last night is gone, baby, gone."

"*Gone* as in dead, or *gone* as in left for parts unknown?"

"Could be either one, Quincey. It's impossible to say."

"Well, then, what do you say we get out and join the rubberneckers? One of us might pick up something useful."

"Works for me. I think I'll bring my bag—you know, just in case."

"Yeah, good idea," Morris said. "Just in case."

Morris went with the slow-moving traffic stream, past Hardwick's house and a couple of blocks beyond. They didn't want to be seen getting out of a car too close to the crime scene, or accident scene, or whatever it was back there.

They approached the small crowd of onlookers at

a slow, steady pace, just another couple out for a walk who've come upon something interesting. By prior agreement, they split up. Somebody who might talk to one stranger might not feel quite as chatty around two of them.

The angle from where he was standing now allowed Morris to see past the ambulance that he had passed earlier in the car. There was a UPS truck parked in the driveway of Hardwick's house. Morris slowly scanned the area for somebody dressed in brown work clothes—and found the uniform being worn by a skinny blond man who appeared to be in his early thirties.

Morris looked more closely. The UPS guy reminded him of somebody who has just finished puking his guts out after a particularly bad drunk—he had the same pallor, the shaking hands, and the look on his face that seemed to combine disgust and weariness in equal measure. He was seated sideways on the front passenger seat of an open police car. Crouching next to him, talking calmly, was a concerned-looking man in civilian clothes. He appeared a little older than the UPS driver, but Morris thought he detected a family resemblance.

After a while, the older man slowly stood up, clapped the UPS guy on the shoulder gently, and walked off, a little unsteady on legs that had probably lost some circulation while he'd been in that cramped position.

Without being obvious about it, Morris placed himself at the edge of the crowd, so that the man would pass close to him on his way back to the street. As he drew near, Morris stepped forward, waving to an imaginary woman and calling, "I'm over here, honey."

The two men collided, but not very hard. Morris immediately said, "Hey, buddy, I'm sorry, my fault completely. I was yellin' to my wife and didn't see you, I'm really sorry." Morris could lose his Texas accent when he wanted to, and he spoke now like most people in the Northeast do who aren't from New England.

"It's all right, don't sweat it, no harm done," the man said, and started walking again. Morris caught up with him in a couple of steps. Clutching his arm lightly, Morris said, "Easy, buddy, you sure you're okay? Don't look too steady on your feet, there."

"No, I'm all right, thanks. Legs are just a little shaky from squattin' down, that's all."

"Well, I was headin' home, anyway," Morris said. "The wife's still gabbin' with her friends over there, and she's not leavin' 'til she's all talked out. You know how the women are. I'll walk with you a little ways, if you don't mind the company."

"Yeah, sure, whatever."

The two made their way toward the street, and Morris silently counted to ten before saying, "Terrible thing, huh?" He was bluffing like mad while holding no decent cards at all, but thought it was worth a try. *Might as well go all in.*

"Yeah, Jesus. That kinda stuff doesn't happen around here. Never has, far as I know."

"What do they think it was, drugs?"

"I dunno. I ain't talked to the cops. My cousin Benny's the UPS guy who found him."

"Really? My God. He got quite a shock, I bet."

"Tell me about it. Benny says this guy, Hardridge—"

"'Hardwick,' I think it was."

"Yeah, you're right. Hardwick. Benny says, he's got a package for the guy, so he knocks on the front door; door swings wide open. Benny don't know whether to close it, leave it open, leave the package, or what, you know what I mean?"

"Sure. How's he supposed to know what the guy wants, right?"

"Right, exactly. So Benny takes, like, a couple of steps inside. He's about to yell, 'UPS man,' or something, but then the smell hits him."

"Christ, it must have been terrible," Morris said.

"Better believe it. Benny says it was like blood, and shit, and rotten meat, all rolled into one."

"Jesus Christ."

"Then he does somethin' I wouldn't of done, not in a million years. But, you know how he is—Benny always had more guts than brains. So he follows this god-awful smell, right into the guy's living room."

"That takes more nerve than I'd ever have, I'll tell ya that much."

"Yeah, well, I bet he wishes he'd just turned around and went back to his truck. He's gonna be dreaming about what he seen for years, I bet."

"Like that post-traumatic thing the guys in the war come home with."

"Yeah, somethin' like that, I guess." Benny's cousin shook his head in wonder. "He says the fuckin' guy—pardon my French—was *turned inside out*. I mean *completely*. Now how the hell could you do something like that? And who the hell'd *want* to, know what I mean?"

"Somebody who wanted to kill a guy and make it hurt," Morris said. "A *lot*."

"Fuckin' nutcase. Pardon my French."

"Yeah, a real psycho," Morris said quietly. "A real damn psycho."

Chapter 16

Libby and Morris stopped at a Perkins Pancake House, and ordered coffee.

"I'm glad you got something for your trouble," Libby said. "All I heard was a theory that the Manson Family was back in business, never mind that Charlie's in San Quentin, serving ninety-nine years to forever—as well he should be. Oh, and I got a nice recipe for strudel, for what that's worth."

The waitress brought their coffee, and Morris stirred sugar into his as he said, "Hey, don't underestimate the value of a good strudel. I knew a fella, one time, survived a knife fight because of a strudel his mom had made him."

Libby gave him a look that said she suspected her chain was being yanked, but then she said, "The sugar gave him the energy to fight better, or maybe run away?"

"Nope." Morris sipped his coffee. "He was carrying it home from his mom's house, when he ran into trouble. Took the strudel, and threw it at the guy with the knife. Knocked him right out. His mom wasn't much of a cook, you see."

Libby smiled and nodded, her suspicions confirmed. After trying her own coffee she said, more soberly, "I guess a strudel wasn't used on the late Mister Hardwick."

"No, not hardly. If he'd been found shot dead, something like that, I'd figure somebody from the poor kid's family came over for payback. But if a guy getting turned inside out doesn't reek of black magic, then I don't know what does."

"For sure. I'm assuming that what I was sensing last night emanated from whoever did that number on Hardwick. I wonder what he did, to piss off somebody like that."

Morris picked up one of the menus the waitress had left. "Well, he messed up the job. Got himself caught, even if the cops did drop the ball and get the case thrown out. And called a lot of attention to himself, in the process."

"Which means," Libby said pensively, "that someone not connected with the law might come along and decide to ask him some questions about why he did it, and for whom."

"Uh-huh. Someone like you and me, for instance. And I guess you could say we have been forestalled, big-time."

Libby picked up her own menu and looked at it without much interest. "So he was killed either as punishment for being careless, or to shut him up."

"Or both, which is my guess."

"Mine, also. Which turn of events leaves us, as my mom would elegantly put it, 'up shit creek.'"

"Shit creek?" Hannah Widmark said, as she slid

248

into the booth next to Morris. "Doesn't sound like a nice place to be." She plucked the menu from Morris's hands, and began to page through it. "So, what looks good?"

"Pardee?" Fenton frowned in concentration, then shook his head. "Doesn't ring any bells with me." He hopped up to take a seat on the counter, next to a pile of Christine Abernathy's papers. "I take it the name has just cropped up for a second time."

"Yeah, I remember seeing it among Annie's stuff, day before yesterday," Colleen said. "It's mentioned in there at least once, maybe twice. Reason I remember, it's the name of a character in a Western that my brother Peter just loves: *Rio Conchos*."

Fenton shook his head. "Never heard of it, but then I'm not too big on Westerns."

"You're not missing much," Colleen told him. "I've sat through it at least three times. I stayed with Pete sometimes, when I was in high school, after I'd have a big fight with my parents. He was always watching that stupid movie—and what was I gonna say? It was his place."

"Yeah, I hear you," Fenton said. "Beggars can't be choosers—of the movies, or anything else."

"Anyway, there's a character in it named Pardee, some ex-Confederate colonel who's trying to re-start the Civil War by giving guns to the Apaches."

"Sounds complicated." Fenton's frown returned. "We're assuming it's a name. There's no such thing as a 'pardee,' is there?"

"Easy enough to check." Colleen produced her iPhone and did a quick Internet search.

"Um. Appears only as a proper name," she said,

a few minutes later. "A big home builder in the Southwest, for one. Lots of smaller businesses around the country. Apparently, a man named Pardee was governor of Arkansas, like a hundred years ago."

"Probably not the one we want, then."

"Nope, not unless he's been resurrected, and I hope to heaven we're not going to have to deal with *that* stuff in this case."

Fenton gave her another sample of the look he had been sending her way a lot, lately. It combined curiosity with a certain amount of suspicion. "I don't suppose any of those Pardee guys—or gals, I guess—is mixed up in black magic."

"Well, I didn't check out all 1.3 million Google hits," Colleen said. She picked up the iPhone again. "Although, you never know…"

"I was kidding, Colleen."

"I know you were. But there's all kinds of stuff on the Internet these days, Dale. And we'd feel like real fools, later, if it turned out that what we wanted was right there in cyberspace, waiting for us."

She applied herself to touching icons on the small screen, one after another. Without looking up, she said, "Fortunately, we don't have to look at all 1.3 million. Let's see what we get by combining 'Pardee' with 'black magic' in our little search."

A minute later: "Nope. Okay, let's try 'sorcery.'"

Then: "Nothing. Hmm, how about 'witchcraft?'"

Then: "Shit. Oh well, it was worth a—"

Fenton was looking off into space, eyes narrowed. "Try 'wizard.'"

"Good one. Although if he didn't show up with the other… well, hello, ladies!"

She looked up at Fenton. "One hit. Looks like a

message board—part of a web page about witchcraft. Not bad, Dale."

As she started tapping the screen again, Fenton said, "A wizard's just a male witch, right?"

"Not exactly," Colleen said absently. "It's a different magical tradition, that draws its power—"

She stopped, then looked up at him. "Why are you asking me about stuff like that?"

Fenton shrugged. "You told me that you read a lot. Figured you might've read something about that subject. Looks like I was right, too. What was it you were saying about a different tradition?"

Colleen went back to the iPhone and shook her head. "Doesn't matter." A few seconds later, she said, "Okay, here we go. Looks like it's part of a long thread on the hazards of witchcraft, mostly about things and people to avoid. Somebody calling himself 'Gandalf 23' had this to say:

'I know just what you mean, Susie B. Buddy of mine, Vince Israel, got involved with a wizard name of Pardee who's bad, man, I mean real fuckin' bad. Dude's magic is the blackest of the black. But Vince wouldn't listen to me, thought he knew everything. Well, this Pardee got him involved in some shit, and now Vince is doing, like, twenty-five to life. They said he killed a little kid. I dunno whether he done it or not, but my point is, some people they're fuckin' poison, and you gotta treat 'em just like snakes in the jungle. I mean, like, cobras and stuff. You run into one, just turn and walk away. Otherwise, you're lettin' yourself in for a world of hurt.'

Colleen sighed, and put her phone down on the counter. "I translated the typos into English as I went along," she said to Fenton. "So this Vince

Israel knows somebody named Pardee, and pretty well, by the sound of it."

"And if you believe the guy on the board, old Vince is in the slam. What's the date on that thread, anyway?"

Colleen checked. "Gandalf 23 posted it on November third, two years ago."

"So, if Gandalf's telling the truth, Vince is most likely still in the system. Unless he got himself shanked in the yard over a gambling debt, or something."

"Good thing his name's not John Smith or Bill Jones," Colleen said. "Shouldn't be too many Vincent Israels behind the walls, I would think."

Fenton nodded toward the iPhone. "Can you get into the Bureau of Prisons database with that thing?"

"One way to find out."

A little while later, she put the phone down again. "No, I can't get access through this operating system. Shit."

"Bet the Boston field office can," Fenton said.

Colleen thought about it. "Yeah, you're right. They probably can."

Fenton looked around the vast, silent warehouse. "Can you think of any good reasons why we need to hang around here?"

"Not even one," she said. "Come on, let's hit the road."

The fifteen desk-chairs were formed in a rough circle, and twenty or so others, not in use, were pushed to the side to make room. Allie Mercer conducted all of her smaller classes this way. When it came to teaching literature, she much preferred guided discussion over lecture, although for her introductory classes, which tended to be larger, the "me-talk-you-listen-and-take-notes-because-it'll-be-on-the-test" approach was sometimes unavoidable.

"So, Goodman Brown grows into old age cynical and bitter," Allie said to the group, "and Hawthorne ends the story with 'his dying hour was gloom.' What's his point here? That ignorance is bliss? Would Brown be better off not knowing that all his neighbors, friends, even his beloved wife, Faith, are practicing black witchcraft in secret?"

"I don't think so, Dr. Mercer." That was from Becky Daniel, who, in Allie's view, was one of the few current English majors who had the potential of one day becoming a true intellectual. "I think what Hawthorne's getting at, is that knowledge comes with a price, and you just have to be willing to pay it. I mean, Goodman Brown sees his…"

That was when Allie Mercer's right hand began tingling in a way that she recognized and understood. A quick glance at her watch told her that the class period had about ten minutes to go, but Allie knew she wouldn't be able to concentrate until she allowed her hand to do what had to be done.

All right, let Becky finish what she's saying, then get them out of here. They never complain when I break class early, anyway.

Becky was saying, "…that having no illusions is a hard thing to face, but we have to face it."

It was an interesting idea, and Allie regretted not being able to follow it up now. Todd Bailey, seated two places to Becky's left, said, "I'm not sure I—"

Allie held up a hand, interrupting him. "Todd, hold that thought, will you? And make a note to yourself about what you were going to say, so we can start at that point next time." To the whole group she said, "We're going to finish a little early today, guys. In fact, we just did."

As the surprised, but not displeased, students began to stand, Allie said, a little louder, "And don't forget to read Gordon Dickson's 'The Amulet' for Friday. That's next on the reading list, in case you forgot."

Allie was concerned that she'd be delayed further if some of them stuck around to talk to her about their term paper topics, but the students all shuffled out the door, and soon the classroom was empty.

With her left hand, Allie reached for the legal pad containing her discussion notes for 'Young Goodman Brown' and flipped to a blank page. Only then did she reach into her skirt pocket for a pen. Her right hand was tingling insistently now, in a way that was almost painful.

She took the pen in her right hand and touched its point to the lined yellow paper. Instantly, Allie was writing. She was not surprised to see the handwriting on the page was not her own.

It took only a few seconds. Then her hand stopped, and the tingling began to subside, soon fading to nothing. Allie stared at the words written on her pad.

The Circle must form, this night at 9:00 EST. It involves a matter of grave importance, and your participation is vital. May the Goddess bless you.

Allie Mercer could feel her heart beating faster. Sister Eleanor, despite an unfortunate tendency toward archaic language when communicating en masse with the Sisterhood, did not use terms like

254

"grave importance" lightly. Allie wished she didn't have to wait almost six hours to find out exactly what kind of shit had hit the fan.

Allie stood slowly, and began to gather together the books, notes, handouts, and other stuff that made up what she thought of as her "professor kit." The specific components of the kit varied from course to course, but the same basic stuff was needed every time.

A guest speaker was scheduled on campus tonight—writer, cultural critic, and sometime porn actress Sharon Purcell, known also as "Shari Sexpert," was giving a talk entitled something like, "Two Drinks Away: Bisexuality and the 'Straight' Woman." Allie had thought it sounded like fun, and planned to go.

But now, nothing was going to prevent her from being home tonight at 9:00pm, lying on her bed and waiting to form the Great Circle.

A knot of anxiety was beginning to form in Allie's stomach. She picked up her professor kit, and headed for the door. Ten minutes of meditation, in her office with the door closed, would help. But she knew that she wouldn't be able to really relax until she found out what the emergency was—and maybe not even then.

"I thought you didn't want to be seen with us, Hannah," Libby Chastain said. "Something abut 'too close to the bull's-eye,' if I remember correctly."

"I think we'll be all right this time, Libby," Hannah said, with a tiny smile. "Especially since the threat to you has been eliminated—at least, the immediate threat."

"Do tell," Morris said. He turned sideways and looked at Hannah closely.

"I imagine this guy," Hannah said, "like those who preceded him, was just a hireling. But from what you've told me about the others, this one was a cut—no, *several* cuts—above."

A waitress came over and asked if they wanted anything to eat. Hannah, still holding the menu she'd taken from Morris, said, "I don't know about these two, but *I* certainly do." She proceeded to order a meal that might make a lumberjack feel a tad overfull. Morris and Libby said they would stick with coffee, for now.

Once the waitress was safely out of earshot, Morris said, "This guy, the one who was several cuts above—I assume he was the one responsible for the bats."

"Oh, yes," Hannah said. "He called them from, I would imagine, miles around. Then he used another spell to change them into something more dangerous. I don't know if you got a close look at any of the little darlings—"

"A little closer than we'd like," Libby said. "In fact, a *lot* closer."

"Some of them fell to fighting among themselves, before this wizard could get everything organized and send them against the motel. A few fell to earth, after receiving mortal damage from one or more of the others. One came near me, and I had a chance to look it over." Hannah made a face. "Nasty things."

"And you were where, exactly?" Morris asked.

"In the hills, but about half a mile away from the bat man. I watched what he was doing through a pair of night glasses I had with me. Once I got a look at how powerful he was, I decided to stay put for a while. People like that—" Hannah stopped herself. "*Creatures* like that have very sharp senses, most of the time. It's difficult to get close without their knowing, and dangerous to try."

"You said 'most of the time,' Hannah." Libby had left the sarcasm behind now. "What's the exception?"

"When they're in the midst of working magic, of course. I realize that you're on the opposite side of things from these... monsters, Libby. But when you're concentrating on a spell, you're not exactly paying real close attention to your environment, are you?"

Libby nodded slowly. "That's true," she said. "I never really thought about it that way before, but you're right."

"So you stayed put, until when?" Morris asked her.

The waitress brought part of Hannah's immense meal, and a fresh pot of coffee for Morris and Libby. Hannah said, "I hope you'll both excuse me," and started in.

After putting away a couple of mouthfuls of pancakes and sausage, Hannah said, "I stayed where I was, until I saw the spell that he was working on the bats. Lots and lots of bats, Quincey, which takes lots of energy." Hannah ate some toast. "And which leaves little energy to spare for other things, like paying attention to what's going on around you."

Morris and Libby nodded agreement, then let her eat undisturbed for a while, since she was clearly very hungry. After a while, Hannah washed down a mouthful of egg with her coffee and said, as if she had not been silent for five minutes, "That's why most military snipers work in pairs: the shooter and a spotter, who also provides security. Putting a round exactly where you want it, from fourteen hundred meters out, takes a lot of concentration, so the sniper has someone to watch his back."

"Unlike the guy last night," Morris said.

"Exactly. Once he started his working, I made my way slowly through the trees to his position. No point in taking chances, after all—just because he was busy didn't make him deaf. It took me a little while to get there, I'm afraid. Long enough for those bats of his to do some damage."

"Quincey and I weren't badly hurt," Libby said, "but a couple at the other end of the unit, senior citizens, I gather, were killed. I guess they just couldn't move fast enough to take shelter in time."

Hannah silently bowed her head over her food, like a monk saying grace. She stayed that way for a while, and Libby actually began to wonder if she was crying. But when Hannah raised her head, her face was unmarked by tears, and her angel's voice sounded normal when she said, solemnly, "I honor the death of the innocent. Always."

"Finish the story, why don't you," Morris said. "I have a feeling you were just getting to the good part."

"Not much more to tell, really. He was so focused on directing and controlling the bats, he didn't even notice me. So, I came up behind him and blew his head off with a shotgun." She might have been discussing the weather in a place she rarely visited.

Morris and Libby looked at each other. So attuned were they to each other by now, words were often unnecessary. Morris's expression said, *I'm sorry you had to hear that*, while the slight movements of Libby's mouth, head and shoulders told him, just as clearly, *Well, that's what we hired her for*.

"Was this guy carrying anything to identify him?" Libby asked.

"Nope. Nothing on his person, except magical stuff. I suppose I could have cut off one hand and brought it along for a fingerprint ID, but the police might have asked some embarrassing questions."

Morris wondered whether Hannah was joking, but decided she'd better not ask.

"I'm not second-guessing your work, Hannah," he said. "Clearly, this guy was nobody to take chances with. But it's a pity you couldn't take him alive. I would have liked to talk to him."

Hannah produced one of her nightmare smiles. "Not to worry," she said cheerfully. "I said 'Hi' for you."

Morris looked over at Libby and saw that she was staring into her coffee cup, a deep frown of concentration creasing her face.

"Something wrong, Libby?" he asked.

Without raising her head, Libby held up an index finger, asking for a little more time before answering. When she did look up, Morris saw a sparkle in her eyes that hadn't been there since this sorry business started.

"I'm an idiot, Quincey, a fucking dyed-in-the-wool lame-brained idiot."

"Don't be so hard on yourself, Libby," Morris said.

"Oh, don't worry, you're a fucking idiot too," she said, and smiled. "We both should have figured this out two hours ago."

"Okay, we're idiots," Morris said, evenly. "Duly stipulated. Now what is it that's so damn easy, we should have figured it out already?"

"What's-his-name, Hardwick, was involved in the child abductions and murders, right?"

"Well, one of them," Morris said. "But the FBI is working on the assumption that they're all connected, and they're probably right. It can't be just coincidence."

"Agreed. And the wizard that Hannah dealt with last night was trying to kill *me*."

Morris nodded. "I can't think of any other explanation that fits. I can't imagine he did it just to get at the two old folks down the way from us."

"Me, neither," Libby said. "So here's the gazillion-dollar question, Tex: *who killed Hardwick?*"

Morris sat there, gently tapping his fingertips against the side of his cup. Finally he said, "You're right, Libby. We *are* idiots."

"Not that it's any of my business," Hannah said between mouthfuls, "but what the hell are you two having conniptions about?"

"Hardwick was killed by black magic," Morris said. "I heard that he was found turned completely inside out."

"And you believe third-hand information like that?" Hannah said.

"Actually, I do, but it doesn't even matter—"

"Because," Libby said, "I sensed powerful black magic at Hardwick's house last night, which is the night he was killed. I told Quincey that stuff was too strong to be coming from Hardwick himself. And the man controlling those bats was a black wizard of considerable power and skill, had to've been. That's no easy job he took on, and, from all indications, he performed it flawlessly."

"Until I ventilated his skull for him," Hannah said.

"Yes, and if I haven't thanked you for that," Libby said, "thank you, Hannah, for almost certainly saving our lives last night." There was no mockery in her voice this time.

"All part of the service," Hannah said. "But how do you know for sure that whoever offed Hardwick was also Mister Batman?"

"Come on, Hannah," Morris said. "This is Kent, Ohio, not New York or London. How many people with that kind of power do you expect to find in a burgh this size, anyway? No, it had to have been the same guy, both times."

"Which means these cases are connected," Libby said. "It's the only explanation that makes any sense. The people involved in this campaign to murder children for their organs, they're the same bastards trying to kill me, for whatever reason."

After that, it was quiet at their table—until Libby got an odd expression on her face and began flexing the fingers of her right hand. Then she pulled an unused paper napkin closer and said, "Do either of you have a pen?"

The message was the same one that was simultaneously being received by Allie Mercer and a number of other women. Once it was complete, and Libby's hand had returned to her full control, she shared the contents with her companions, and briefly explained what they meant.

"So, you're going to be doing it again, that

astral transference you used to talk to me in L.A.," Morris said.

"Pretty much, except my destination won't be anywhere on this plane. We'll be meeting in, it's hard to explain... somewhere else."

"Save a lot of money on hotels that way," Hannah said, without smiling.

Later, after most of the plates were cleared away, Morris said, "Well, I'm sure enough glad not to've ended up as bat food last night, but that means we're still up shit creek, Libby. Hardwick was the only lead we had. Once he was taken out of the picture, the guy who killed him became our only lead, even though we didn't know it at the time. And once Hannah did her number on *him*—the number of our leads went down to zero. We've got diddly-squat, now."

Libby seemed about to say something, when Hannah said, "Know what? I may be able to help you with that."

She produced her cell phone, a sleek, black-covered instrument, not unlike Hannah herself, and said, "Let me just make a couple of calls."

Chapter 17

The institution's official name is Massachusetts Correctional Facility, Cedar Junction, at Walpole, but everybody involved in corrections (on both sides of the law) in New England just calls it Walpole. Like every maximum-security prison in the world, it is a cold, gray place, made of stone, brutality, barbed wire, and despair.

FBI Special Agents Fenton and O'Donnell were shown every courtesy by the prison administration, once it was made clear that they were not at Walpole to investigate any of the many accusations of human rights violations that had been leveled by inmates over the years.

They had been waiting in Interview Room 4 for about ten minutes when they heard an iron door opening and closing nearby, then another, followed by the sound of approaching footsteps.

Vincent Israel, hands shackled to the heavy belt that was fastened around his waist, was brought in by a bored-looking C.O. who looked a question at Fenton, then left after receiving a nod in return.

Israel didn't look a lot like his mug shot, taken at the time of his arrest three years ago. His head was shaved now, and he had scar that ran down the right side of his face, parallel to his eye and about half an inch away. The slash that caused the scar must have missed Israel's eye very narrowly. The man's muscular arms, revealed by the short-sleeved prison shirt he wore, bore several crude tattoos that had probably been acquired after Israel's incarceration. A stylized swastika was prominent on one arm, the initials "A.B." dominating the other one. From the moment he'd entered the room, Israel's eyes had been on Colleen, whom he was staring at with the kind of intensity that a long-time dieter will give to a hot fudge sundae.

Colleen and Morris both displayed their FBI identification as soon as Israel was seated. Now Fenton, who was looking at the "A.B." tat, said, "I see you've gone and hooked up with the Aryan Brotherhood."

Israel tore his eyes off Colleen long enough to answer Fenton. "Man does what he's gotta, to survive. In here, you don't belong with somebody, then you're meat for everybody." He looked Fenton up and down, with undisguised contempt. "First week I was inside, three… *African Americans* jumped me, and beat the livin' shit out of me. They took my smokes, my lighter, and my watch. Then they gang-fucked me for about an hour, although it seemed a hell of a lot longer. That shit don't happen no more, now I'm with A.B." Israel had clearly wanted to say "niggers" instead of "African Americans," but was probably unsure whether he could afford to piss Fenton off.

Fenton gave him a broad smile and said, "I'm a little surprised those Nazis would be interested in a guy named, you know... 'Israel.'"

"You think I'm a kike, because of the name?" Israel made a disgusted sound. "Ain't none of them in *my* family. Way I hear it, one of my ancestors was some kind of preacher in Massachusetts, 'round the time the Puritans come over from England. His real name was probably Smith or Jones—some shit like that. But he was such a holy roller, he changed it to Israel, maybe to prove that he'd read the Bible. And the name stuck. I ain't no fuckin' Jew, no way."

"Before we talk any more, there's some things you need to get straight," Colleen told him. "We can't get you a transfer out, or a new trial, or an appeal that your lawyer didn't try already, and get thrown out of court."

Israel looked up from her body to her face, then gave a small nod of something that might almost have been respect. Behind the walls, hope is the thing that will hurt you worse than a shank between the ribs, once it comes crashing down around you—as it always does. By refusing to offer him any false hope, Colleen was showing the only kind of honesty that Israel was prepared to accept.

"Okay, so that's what you *ain't* got." Israel went back to his close examination of Colleen's breasts. "What *have* you got, and what do you want out of me in exchange for it?"

"We might be able to make your life in here a little better," Fenton said. "No guarantees, but if we tell the Deputy Warden that you cooperated in our investigation, and make a specific recommendation on how he might express our gratitude, I think he'll take it seriously. Might be able to get you a better job. Where are you now, the laundry? I think we could help with that, if we had a reason to."

"We also have a few bucks that we're allowed to use, to pay informants," Colleen said. "We could make sure some of it gets into your commissary account. Get you some extra smokes and candy bars."

"All that? Damn!" Israel's sarcasm wasn't subtle. "And what is it you're lookin' for, in return for all that generosity?"

"We want Pardee," Fenton said. He had been watching the man's eyes as he'd said the name. Most cons are good liars, and even better at reaction concealment. But dilation and contraction of the pupils is an autonomic response, outside the control of the will, that is geared to strong emotion.

Fenton had seen Israel's pupils contract, an instant after he'd said Pardee's name.

"Pardee?" Israel pretended to consider his list of friends and acquaintances. "Nope, don't think I know the name."

"We hear otherwise," Colleen told him.

"That right?" Israel said to her chest.

"We've been told, by somebody who would know, that Pardee's the guy got you involved in all this occult bullshit," Fenton said. "That he's the one, put you up to snatching that kid, and cutting him open."

"That wasn't me, man." Israel didn't even bother to act indignant. Protesting his innocence was probably just a reflex by now. "The cops got the wrong man, and their evidence at the trial wasn't worth shit."

"The jury thought otherwise, though, didn't they?" Colleen said. "Took them less than three hours to come back with a verdict, too. Guilty on all counts: kidnapping, felony assault, and aggravated murder in the first."

Israel gave an exaggerated shrug, which caused his shackles to jingle briefly. "What can I tell you? I'm innocent."

"So you didn't snatch the kid, you didn't kill the kid, and you never heard of anybody named 'Pardee,'" Colleen said.

Israel grinned at her. "That's a big ten–four, honey. But say 'snatch' again for me, will you? I love it when chicks talk dirty."

"Too bad," Fenton said, and pushed his chair back. "Because if you don't know anything about Pardee, then you've got nothing of interest to us."

Colleen, playing along, began to gather together the papers she had laid out in front of her.

"Aw, shucks," Israel said. "Now I'll never get that job in the library. And just think of all them candy bars I'm gonna miss out on."

Instead of standing up, Fenton said, "I think I hear you saying you don't care for our offer."

Israel shrugged again.

"Just for the sake of discussion," Colleen said, "if we *were* able to come up with something you found interesting, what could we get for it?"

"Well, for instance, if I did remember this guy, Pardee," Israel said, "I'd tell you everything I know about him."

"Including where he is now?" Colleen asked.

"Get real, lady," Israel said. "I been in here going on three years. Don't know for sure where anybody is now. Except my mom. She writes once in a while, and her return address ain't changed."

"If you don't now where Pardee is now…" Fenton let the sentence trail off.

"I might be able to tell you about a real nice deal that this Pardee fell into. Where somebody with a whole pile of money was willing to spend some of it on Pardee and his magic tricks. Something that sweet, a guy wouldn't be in a hurry to walk away from it. There's a good chance he'd still be with this rich guy. I might know the name."

"Uh-huh. All right," Fenton said. "Say we thought this was interesting enough to go to some trouble over. A better job and more commissary money doesn't do it for you. So what *do* you want?"

"Despite what you hear about prison," Israel said to Fenton, "it's possible for a man to find some of life's little luxuries in here, if he's got money, or the right connections, or maybe if he does favors for the right people. Booze? Yeah, sure, there's booze. I mean apart from stuff like raisin jack, that you can make yourself. Not impossible to get yourself on the outside of a pint of mediocre Scotch, brought in from outside. Weed, same thing. Stuff from the pharmacy, yeah, that's around. Even coke, if you know a friendly guard who's maybe gettin' behind in his car payments. But there's one thing ain't available behind the walls. California, maybe, but not in this state." Israel turned and looked at Colleen again, and now the hunger in his eyes was almost palpable. "Pussy," he said. "That's the one thing I can't get in here."

"Watch your mouth, asshole," Colleen snapped. "The same juice that lets us get you a better job also gets you a month in the Hole, if we want it that way. Maybe two months."

Israel gave her a crooked smile. "Threaten me all you want, honey. It just gives me a hard-on to hear you talk about juicy holes."

Then he turned back to Fenton. "You wanna find Pardee, I'll tell you how. Give you everything I know about him. But first, you get me a woman. And until you find a way to *juice that*, we got no more to talk about."

Israel turned toward the door and called out, "Sir? I'm all done in here, now."

As the C.O. who had brought him in reappeared, Israel looked back at Fenton and Colleen with a nasty grin. "You folks be sure and come on back, whenever you're ready to continue our conversation." Then he gave Colleen a wink, and allowed the guard to lead him out of the room.

Once they were alone, Fenton looked at Colleen. "Well, shit. Think he means it?"

"Take it from the woman he's gonna be thinking about when he jerks off tonight," she said, and shuddered. "He means it, all right."

The Ouroboros Bar and Grill occupied the middle of a block on one of downtown Cleveland's less busy side streets. Business was slow around four o'clock in the afternoon, as Libby and Morris followed Hannah Widmark through the door. The sunny day made the interior gloom of the place seem darker than you'd expect, even for a bar.

As soon as they were inside, Hannah made a head gesture toward a nearby empty table. "Just sit and chill for a second, while I have a word with Frank.

He's kinda jumpy sometimes, and he gets nervous when strangers come in."

"You mean he might run?" Morris asked quietly.

"No," Hannah told him. "That's not what I mean."

She walked over to the bar and took a seat. After a moment, the bartender wandered over. Morris couldn't see him clearly, since his eyes were still adjusting to the gloom, but Hannah's friend looked tall and thin and very pale. But there was nothing about the way he moved or stood to suggest weakness.

The bartender served Hannah a beer that she let sit on the bar in front of her. The two of them spoke quietly, and once Morris saw the man looking toward the table where he and Libby waited. Finally, Hannah turned their way and made a beckoning gesture.

They sat at the bar, one on either side of Hannah, who performed introductions. "Frank, this is Quincey and Libby. Guys, meet Frank."

Morris was a little surprised when Frank leaned over to shake hands. He found the man's grip to be very strong, but Frank didn't use it as if he had anything to prove. As they shook, which took a second or two longer than it should have, Frank looked carefully into Morris's face, then gave a little nod and released his hand.

He did the same with Libby, only he extended the handshake even longer than he had with Morris. Frank released Libby's hand gently and looked at her with open curiosity. "Hannah didn't tell me you were a witch." The man's quiet voice made it a fact, not an accusation.

Libby returned the interested look. "I won't ask how you know, because I felt something, too. Um, you should also know—"

Frank gently raised a forestalling hand. "It's okay, Libby. You're one of the good guys. I could tell that, too." He took a step back. "Now, what are you folks drinking? On the house."

Morris ordered bourbon and water. Libby said, "Vodka, please. Ice cold if you've got it, on the rocks otherwise."

Frank filled the orders promptly. He placed a frosted glass of vodka in front of Libby. "Gray Goose," he said. "I think you'll like it." Frank wasn't serving the house brand, Morris realized. Gray Goose was top-shelf. Morris took a sip of his bourbon, and could tell by the way it caressed his tongue that Frank hadn't given him the cheap stuff, either. Hannah still hadn't touched her beer.

Hannah's friend Frank looked to be in his mid-fifties. He had the kind of lived-in face you associate with dissolute rock stars like Mick Jagger and Steven Tyler, but Morris would have bet that the lines and creases Frank bore hadn't come from years of hard partying. His forehead was broad and high, below straight brown hair that was combed back to reveal a severe widow's peak. Morris noticed that Frank's brown eyes seemed to move constantly. Morris would have bet that they noticed everything, and were surprised by nothing.

Frank took a quick look around the bar, probably to see if any of his half-dozen other customers needed a refill. Satisfied, he reached into his shirt pocket for a pack of filtered Lucky Strikes. Holding the pack up so the other three could see it, he asked, "You folks mind?"

Nobody did, and Frank lit up, then produced a heavy glass ashtray from beneath the bar.

Frank leaned on the bar, thus keeping their conversation private, but Morris noticed that he turned his head away whenever he exhaled smoke. He could have blown it in their faces, if he'd wanted. It was his bar, and his booze, and Hannah's friends were coming to him for help and thus in no position to object. But Frank chose to blow his smoke away from them, and Morris thought he kind of liked the guy for that.

"Hannah says you folks are looking for some information," Frank said. "I don't know if I'll be able to do anything for you—I've kinda been out of the loop, the last few years. But still, I hear stuff once in a while." Frank pondered the glowing tip of his cigarette. "What is it you want to know, exactly?"

Libby and Morris took turns summarizing the two areas they'd been investigating, which had now apparently merged into one. Hannah chimed in from time to time.

Two cigarette butts, smoked down to the filter, were squatting in the ashtray by the time they all finished. Frank lit up his third smoke, pensively.

"Yeah," he said. "I might know something that'll help you."

Pardee had a workroom set up at Grobius's Idaho mansion, separate from the spacious office he used for administrative and recreational purposes. Pardee's office was relatively accessible to the staff, when Pardee wanted it to be. But this room, with its boarded-over windows, had a good, stout lock on the door, to which Pardee held the only key. It was also protected by other, less obvious measures.

Even Grobius did not come here. Pardee could not, of course, forbid the man access to a room in his own house, but he had implied that any interruption while a wizard was working at his craft could have disastrous consequences for everyone in the vicinity—a claim that was not very far from the truth.

The scrying was almost ready. Pardee had filled the big, intricately decorated bowl with distilled water, then added the necessary ingredients while reciting the words of the spell, which he had memorized long ago. Soon he would be able to learn where that bitch Chastain was now, and determine the best method of overpowering her for transport back to Idaho. And if the man Morris, or anyone else, tried to interfere—well, Pardee wanted Chastain alive, but that courtesy did not extend to anyone else of her acquaintance.

Pardee had misled Grobius, and not for the first time. The wizard did not, in fact, believe that sacrificing Chastain at the climactic moment would add anything significant to the power of the summoning spell contained in Alhazred's *Book of Shadows*. But after she had frustrated his attempts to have her killed, not once but twice, mind you, Pardee had decided that a quick death was more than she deserved. The cunt had just pissed him off once too often. Besides, he owed a little something to Chastain, a debt that went back a number of years. In three days, or, more precisely, three nights, he would make payment, in full and with interest. And Pardee was always generous when it came to paying that kind of interest—crossing him always brought a high rate of return.

Pardee now needed just one more ingredient to complete the scrying spell. It didn't have to be from a human, but it must be fresh.

There were a few members of the staff whom Pardee had allowed to know the location of his sanctum, although they would never, of course, be allowed inside. He picked up his cell phone and called one of them, a small oily man named Jernigan. When the man answered, Pardee said, "That stray cat that's been hanging around the kitchen and people have been feeding—someone mentioned that it had a litter the other day." Pardee listened for a few seconds. "That's what I thought. I'll meet you outside my workroom in ten minutes. Fetch one of the kittens and bring it to me."

Chapter 18

"Forget it!" Fenton said. "No fuckin' how, no fuckin' way! If that's not the dumbest, most depraved fuckin' idea I've ever heard, then it's for sure in the top ten, and moving up the charts fast."

He stopped pacing—which is just as well, since the typical room at a Holiday Inn affords little room for that activity—and faced Colleen, who was seated on the edge of the room's king-size bed, waiting for the storm to blow over, or at least to wind down a bit.

"I don't know if you've lost your mind or what, Colleen, but that's just insane. I forbid it!"

Colleen, who had been in her normal slouch, sat up straighter at once.

"*Forbid*, Dale? I'm not all that sure you're in a position to *forbid* anything. And stop talking like my father!"

"I'm not your father, I'm the senior agent, damn it!"

"You were two classes ahead of me at Quantico, which doesn't amount to one hell of a lot of seniority, does it?"

"Doesn't matter, I was named the senior agent on this team, and you know it."

Colleen took a very deep breath, and let it out. When she spoke, most of the edge was gone from her voice.

"Dale, this isn't the way we deal with each other, you and me—yelling and pulling rank, all that crap they did when we went through training. We're a team, Dale, aren't we? And a pretty damn good one."

Colleen had been tempted to add a little magical *push* to those words, to make Fenton more receptive. But she quickly rejected the idea. This was her partner, and a man she considered her friend—not some two-bit informant on a street corner somewhere.

Fenton glared at her a moment longer, then took and released a deep breath of his own. He turned away, and dropped into the room's single easy chair. He cleared his throat and said, almost calmly, "I'm sorry I flew off the handle, Colleen. I apologize for the way I talked to you. I was pissed off, but that's no excuse to treat my partner that way."

She inclined her head, graciously. "Accepted, Dale. Now let's just forget it happened."

"Be happy to do that," Fenton said. "But that doesn't mean I'm gonna go along with this idea of yours, which I swear is gonna be used as an example in the next Merriam-Webster's, right under the definition for 'stupid-ass brainstorm.'"

"I didn't just give it to you off the top of my head, Dale. I gave it a lot of thought, during our drive back from Walpole."

"Wondered why you got so quiet. You'd have been better off talking—about anything, except this nonsense. Colleen, you can't just go back in that interrogation room and *do* this guy."

"It's not something I look forward to, Dale. Not even a little, tiny bit. But if you've got a better idea, believe me, I am all ears."

Fenton leaned back, resting his head on the back of the chair, and closed his eyes. After a while he said, without opening his eyes, "If you really think giving this creep what he wants is going to get us anywhere... okay, then, we bring him a hooker. A high-class working girl in a business suit, carrying a briefcase."

"Interesting," Colleen said. "But, to get into one of those private interrogation rooms, as opposed to a public visiting area, you've either got to have a law enforcement ID, or pass a federal background check. What do you suppose will happen when they run your hypothetical working girl's prints?"

"Jesus, Colleen, your way, there's about a zillion things that can go wrong. And the worst one, and I mean this, is the effect it's going to have on you. You're *not* a working girl, Colleen. Or a porn star. Having sex with a stranger just because you want something from him... that's gonna change you, inside where it really counts. It's not worth it."

"It just might do that," she said. "If I were really there."

"Say *what*?"

"I've studied Zen meditation techniques most of my adult life, Dale. I know all kinds of ways to manipulate my consciousness. Mentally, I'll hardly be there at all. I'll keep just enough Mind focused on the here and now to do what has to be done." She gave him a lopsided smile. "It won't require very much, trust me. And an hour later, it'll be like a dim memory of something that happened to somebody I used to know a long time ago. I'll be all right."

"Colleen, Jesus, you can't just—"

"Dale, I want you to do something for me."

His face became wary. "What?"

"Open up your laptop."

He gave her a suspicious look, but went over to the closet shelf where he had stored his computer, took it down, and returned with it to his seat.

He opened it up and said, "Okay, now what?"

"Access the NCIC database."

A couple of minutes went by before he said, "Okay, I'm in."

"Now go to 'Reports of Crimes by Local Jurisdictions,' or whatever it's called."

"Yeah, that's what they call it. Okay."

"For timeframe, choose 'Prior forty-eight hours.'"

"Got it. Colleen—"

"You're indulging me, remember? Select category 'Homicide.'"

"Done."

"Sort by 'Age of Victim.'"

"Okay."

"Select 'Juvenile.'"

"Colleen come on, you don't have to—"

"Are you going to work with me, or not, Dale?"

"Yeah, yeah, all right. 'Juvenile.' Got it."

"Eliminate 'Gang-Related.'"

"Done."

"Eliminate 'Domestic Abuse.'"

"Done."

"How many does that leave?"

"Um, twenty-four."

"Cross-reference with 'Abduction.'"

"Got it."

"How many now?"

"Eight."

"Ante-mortem removal of bodily organs would be classified under 'Torture,' wouldn't it?"

"Yeah, I think so."

"Cross-reference with 'Torture.'"

"Done. Before you ask—three. Three cases."

"Give the case summaries a quick scan. You know what to look for."

"Yeah. Yeah, I know."

When he finally looked up from the keyboard, his face told her what she wanted to know.

"Remember the term they used to use in the Con. Law class at Quantico, Dale? *Res ipsa loquitur*?"

"'The thing speaks for itself.' Yeah, I remember."

There was silence in the room then. They could hear the growl of rush hour traffic in the street below.

Finally, Fenton said, in a near monotone, "We are gonna lose our jobs over this, you know."

"Only if we get caught, Dale. Only if we get caught."

"All right, let me start by telling you what I *don't* know," Frank said, "and that covers a lot of territory. First of all, I have no idea who's behind the organized murder and mutilation of these poor kids—although I wish I did." As he said those last few words, something changed in Frank's face. It was nothing dramatic, but it might suggest to you, if you knew what to look for, that Frank had not always been the owner of a sleepy little bar in Cleveland, Ohio. Quincey Morris knew what to look for. It told him that Frank had once been, and might still be, someone you really don't want to get on the bad side of.

"And I'm afraid I don't know who's trying to kill you, Libby, or why." Frank took another long drag of his cigarette, and his face had resumed its normal, melancholy expression. "But I have heard a few bits and pieces that might bear on your problem—both aspects of it." He looked directly at Libby. "Have you considered that you may not be the only one who's being targeted? Could be, you know, they're after you not because of *who* you are, but *what* you are."

Libby seemed to think about that, then shook her head in puzzlement. "I'm not following you, Frank, sorry. I didn't get a lot of sleep last night, what with one thing and another, and I'm probably not as sharp as I should be."

"It's my fault for being cryptic, Libby," Frank said. "What I'm getting at is, I've heard that two white witches have been murdered over the last ten days or so. Maybe you were intended to be number three."

Libby's face lost a lot of its color, in a hurry. "Who? Did you get names? Who died, Frank?"

"I never heard any names, Libby, sorry. One was in Cincinnati, I know that... the other one was someplace out west—Oregon, or maybe Washington."

Libby drained the remains of her vodka in one gulp. "Do you think I could have another one of these, Frank? I'm happy to pay for it."

Frank took her empty and returned shortly with

another frosted glass. "No charge, Libby. Consider it medicinal, and don't worry about it. I'm tight with the owner."

Libby didn't touch her fresh drink immediately. "I can't think of any Sisters who live in Cinci." She spoke softly, almost as if talking to herself. "We don't all know each other, of course. It's not like we have yearly conventions, or anything." She took a sip of vodka before saying, "I do know two or three who live in the Pacific Northwest, but that covers a lot of territory, so..." She looked at Frank and said, "As it happens, the Sisterhood is having a kind of... conference call tonight. I'll be sure to give them the news, and hear what they have to say."

Morris leaned forward and, talking past Hannah said, "Have you considered that 'as it happens,' may not be the case at all, Libby? What if the reason for the confab is to discuss the fact that somebody is apparently having members of the Circle murdered?"

Libby nodded slowly, her face pinched with worry. "Quite right, I hadn't considered that. In fact, the more I think about it, the more I'm sure that's exactly the reason for the 'confab,' as you call it, Quincey."

Hannah glanced at Libby, than said to Frank, "Why would someone want to kill white witches? They don't hurt people—they can't. It's part of their code."

Frank stubbed out the butt he was holding and sent it to join the others. "Just because they don't make voodoo dolls, or something, doesn't mean they can't make enemies. Way I hear it, Libby's sisters often tangle with those who follow the Left-Hand Path—getting in their way, and so forth. So revenge isn't out of the question."

Frank had the deck of Luckies in his hands and was absently tapping another cigarette out when he said, "Maybe it's not even revenge, but—what's that word—preemption?"

"Stopping the Sisterhood from doing something?" Morris shook his head. "I don't know Frank, that sounds like a bit of a stretch."

Frank got his cigarette going and said, "Maybe it is. But there's something else that may be a relevant factor." He looked at each of them, in turn, before saying, "Can I assume that everybody here knows what the thirtieth of this month is—after sundown, anyway?

Morris and Libby said, almost together, "Walpurgis Night," and Hannah nodded.

"Walpurgis Night comes around every year, Frank," Morris said. "Sometimes bad stuff happens, but nothing catastrophic." He looked at Frank closely. "There's more to it, isn't there, podner?"

"Well, yeah. There is," Frank said, "especially if, like me, you keep track of the phases of the moon."

Libby was the first one to catch his meaning, and did a quick calculation in her head. "Oh, dear," she said. "Oh, goodness, gracious me."

Morris found his stomach tightening. Most people swore when they were angry or upset. Although Libby could toss obscenities around with the best of them, when she was really thrown by something, she would sometimes revert to an excessively dainty and refined mode of speech. Morris had never understood whether it was supposed to be some kind of ironic understatement, or simply something the Sisterhood had taught her.

Then his mind caught up with hers, and he suddenly

knew the cause of her reaction. "The full moon," he said. "It's going to be full during Walpurgis Night this year. Christ, that's the first time since…"

"The 1930s," Libby said, and her voice contained no emotion at all. "The year 1939, to be exact."

Pardee ground his teeth as he stared in frustration at the blank surface of the scrying pool. He should have located Chastain by now, especially since he knew where she had been as recently as twenty-four hours ago.

The bitch must be putting up some kind of a cloaking spell to frustrate his scrying. Defying him again.

Pardee's lips were pressed together in a thin, bloodless line. He had schooled himself long ago not to give vent to cursing, or any other overt expressions of anger, in his workroom. There were too many Powers close by, watching, waiting, eagerly hoping for an opportunity to pounce.

Well, perhaps in three days' time they would have their chance—but Pardee would not be their victim.

He tossed a lifeless ball of fur into the barrel he used for waste disposal. Chastain would relax her vigilance eventually. No one of her inferior status could keep up indefinitely the effort needed to keep him blind. She would weaken, and then Pardee would be ready to do some pouncing of his own.

He picked up his phone again. Jernigan being no fool, answered on the first ring. "I'm still in my workroom," Pardee said. "I'll meet you in the hall outside. Bring me another kitten. No, wait—bring all of them."

Chapter 19

As he pulled into an empty slot in Visitors' Parking Lot C, Fenton said to Colleen, "You realize, if he tells you what we want to know before you come across, you could just laugh in his face and leave, and he couldn't do diddly-squat about it. And old Vince knows that, too. He's never gonna go first."

"I know that, Dale. He'll want to *come* first, instead."

"Jesus, Colleen..."

She touched his arm for a second. "I'm sorry, Dale. I don't mean to rub your nose in it. But try not to make more of this than it is, okay? I mean, I haven't got the track record of somebody like Jenna Jameson, but I'm not a sheltered virgin, either."

"A nice, Irish Catholic girl like you." Fenton seemed to be trying for a light touch, which he failed to achieve.

"A nice, Irish Catholic girl, who left home the day after high school graduation and never went back."

"Didn't get along with the parents, huh?"

"I wouldn't say that, exactly. I got along with Dad

quite a bit better than I ever wanted to."

The silence that followed made her last utterance seem to hang in the air like an echo.

Finally Fenton managed, "Colleen, are you saying that your—"

Colleen O'Donnell opened her door, said "Come on, let's get this over with," and got out of the car.

As they walked toward the gate, Fenton tried again. "Colleen, look, what you were saying back in the—"

In an odd gesture, Colleen slipped her arm under his and held it there, as if Fenton were escorting her to the senior prom. "Leave it be, Dale. The past is dead, as they say, and I'm alive, and that's what's important. I was just trying to make the point that, although this is going to be unpleasant, so is cleaning toilets in a bus terminal. People do that, and I can do this, and I will not be emotionally or physically shattered when it's done. And if we get what we came for, that puts us a step ahead, the way I look at it."

"Yeah, okay, but what if you, uh, do the deed, and then he laughs in *your* face? That's just the kind of thing a bastard like him would do. If you're gonna put yourself through this, it shouldn't be for nothing."

"It won't be, Dale. Trust me. If he knows Pardee's whereabouts, and I believe he does, he'll tell me, and he'll tell the truth."

"How the hell can you be so sure? You're not thinking of... doing something to him to get him to talk, are you? Because that's sure to leave traces— bruises, cuts, whatever—that he can—"

"Dale, I hate to keep interrupting you, but stop

worrying. The only thing I'm going to do to him is what we've been arguing about since yesterday. Now, hush."

They were at the Official Visitors' Gate now. The guard on duty examined their ID, then called the main building, to make sure they were expected.

Once the gate guard sent them forward, and they were out of earshot, Fenton said, quietly, "I just hope the Deputy Warden buys into our little national security story and turns off the surveillance camera in that room."

"He pretty much has to, Dale. He'll probably ask us to sign a waiver of some kind, but then he'll do it. It's no skin off his nose, anyway."

"Yeah okay, you're probably right. Look, once you're in there, I'll talk to the guard like we planned, try to keep him occupied, but if somebody insists on getting in that room that I can't keep out..."

"Argue with them. Loudly, and for as long as you can. That'll give me a warning and buy me some time, as well."

"I'll do my best, but you may not have long to, uh, you know, get dressed."

"I won't have a lot of dressing to do—no way I'm getting naked for this chump."

"Then, how, uh..."

She laughed, a little. "Stay as sweet as you are, Dale. Look, if I wear a skirt like this one, official business and all, bare legs are a no-no. I've gotta wear pantyhose underneath it, right?"

"Yeah I guess. Never thought about that. But I can see you've got 'em on now."

"No you can't, 'cause I don't."

"Huh?"

"Remember that stop we made at Rite-Aid last night, after dinner? I said I needed to pick up a few things, and you wandered off to look at the paperbacks."

"Yeah, I didn't want to follow you around, figured you were buying some kind of... female stuff."

"You're right, I was. I bought two things. Well three, if you count the pack of Juicy Fruit. I picked up a tube of KY Jelly, and I hope you're not going to ask me what for."

"No, ma'am, I am not."

"Good. Well, the other thing I picked up was a set of nylon thigh-highs. That's what I've got on now. No pantyhose."

"I see."

"No panties, either. That's why I won't have much dressing to do, afterward."

"Uh, Colleen...?"

"Too much information?"

"Fuckin' A."

"I can't believe that I didn't notice that the full moon occurs during Walpurgis Night this year," Libby said. "If nothing else, the Sisterhood should have caught it."

"Maybe they did," Frank said. "Could be that's why some of them have been killed, and you almost were, Libby."

"It's like a perfect storm of the occult," Morris said gloomily. "Either one of those alone can be bad—I mean, werewolves transform under the full moon for a reason, and murder rates go up, worldwide—but on Walpurgis Night..."

"Yeah, I hear you," Frank said. "The Witch's

Sabbath." Frank reached for the pack of Lucky Strikes. "Feasting, dancing, initiations, and a whole lot of crazy sex, topped off by a visit from Old Nick himself." Lighting up his smoke, he dropped the spent match into the ashtray, which was starting to get pretty full. "At least, that's the legend."

"You believe that last part?" Morris asked. "About Satan showing up?"

"No, I don't." Frank said. "Most of the authoritative writings say that Satan doesn't come to this plane of existence. Minor demons, sure. They'll show up, if invoked properly. Even major players like Lucifuge Rofocale or Baal sometimes, if you know how to call them, and you're willing to take the risk. But the big guy?" Frank shook his head. "He doesn't visit, even on holidays. Which is probably just as well."

"Why's that?" Hannah asked. Although saying little, she appeared to have been following the conversation closely.

"If Satan were ever brought to Earth," Frank said, "who would have the power to send him back?"

The others contemplated that in silence for a while, until Morris said, "Were you just pointing out this confluence of events as an interesting phenomenon, Frank, or do you know anything specific?"

"I've heard something," Frank said, "although it's not real specific. But an event's been planned for Walpurgis Night this year, some kind of big deal, and it's supposed to take place in North America. There have been stirrings for months among people who follow the Left-Hand Path. Nobody seems to know much, but all of them have heard something, it seems like. And, most likely, those who know the most have the least to say."

"I'm afraid that doesn't really help us too much Frank," Libby said.

"Well, there is one name that's cropped up a couple of times in different places. I don't know if it means anything, or even if it refers to a real person. Any of you guys ever hear of somebody called Pardee?"

Libby Chastain gave a little gasp, but the loudest response to Frank's uttering of that name was the sound made when Hannah Widmark's still-full beer glass hit the floor behind the bar and shattered into a million pieces.

Hannah thinks all the fuss over this Y2K business is a lot of nonsense, hyped either by hucksters with something to sell, or the kinds of professional doomsayers who are forever seeing the Apocalypse around the next corner. But Martin is a little concerned, especially about the computers.

"The world's run by computers these days, honey, and the people who programmed 'em didn't think ahead to the turn of the millennium. Computers, when you get down to it, are just big dumb adding machines, and if they don't know what number comes after 1999, they might just shut down."

"But haven't the people who program these things been working on the changeover for years?" Hannah asks. She's just making conversation, really. Having the family spend New Year's Eve at their cabin in the hills sounded like a fine idea to her—a nice change from the boozy parties that their friends throw and expect the Widmarks to attend. This year, they have

an excuse that might amuse a few, but would offend nobody.

"Some have been working on it, yeah, but others didn't start taking it seriously until this year, and that just might be too late. Several of my clients have been very concerned."

As a patent attorney, Martin spends a lot of his time with inventor types, some of whom might charitably be called "eccentric," or, less charitably, "a little nuts." Martin is a good husband, a great father, and Hannah loves him utterly. A little paranoia once in a while is a small price to pay for the life they have made, together with their two children.

Marshall and Jennifer are actually quite excited about the departure from mid-winter routine. And Hannah has promised they can stay up this year and listen to the Big Moment on the radio she is bringing to the otherwise low-tech cabin—always assuming the two of them can manage to remain awake that far past their usual bedtime.

Which is how the Widmark family finds itself spending the turn of the year/century/millennium in their isolated cabin. It is the last New Year's they will ever have together.

At a little past 11:00pm, Hannah is readying some popcorn for the kids to heat over the wood-burning stove, when the front door of the cabin, reinforced to keep the bears out, and double-locked besides, bursts open with a terrific crash.

As parents and children stare open-mouthed at the empty doorway, three men stride through it and into the cabin. Two are dressed in ordinary winter clothing, and there is little remarkable about them.

The third man, however, would be remarkable

anywhere. He is tall and very thin, head shaved, wearing a rough robe of the kind she associates with monks and friars.

Brave, foolish Mark does his best to defend his family. There are no firearms in the cabin—out of deference to Hannah, who hates guns—so Mark grabs up the axe they use to chop wood and charges at the man in the robe, who is clearly the leader of the invaders.

Mark has barely taken two quick paces when the robed man points his left index finger at him and shouts a single word in a language that Hannah has never heard before. Poor Mark drops like a steer in a slaughterhouse, the autopsy later revealing that his heart has simply burst within his chest.

Her husband is dead and her children are screaming in terror and Hannah Widmark, who has never in her life hurt anything bigger than a spider, and that only reluctantly, screeches like a banshee and attacks her husband's murderer with her bare hands.

She half expects to be struck dead like poor, dear Mark, but the man lets her reach him, only to sidestep her rush, then grab her around the throat with a grip like a steel trap.

"Sorry for the intrusion," he says, like a party guest apologizing for dropping an hors d'oeuvre on the rug. "But I have need of these two brats of yours. This is a most propitious night for a little celebration of my own devising."

He lifts her off her feet with strength no one his size should possess. Looking into Hannah's face with little interest, he tells her, "My name is Pardee. I just thought you'd like to know."

Then the sensation of flying through the air that seems

to last forever until she crashes into the woodpile, and she vaguely feels something slash her face on one side before the world, blessedly, goes dark.

Hannah returns to consciousness to find other men on the cabin, two of whom wear paramedic uniforms and are gently lifting her onto a stretcher. She feels a thick gauze bandage tight on one side of her face. "Don't try to move, please, ma'am," one of them says. "The way you were lying, we thought at first your neck was broken. It's not, but we won't know what kind of damage you're got until you're X-rayed at the hospital. Please, just lie still, now."

Another man, this one in a State Trooper's uniform, kneels beside the stretcher. "Take it easy, ma'am. You're in good hands, now. Looks like you had some luck." He glances around the ruin of the cabin, which includes the sheet-covered form over near the fireplace. "And I guess you were due. Couple of guys from town decided they'd rather hunt this morning than nurse their hangovers. They passed by your place here, and noticed that the front door was gone. Came in, saw... everything, and one of 'em called 911 on his cell. Otherwise, you could've been here for Christ knows how long."

"Trooper, we've got to get her out of here," one of the paramedics says.

"I know, I know. Just give me a second."

He brings his face close to Hannah's. His breath, she thinks crazily, smells like bratwurst.

"Ma'am, I won't keep you from the ambulance, but can you tell me anything about who did this to... your family?"

When Hannah speaks, her voice is little more than a croak. "Some men came. One was dressed like

293

a monk, said his name was... can't remember. He said, he said... oh my God, where are the children? Marsh, Jen, where are they? Are they all right?"

"There'll be officers at the hospital who can talk to you about that, Mrs. Widmark." Suddenly, the trooper is no longer looking her in the face. "They'll have a lot more information than I do. Try not to worry about it right now."

Then the paramedics lift Hannah's stretcher, and carry her out. They must be rattled by what they have seen behind the cabin, because they have neglected to fasten the restraining straps that are used to keep patients from falling out of the stretcher. That is why, when she hears a man's voice from behind the cabin call, "Hey, Sarge, can we cut 'em down, now?" Hannah gasps and instantly rolls out of the stretcher before the paramedics can stop her. One of them makes a grab for her and misses, and then Hannah is sprinting toward the corner of the cabin, coming face-to-face with a young trooper, his face ashen, who has just rounded the corner from the other direction. His eyes widen at the sight of her, and he says, almost desperately, 'Ma'am, ma'am, no, you don't wanna go back there! Ma'am!" He reaches for her.

Hannah, who played basketball all through college and even made Second Team All-American, instinctively fakes left and goes right. The trooper falls for the fake and in an instant Hannah is past him and tearing around the corner of the cabin and she runs three more steps then slows, then stops dead. Other troopers immediately surround her, but before one of them can cover her face with his Smoky the Bear hat, Hannah sees what has been left *there behind the cabin after the bald man and his minions were finished. She sees... everything.*

Hannah Widmark is still screaming when they finally get her loaded into the ambulance, and the paramedics have to hit her with two injections of Thorazine, right into the vein, before she finally stops.

Frank contemplated the mess on his floor, then looked up at the woman in black. "Are you okay, Hannah?"

"Sure," she said. "I was just getting up to go to the john, and I forgot the glass was there. Sorry about the mess, Frank."

"No big deal, don't sweat it," Frank said, and went off to get a mop.

Morris studied Hannah's face. "Did that name, Pardee, mean anything to you?"

"Nope, never heard it before. Excuse me, folks. Hannah's gotta go pee."

After Hannah had left for the ladies' room, Morris watched Frank mop the floor for a while.

"She says she never heard the name Pardee before, Frank. You believe that?"

"Sure, I do," Frank said, with a shrug. "But then, I believe in the Easter Bunny and the Great Pumpkin, and I always set out milk and cookies for the fat guy on Christmas Eve."

Morris nodded his agreement with Frank's skepticism, then looked at Libby. "Seemed like it rang a bell with you, Libby."

"Yes it did. And, unlike Hannah, I'm not disposed to lie about it."

When Libby did not continue, Morris said, "Care to share it with us?"

"Sure, but I might as well wait until Hannah gets back. What I have to tell isn't all that big a deal, but maybe it will jog her memory, a little."

Morris turned to Frank, who had just finished putting the mop away. "I don't know where this whole mess is going to lead, Frank, but it looks like we could use all the help we can get. You seem like a fella who knows a lot about the kind of thing we're dealing with here. Care to saddle up and ride with us? I'm pretty sure I can squeeze some money out of the FBI for you. If not, I'll pay you out of my own pocket."

From a nearby tap, Frank drew a glass of what looked like soda water, and drained half of it in two or three gulps. He looked from Morris to Libby and back again before he spoke.

"I used to work with some people, about ten years ago, who were worried that the turn of the millennium was going to cause all the supernatural shit to hit the fan. You may have noticed that it didn't, and I like to think our group had something to do with that, before the whole organization went to shit. But that was then." Frank sipped the remaining soda water.

"I live a pretty quiet life these days," he said. "Sure, I keep my eyes and ears open, and since I know a lot of people, I sometimes stumble across information that's useful in the struggle—which continues, as you folks well know. If I come across something interesting, I pass it on to somebody else, who might know somebody who can do something about it. But beyond that..." Frank shook his head slowly. "My daughter Jordan's in college now. I'm the only family she's got left—her mother died quite a few years ago. She's all I really care about anymore."

"Where does she go?" Libby asked. "To college, I mean."

Frank looked at her for a long moment before saying, "Someplace a long way from here. We don't see each other all that much, but we talk on the phone and exchange email all the time."

"If you guys get along so well," Morris said, "how come you don't see each other more often? Air travel makes it pretty easy, these days."

"I go and visit her once in a while," Frank said. "But I've asked her not to come here. I don't want her close by, in case something catches up with me one day, looking to settle an old score."

Libby frowned at him. "In case *something* catches up with you? Don't you mean some*one*?"

Frank gave her a sad-looking, lopsided smile. "Do I?"

The three were silent for a little while. Frank went off to check on his other customers. When he came back, Hannah had returned to her seat at the bar. Morris turned to Libby and said, "Now that we're all together again, why don't you tell us about your encounter with the mysterious Pardee."

"All right," Libby said. "It was about nine years ago. He's considerably more powerful now than he was back then. Or so I hear."

"I really wish my parents would stop interfering with my life," the young woman says. "I'm twenty-six, which means I'm old enough to make my own decisions. And I'm afraid they've sent you on a fool's errand, Miss... I'm sorry, I'm terrible with names."

"*Chastain. Elizabeth Chastain. But my friends call me Libby.*"

"*No offense, Miss Chastain, but I don't think you and I are likely to become friends.*"

Gabrielle Stafford turns her back on Libby, ostensibly to enjoy the magnificent view of Lake Michigan afforded by her condo's immense living room window. Although her tone is dismissive, Libby notices that she hasn't buzzed for someone to show Libby out (a term the rich use when they have one of their flunkies throw you out on your ass). There are conflicting impulses at work here, Libby thinks. Good. At least she is not completely in the bastard's thrall—yet.

"*Your parents aren't trying to interfere,*" Libby says. "*But they're very concerned that you may have given your trust and affection to someone who... might not have your best interests at heart.*"

Gabrielle turns back from the window and gives Libby a withering look. "*You don't need to be tactful, Miss Chastain. I know they think Lewis is only after my money, they've made that abundantly clear. As if I haven't had enough experience with gold diggers to tell the difference. No, Miss Chastain, Lewis loves me, and I love him. Very, very much. Tell my parents that. They won't take my word for it, God knows. Maybe they'll believe it if it comes from one of their... employees.*"

Libby ignored the snub. "*I'm only working for your parents as a consultant, Miss Stafford. They're kind of concerned, because you've given a great deal of money to Mister Pardee over the last four months. That's your right, of course. Your grandmother left it to you, I understand, to do with as you wish.*"

"That's right, she did! And if I choose to share it with the man I love, that's my business, and none of their own. And certainly not their consultant's."

"Of course," Libby says. "As you say, it's your own money. But your folks are also concerned that your fiancé has involved you in a lifestyle that may be, um, unhealthy."

"Oh, for shit's sake, is that what this is about? The week Lewis and I spent at Decadence, in Jamaica? It's a beautiful, exclusive resort, all the best people vacation there." She slowly looked Libby up and down. "I don't imagine you've been there, yourself?"

All right, relax, Libby tells herself. It's not her fault, not really. Of course, being in thrall to a black wizard doesn't preclude the possibility that you might also be a bitch.

"Since you've relieved me of the burden of tact, Miss Stafford, let's call it what it is. Decadence is a sex club for what used to be called the jet set. Quite notorious in some circles."

"Our sex life is our business. And if Lewis and I choose to invite others to share in it occasionally..." She waved a dismissive hand.

"Uh-huh. You got whacked on a combination of booze, pills, and coke and then let yourself get gangbanged. Three men at once, one for each hole. A number of other people watched the show, including your fiancé, Lewis." Libby just shakes her head. "And somebody in the audience, or maybe one of the employees, took pictures."

"I thought that was all taken care of," she says, sounding more like a whiny adolescent than a supposedly mature woman. Hearing Libby describe

her activities so bluntly seems to have rattled her.
"My parents paid off that terrible person before he could post those... pictures on the Internet."

*"Yes, the combination of a fat check and the threat of legal action did it—*this time. *But you and Lewis have reservations there for next week, don't you?"*

"Lewis says we need to experience everything life's rich banquet offers, and what the fuck do you care, anyway?"

Libby catches the note of hysteria in the young woman's voice. This one's not quite as content with her new "lifestyle" as she claims to be.

"You're right, Miss Stafford. How consenting adults amuse themselves is not my business. As long as you were *consenting?"*

"What are you talking about? Nobody forced me." Her laugh has a bitter undertone. *"If you saw the pictures, you must have seen that much, honey. Nobody held me down. I did it of my own free will."*

"That's an interesting phrase, 'of my own free will,'" Libby says thoughtfully. *"It sounds like a term that certain... practitioners* use.*"*

"What do you mean, doctors?"

"Not in the classic sense, no. Doctors usually try to help people, or so I hear."

"I'm not going to stand here and play word games with you, Miss Chastain. I'll have to ask you—"

"I was asked *to bring you a gift."*

That got her attention. This lady isn't the type to turn down presents.

"Really?" Gabrielle says. "Who from?"

"Your parents gave it to me to pass on to you. They said it belonged to your grandmother."

Libby reaches into her voluminous handbag and comes up with a shiny white box, the kind jewelry stores use. She walks toward Gabrielle, the box extended. "Your mom said your grandmother would have wanted you to have it."

Gabrielle opens the jewelry box, with a deft flick of the wrists that bespeaks much practice, to reveal a slim chain that looks like silver, from which hangs a matching pendant. It is heart-shaped, the kind that is hinged to swing open, usually to reveal a picture inside. Gabrielle tries to open it, but to no avail.

"This damn thing won't open up," she says.

"Why don't you see how it looks on you," Libby says, and gives a slight push of magic along with those words. "Then we can see about getting it open."

"Good idea." Gabrielle stands before the nearest of several mirrors in the room and brings the two ends of the chain up to the back of her neck. She fumbles with the catch that will join them.

"Here, let me give you a hand," Libby says. "I'm pretty good with these things."

She is as good as her word. In a few seconds, the chain is fastened.

As Gabrielle is admiring her reflection, she sees in the mirror that the Chastain woman is resting her fingers on Gabrielle's shoulders, and her lips appear to be moving.

"What are you doing? Are you talking to yourself?"

Libby hands tighten imperceptibly. "Sshhh. Be still."

The annoyed expression drops from Gabrielle's face and she stands there, uncertain.

Libby continues speaking under her breath for a few moments longer, then reaches her hands up to gently cup the young woman's ears. "Ephphatha. Ephphatha. Ephphatha." It is ancient Aramaic, the same word said to have been used, long ago, by a troublesome Galilean preacher who once gave a deaf and blind man the greatest gift imaginable.

Gabrielle does not protest this intrusion upon her precious person, nor does she object when Libby rests her hands over the young woman's eyes, to say the same word, three more times.

The word means, "Be thou opened."

Libby steps back, then walks around to face Gabrielle Stafford again.

Gabrielle does not look angry, but perplexed. "What did you do? I feel... strange."

"We were talking about your fiancé, Miss Stafford, about Lewis. You were telling me how he wants you to try new things, experience new sensations."

Over the space of about ten seconds, the young woman's facial expression morphs from confusion, to surprise, to shock, then finally to what can only be described as shame.

"Oh, my God!" she says quietly, as if talking to herself. "What did I... what have I...?"

She moves on unsteady legs to the nearest chair, and collapses into it. Libby returns to her chair, as well.

"Go on," Libby says. "What were you about to say, about Lewis? About the things you've done, just because he told you to?"

Gabrielle's eyes dart back and forth wildly, seeing nothing, as her mind processes memories, emotions, suppositions, conclusions... but mostly memories.

"*Sweet merciful mother of God!*" Gabby breathes. "*Lewis said I should, I had to... My God, I let three guys fuck me, all at the same time! While people* watched!!"

She puts her head in her hands, and sobs, as if from the cellar of her soul.

Libby takes no joy in Gabrielle's pain, but she is made joyous by what it represents—the spell that the black wizard cast over her is broken, before it could destroy her will entirely. The girl's parents had been right when they'd told Libby that Pardee had bewitched their daughter—they just did not realize how right they had been.

But there is more to be done, before Libby confronts Pardee himself.

"*Your fiancé, is he out for the afternoon?*" Libby already knows the answer to that question, but she wants Gabrielle to consider its implications.

"*Yes... yes, he's out shopping for clothes, and that usually takes him hours. Lewis likes nice things.*" Then her voice changes. "*Nice things that I'm paying for... oh, my God, so much money. I've given him so much...*"

"*Is it possible that some of the financial arrangements you've made with Lewis might be revoked, without Lewis's knowledge or consent?*"

Gabrielle wipes a manicured hand over her tear-stained face. "*Yes, yes I think so. A lot of it is in joint accounts, with both our names on them. Either signatory can withdraw funds, or even close the account, without the consent of the other.*" She sounds as if she is quoting from a financial document she read a long time ago.

"Do you think perhaps some phone calls might be in order?" Libby asks gently.

Gabrielle's full lips are now compressed into a thin, hard line. "Yes, I most certainly do." She looks at Libby. "I'm sorry I was rude to you before, Miss Chastain. I don't know what you did, but the fog is gone from my brain for the first time in... months. Thank you. Thank you very much."

Libby inclines her head a little. "You're quite welcome. And as for what I did—it was nothing more than open your eyes, to let you see what's real."

"Well, I'm really glad you did it. Now, if—"

"Don't you think it would be a good idea if I stayed a while longer?" There is a gentle push behind those words. "Just in case your mind starts to feel foggy again."

"Yes, yes you're right. You sure you don't mind?"

"Not at all. There's nowhere I have to be."

Except right here, when Mister Pardee comes home. It's time he and I had a chat.

Libby feels a little bad about using her magic to manipulate Gabrielle Stafford. But compared to what Pardee's black magic had done to her, Libby was giving her a mere gentle touch on the shoulder, and it should all be to her benefit, as it had shown to be already.

"Miss Chastain, will you—"

"Why don't you call me Libby?" No push there, just an offer.

"I will, thanks, Libby. I'm Gabby." She thinks about how odd the phrase sounds. "You know, that's going to be kind of funny some day. But not today."

Gabby stands up. "Will you excuse me for a minute, Libby? I want to wash my face. Then I have phone calls to make. If you'd like anything to drink or eat, just push that button to your left. One of the staff will be happy to get whatever you need."

Libby isn't hungry or thirsty, and she always feels kind of awkward asking servants to do things for her. So she uses the few minutes Gabby is gone to ready some of her gear for the coming confrontation with Pardee. She has studied the wizard from a distance, and is confident that her power is greater than his— at least, at this stage in his development. But with black magicians, you never, ever take chances.

Libby makes sure her wand is at the top of the other objects in her bag.

In fact, Pardee does not make an appearance until almost 6:00pm.

He lets himself in with his own key, and he does not close the door behind him gently. Libby is sitting where she can face the entrance to the living room, and has asked Gabby to sit on the sofa to her right.

Lewis Pardee, sporting a full head of thick, black hair, is carrying several bags and boxes with the names of expensive men's stores on them, but this exercise in retail therapy does not appear to have made him happy. In fact, as he enters the living room, he looks distinctly pissed off. Then he sees Libby Chastain and slows his progress, his face slowly changing from angry to wary.

His eyes are on Libby from the moment he enters the room. She can feel his witch sense probing her, testing, looking for weaknesses. Pardee tosses his purchases carelessly on a nearby chair, staring at Libby with intense interest and no small amount of hatred.

"I should have known," he says, "when I found that my credit cards had been cancelled—every fucking one of them. I should have known."

From the sofa, Gabby says, angrily, "Lewis, we need to—"

"Shut up!"

"I will not shut up, you bastard, and you will not talk to me like that way, any more. I've always hated it, and I've stopped putting up with it, effective right now."

Pardee stares at Gabby as if seeing her for the first time, then turns and looks at Libby again. "Well, now," he says. His quiet voice is a chilling contrast to the tone he has just used with his fiancée. "We have been busy, haven't we?" Then he forces a semblance of a smile onto his face and starts toward the chair where Libby sits.

"I suppose proper hospitality calls for introductions, even under difficult circumstances," he says in an almost normal voice, extending his hand as he approaches Libby. "I'm Lewis Pardee, but then I guess you know that. And you are..."

"Stop right there!" Libby says, and there is more than a little push in the words. She moves her hands a little, so Pardee can see the wand she holds in her right.

Pardee stops dead in his tracks.

"I'll not shake your hand, wizard, and my name doesn't matter," Libby says firmly. "You know all you need to know about me." In magic, black or white, names are power. No way is she giving this creature her True Name.

Pardee feigns disappointment. "Tsk, tsk," he says. "I would have assumed the Sisterhood taught better manners."

"They teach more important things than that, Lewis Randall Pardee." Let him know that she has his True Name, even as he had not learned hers.

Libby rises from her chair, the wand ready in her hand. She walks slowly toward the sofa and eases behind it, so that she stands over the still seated Gabby Stanford.

"Lewis Randall Pardee," she intones, "I charge you to leave this woman in peace, and never to return to her, in any form, physical or spiritual. I charge you to have no contact with her by any medium whatsoever, whether those of man or magic. I further charge you to do her no harm of any kind, now, or at any other time."

Libby steels herself. If it is going to hit the fan, it will do so now. "And finally, I charge you to leave this place, and never to return, in any form. In furtherance of these commands, I place my geas upon you now." Libby points her wand at Pardee like a pistol, and says something in a language Gabby has never heard before, but which the wizard knows all too well.

He tries to fight her. Without moving a visible muscle, he sends his Will and his Power against Libby's geas, but despite an effort that brings sweat to his forehead, he cannot dislodge it.

Neither form of magic, white or black, is more powerful than the other. When the two come into conflict, the outcome is determined by the magical strength and skill of the practitioners. A white witch may not use her magic to destroy a black one (although the reverse is not true)—but that does not mean that a black witch—or wizard—

*may not be rendered temporarily impotent by the
superior strength of a white magic practitioner.*

*Once Pardee realizes that he will not prevail, he
looks closely at Libby Chastain, as if planning to
paint her portrait from memory. Finally he says, in
that quiet, deadly voice, "I think it likely that we
shall meet again. And I think it very likely that the
outcome shall be different on that occasion, much to
your sorrow."*

*Libby says nothing. She merely stands there, her
Power and her Will serving as both her sword and
her shield.*

*Pardee turns on his heel and leaves the room, and
then the condominium. Libby keeps magical track
of him until he is out of the building. He never
returns.*

As he drove back to the hotel they had checked into
earlier, Morris said over his shoulder to Hannah,
"Your buddy Frank seems like the kind of guy
I wouldn't mind having at my back. Pity he's so
burned out."

"Yes, he's been through a lot." Hannah was sitting
sideways in the back seat, so that she could check the
traffic behind them for a tail. "With some people,
that breaks them down, over time." After a moment's
pause, she went on. "Others, it just hardens."

"You agree with Nietzsche, then?" Libby said
from the front seat. "*That which does not kill us
makes us stronger.*"

"Yes I do." Morris and Libby each noticed an odd
note in Hannah's voice, but neither commented on
it. "I most certainly do."

A little later, Libby said to Morris, "Well, we've

got some information, and a name. I'll be passing all that on to the Sisterhood tonight, but what are *we* going to do with it?"

"Fenton's got access to the FBI's information network, and through them, the whole federal government," Morris said. "We'll give him the name 'Pardee,' see if he can run it down. If it's anywhere on record, he'll find it."

Morris was thinking about their departure, a few minutes earlier, from Frank's bar. All three had wanted to express their thanks for his help and hospitality. Morris and Libby had each shaken the man's hand. Hannah had been last. But instead of shaking with Frank, she had turned her hand palm down, made a fist, and extended it slowly toward him. After a moment's hesitation, and a quick glance in Morris and Libby's direction, Frank had leaned forward and lightly pressed his own fist against Hannah's. "This is who we are," he'd said quietly. Hannah had nodded. "This is who we are."

At the next red light, Morris said to Hannah, "You know, if Frank is who I think he is, calling his joint the Ouroboros Bar and Grill may not exactly be the best way to hide."

"I don't think he's hiding, Quincey," Hannah said. Her voice sounded normal again now.

"What's he doing, then?"

"Waiting."

Chapter 20

Fenton and Colleen listened to doors slamming again, and soon a shackled Vincent Israel was brought into the interrogation room.

Colleen glanced toward the surveillance camera mounted high on one wall. The little red light that had glowed during their last visit was out. The camera, as requested, has been turned off.

Once the guard had left the room, Israel gave them the ratty grin again. "So, you guys decide that you're gonna get me a piece of ass? Dine in or carry out, either one works for me."

"That's a ridiculous demand, and you fucking know it," Fenton said. "We came back to see if you decided to be more reasonable, and ask for something we can actually provide."

Israel gave them raised eyebrows. "That all? Too bad you wasted your time. Didn't waste mine, though. Me, I got all the time in the world."

He stood up, and turned toward the door through which he'd just entered.

"Sit the fuck down!" Fenton snapped. "I'll tell you

when it's time for you to leave."

Israel looked at Fenton for a moment, then plopped back down in the cheap plastic chair. He stared from one of them to the other, back and forth a couple of times. "So?"

Fenton turned to Colleen, his face impassive. After a second's hesitation, she nodded. Without another word, Fenton stood up and left the room, closing the iron door behind him.

Israel looked at Colleen, and a grin, much more genuine than the usual smirk, spread across his face. "I sure hope this means what I think it means."

"You told us you know the name of the rich guy that hired Pardee shortly before you got busted," she said, her voice a little husky.

"That's right, honey." The happy grin was still in place. "I know his name, and a guy with that much cash, he shouldn't be hard for you feds to track down. Hell, just ask the IRS—he's probably their biggest customer. Either that, or they're trying to put him inside, for not paying all the taxes he owes."

"And you'll give me that name, if I fuck you."

The latter part of that sentence seemed to hang in the air, and Israel relished it, like a wine snob sniffing a nice Bordeaux. "You got it, sweet buns." The grin was, if possible, even wider now. "And no blowjobs—I can get that in here for a carton of smokes. Just close my eyes and pretend it's Angelina Jolie." Israel shook his head a couple of times. "Uh-uh. Gotta be the real deal." He tilted his head a little to the side as he devoured her with his eyes. "You *are* serious about this?"

Colleen stood, and took a step back from the table. "I'll show you how serious I am." The huskiness in her voice was stronger now. She reached down, grasped a fistful of her full skirt with each hand. Then she slowly raised the garment, until the hem was above her crotch.

The grin on Israel's face was gone, replaced by a look of longing that might have been pathetic under other circumstances. "My God, look at that beautiful thing," he said, softly. "And you even shaved it for me. That's nice. That's real nice."

Colleen let the skirt drop back in place. Trying hard for a flirtatious tone, she asked, "Like what you saw?"

The grin was back in place now. "Like it?" Israel looked down at the crotch of his prison-issue jeans. "Honey, that boner I just got didn't appear on its own. Yeah, I guess you could say I like it."

"All right, then," Colleen made herself say. "It's yours—one time."

Israel licked his lips. "Okay, first thing," he said, "let's get these shackles off me. I wanna feel you all over, baby."

"Uh-uh," Colleen said. "The shackles stay on. We'll just have to manage, somehow." She took in and exhaled a deep breath, staring hard into the man's eyes. In the most seductive voice she could manage, she said, "If I do this, if I let you stick your big, hard cock inside my wet pussy, and fuck me 'til I come real hard, over and over, you'll give me the name of Pardee's boss."

Israel's voice was a little husky now, too. "That's right, baby. I'll shout it from the fuckin' rooftops, that's what you want."

Then Colleen said, putting as much *push* into the words as she could, "You go first. Tell me his name, *now.*"

Israel opened his mouth, then quickly closed it again. He squeezed his eyes shut and shook his head, like a wet dog shaking water off itself. Then he opened his eyes and stared at Colleen. "What the fuck was *that*? Some kind of hypnotism?"

Colleen was silent, not letting her disappointment show. She'd thought she had a good chance, using a strong *push* on Israel, to get the name out of him when he was so excited. If it had worked, she would, with no regret whatever, have declined to keep her part of the bargain. Deals with the devil allow cheating on both sides—that was the way Colleen looked at it.

But a *push* did not work on everyone, as Colleen knew from both training and experience. Some people were very suggestible, some moderately so, and others not at all.

It was now clear that Vincent Israel was in the third category. *Fuck!*

Israel looked at her speculatively. "Is that what you had in mind, honey? Get me all worked up, then try some kind of hypnotic *mojo* on me? There's a guy in here, kind of a buddy of mine. Before they caught him fucking his baby daughter, he used to do a mentalist act with some carny. Knows a lot about hypnotism. He tells me I'm a lousy subject for it." The grin was back in place. "Guess you'll really have to come across, now."

She stood looking at him, her face expressionless, for the space of a slow count to ten. Then she reached for her bag, rummaged inside for a moment, and tossed something onto the table: a foil-wrapped Durex condom.

314

Although between boyfriends currently, Colleen had what most people would describe as a healthy sex life. Thanks to help from some of her Sisters, and years spent seeing a good therapist, Colleen was able to enjoy consensual, passionate, loving, orgasmic sex, when she chose to.

But she also knew how to just lie there and let a man fuck her. Her father had taught her that, both early and well.

Colleen had not lied to Fenton about her ability to disassociate. Both her ugly personal history and the magical training she'd received from the Sisterhood had taught her how to send her mind off to a Good Place, no matter what was being done to her body. And she wished she could go there right now, but she had a job to do, and it had little to do with Vincent Israel's thrusting and grunting. Sexual intercourse is the most intimate thing that two people can do, physically. It creates a connection while it is occurring, and the connection goes beyond genital friction, no matter what the circumstances. And some individuals know how to tap into that connection. Colleen O'Donnell was one of them.

Objectively, Colleen was lying half naked on her back while a shackled criminal rammed his penis into her. But she transcended that. With all the skill that her Sisters had patiently taught her, she carefully reached out to Vincent Israel's mind.

It took about three minutes, all told, before Israel's breathing began to quicken into short gasps that came faster and faster, until he groaned like a man in pain and thrust into Colleen harder than ever. Then, mercifully, it was over.

Even then, Colleen's work wasn't finished. She had

to remove the condom from Israel's rapidly shrinking penis and, with no small amount of disgust, tie a knot in it, wrap it in some tissue, and stash it in her purse for disposal later. Having someone find it in this room's trash could raise the wrong kind of questions.

It took Colleen only a few seconds to get her skirt back on and zipped. But Israel was hampered by the shackles, and she had to help pull up his dirty undershorts and jeans, which had been pooled around his ankles. She left him to do the zipping and buttoning himself.

When Israel looked more or less the way he had when he was brought in (barring the flush on his face and the shit-eating grin), Colleen said briskly, "We shouldn't have to sit down again. All I need is a name. Who does Pardee work for?"

"Can I ask you something, first?"

"Make it quick."

"Was it good for you, too?" The giggle that followed was almost enough to make Colleen vomit, even though she had deliberately skipped breakfast.

"No," she said flatly. "Now answer mine. Pardee's employer."

Israel said, "You know, it was right on the tip of my tongue when I came in, but I just can't seem to remember it now. It'll come to me though, don't you worry." The smirk he wore was the kind you want to wipe off, preferably with a chainsaw.

"Why don't you come on back tomorrow, but this time leave your nigger boyfriend behind. And, uh, wear the same outfit. You never know what might jar my memory."

Colleen just stared at him. Finally, she said in a

318

soft, emotionless voice, "Pardee would be proud of you."

"You think?" More of the giggle.

"Absolutely. And so would his boss, Walter Grobius."

Israel gaped at her, but Colleen just turned away and walked out of the room, ignoring the shouted "Hey! Wait!" from behind her.

Fenton was a little way down the hall, making chit-chat with the guard who had brought Israel in, while managing to stand between the man and the door of the interrogation room. As soon as Colleen opened the door, Fenton and the guard both looked her way. Colleen walked up to them and said to the guard, "I've finished questioning the prisoner, officer. You can bring him back to his cell now, if you would."

The guard said, "Yes, ma'am, thank you," nodded amicably to Fenton, and went into the room Colleen had just left.

"Let's go," she said to Fenton. As they walked side by side down the corridor, Fenton kept sneaking glances at her. Finally, he said, "Are you all right, Colleen? Can I do... I mean is there anything... Aw, fuck, I don't know what I'm trying to say."

She gave him a small but affectionate smile. "It's okay, Dale. *I* know." She gave his arm a quick squeeze. "Well, there are three pieces of good news."

"Yeah? Let's hear 'em."

"One, it's over. Two, I'm okay, so try to relax a little. And three, it paid off."

"He told you? The motherfucker gave you the name."

"Yes, he did, and I'd bet my next three paychecks that he was telling the truth. Pardee works for, or at least used to work for, one Walter Grobius."

"That name rings some kind of bell, but faintly," Fenton said. "The phrase that popped into my head when you said it was *shit rich*."

"I read a magazine article that mentioned Grobius, a while back. If I remember it right, *shit rich* is something of an understatement."

"Sounds like somebody who can afford to have this bastard Pardee on the payroll. Speaking of which, I've got a weird coincidence for you."

"I'm all ears," she said.

"While you were, uh, you know, in there, I got a text message from our friend Morris."

"We haven't heard a lot out of him, so far. I hope he's putting some effort into his end of the investigation."

"Well, the text I got would suggest that he is."

"You've milked it for suspense enough, Dale. What did it say?"

"It said, quote, 'Need all info you can find on Lewis Pardee, ASAP.'"

"Well, well." Colleen did not slow her pace. "We can call him and see what he's got, but first we are going to drive back to the hotel at the maximum safe and legal speed, so that I can take off these clothes, which I may burn later, and get in the shower, where I plan to spend quite some time."

"Don't blame you for that. Hell, I'll even turn on the siren for you."

"That's sweet, Dale, thank you. But let's not call a lot of attention to ourselves today."

"Okay fine. Uh, Colleen?"

"If you're going to keep asking me if I'm all right—"

"No, that wasn't it. I was just curious about something, but if you don't want to talk about it, that's cool."

"Try me."

"Well, that bastard Israel could've just told you to fuck off, or maybe said that Pardee's an elf, works for that criminal mastermind, Santa Claus, some shit like that. Once he'd already... you know... how'd you get him to tell you?"

"It was easy, Dale. I just made him an offer he couldn't refuse."

Chapter 21

Pardee gave Grobius a tour of the grounds in an electric-powered vehicle that looked something like a glorified golf cart. Grobius had bought half a dozen of these customized models for the groundskeepers, so they could attend to the topiary without either tearing up the grass or making undue noise. Of course, given whom these toys belonged to, each was equipped with satellite radio, a GPS, and a fast Internet connection. Grobius's request for mounted .50 caliber machine guns had been politely declined by the manufacturer.

This was Grobius's own property, but much had been done to the grounds in the past couple of months, and Pardee welcomed the chance to show it off.

"Over here are more of the fire pits, where the individual practitioners will work their rituals, independent of each other, but nonetheless in concert."

"How many of these did you install, anyway?"

"Twenty-five," Pardee said. "That's probably

more than we'll need—I don't think that many practitioners will show up, but it never hurts to plan for success."

"All the money I gave you for this project, and you couldn't even come up with twenty-five of these people?" the old man said grumpily.

"Actually, there aren't all that many followers of the Left-Hand Path in this country—or worldwide, for that matter."

"Why not? Judging from the kinds of things I've seen you do, I would have thought there'd be thousands of people, if not millions, who would want that kind of power."

"I appreciate the compliment, but it took years of study and practice to attain my level of proficiency," Pardee said. "But, you're right, in a way. There are, in truth, quite a few people who start on the Path, more or less for the reason you mentioned: the power. We have more fire pits over there, as you see."

"Many are called, but few are chosen, eh?" Grobius laughed at his witticism. Unlike everyone else who worked for the old man, Pardee felt no obligation to join in.

"Something like that," Pardee said. "A number of them lose interest, once they realize the amount of work, time, and sacrifice involved. No commitment, you see. Whereas others have the commitment, but not the aptitude. Quite a few of them are killed every year, in the occult equivalent of laboratory accidents."

"Get blown to pieces by their own potions, you mean,"

"That, or something worse." Pardee brought the cart to a gentle stop.

"Here's the main altar, which you've seen from the house. I don't think you've had a good look at it from ground level, yet."

Grobius took in the stone steps leading up to the central platform, on which sat a construction that might well have served as a table for the gods, especially if the gods were messy eaters. Symbols were carved into the altar and surrounding stones.

"Is this *marble*?" Grobius asked.

"Yes, as a matter of fact, it is. Italian, from the Carrera Quarry, the one that Michelangelo used. As I've told you more than once, we have to go first class if we are to welcome such a distinguished guest."

Thirteen feet beyond the altar was an elaborate circle painted on the marble. It was surrounded by other painted symbols, most of which Grobius didn't recognize.

"That's where he will appear?" he asked Pardee.

"Exactly. He will be confined within that circle, of course. I have no doubt he will be willing to do my bidding."

"What if he gets out of the circle?"

"He will not." Pardee might have been stating the law of gravity.

"How can you be so certain?"

"Because I have researched this ceremony for years, and I have been a practitioner of the Art for many years more. He will not escape, I can assure you."

Grobius looked around at the huge, elegant, and expensive structure.

"I will trust in your judgment," he said. "You've never let me down before, Pardee."

"Nor will I this time."

Then, after an uncharacteristic moment of hesitation, Grobius said, "You're sure he can cure me."

"Without doubt. With the power he possesses, he can cure any illness, if he has a reason to."

"And... extend my life, indefinitely?"

"Indefinitely, yes. Eternally, no. Eternal life, sad to say, is not possible on this plane of existence, according to conditions laid down by G... the one who made it. But five hundred years, six hundred years is not impossible. I have known him to grant this boon to others."

"Well, I suppose that will have to do." The old man essayed a crooked smile. "As long as you're satisfied with the arrangements."

"I am."

"Wait—didn't you say something about sacrificing one of the white witches, as the capstone of the Ceremony?"

"I did, and that is still my intent," Pardee said. "I have reason to believe the one I have chosen for that honor will be available very soon now."

"And that will guarantee success?"

"In the Art, guarantees are hard to come by. But a great deal of power will be brought to bear Wednesday night, more than has ever been concentrated to one end before, I believe."

"The Devil, you say." Once again, Grobius chuckled at his own wit. This time Pardee joined in, with what seemed to be genuine amusement.

"And if after all this, it fails..." Grobius was not laughing now. "There will be the Devil to pay."

"Indeed, sir. There will, indeed."

* * *

Morris and Fenton had talked on the phone at some length that morning, agreeing on how they would divide their labor, and it was evening before they spoke again. Each had been busy, and so had their partners.

"Grobius is almost a caricature," Fenton said. "The Reclusive Zillionaire. Like Howard Hughes, but without the foot-long fingernails."

"Yeah, I saw that movie," Morris said.

"Even Google hardly knows this guy," Fenton said. "I got like twelve hits off his name, and they all link to brief mentions in articles published over the years. I thought rich people were always sponsoring charity events, getting their faces on the society pages."

"I think maybe it's the other way around. Those who do the charity stuff are the ones we hear about. Those who don't want publicity are able to buy a lot of privacy. Just how rich are we talking about, do you know?"

"I talked to a guy I know at Treasury. He did a little digging around over there, but they haven't got much about Grobius either. My guy says that's because his holdings are so spread out, and they involve so many holding companies and shit like that, nobody outside the operation, and probably damn few inside it, knows what's Mister G's and what isn't."

"Fella's like Keyser fucking Söze," Morris said.

"Yeah, and like Keyser, there's no official evidence to connect Grobius to anything illegal. The guy's either real clean or real careful."

"Libby and I called a lot of the people we know who are involved in the more esoteric side of things. Grobius's name rang a couple of bells, but small ones. There's a rumor going back maybe five years, that Grobius was sick with something lingering but fatal. I don't know if it was AIDS, or what. The docs apparently told him to make out his will, so he went looking to the magical community for help."

"There's nothing illegal about that, Morris. It's even kind of understandable. I mean, if you're looking the Reaper right in the eye, and you've got a bunch of money that's no good to you when you're dead, you'll try anything that offers hope—Laetrile, crazy diets, and maybe magic."

"Yeah, but don't forget, there are two kinds of magic, white and black. Libby says that neither one can cure a fatal illness. Prolong your life a while—maybe. Cure you—no. But there's a difference between the two sides."

"Which is..."

"White magicians don't lie about what they can accomplish. Black ones sometimes do."

"Black ones like Pardee, maybe."

"Uh-huh, that had occurred to me."

"That still doesn't explain the dead kids with the missing organs, Morris."

"No it doesn't... except..."

"What? Except what?"

"Well, shit. I had an idea, but lost it in the fog of sleep deprivation. I'll let you know if I find it again. But there's something else, Fenton. Remember, I told you what Hannah's buddy Frank said: something big and nasty is supposed to be going down in North America on Walpurgis Night, which coincides with the full moon, this year."

"There was a time when I would've said 'occult bullshit' to that, but I think I'll hold that opinion in abeyance for now."

"Smart man. Thing is, Libby and I both got confirmation from some of our sources. There's a lot of stirring among the followers of the Left-Hand Path lately, and some of them are talking about a big deal coming up on the thirtieth."

"Which is two fucking days from now."

"Which is precisely two fucking days from now. But one of the guys I talked to had also heard the name of a place that's been associated with these revels."

"And Colleen accuses me of milking stuff. Just tell it, will you?"

"Coeur d'Alene, Idaho."

There was silence on Morris's phone.

"Fenton? Hello?"

"Yeah, sorry. 'Coeur d'Alene' rang the chimes. I was just checking my notes, wait... yeah here it is. Morris..."

"I'm here."

"Grobius has a place in Coeur d'Alene, Idaho. Big estate, apparently."

"Well, fuck my ass and call me Shirley."

"Say *what*?"

"Just an expression."

"Something else I'm lookin' at, that's interesting about this estate. They only started building it five years ago. That was about the time that Grobius supposedly took sick, isn't it?"

"You know, I wonder if Libby can do a scrying of Grobius's place in Idaho, see if there's anything there besides cows."

"What the fuck, man, go for it. I know Libby has done some pretty impressive stuff in the past. Go on, ask her."

"I will, as soon as she gets back. The Sisterhood is having a… meeting, I guess you'd call it, supposed to start in a little while."

"She gonna be back tonight?"

"Oh yeah, couple of hours, max. It's kind of like a conference call. Say, is your partner there with you?"

"Colleen? No, she's lying down for a while. She's dealing with some shit that happened this morning. Asked me not to disturb her for a while. Why?"

"Nothing important. Thought I remembered where I might've met her, some years back, and I wanted to ask her about it. It'll keep."

"Okay. If Libby can do the scrying, let me know what she turns up, even if it's nothing but cows. I just won't put the scrying stuff in my report for the Bureau."

"Yeah, I'll call you either way. But what do we do if she can't make it work?"

"Beats the pure fuck out of me."

Libby Chastain checked the time and saw she had ten minutes until the Circle would form. As she always did on these occasions, she went into the bathroom to take a simple precautionary measure. Then she made sure her hotel room's door was triple locked, and that the wards she had placed there earlier were still in place and functioning. Quincey Morris was in the adjoining room, the connecting door closed but not locked, and he had promised to remain there until Libby was back in her body again.

She lay on the bed, loosened her clothing a little to make sure she would remain comfortable, and closed her eyes. Libby began to repeat in her mind the mantra she had been taught years ago, while seeing in her mind's eye the image of a circle. She needed to focus on keeping that circle perfectly round, perfectly round...

"Greetings, Sisters, and may the peace of the Goddess, and the love of the Earth, our mother, dwell in your hearts." Eleanor Robb sat at the head of a long conference table, in a luxuriously appointed boardroom. The carpet beneath Libby's feet was beautiful and wonderfully soft. Sunlight streamed gently in from several windows, and yet none of it shone in anyone's eyes. The air held just the slightest odor of sandalwood, and from somewhere came the music of a beautifully played Spanish guitar, just loud enough to be audible.

All of this was an illusion, of course, created by Eleanor Robb. Her predecessor, Jamie Carruthers, had favored sun-dappled glades with a brook bubbling in the background. The physical bodies of the Sisters sitting around the polished table were also illusions. They had brought their spiritual essences together in a place where they could speak, hear, and exchange information, blessings, and love. When they returned to their corporeal bodies, they would remember everything that transpired here.

"Sisters," Eleanor Robb said solemnly, "many of you know something of the sad news that brings us together, but perhaps few of you know all of it. It is my sad duty to report to you that eight of our number have been taken from us within the past few months, all apparently at the behest of a single mind. Further, three others are missing and must also be assumed to have gone on to the next life. Sister Rachel will read the names of the deceased, for whom we will offer prayers, both now, and daily, as long as each of us shall live."

The names were read, tears were shed, prayers offered, reminiscences shared. Then, after a time, Eleanor spoke again. "Our purpose must be not only to mourn the dead, but to protect those of us who remain. We must determine who is responsible for these evil acts, and why, and what countermeasures should be taken. Although our commitment to the White forbids us the use of our power to commit physical violence, except in the most extreme circumstances, these murders are also civil crimes, and it may be that they can be punished by the civil authorities. But first, we must know who is doing this to us. Can any of you shed light on this mystery?"

Libby did not wish to seem importunate. Self-effacement was one of the Sisterhood's values. But when none of the others came forward, Libby stood, and waited to be recognized.

"Sister Elizabeth," Eleanor Robb said immediately, with a touch of relief in her voice. "I had hoped that you might be able to offer insight into the nature of these depredations."

"I can, Sister. And as the saying goes, 'It ain't pretty.'"

Morris was curious to see which particular hand basket the world was going to hell in today, so he turned on the TV and watched the local eleven o'clock news. When it was replaced by *The Tonight Show*, he decided to check on Libby. She'd said the nine o'clock confab (as Morris kept thinking of it) would be over in about two hours, but she had yet to stick her head through the connecting door to let him know that she was here in spirit, as well as in body.

He knocked at the door gently, then a little more loudly. "Libby?" Nothing.

Morris opened the door a foot or so. "Libby?" More nothing. Of course, if she was still taking part in the confab, that was to be expected, since the bed would contain only her lifeless form. But still…

"Libby, I'm coming in, so if you're not decent, now's your chance to cover it up."

Morris waited a few seconds, then pushed the door slowly open.

Libby Chastain's body, lifeless or otherwise, was not on the bed.

Morris listened for the sound of the shower running. Silence from the bathroom. He went and checked, anyway—the bathroom door was open, the little room dark. He flicked on the light. No Libby.

It was highly unlikely that Libby would "return" from the confab, and just leave through the room's main door, but he looked around for a note, for anything that would give him a hint of where she'd gone. *Nada*.

Then it occurred to him to check the door itself. It was triple-locked, and two of those locks could only be engaged from inside the room. He also saw that Libby's magical wards were still in place on and around the door.

A sudden thought chilled him, and he quickly went over to the window. They were on the ninth floor. If someone had managed to steal inside, and slip her limp body out the window…

Apparently Ramada Central had something similar in mind, give or take the magic part. The big window had no hinges or latches. It was designed to let in light and provide a view, no more.

It was then that Morris's subconscious decided to give his forebrain a wakeup call, and he realized there was a faint odor in the room that had nothing to do with Libby, or any perfume she might have brought with her.

Black magic has a scent all of its own.

Morris stood there in the middle of Libby's hotel room and did ten slow, very deep breaths, using his stomach muscles to push the air out hard. He did this to help quell the incipient panic that threatened to send him over the edge.

He went back to his own room and picked up the phone.

"Fenton."

"It's Morris. Forgive the melodrama, but they've got Libby."

Silence, for three slow heartbeats, then Fenton's voice: "Tell me. Take your time with it."

Morris related what he knew, then answered the questions that any intelligent cop would ask under these circumstances: was Morris sure he hadn't fallen asleep while Libby was "napping." Had Morris been drinking or, God forbid, using any kind of drug? Did Morris and Libby quarrel about anything before she disappeared? And so on. Morris didn't take offense, but he was glad when the litany was done. Then he asked Fenton, "Is your partner up and around again?"

"Yeah she is. She seems okay."

"Is she there?"

"In the next room, why?"

"Get her, please. I need to talk to her."

More silence. Then, "Hold on."

Less than a minute later, a female voice was saying in Morris's ear, "This is Agent Colleen O'Donnell."

"Did Fenton tell you why I called?"

"He said Libby Chastain's missing from her room."

"Yeah she is, and there's a faint whiff of black magic in the air."

"Mister Morris, maybe you should confine yourself—"

"I know you're in the Sisterhood, Agent O'Donnell."

It got so quiet, Morris wondered if he'd lost the connection. "Hello?"

"Did Libby tell you?"

"No, I realized it the first time we met, in L.A. I have something of a nose for magic, both white and black."

"Yes. Yes, it would appear that you do."

"Listen, I realize that Fenton doesn't know. I didn't tell him—I figured that was between you and him. I'll do whatever you want to help preserve your cover, but—"

"Fuck that, there are more important things to think about. In fact, I guess I'll tell him after we're done here. It's time, anyway."

In the background, Morris heard Fenton's voice say, "Tell me what?"

Morris heard mumbling for a little while, so he assumed that a hand was over the phone at the other end. Then the mumbling stopped.

"Agent O'Donnell?"

"Maybe, all things considered, you might as well call me Colleen."

"All right, Colleen, I'm Quincey. So, can I assume you were at the confab tonight?

"The what?"

"Sorry that's my name for it. Where the Sisters leave their bodies and convene someplace."

"Yes, I was there."

"Did you uh, 'see' Libby there?"

"Yes I did. In fact, she was very helpful in bringing us up to date with the facts and suppositions—hers, yours, and the FBI's."

"Did you all leave together, if that's the right term?"

"Yes, we did. No one leaves until the Circle is dissolved. Then we all go back... where we came from."

"Forgive my ignorance of the way these things work, Colleen. But is it possible for Libby's 'spirit' to end up someplace other than back in her body?"

"Absolutely not. The spirit instinctively seeks its home, which is the body. There are various theories about what might happen if a Sister's body were destroyed, say, by an explosion, while her spirit was elsewhere. But that has never happened in the Sisterhood's recorded history, which goes back a long way. And it doesn't sound like that's happened here, anyway."

"No, I reckon not, but we still don't know that the fuck *did* happen."

"Well, given what you've described, I think I know the what, if not the who, or the why."

"I'll take anything you got."

"It seems obvious that a black magician or witch entered Libby's room through magic, grabbed her unoccupied physical form, and left with it."

"What the hell would happen to Libby's spirit, then?"

"Once the circle was broken, as I told you, the spirit returns to the body. Libby's spirit would go to wherever her body was, and rejoin it."

"So Libby's going to wake up somewhere, and find herself in very deep trouble."

"Yes. That's probably true. Whoever managed to pull this off has both a lot of Will and a great deal of Power, Mister Morris."

"Quincey."

"Quincey, sorry. I'm going to get in touch with El—uh, the head of our Circle, and appraise her of what's happened. After we've talked, I'll get back in touch with you. I assume Dale has your number?"

"Who? Oh, you mean Fenton. Yeah, he has it."

"Keep your phone close by, will you?"

"Sure. And I'll be happy to talk to your mysterious El, or you, or Fenton, or Glenda the Good Witch of the East. But I doubt any of that's going to change my plans."

"Um, would you care to share those with me?"

"Sure." The expression on Morris's face would have been instantly recognizable to anyone familiar with his gunfighter ancestors.

"I'm pretty sure Libby Chastain's in Iowa," he said. "And I aim to go and get her."

V

DIES IRAE

Chapter 22

Libby Chastain came fully back into her body with the knowledge that, while she'd been away, something had gone very wrong.

Her hands were secured above her head with some kind of metal fetters, and there was something stretched across her mouth that would make coherent speech impossible. She tried, very cautiously to move her legs, and found they also were secured. She lay there (wherever *there* was) without moving or opening her eyes. Libby wanted to find out as much as she could about her situation before letting anyone know that she was one whole entity again.

But she learned that her pretence was all for naught when she heard a familiar voice say, "Don't try to play possum with me, you worthless piece of shit. I could sense your life force as soon as it returned to that sagging bag of flesh you call a body." The voice belonged to Lewis Pardee.

Libby opened her eyes to see that she was lying on a bed, obviously not the one she had been occupying in Cleveland. This room was considerably more luxuriously appointed, not to mention quite a bit larger. But Libby didn't waste time and attention on the surroundings—not when Pardee was sitting in a chair next to her bed, grinning.

"As you've no doubt figured out, I have removed you from the safety of your hotel room, to someplace which you will find to be considerably less safe. Your pitiable defenses wouldn't have stopped me if I had wished to enter by the door, but it amused me to pass through the outside wall, and take you back with me the same way. Your boyfriend Morris never heard a thing. I could simply have killed him, but I like imagining the expression on his face when he finally goes looking for you."

"He's not my boyfriend," Libby tried to say, but the gag, or whatever it was across her mouth prevented her from uttering anything beyond an inchoate moan.

"I've been contemplating all sorts of delights to visit upon you between now and Wednesday night," Pardee said. "Using my superior magical power to bounce you off the walls and ceiling for an hour or so would be amusing. So would a bit of rape. Oh, I wouldn't touch you—I like the women I fuck, even the unwilling ones, a lot younger and considerably better looking. The years haven't exactly been kind to you, have they, Libby? You don't mind if I call you Libby, do you? After all, we're old friends, aren't we? How is dear Gabby these days, I wonder? Do the two of you ever get together over cups of tea and reminisce about how you were able to gain the advantage of me when I wasn't expecting trouble? *Do you?*"

The last two words were almost a scream. Libby realized that what had been a fairly minor exercise for her, almost forgotten by now, had been for Pardee a defeat of ego-shattering significance. She wondered how much of his outrage came from having been bested by a woman, in front of another one, whom he'd had in his thrall.

"You know, I thought about paying little Gabby a painful, humiliating visit, to show both of you cunts just how little power your pathetic geas has over me now. But I didn't want you to become aware of my superiority until a time of my choosing. Which has now come round at last."

Pardee's grin was so wide it threatened to split his face in two. "Now, where was I before you got me distracted. Oh, yes, rape. Well, although the prospect of ravaging your pussy doesn't appeal to me, I could probably find a few dozen men who aren't quite so picky. Or I could call up a few demons and allow them to amuse themselves with you for a day or so. I don't know if you've ever been fucked by a demon, Libby, but I understand they are insatiable, just insatiable. And ever *so* well hung."

He stared at her face, as if expecting some kind of reaction. Tears, perhaps, or an attempt to beg for mercy through whatever was across her mouth. But she just looked at him.

Pardee shrugged, his good mood in no way diminished by Libby's refusal to be baited.

"But I thought, no—such petty brutality is unworthy of one such as me. After all, I am the wizard who is going to usher in a whole new era for this world of ours, in a few days' time. I really should behave in a way consistent with what will soon be my elevated station. And you have no idea, Libby dear, just how far I am going to be elevated, once the new order takes power. Many will die, it's true, and many more will suffer. But a select few, such as my humble self, will be richly rewarded."

Libby stared at him impassively, but she was thinking, *Sweet Goddess, he's crazy as a bedbug. I don't know what this big plan is that he's blathering about, but even if he fails, he can cause a great deal of harm in the process.*

"Well, there's no sense bragging in front of such an unappreciative audience," Pardee said cheerfully. "You'll find out what it's all about soon enough, during the final moments of your life.

"But here are a few tidbits to tide you over: my employer is going to get what he wants on Walpurgis Night, but also rather more than he has bargained for. And you will have the honor of playing a key role in the ceremony. For at the crucial moment, I am going to cut you open, the same way one butchers any species of pig, and then I'm going to rip out your major bodily organs, one by one. I'll show them to you, if you like, and I guarantee that my superior magic will keep you conscious and aware until the very end, awake and screaming. Oh, yes, I'll remove your gag for that. I want to hear every syllable."

Pardee stood up in a single fluid motion that reminded Libby of a cat she had once owned. "In the meantime, you won't be working any of your so-called magic. The fetters that bind you to this bed have my spell on them. You're not going anywhere, until I decide it's time for your final journey. And you'll have lots of time to think about... things."

Pardee walked to the door, then stopped and

turned back. "I'll have some glucose put into you intravenously later. We can't have you departing this vale of tears prematurely. Nothing to eat or drink, of course—that gag stays on until very near the end. Oh, and if you feel the urge to piss, or take a shit, at any time, dear Libby, feel free. You're the one who's going to have to lie in it, after all."

Then he was gone, the heavy wooden door clicking solidly shut behind him.

"I don't mind talking to you on the phone," Morris said, "but I'm a little surprised that you're not visiting though astral projection."

"I would, if it were necessary, Mister Morris," Eleanor Robb said. "But I don't see the need at the moment, and I'm already quite exhausted from attending that meeting of the Circle earlier this evening. It takes a great deal of psychic energy to go out of one's body, you know."

"I didn't, but I'm not surprised. All right, I assume you're calling because you've heard from Colleen O'Donnell."

"That's right, I have. She tells me that Libby is... missing, under suspicious circumstances."

"'Suspicious' is something of an understatement, Sister."

"Perhaps you should just call me Ellie."

"All right, Ellie, I will. Did Colleen give you the specifics?"

"She did. Do I understand that all of Libby's wards were still in place when you checked her room?"

"Yes, ma'am, they sure were. Whoever it was, they didn't get in through the door."

"That's rather troubling. I say that, because—"

"Because it means that whoever took Libby is one magical bad motherfucker."

"Admirably put, Mister Morris. Crudely, but admirably."

"Call me Quincey, since we're being informal, and all."

"Very well. You see, a discorporation/reincorporation spell is difficult to perform, and to do so while carrying another person is... well, there are few among the Sisterhood who could pull it off successfully."

"And few outside the Sisterhood?"

"Let's just say it would be a formidable undertaking for any practitioner of the Art, whether white or black."

"Is it within the capabilities of a fella named Pardee, do you think?"

There was a tired-sounding sigh in Morris's ear. "Quite possibly. The Sisterhood has not had any direct contact with this man since Libby's encounter some years back, but we do keep an eye on the other side's 'rising stars,' as it were."

"More like 'falling stars,' isn't it?"

"All depends on one's point of view, I imagine, but I get your meaning," Ellie said. "We don't know a great deal about this Pardee, but reports are that he has been gaining a great deal of magical power, source unknown, over the last few years. It is not unreasonable to posit that he would now have the ability to carry out Libby's abduction, under the conditions you've described."

"The question is, *why*? All the other recent attacks on the Sisterhood, that we know about, have been murder attempts, whether successful or not."

"That's true. It's difficult to say with any degree of certainty what Pardee has in mind, assuming he's the one responsible—although, I suppose…"

"You suppose what?" Morris asked.

"I don't want to upset you, Quincey. But it's possible that his defeat at Libby's hands years ago may have festered into a desire to take her life in a… more prolonged and painful fashion."

"Yeah," Morris said tightly. "That had kinda occurred to me, too. But why *now*? If he's been some kind of a magical heavyweight for a while, why make a move on Libby now?"

"I wish I had an answer for you, Quincey, I really do."

"Shit." Morris massaged the bridge of his nose between two fingers. "I assume Colleen has also told you about the Walpurgis Night business."

"She did. Libby was incorrect, by the way. The Sisterhood was not unaware of the confluence of Walpurgis Night with the full moon this year. Some of us were keeping our eyes open, but we weren't really worried about anything very serious transpiring."

"Libby said the last time this happened was 1939. Seems to me that something pretty damn serious transpired back then."

"I think the start of World War Two that year was probably something of a coincidence."

"You just said 'think,' 'probably,' and 'something.' That's three qualifiers in one sentence, Ellie."

There was silence on the line for several seconds. Finally, Eleanor Robb said, "You're quite right. I was hedging. In truth, I *am* somewhat concerned. But the world is not on the brink of war today, as it was in Thirty-Nine. I think the Left-Hand Path's capabilities for mischief are fairly limited, the Goddess be thanked."

"Colleen also told you that Libby and I picked up a rumor in Cleveland that something big is planned for the revels this year, right?"

"Yes, but that could just be big talk to draw a large attendance to the one in, where was it, Iowa?"

"Idaho. Walter Grobius's estate in Idaho."

"Well, Walpurgis Night is mostly just a big party night for the people of the black. It's one of two nights a year they can crawl out of the shadows and feel—"

"What did you say?"

"I said, the eve of the Feast of St. Walpurgia and Halloween are the two nights of the year—"

"No, something about shadows."

"It was just a metaphor, Quincey. I was trying to—"

"Quiet! Just give me a second, will you?

Whether insulted or not, Eleanor Robb kept silent. Morris heard again the voice of his friend, John Wesley Hester: "*Some blokes in Baghdad found out recently that the Book of Shadows is missing.*" Then he heard John saying, "*You know what kind of stuff's supposed to be in that bloody thing. Imagine an adept of the Left-Hand Path with that book, along with all the magical power gained from those nasty kiddie sacrifices you've been talking about.*"

Then he heard his own voice, in Frank's bar in Cleveland, talking about Walpurgis Night taking place during the time of the full moon: "*It's like a perfect storm of the occult.*"

Into the phone, Morris said, "Forgive my rudeness just now, Ellie, but something popped into my head, and I wanted to get a look at it before it disappeared again."

"And did you?"

"Yeah, I did. Listen, Ellie—if you're not sitting down right now, maybe you should."

"Why's that, Quincey?"

"Because *I'm* about to upset *you*."

The next morning, after a mostly sleepless night, Morris heard from Fenton.

"Looks like we finally caught a break," he told Morris.

"Good, we could fucking use one. What happened?"

"While I was brushing my teeth this morning, I remembered that at the last reunion I attended, a college buddy of mine said he'd gone into the Air Force not long after graduation. Officer Candidate School, and all that. Told me he was one of the top guys in the Idaho Air National Guard, now. Well, I got him on the phone, and he's still there. In fact, he's been moving up pretty good—Deputy Commander of the whole fuckin' air wing."

"I guess that's good," Morris said, "but I'm not sure I see exactly how, unless you can get him to drop a few tons of bombs on Grobius's place out there and call it a training exercise."

"No, can't do that. But there's more than one kind of training exercise, and Charlie *is* willing to send one of their reconnaissance aircraft over the place, with its cameras running."

Morris sat up straighter. "Okay, that *is* good news. Maybe we'll learn what the hell Grobius and his pet wizard have in mind for tomorrow night. Wait, though. Shit!"

"What's wrong?"

"If Grobius and his boys figure out that they're under surveillance, they might decide to cut their losses and close down operations. That would probably include disposing of all potential witnesses, including Libby."

"Don't sweat it, man. Charlie tells me the plane'll be at fifty thousand feet—maybe higher, depending on the cloud cover. And it'll be over Grobius's place and gone before anyone even notices it's there. With the kinds of cameras and shit they've got today, apparently one pass is all you need to get a whole bunch of good pictures of anything on the ground bigger than a gopher."

"Okay, then. Not bad, Fenton. Not bad, at all. But the sooner we get this done, the better. When's your pal gonna send the plane over?"

"What time is it now?"

"About eight forty-seven, Eastern."

"It's already airborne."

"Have you got it, Ellie?"

"It's loading now. My Internet connection is kind of slow, so this may take a minute."

Morris sat in front of his laptop, the mouse in one hand, his phone in the other. After a short wait, he heard Ellie Robb's voice again.

"Yes, all right. I've got it."

"I'm sending another one, now. It can be loading while we talk."

"I'm looking, Quincey, but I'm not sure what

it is I'm seeing. I'm not trained in aerial photo interpretation, you know."

"Me, neither," Morris told her. "But, fortunately, I just spent twenty minutes on the phone with an Air Force tech sergeant who is. He worked with me, and I'll work with you. What does the image look like?"

"Well, clearly it's a stretch of land. Most of it looks like it's been landscaped, but some of it appears to be wild. I also see what I suppose are buildings—one large one, more or less in the center, and several smaller ones, in different places around the area."

"Anything else?"

"I don't know—there are some other things spaced between the buildings, at what look like regular intervals. They're just dots in the photo, although one them appears a tad larger than the rest."

"All right, good. As I'm sure you've figured out, Ellie, you're looking at an aerial photo, taken by a military aircraft, of the Coeur d'Alene estate of one Walter Grobius, reclusive zillionaire."

"That's all very well, Quincey, but this is the best the Air Force can do—"

"It's not. They've got state-of-the-art magnification equipment, as well as computer programs that can fill in the gaps, based on mathematical probability. Or something like that. Go to the next photo, please, while I send you a third one."

"All right, it's loading."

Half a minute or so later, Eleanor Robb said, "Okay, I can tell that it's the same image, but blown up. Quite an improvement."

"Good. So, what are you looking at now?"

"Well, the buildings are much clearer. The big one

looks to be a house, quite a large one. The others appear to be outbuildings."

"What about the dots?"

"Hmmm. They look like excavations of some sort. Similar in size, if I'm any judge, and evenly spaced around the grounds."

"Okay. Now, what about the thing you described as the bigger dot?"

"I can see now that it's some kind of structure, not one of the excavations. Hard to say how big it is, but it's smaller than the outbuildings, I can tell that much."

"All right, then," Morris said. "I'm sending the third photo, which is an even better enlargement. Once it loads, tell me what you see."

"Will do."

Morris clicked "Send," and waited. Thirty seconds went by, but he did not hear from Eleanor Robb. He waited another half minute before speaking.

"Ellie? What's wrong? Didn't it load?"

"No, Quincey. It loaded fine." Morris thought there was an odd note in Eleanor Robb's voice.

There was more silence on the line. "Ellie? Hello?"

She cleared her throat before speaking. "The smaller excavations are fire pits, of a very particular kind. I've seen these before, but never more than one at a time. I have never even imagined, wait... twentyfive of them in one place."

"What are they for, Ellie?"

"They are used in conjurations—black magic rituals for calling up demons."

"So, someone is planning to call up twenty demons at once, you think?"

"Perhaps... but probably not."

"Why do you say that?"

"That *thing* in the middle of it all. Quincey, it's an altar. The most elaborate, complex black altar I have ever seen. And for those of the Left-Hand Path, altars are places of sacrifice."

"Sure, Ellie, but Catholics do the same thing. Episcopalians too, I guess."

"True, but those sacrifices are purely symbolic. In black magic, the sacrifices are very real, and invariably bloody. Usually, it's some kind of animal. But not always. The sacrifice is designed to please the Infernal Powers. The bigger and more important the sacrifice, the greater the favor to be gained from the other side, and hence the more power present in the conjuration. And having multiple rituals going on at once would *further* increase that power."

"All right, Ellie. Given what you're looking at, give me your best guess as to what these people intend."

Silence.

"Ellie?"

Still silence.

"Ellie? Are you there?"

"Quincey I can only come to one reasonable conclusion, and it hurts my head just to have the thought in there. It's just... inconceivable—except the evidence is right in front of me that someone *has* actually conceived it, and intends to carry it out. Or try to."

"I need to hear you say it, Ellie. Carry *what* out?"

"A conjuration that will, Goddess save us, bring Satan himself to Earth."

Chapter 23

Walpurgis Eve

It is not known for certain either when or why Walpurgis Night became the night of the Witches' Sabbath. Its name derives from Saint Walpurga, whose feast day occurs on May 1. There is nothing sinister about the reputation of this good and pious woman, who in her lifetime was known for speaking out against witchcraft and sorcery. Some say the date was first chosen because it is the mirror of Halloween, being exactly six months away from that other night held sacred by followers of the Left-Hand Path.

Reports that the night of April 30 was being used for revels in worship of the Evil One began to surface in the Middle Ages, although some scholars claim this dark observance goes back to the Roman Empire. The first Walpurgis Night revels probably took place on The Brocken, the name given to the highest peak of the Germany's Hartz Mountains, although they have also been known to occur in other places throughout Western and Central Europe and, more recently, North America.

These days, The Brocken is a tourist attraction on Walpurgis Night. But there is another peak in the Hartz Mountains from which strange lights and even stranger noises emanate on the night of April 30. The good Germans who live near there stay indoors on Walpurgis Night, and there are no tourists at all—not after what happened to the first group who tried to crash the party, some thirty years ago.

Their charred remains were eventually identified, through dental records.

Every year, the daylight hours preceding Walpurgis Night are occasions for frenetic activity in certain circles, although this is rarely noticed by the public. This year, the forces aligned with the Light—as well as their counterparts, the Children of Darkness— were even busier than usual.

Coeur d'Alene Idaho
9:14am

Pardee walked the grounds of the Grobius estate, telling himself that it never hurt to give the preparations a final check. The truth was, he needed to move about in order to channel some of the nervous energy that had been growing in him ever since arising, which stemmed from the knowledge that today was the day—or, more precisely, that tonight would be the night.

A few hundred yards away, Walter Grobius lay in his immense bed, waiting for the pain medication to start working before he got up. Although this usually made him grumpy, Grobius consoled himself with the knowledge that this was the last morning for a very long time that he would have to worry about pain. Starting tomorrow, everything was going to be different.

Outside, Pardee looked up at the sky, imagining it filled with the brooms and other conveyances by which his guests would arrive after dark, although some were planning to employ more mundane means of transport.

Beginning tomorrow, everything was going to be different.

In the air, over western Iowa
10:03am

Quincey Morris had a window seat on United Flight 448, but he wasn't staring at the cloud formations as the plane made its way toward the connection that would bring him to Idaho. In his lap, he held an aerial photograph, the in-flight magazine tucked underneath for stability. The photo showed a view of a large patch of land with some buildings on it, and a number of holes dug throughout the property at regular intervals. Morris had a pencil in his hand that he used to make occasional marks on the photo, but he was not doodling.

He was working out a battle plan.

Six rows behind Morris sat a tall, slim woman dressed all in black. She was attractive by most standards, barring the long scar on one side of her face, which she had made no attempt whatsoever to cover with makeup. The woman, like Morris, had a window seat, and she was taking in the view, although the set of her face suggested that it did not please her. The seat next to her was empty, and the man sitting on the aisle had tried to make pleasant conversation precisely once. The look the woman in black gave him had guaranteed that he would not try again.

Eleanor Robb, who had a lucrative consulting business, sat in First Class and frowned over the legal pad she held in her lap. Eighteen of the Sisterhood were able and willing to rush to Idaho on extraordinarily short notice. Ellie had no way to know whether that would be enough to stop the madness that loomed on the horizon like a Class Five tornado. She prayed silently to the Goddess that it would be.

When the beverage service came around, she declined the flight attendant's offer of champagne and instead asked for black coffee. Ellie needed to work, even though she had been up all night, and the prospects for sleep tonight were uncertain, at best. Of course, if she and her allies failed in their task, they would have all eternity to rest in—along with, quite possibly, most of mankind.

Their connecting flight to Spokane scheduled to leave in twenty-five minutes, FBI Special Agents Fenton and O'Donnell sat in the departure lounge near their gate, neither one looking very happy.

"At the risk of starting another argument," Colleen said, "what's the matter, Dale? You've hardly said ten words since we left Boston."

Fenton had been staring at his shoes for the last ten minutes. Without looking up, he said, "You happen to notice how I paid for those airline tickets of ours?"

"No, I can't say I was paying attention. I assumed you used the credit card the Bureau gave you for business travel."

"You assume wrong," Fenton said tonelessly. "I used my own Amex card."

"Why? I mean, you can get reimbursed, after filling out a small mountain of paperwork, but why go to the trouble?'

"I won't be asking for reimbursement, because I don't want any official documentation connecting us with this little trip."

"But we had to show picture ID before they'd issue the tickets," she said. "That's standard procedure, to stop people from avoiding the No-Fly List by traveling under an alias."

"Yeah, I know," Fenton said. "Nothing we can do about that. But nobody should have any reason to check the passenger manifest for our names, as long as we don't let them know that we were within five hundred miles of Coeur d'Alene, Idaho. Far as the Bureau's concerned, you and I are still in Massachusetts, following up some leads we got from that scumbag in Walpole."

"Well, they won't hear any different from me."

"Do you know why I did that, Colleen?"

"Yeah, probably, but I guess you're going to want to tell me, anyway."

"I did it because I'm pretty damn sure that something bad is going to happen, once we get to Idaho. It's gonna be bad, and it's probably gonna be illegal, and we're gonna be involved in it up to our necks."

Colleen gave her own footwear a certain amount of study before saying, "Yeah, I expect you're right. On all three counts."

"Can't act officially. If we tried to get a warrant to search Grobius's property based on the evidence we've got, the judge would not only turn us down, he'd have us committed. And as for an arrest warrant..." Fenton just shook his head.

Colleen nodded solemnly. "Yep. Right again. And yet, here we are. More to the point, here *you* are. How come?"

Fenton gave his shoes another thirty seconds or so of analysis before saying, "You know that line from Shakespeare, Hamlet I think, that goes, 'There are more things in heaven and on earth than are dreamt of in your philosophy, Horatio'?"

"Yeah, I believe I've come across it," she said.

"It's kinda like that for me, I guess. Starting with that hairy business last year that Van Dreenan and I got sucked into, I've seen too much shit that can't just be explained away as hallucinations, or hysteria, or fucking swamp gas."

"It says a lot for the openness of your mind, Dale. Most agents of the Bureau..." She let the sentence trail off.

"Yeah, well, most of 'em don't have a witch for a partner. Even of the 'white' variety."

"That's most likely true."

"By the way, someday you and me are gonna have

a conversation about the racial prejudice inherent in the terms 'white magic' and 'black magic.'"

"It's got nothing to do with race, it's from... Oh. You're messing with me, aren't you?"

"Gotta do something," he said. "And that's better than screaming, which is what I *really* feel like doing. See, Colleen, it's not that I believe that Grobius and Pardee are actually gonna call up Satan tonight out there in Coeur d'Alene. And if they do manage to pull that trick off, I don't believe that they won't be able to control him, he'll get loose, and as the saying goes, lay waste to the world. I don't believe that, okay?'

"Okay. Then why are you—"

"I'm here because I don't fucking *disbelieve* it. And if that shit's a possibility, I mean if it's even a one percent chance... then I gotta go do what I can to stop it."

She reached over and squeezed his shoulder for a moment. "You and me, Dale. You and me."

On the ground, north, south, east,and
west of Coeur d'Alene, Idaho
12:03pm

All around America, practitioners of magic (both the white and black varieties) were either in transit or preparing for departure. Most were in airplanes, others rode in cars, a few would travel by train at least part of the way, and certain others planned to use less conventional means of transportation, once the sky was dark enough to hide their passage. From time to time they offered prayers, to whatever deity they worshipped, that their work tonight would be successful. None of them knew for sure whether those prayers would be answered.

Spokane, Washington
2:01pm

Quincey Morris walked into Meeting Room B at the Holiday Inn, which had been reserved for the occasion by something calling itself QM Reclamations, Inc. The witches were already waiting for him.

Morris scanned the nineteen faces, to see if he knew anyone present, but they were all strangers to him. Their ages, at a rough guess, went from late twenties to mid-fifties, and their attire ranged from blue jeans to business suits. He had known better than to expect anything unusual in their appearance. Witches, whether white or black, look like anybody else. It is only their deeds that are, sometimes, extraordinary.

One of the women stood as Morris came in, and went over to him. She was one of the older witches present, which in her case Morris guessed to be a vibrant-looking fifty-five. Her sharp green eyes studied him as she approached.

Morris extended a hand. "Eleanor Robb, I presume?"

"You presume correctly, Mister Morris. Normally I would go around the room and introduce my Sisters, but I gather that time is important. However, if you prefer introductions…"

"No, that's fine, you're quite right." Morris raised his voice a little, so that all could hear him. "Howdy, ladies, and welcome. I hope to meet each of you and offer my thanks individually, once this is over. In the meantime, I hope you won't think it rude of me to forgo introductions."

Morris walked quickly to the front of the room, and invited Ellie Robb to join him.

"I assume Ms. Robb explained to you what's going on, or you wouldn't have put your busy lives on hold to rush out here," he said. "We haven't got a lot of time, but if any of you have questions, I'll try to answer 'em."

One of the witches, a thin woman of around thirty, asked, "If all the action is going to be in Idaho, what are we doing in Washington?"

"You probably would have flown into Spokane, anyway," Morris told her. "It's the only big airport in the area. So what we've got right here is what the military calls a 'staging area'—a place to get organized before moving into... the area of interest." Morris had been about to say "battle," but he didn't want to sound like some macho nitwit who thought he was George Patton. Besides, he didn't want to scare any of them who might already be developing cold feet. "We don't want to show up in Coeur d'Alene until it's almost time to begin the work that you've come here to do. It's a small place, and the presence of twenty or so strangers would be noticed, and probably reported to Grobius, or one of his..." Morris searched for the right word.

"Henchmen?" another woman said, and there was nervous laughter around the room.

"That's not quite the term I was going to use," Morris said. "I didn't want you folks to think we'd all wandered into the middle of a Batman movie."

Louder laughter this time. Morris was glad to hear that. It would help to reduce the extraordinary tension they must all be feeling. Who wouldn't? You get a phone call from somebody who says, "We'd like you to drop whatever you're doing and come out to Idaho immediately, to help prevent the end of the world." *No pressure, or anything. No, siree.*

Once the laughter died away, he said, "Anyway, if we used Coeur d'Alene, or anyplace nearby, as our base, Grobius would probably hear about it, and we don't want him knowing we're in town, until it's too late. Besides, I understand that this many of you all in one place might be sensed by some of those on the other side."

There were some nods. Morris turned to Ellie Robb, "I assume you've been putting out a cloaking spell to shield this room from the bad guys' radar?"

Ellie gave him a crooked smile. "That's not exactly how it works, but, yes, the room is well shielded. None of those from the Left-Hand Path should become aware of our presence."

Another woman, a pert-looking twenty-something, raised her hand. "So, when do we leave here?"

Morris looked to Ellie again. "You said their revels should start at nine, right?"

"That's right," she said. "It's traditional. Three hours to do... what they do, and it all stops at midnight."

"This year, the party's going to break up early," Morris said.

Someone from the back asked, "How are we gonna get there, anyway?"

"I rented three Ford Econoline vans. We leave at eight sharp, so please be ready, with all the gear you think you'll need."

A Latino woman grinned at him. "Gear? How do you know we call it that?"

"One of your Sisters is a good friend of mine." There was something in his voice that told some of the more discerning Sisters just how worried for Libby Chastain he was.

"Three vans, Quincey?" Ellie Robb asked. "Not my business, but I'm pretty sure we could all fit in two, if they're the big ones."

"I'm sure you could," Morris told her. "But with three, if one of them has mechanical trouble or a flat tire on the way, we can just stop the caravan and transfer its passengers to the other two vans. We won't lose much time, that way."

Ellie pursed her lips, then nodded slowly. "Not bad. Not bad, at all. I begin to see why Libby speaks so highly of you."

"Thanks," Morris said. "And if everything goes just right tonight, maybe she'll have the chance to do it again."

Coeur d'Alene, Idaho
2:40pm

Libby Chastain, shackled hand and foot to the metal bed frame, used meditation techniques to quell the incipient panic within her. She had relied on the same disciplines to slow her metabolic rate, and was thus able to avoid the discomfort, not to mention the odor, of voiding her bladder or bowels. Periodically, she tensed and released her major muscle groups, one after another, to keep her body from growing stiff in its confinement.

She had not been greatly worried about Pardee's threat to have her raped, whether by humans or demons. The only one Pardee wanted hurting Libby Chastain was Pardee himself. And he intended to hurt her very badly, indeed.

If she had been wrong about the rape, Libby could have used some other techniques the Sisterhood had taught her, to lose consciousness at will, and thus avoid at least the immediate horrors of sexual assault. But rape would have caused her another problem that could not be overcome through meditation and self-hypnosis, so Libby was doubly glad that her estimate of Pardee's character had proved accurate.

The shackles securing her had been made far too strong, first by the manufacturer and then by Pardee's magic, for Libby to have any realistic hope of freeing herself. Her only chance, slim though it was, would come when she was on the altar of sacrifice, in the seconds between when Pardee removed her clothing (to humiliate her and make her disembowelment easier) and pulled off her gag (to hear her pleas for mercy, followed by her screams when mercy was not forthcoming) before plunging his blade into her body. Libby made herself visualize the scene, Pardee's likely behavior, and her own desperate actions, which could be varied depending on the specifics of the situation.

When the time came, Libby would have to be very quick. But if she managed somehow to be just quick enough...

Chapter 24

The knock on Morris's door came as he was sharing a hastily ordered meal from room service. He hadn't been especially hungry, but was concerned that low blood sugar later in the evening could make him slow and stupid just when he needed to be quick and smart.

He opened the door to admit Eleanor Robb. "Sorry to be late," she said, "but I thought a bit of a pep talk might... Oh. Am I interrupting?"

"Not at all. We were just having some pre-operational chow," Morris said. "Ellie, meet Hannah Widmark. Hannah, Ellie Robb, who I've told you about."

The woman in black had stood, and Ellie approached her slowly. "Hannah Widmark," she said. "If half the stories I've heard are true, you must be a remarkable woman."

"Oh, I am," Hannah said, deadpan. "Absolutely." She extended her hand.

"You know," Ellie said, "as a member of a sect that embraces life and opposes violence, I cannot say that I approve of you."

Hannah said nothing, but lowered her hand.

"But as someone who has seen the evil wrought in this world by those whom you hunt, I cannot say I disapprove, either." She smiled and extended her own hand. "Pleased to meet you, Hannah."

Once they were all seated, Morris offered Ellie something to eat. She declined, but did accept a cup of coffee.

"As I started to say, I just finished spending a few minutes with each of the Sisters," Ellie said as she added Sweet 'n Low to her coffee. "They are brave women, or they would not have come—I did not lie to them about the dangers involved. But still, they fear for their safety, even if none of them have said so aloud."

"Hannah and I were just talking about that," Morris said. "Certainly, once Grobius or his people realize what your Sisters are doing, he'll try to stop them. Will he have Pardee use magic, do you think?"

"I doubt he'll have any to spare," Ellie said. "What they are trying to accomplish"—she shook her head at the sheer insanity of it—"will require all the magical power that can be brought to bear. Even then, it may not be enough, be we can't count on that, of course."

"Hannah and I had thoughts along the same line," Morris said. "But Grobius has security people, and we know they have weapons. There are licenses on file for his corporation's purchase of rifles, pistols, and shotguns. Whether their arsenal includes anything illegal, like automatic weapons or grenades, I'm afraid we're only going to find out the hard way."

"You *must* do what you can to protect my Sisters, Quincey," Ellie said. "They know they are risking their lives, bless them, but I will *not* have those lives just thrown away, no matter how great the cause."

"They won't be," Hannah said. "The ones throwing away their lives will be those who try to harm your Sisters."

Ellie Robb looked at her, then back at Morris. "This is one of those matters that I would prefer not to ask about," she said. "But in this instance, I'm afraid I must."

"We'll explain it all," Morris said. "But there are two other people who should be joining us shortly. Their plane landed about twenty minutes ago, and they called me from the Avis counter at the airport. They'll be here pretty soon, and we'll all work out the details of the plan that Hannah's come up with."

"It's a simple plan, really," Hannah told her.

"She's right," Morris said. "But then, a broken neck can be described as a simple fracture. Are you sure you wouldn't like some salad, or something, Ellie?"

They were almost done with the remains of the coffee when someone knocked at the door of Morris's room. He opened it to welcome an African-American man and a white woman. Ellie rose—to meet the man, and to embrace her Sister, Colleen O'Donnell.

* * *

Morris had the aerial photos of Grobius's compound spread out on the low table where the five of them sat. "As you can see, the walls form a rectangle," Morris said. "Four sides, four gates. These circles I've drawn around the outside represent the approximate positions that the white witches will take, to conduct their own rituals."

"Why those particular positions?" Fenton asked.

"They give the lines of power the best angles to intersect," Ellie said. "This kind of magic, where you have a number of practitioners working toward the same goal, takes advantage of what management theorists call 'the assembly effect'—a group of people working together will produce something greater than the total of their individual efforts."

"I didn't think magic used the language of management theory," Fenton said, smiling a little.

"It doesn't, but I do," Ellie told him. "Just for explanatory purposes. And keep in mind that those... *others*... inside the compound are attempting the same thing. The Sisters must work together if we're to have any hope of offsetting their magic."

"It only stands to reason that someone inside the compound, probably Pardee, will realize what's going on outside and try to stop it," Morris said. "Ellie says he won't be able to spare any magical resources to do that—"

"Yes, she's right about that," Colleen said. "They can't afford to break their circle, once it's been formed."

"I hear you," Morris said. "So what Pardee's got left are Grobius's security people. We don't know how many for sure will be on shift tonight. Maybe all of them, and the three shifts total thirty-six people. And they're armed."

"What with?" Fenton asked. "Handguns?"

"Rifles and shotguns, too, for certain," Morris told him. "And I wouldn't be surprised if Grobius has circumvented the federal firearms laws and bought those fellas some automatic weapons to play with, as well."

"Yeah, rich fucks like that always figure the law doesn't apply to them," Fenton said, then looked up. "Pardon my language, ladies."

Ellie smiled at him. "I've been known to use the work *fuck* myself once in a while, Agent Fenton," she said.

"Yeah, don't fuckin' worry about it," Hannah said. She didn't smile, but there was a touch of levity in her voice.

"Fuckin' A," Colleen said.

"Of course, what applies to those inside the compound is also true for us," Ellie said. "Once the Sisters are engaged in their rituals, they won't be able to use their magic to protect themselves against any attack—whether by people with guns, or anything else."

"That leaves it up to us," Hannah said. "Excuse me a moment."

She stood up and went to Morris's closet. Pushing aside the sliding door, she removed, one at a time, four long, heavy boxes made of some shiny, dimpled metal. Each had a carrying handle and several locks.

Hannah laid the boxes out on the floor, and produced a set of keys. Ellie Robb watched in obvious fascination. The others appeared interested, but not especially curious. They had all seen rifle cases before.

Fenton shook his head once and muttered, "Knew it was going to come down to something like this."

"You wouldn't believe what it cost me to have these shipped as cargo in each plane that Quincey and I took to get here," she said, while unlocking the cases. "We had to change planes twice, and my biggest worry was that some baggage handler would get careless and send them to Pittsburgh, or someplace, by mistake." She opened the cases, one by one. "I could have bought replacements locally, but nothing nearly as good, and no time at all to zero them in."

The weapons that Hannah had revealed were not identical, but they had several features in common. Each had a telescopic sight attached, a light coating of oil, and the appearance of uncompromising lethality. These all looked exactly like what they were: extremely well-made killing machines.

Hannah rested her hand on one of the cases and looked at Fenton. "You should recognize this one, Agent Fenton. You went through the USMC Scout Sniper School, didn't you?"

Fenton nodded glumly. "I won't even ask how you know that," he said. "And you may as well call me Dale. I'm sure as shit not here in any official capacity."

"Okay, Dale," she said. "Well, this one's yours, for obvious reasons. It's zeroed in for five hundred meters, but I'm pretty sure we'll be closer than that, so you'll have to adjust your point of aim accordingly."

Hannah looked at Morris. "I remember you telling me, years ago, that you once did the Austin SWAT team's sniper course, Quincey."

Morris nodded. "Yeah, a cop buddy of mine cleared it with his boss, so I could take the course. I never thought I'd be using it to save the world, though. Just shows you."

"All right, then," Hannah said. "That just leaves you, Colleen. You ever work with a long gun before?"

"My family's full of hunters, me included," Colleen said. "Sometimes we'd go up to Montana, after Bighorn Sheep. We used rifles something like these here. It's been a while, but..."

"You ever hit any of those wild sheep?" Hannah asked.

"Stop down to the family home sometime," Colleen said. "All our trophy heads are still mounted on the wall. Eight of them have my name underneath."

Hannah looked at her for a few seconds, then nodded. "I guess you'll do."

"At the risk of seeming stupid, I need to ask just what you plan to do with these guns," Ellie said.

"Each of us will set up in range of one of the four gates to Grobius's compound," Morris said. "If the guards come out, and they probably will, they've gotta come through there. So when they do—"

"We kill them," Hannah said.

"Hold up a second there, lady," Fenton said.

"I'm not a lady, Dale," Hannah said, matter-of-factly. "I haven't been for quite some time."

"Whatever," Fenton said. "My point is, we can try to wound them. It'll serve the same purpose, protecting the women."

Hannah looked at him. "Dale, have you ever tried to 'shoot to wound' with a weapon like this, at three hundred meters or more, and at night, besides?"

Fenton looked at her, but said nothing.

"You know as well as I do, there's only one thing you can do," Hannah said. "You put the crosshairs on the center of body mass, and you service the target."

"You sound very professional, Hannah," Ellie said.

"That's because I am," Hannah said. "And so is Dale, I bet, once he gets past all that FBI 'Come out with your hands up' bullshit. They didn't teach you to 'shoot to wound' in the Corps, Dale."

"That was in a war," Fenton said. His face had gone tight.

"And what do you think it is we've got here—a game of lawn tennis?"

"There's something else we can do," Morris said, and all their eyes turned toward him.

"Dale's got a point," Morris said. "The goal is to keep the Sisters safe, not necessarily to kill Grobius's security people."

"I don't see—" Hannah began.

Morris held up a hand, palm out in a 'Stop' gesture. "Just listen, Hannah. Please?"

After receiving her reluctant nod, Morris went on, "Let's say you're one of Grobius's guards, and you get orders to go outside the walls and do something about those pesky white witches. But when you approach the gate, doesn't matter which one, somebody you can't even see puts a round into it, about two feet from your head. What do you do?"

"You take cover," Fenton said, looking happier than he had since entering the room.

"Exactly," Morris said. "And if you stick your head up, another round hits close by, so you duck back down again. I figure any of us can keep those fellas pinned down long enough for the Sisters to do their work, and we won't have to kill anybody. Probably."

"I like the way you think, Morris," Fenton said.

"Well, I don't!" Hannah said. "Pussyfooting around with half-measures is a good way for people to get killed. Our people."

Morris shrugged. "I guess each of us is going to have do decide where we're going to aim. You do what you think best, Hannah."

"Oh, I will, believe me. And by the way, what happens if these penned-up guards get smart and try coming out inside a vehicle?"

"Then," Morris said, "I guess we'll have to kill people."

Coeur d'Alene, Idaho
5:25pm

"Are you excited, to know that your deliverance is at hand?" Pardee asked.

"Oh, yes," Walter Grobius said. "Very much so. I've been living under a death sentence far too long. If it weren't for you, I imagine I'd be dead already."

"Well, there is that possibility," Pardee said modestly. "But everything will be different tomorrow."

"So, the ceremony starts at nine? My memory, these days…"

"That's something else you won't have to put up with after tonight, sir. In any event, it's the revels that start at nine."

"That's right, I'd forgotten. The big black magic sex orgy."

Pardee smiled. "As good a description as any, I suppose."

"It just occurred to me. These are all women, right?"

"Yes. That's traditional."

"So, who are they going to... orgy with? Each other?"

"To a large extent, yes. Witches of the Left-Hand Path are not known for their sexual inhibitions."

"Bunch of dykes, are they?"

"Not exactly. I'd describe them more as ravenously pansexual."

"You said something about 'to a large extent.' If they don't fuck each other, who's left?"

"Their familiars, of course. Each will arrive with one."

"They're going to have sex with fucking *black cats*?"

Pardee permitted himself some polite laughter. "That's just a cultural stereotype, sir. All kinds of animals can be used as familiars. Cats, dogs, baboons..."

"Bestiality? Now *that* should be interesting."

"I have no doubt. But a familiar is just a minor demon in animal form. On an occasion such as tonight, some of their mistresses will permit them to return to their natural states."

"They'll become demons again, you mean."

"For a few hours. Others will remain in the animal

shape, but may be made to become, um, somewhat *larger*."

"Sounds like quite a party," Grobius said. "Pity I'm in no condition to partake. Still, next year will be a different matter."

"Indeed. For now, would you like to be present as an observer?"

"Being that close to the banquet without being able to dine? No, the frustration would be maddening. I'll watch from up here, through the binoculars. What about you? Planning to join in?"

"With regret, no. Once I get things going, I'll retreat to my workroom for final preparations and a spell of meditation, to clear my mind and spirit for what's to come."

"Probably wise. Will you need help getting what's-her-name…"

"Chastain. Elizabeth Chastain."

"Yes, of course. Do you need anyone to help you get her to the sacrificial altar?"

"No, but thank you. She is completely under my control, and I will give her no opportunity for mischief, you may count on that."

"So, when will it… happen?"

"The ceremony will start at eleven. It should reach its peak about eleven forty-five, at which point Miss Chastain's day will take a sudden turn for the worse."

Grobius gave a snort of laughter. "And that's when he will appear."

"Very shortly afterwards. I'll be rather busy, but there are people ready to take you down when it's time, and bring you to the place of honor."

"Will I be able to… speak to him?"

"Oh, by all means. I expect he will find that very interesting. As will you, of course."

"If you can make this work, Pardee, you can have anything you want, anything."

"I have no doubt that my reward will come. None at all."

Chapter 25

Quincey Morris settled in and tried to get comfortable. The position he had chosen gave him a clear field of fire about 200 yards from the south gate of Grobius's compound, a two-acre plot of land surrounded by a concrete wall twenty feet high. The daylight was just giving way to the black of night, following a blood-red sunset that Morris hoped would not prove prophetic.

Morris wore one of the light headsets that Hannah Widmark had picked up at a specialty electronics store in Spokane. It consisted of an earpiece, a battery-powered transceiver, and a slim microphone that was positioned about four inches from his mouth. Duplicate sets, tuned to the same frequency, were now being worn by Hannah, Fenton, Colleen O'Donnell, and Ellie Robb. All of them were now in their pre-selected positions at different points around the compound's perimeter.

Morris pressed the "Transmit" button and said, "This is Q. The doves are in position, and so am I. Acknowledge." A moment later, a woman's voice, still lovely despite the static said, "This is H. Got it." Then he heard a man's voice say, "This is D. Acknowledged." Once he had heard from Colleen and Ellie, Morris settled the rifle across his knees and tried to relax. He would probably be here a while.

He had just finished leading the white witches to their predetermined positions, using a GPS device to find the precise spots that had been determined from viewing the aerial photographs of the area. Each had with her a backpack or carryall or some other container for the "gear" she would use to cast a spell to counter that being made by the black witches inside the compound.

Morris had wanted Fenton in the position covering the front, and largest, gate. To his surprise, Hannah had not argued, and had readily agreed to take the north gate, on the side opposite from Morris. Colleen O'Donnell was covering the back. Morris had assumed that Hannah would want the front, which would likely offer the greatest number of targets. He was certain that she had no intention of merely keeping the guards in her scope pinned down by fire, which was why he wanted her somewhere else. Hannah's ready agreement had pleased him at the time, but now he wondered if she were playing some more devious game. Then he mentally shrugged, and let it go. *Wheels within wheels. You think about that stuff too much, you can drive yourself nuts.*

Morris's own plan was crude, but the best he could come up with. Once his fire had sent any guards near the south gate scurrying for cover, Morris was going to move in as closely as he could without being seen. By then, if the guards had been called to some other part of the compound, all well and good. But if any remained, Morris planned to shoot them dead, before charging the gate to gain entry to the compound. Hannah would probably have accused him of being hypocritical; however, Morris was not planning to kill guards out of bloodlust. He did not want to kill anyone, at all. But he was going in after Libby Chastain, and God help anyone who got in his way.

Morris decided to spend the time until action doing something useful. He prayed.

8:12pm

It was full dark, now. Pardee strolled the grounds, trying to keep his excitement under control by running down his mental checklist, to see if there was anything he had missed. He could not think of a single thing.

Several of the invited black witches had arrived by car during the afternoon and early evening. Each had been greeted with great courtesy, shown to a spacious private bedroom with bath, and told to call housekeeping if she needed anything at all. But now that it was dark, the others should...

Pardee looked up, just in time to see a silhouette pass between him and the risen full moon. A grin split the wizard's thin face. The figure he had glimpsed in outline had not been wearing anything as silly and impractical as a conical hat.

But she *had* been riding a broom.

* * *

"My sisters in Satan, I bid you welcome!"

Pardee stood upon the highest of the marble steps that led to the great altar, and looked down at the twenty women who stood in a ragged semicircle before him. Their ages ranged from twenties to fifties, and their garments spanned the gamut from goth, to biker chick, to hippy, to punk, to almost nothing at all. Most of them had animals of various species either in their arms, on their shoulders, or by their sides.

"By these revels tonight, we bring about a new age of our faith, for we shall, by making use of this ancient ritual, which has been hidden for centuries, successfully call upon the one whom we all worship, and whose favor we all hope to gain, both in this world and in the next."

Pardee made a sweeping gesture to include several long tables that had been covered in white cloths, which were even now being removed by trusted servants.

"For our revels, I offer you the finest drink, the most sumptuous food, and the most intoxicating herbs, and I bid you eat, drink, dance, get high, fornicate, and enjoy yourselves any fucking way you wish, until the witching hour is almost at hand, and the true work of the evening can begin. Until then..." Pardee drew in a deep breath, and what followed was a joyous shout: "*Let's party!*"

That was the cue for the music, which instantly boomed from a dozen huge speakers spaced around the area. The first song on the playlist was, appropriately, by Black Sabbath.

9:02pm

As the first strains of "Heaven and Hell" blared forth from inside the compound, Morris shook his head. Then, after a moment, he checked his watch. *Well, at least they're punctual. Trite, but punctual.*

He reached for the airline carryall bag he'd brought with him and unzipped it. Not wanting to show a light, Morris rummaged past the boxes of rifle ammunition, a St. Christopher's medal, a large revolver, and other necessities to find an energy bar, which he brought out along with a bottle of water. Might as well chow down and enjoy the show, if *enjoy* was the proper word.

Look on the bright side, Quincey. If those assholes are planning to make us listen to almost three hours of heavy metal, getting shot at when it's over is gonna come almost as a relief.

9:03pm

From her concealed position 180 yards from the north gate, Hannah Widmark was bobbing her head to the beat coming from the other side of the wall. She quite liked heavy metal music, and was glad to learn that the Forces of Evil had decent taste in something.

Even though she knew it was likely to be several hours before she got to kill anybody, Hannah checked her equipment, using touch alone. Ammo—check. Combat knife—check. Tampax (just in case)—check. She spent extra time on the two Colt .45 automatics that she wore, butts forward, in twin holsters under her armpits.

Her pistol craft instructor, a shadowy, enigmatic man named Cranston, had insisted that the .45 Colt, although foolishly abandoned by the U.S. military ten years earlier, was still the best combat handgun in the world. Its rate of fire was as fast as anyone could want, it would never jam if you kept it clean, and the big, slow .45 round was a guaranteed one-shot stop, no matter where on the body you hit.

Cranston had taught her, with care and patience, how to fire both weapons simultaneously and hit what she was aiming at, with either hand, every time. Two hours a day, every day, for more than a year, Hannah had watched and learned and practiced. Cranston used to say, with that weird laugh of his, "The weed of Satan bears bitter fruit, Hannah. And these are your weed-cutters."

Hannah hoped they'd play some Def Leppard over there before the evening was done. Those guys were her faves.

9:28pm

Sitting in his darkened office, Walter Grobius watched the witches' revels through state-of-the-art binoculars that showed him every detail. He could almost have counted individual strands of pubic hair, except many of the ladies of the Left-Hand Path seemed to prefer having none at all.

Grobius watched the witches as, in various pairs and combinations, they got it on with each other, with familiars in the forms of baboons and large dogs, and with bizarre-looking creatures that he assumed were the minor demons Pardee had referred to.

It was the most erotic thing he had ever seen in his life.

For the first time in years, Grobius found himself getting an erection. Something so rare was too good to waste. He reached for his telephone.

"Send one of the secretaries up here. No, I don't care—whoever's handy."

Grobius put the phone down and smiled contentedly. Getting your cock sucked a few hours before achieving virtual immortality was not a bad way to spend an evening. Not bad, at all.

11:21pm

"Well, dear Libby, it's time," Pardee said.

Libby Chastain looked at him impassively. She had heard the music start a few hours ago, knew what it portended, and had estimated the passage of subsequent time with fair accuracy. She had not been surprised when Pardee, shit-eating grin in place, had opened the door.

She had spent most of the day in meditation, so her mind was calm and clear. She had practiced several other mental disciplines, as well. The last hour or so had been given to a series of muscle contraction routines, including some Kegel exercises that Libby thought might prove very beneficial in a short while.

Pardee approached the bed, and sniffed loudly. "What's this—you haven't soiled yourself? Such discipline! However, I fear it will prove all for naught. When I plunge my sacrificial knife in your lower belly and start working my way up, I'm afraid both your bladder and bowels will give up all their contents."

He stood next to the bed now, and was staring into her eyes. "But do you know what?" he said. "I'm not going to let it spoil my enjoyment, not even a little bit. In fact, your sudden incontinence might even add to it. Now, then."

Pardee reached out one hand and cupped it over the top of Libby's head. He noticed her right hand suddenly form a fist; clearly, she was not as composed as she pretended. Good. Pardee said a short phrase in some arcane tongue and Libby instantly went limp, eyes closed, head lolling to one side.

"Can't have you putting up a fuss along the way, dear girl. Although I doubt you would prove very much of a problem."

Pardee touched the shackle binding Libby's right hand and said another word in the same language. The manacle dropped free, then slid off the bed to hit the carpeted floor with a soft thud. He repeated the operation three more times, then picked up Libby's limp form and carried her out of the room.

The grin remained in place. If possible, it was even wider.

11:26pm

Pardee, now clad in black ceremonial robes, dumped Libby Chastain onto the altar as if she had been a load of dirty laundry. He then faced the witches, most of whom, being engaged in various forms of debauchery, had not yet noticed his arrival. Pardee watched for a few moments, finding special interest in a chunky, tattooed blonde and what she was having done to her by both a minor demon, covered in scales like an alligator, and her familiar, which had taken the form of a large, clearly aroused, Great Dane.

Then Pardee raised his arms skyward, the signal to cut the music. Def Leppard was silenced in mid-screech, although the orgy down below tapered off more gradually. When he was sure he had their attention, Pardee said, "The time is come, my sisters. Go to your positions, ready your materials, and prepare to welcome the new king of this world!"

The witches, some of them walking a bit unsteadily, got to their feet and began to move toward their designated fire pits. Some pulled their clothes on first, while others chose to remain skyclad. Soon, flames began to rise from several locations, and soon all twenty of the pits being used were burning. The body organs of dead children would be burned in those pits, accompanied by suitable incantations.

"Sisters, I bid you begin your rituals now!" Pardee cried.

Then he turned to the altar and began tearing off Libby Chastain's clothing.

11:27pm

When Ellie Robb noticed that the awful music had finally ceased, she closed her eyes and concentrated, sending the same message, over and over, to the white witches who had accompanied her: *Begin, my sisters, Begin, my sisters, Begin, my sisters...*

Then she opened the backpack she had brought with her, and prepared to join her own efforts with those of the others. She sent a quick prayer to the Goddess that they would be enough, in number and in power, to stop the abomination that was beginning behind those concrete walls.

11:28pm

Pardee had just finished stripping Libby Chastain, and he was looking with interest at her nude body when he sensed something... wrong.

He focused all his concentration, and suddenly knew what it was. There was white magic being practiced in the immediate vicinity, and from a number of individual sources. *So the Whities have figured out what my plans are, and have assembled outside somewhere to try and stop them. Well, we'll just have to see about that, won't we?*

Pardee reached under his robes and produced a cell phone with a walkie-talkie function. He depressed the button and brought the device to his mouth. "Hannigan! Hannigan, pick up damn you!"

The voice of the security detail's commander sounded in his ear. "Yes, sir, Mister Pardee."

"Hannigan, there are some people, probably all women, outside the wall somewhere. They are disrupting my ceremony here. Send your people out there and stop them! At once!"

"Yes, sir. Uh, when you say 'stop them,' do you mean we should—"

"Hannigan, I don't care if your goons shoot them, hit them on the head, arrest them, or tie them down and fuck them. Just stop them! Now!"

"Uh, yessir, Mister Pardee. Will do. Hannigan out."

Pardee had no way of knowing that behind him, Libby Chastain's eyes had cracked open, briefly, before closing again.

He turned back to the altar, and made sure his sacrificial knife, which he had made with his own hands, was nearby. He pushed down on Libby Chastain's knees to make her body lie flat. He would wake her up and remove the tape from her mouth just before he was ready to put the knife into her. He hoped she would give a good long scream to welcome the Lord Satan to His new kingdom.

Pardee began to recite the "Ritual for Calling forth Shaitan" from Abdul Alhazred's *Book of Shadows*. It had taken him months to memorize, but he knew the thing by heart, now.

Pardee had just completed the first section, and was rewarded by a shimmering in the air over the Sacred Circle. His Lord was not here yet, but was on his way. Pardee had no idea whether the magic circle would contain Satan's power—but, then, it was never his intent to contain it. If the circle proved a barrier, Pardee would simply break it, to allow his Lord ready access to the world he had coveted for so long.

Pardee was well into the second part of the ritual, the section that would end with Libby Chastain's slow disembowelment, when his concentration was disrupted by the sound of gunshots—*lots* of gunshots. And some of them, by the sound, were being fired by heavy rifles, which were *not* part of the arsenal provided to the compound's security people.

Pardee turned his back on the altar again and produced his walkie-talkie phone. "Hannigan! What the fuck is happening? Hannigan!"

Behind Pardee, two important things were taking place. One involved the Sacred Circle, where the shimmering in the air had increased noticeably, and the vague outlines of a humanoid form could now be perceived. The second event involved Libby Chastain, who slowly spread her naked legs wide and began to bear down hard with certain muscles that she had trained to suppleness over the last twenty-eight hours.

"Hannigan!"

11:35pm

When that heavy metal crap had stopped screeching from inside the walls, Fenton knew that the time for action was very nearly upon him. He was in a good position, concealed by some brush, a clear field of fire to the front gate, the weapon's stock tight against his shoulder. It wasn't long before there was a flurry of activity inside the big gate, and then it swung open.

All of the entrances to Grobius's little fortress were well lit by floodlights, so vision was not a problem. Fenton had been worried they might have to rely on nightscopes for their rifles, and those things were not only heavy and clumsy, but also unreliable.

Fenton had decided the best way to show the dudes in the khaki uniforms that he meant business was to drop one of them. Not kill him—not unless absolutely necessary. But despite that bitch Hannah's sneers about shooting to wound, Fenton was betting he was still a good enough marksman to maim a stationary target, especially one who had no idea that Fenton was even in the neighborhood.

A heavyset guy with sergeant's stripes on his

khakis was standing out in front of the gates, apparently giving orders to his crew of guards. Fenton interrupted the briefing by putting a round into chubby's leg from what he estimated to be 320 meters away. Sarge dropped like a marionette with the strings cut, and after a second for the sound of the shot to catch up with the bullet, the rest of the group scrambled for cover.

Center of body mass, my smooth black butt. Put that pipe up your ass and smoke it, Widmark!

* * *

11:37pm

"All right, then, have them split up and go out the side gates, both groups at the same time," Pardee said. "This isn't fucking World War Two, Hannigan. It's just one man with a rifle, and he's at the main gate, which is the logical place for him to be. It isn't physically possible for him to cover the front and both sides at once. And if you don't get your people moving *right now*, Hannigan, I promise you, getting fired is going to be the *least* of your worries. Do you understand me? Then do it!"

While Pardee had been yelling into his walkie-talkie, Libby Chastain had carefully pulled from her vagina an object about the size of a thick pen. It was still slick with the thick coating of KY Jelly she had applied before inserting it, just prior to taking part in the Circle the other night. It wasn't that Libby distrusted Quincey's vigilance, but this was something she did every time she had to send her spirit out of her body—it made her feel more secure, knowing that she had a collapsible, fully charged magic wand secreted inside her body, just in case. *Well, Libby, welcome to "Just in case."*

Libby grasped the wand at both ends to extend it to its full length. She had to move slowly, carefully, since the thing was so slick, and to drop it now would be to send disaster an engraved invitation.

She had just gotten the wand extended when Pardee turned back toward the altar and looked right at her.

11:40pm

Any soldier who's fought in a war will tell you how important luck is when it comes to staying alive in combat. Your buddy happens to step on the mine, instead of you; the mortar shell lands in somebody else's foxhole, instead of yours. No matter how brave, or quick, or well-trained you are, luck, whether good or bad, has a lot to do with making that age-old distinction between the quick and the dead.

In the small war that took place around Walter Grobius's compound that night, luck also had its role to play. Captain Seamus Hannigan, who had assumed personal command of the security detail after Sergeant Willner was wounded, divided his troops into two groups, acting quickly and arbitrarily. The group you were assigned to was determined by where you happened to be standing when Hannigan made his selection.

One group of ten men was lucky. They were sent out the south gate, where Quincey Morris was waiting to shoot above and around them, thus urging the wisdom of their staying exactly where they were.

The other group was arbitrarily assigned to the

north gate, where Hannah Widmark was prepared to receive them. They did not fare as well.

The men who, at Hannigan's command, had surged out the south gate, surged back in shortly thereafter. Their only casualty was a man who had been hit in the eye by a splinter of stone that was sent flying when one of Morris's rounds hit the wall close to his head.

Of the ten men who charged out through the north gate, only six returned, one of them bleeding heavily from a wound to the arm that looked as if it would require amputation below the elbow.

None of the security guards had tried to leave by the rear gate, so Colleen O'Donnell never got to see how badly she could scare them with near misses. After a while, she began to doubt that the rear gate was figuring in the plans of anyone inside the compound. Colleen was not impatient by nature, but she was acutely aware of how precarious was the situation that pitted her Sisters' magic against that of the unknown number of black witches inside.

Finally, when the shooting from the side gates had died down, and with no activity at all at the rear, Colleen put down her rifle close to hand, and opened her carryall to remove the implements of her craft. Within three minutes, she was adding her power to the ritual being performed by her Sisters all over the property. It was, she concluded, the best use of her time and talents.

11:41pm

Walter Grobius, with the help of two trusted employees, had been brought to the scene of the ceremony just as Pardee ordered the music stopped. Grobius was glad—all that noise, which apparently passed for music in some degenerate circles, made his head pound.

His people had led him to a throne-like chair that had been set up on the other side of the Sacred Circle from where Pardee was presiding over the altar. From the moment the air began coruscating over the circle, Grobius was mesmerized. Once the dimly perceived shape of The One could be seen, he was positively transfixed. He paid no real attention to the distant gunshots, or even to what difficulties Pardee might be having up on the altar. Walter Grobius knew that his time was at hand, and he sat ready, in breathless anticipation of his coming glory.

11:42pm

As soon as Libby Chastain had seen Pardee turn around, she had rolled her naked body away from him, off the altar and onto the marble floor. The drop of three feet had hurt like a bastard, but Libby was pleased by what followed her to the floor a second later: Pardee's ceremonial dagger. Libby wasn't sure exactly what use it would be to her, but at least if she had it, Pardee couldn't use it to slice her open like a Christmas goose.

And Libby had maintained possession of her wand.

Pardee rounded the corner of the altar quick as a cat, already declaiming a spell, which was no doubt intended to subdue her in some way. As he came into sight, Libby pointed her wand at him and began reciting the words of an all-purpose defense spell that might not stop Pardee, but would surely slow him down.

And Libby could hear the shots, too. She had never doubted that Quincey would find her, and he had not only found her in time, but brought help with him, by the sound of it. Libby was fairly certain that time was on her side.

But then Pardee bore down, and she felt the full force of his power. It might have been Libby's weakened state (not having eaten in almost forty-eight hours) or maybe it wouldn't have made any difference, anyway. Because Pardee had been right about one thing.

His magic was stronger than hers.

11:44pm

Frank Durkin was a smart guy. He knew it, even if the other guys he worked with were too jealous to admit his intellectual superiority. While everybody else was running in and out of the front and side gates like headless chickens, getting shot at each time, Durkin realized that nobody had tried getting out through the back.

Sure, he knew he was taking a chance. The people attacking, whoever they were, might have the back gate covered, too. But it was one thing to hit somebody who was part of a bunch of guys all coming out together. It was something else to nail one guy who you weren't expecting, in the first place. Especially if the guy in question was Frank Thomas Durkin, who had been a track star in high school, and never let anybody he knew forget it.

Durkin approached the back gate slow and

sneaky, so he wouldn't be seen coming by anybody who might be lurking out there in the dark. If he made it through okay, he'd break left, then find some of those chicks that Captain Hannigan had said Mister Pardee was so pissed off about. He'd take out a couple of them, which none of the other guys had been able to do, and be the fuckin' hero. Hell, he might even get a big, fat check from Mister G for being the only guy on the security detail with enough brains and balls to try something like this. Thinking out of the box, that's what they called an idea like his.

Durkin was at the gate now, a few yards to the left of the entrance.

Okay, running start, slam the gate open without stopping, then run like hell off to the left and into the trees. No problem at all. Ready, set, and here's the starting gun! Go!

11:45pm

Colleen O'Donnell was about a third of the way through the Sisterhood's most powerful anti-black magic ritual when she saw the man in khaki burst out of the back gate and run, very fast, off to the left. She put down the religious implements she held (she could not bring herself to drop them; her training had been too thorough for that) and grabbed the rifle, but the man was out of sight even before she could bring the weapon to her shoulder.

Fuck! Cocksucking motherfucker. SHIT!

She heard several fast gunshots then, but they were too far away to have anything to do with the guard she had just, through her own negligence, let through.

Colleen O'Donnell put the rifle back down, got to her feet, and ran.

11:45pm

Hannah Widmark had approached the north gate at an oblique angle, in the dark, wearing her usual black clothing. The group of guards milling around just inside the gate, wondering what to do next, had no idea she even existed until she casually walked through the gate and stood facing them, hands on hips. "Hello, boys. How's everybody tonight?"

No one knows what might have happened if they had just continued to stand there, dumbfounded, and let her pass. Because some fool decided to go for his gun.

The twin shoulder holsters that Hannah wore each had a thin nylon cord that hung down from the bottom. This was designed to be tied to the belt of the wearer, to prevent the holster from snagging when the gun it held was drawn very fast. Hannah had both those cords fastened securely to the wide belt she wore, and her holsters did not snag the twin .45s as she drew them, very fast indeed.

The guard who had gone for his weapon was the danger man, so Hannah shot him first, aiming for center of body mass, just as Cranston had taught her. The big .45 slug caught him in the sternum, sending the man to the asphalt as quickly as if the hand of God had reached out and pulled him down.

By then, of course, the other five guards had no choice. No choice at all.

Hannah took the two on the outside first, left and right, one round from each of the .45s doing the job nicely. Then she dropped the next two, who had yet to clear leather with the Walther PPKs they wore on their hips. Then there was only one man left; he had actually managed to draw his weapon, and was bringing it to aim when two of Hannah's slugs blew his heart out between his shoulder blades.

Without any hesitation, Hannah turned left and ran, toward the area where the aerial photos showed the sacrificial altar to be. That was where she would find Pardee. She changed clips as she ran, replacing the half-expended ones in her guns with fresh clips containing the full eight-round combat load. Hannah had no idea what she was going to encounter on her way, but she was not interested in running out of ammunition when she dealt with it.

And she wanted plenty of ammo left for when she saw Pardee again.

11:47pm

Libby Chastain was forced to face the fact that, for reasons either temporary or permanent, Pardee was stronger than she was. That meant she was going to die in the next few minutes, unless she did something extraordinary.

She decided to do something extraordinary.

White magic does not employ blood sacrifice. Unlike its black counterpart, which is dedicated to death and destruction, white magic is about life, and nature, and growth. Thus, no grisly symbolism plays a role in its practices.

With one exception.

White magic does allow for one kind of blood sacrifice—when the practitioner deliberately offers up her own blood. Since this does not involve doing harm to another, and instead represents the voluntary giving up of one's own life essence, it is consistent with the philosophy, laws, and practices of those who follow the Right-Hand Path. It can, done properly, temporarily increase the practitioner's magical power as much as tenfold. Of course, if too much blood is sacrificed, the practitioner dies. And the sacrifice may be made only in the direst of circumstances.

Libby Chastain regarded her present circumstances as *pretty fucking dire*.

Libby had never done a blood sacrifice, only read of it in the Sisterhood's books on magic theory. Plus, she tended to be something of a baby about pain. But she had never turned away from grim necessity in her life. She was not about to start now.

Which is why, without ever taking her eyes off Pardee, or lowering the wand she held in her dominant right hand, Libby seized the sharp ceremonial dagger with her left, quickly brought it down to the inside of her bare left thigh, and with one get-it-over-with-before-I lose-my-nerve movement, deeply slashed her leg, severing the femoral artery.

11:49pm

Quincey Morris approached the south gate cautiously. It appeared unattended, but there was no way to know, until he was inside, whether any guards were lurking in the vicinity. Morris hoped there weren't any around. He didn't want to kill anybody tonight—but time was running out. He was going to find Libby, if he had to do it over the bodies of Grobius's entire security unit, then that's just what he would do.

He was nearly at the gate when he heard gunshots from inside. Nobody was shooting at him—there were no muzzle flashes, and no bullets went whipping past. And he thought he recognized the distinctive report of a .45. It would appear that Hannah had gotten tired of waiting, too.

When Morris cautiously poked his head around the corner of the gate, he saw that the few guards in the vicinity were running hard toward the north gate. He slipped inside then, keeping to the shadows as much as possible, and headed for the altar of sacrifice. At first he went at a fast walk, looking everywhere, prepared for trouble. But soon, encountering no challenge, he began to run.

11:50pm

Colleen O'Donnell was in the undergrowth for about thirty seconds when she realized that her eyes weren't going to help her much. Despite the full moon overhead, it was impossible to track the man's passage in this light, through this undergrowth. Then Colleen did something smart. She stood still. And listened.

There was crashing through the brush, ahead of her and maybe ten yards to the right. She quickly developed a technique that worked. Move twenty or thirty feet ahead. Listen. Catch the noise the guard was making. Adjust course, if necessary. Move forward. Repeat as needed.

Then she heard a voice. A man's voice. Moving slowly, pistol drawn, she followed it.

"Lady what the fuck are you doin' here?" the voice said. "Coming around, upsetting Mister G. and all that. You can't do shit like that, lady. Not and keep livin'."

Colleen was close enough to hear the click of a hammer going back. She ran forward now, yelling, "FBI, hold it!"

She broke through the last of the brush into a small clearing. One of the Sisters, Colleen couldn't remember her name, was kneeling on the ground, her magical implements arranged around her, clearly terrified of the man who was holding his gun on her, even though he was now looking at Colleen.

"FBI!" she said again, pointing her Glock at him. "Drop your weapon! Do it!"

The man seemed to sneer in the moonlight. "FBI, yeah right. Where's your fucking ID, Miss FBI Man?"

Her ID was back at her firing position. *Shit!* "I'll be happy to show you my ID in a second. But, put your weapon down now!"

The man was shaking his head. "I don't think so, sister. You ain't taking this away from me. It's my big chance." Then he pivoted at the hip and pointed his pistol, some kind of automatic, right at Colleen.

She double-tapped two rounds into his chest, and killed him.

11:53pm

Libby Chastain, stark naked, sat in a growing pool of her own blood and felt the magical power within her

401

grow stronger, even as her body became weaker. Pardee was staring at her, his eyes wider than Libby had ever seen them. The shit-eating grin was gone now.

Although she was starting to feel light-headed, Libby forced herself to concentrate, to focus on the sacrifice she was making. *O Goddess, I make you this gift of my blood, my life force, my very essence, I make it of my own free will, and I beg of you to give me the power to defeat this Son of Darkness. Then, if you would have my life as recompense, it is yours to take.*

Libby could feel the power swell within her. Pardee was driven a step back, then another, then, in a final surge, Libby could feel her power wrap around Pardee's, wrap around it and smother it and crush it until it lived no more.

Pardee lowered his hand and just looked at her. He knew it too, she could tell: his magic was gone. Maybe for an hour, a day, forever. But as he stood before her now, he had no magic whatever.

Libby's vision began to blur, and she saw Pardee's face twist as he started toward her. He might be without magical power, but soon Libby would be so weak that any mortal man would be able to kill her. And Pardee seemed to think that he was just the man to do it.

Libby tried to keep the wand raised, tried to focus, tried to stay alive. Her vision was fading and there was a roaring in her ears now, but it did not prevent her from hearing the voice that spoke from behind her, a female voice, beautiful as an angel's, that said, "Looks like a fun game, kids. Can anybody play?"

* * *

"Hannah!" Libby cried, although her voice came out as little more than a croak. "I took his magic, Hannah. He has... no... power..." Then Libby lowered her hand, her eyes closed, and fell over, into the pool of bright red, arterial blood that continued to grow larger by the second.

Pardee and Hannah stared at each other. Then recognition, or *something*, seemed to dawn in Pardee's eyes—which may have been why he turned and ran.

Hannah started after him, but, after a second's hesitation, stopped and knelt next to Libby Chastain, whose eyes fluttered open.

"Libby," she said, in that voice of heartbreaking beauty. "What can I—"

"Go," Libby croaked. "Go get him. My life's... with... Goddess now... her will. Now, *go!*"

Hannah looked at Libby for just a second longer, but a great deal passed between the two women in that brief space. Then Hannah whispered, "Goodbye, Sister." Then she was gone, sprinting off into the night.

11:58pm

Quincey Morris had finally reached the place of sacrifice. Most of the black witches were still busily engaged in their ritual, although a few had broken off and were staring, wide-eyed, toward the big altar that looked like it was made of marble.

Although everyone else in the world who owned a handgun seemed to have gone over to automatics,

Morris perversely stuck with a revolver, maybe as a *homage* to certain of his forefathers, one of whom, it was said, had ridden with the Dalton Gang. Morris carried a Colt Python chambered for .357 Magnum, and when he aimed it over the heads of the black witches and fired, it sounded like a small artillery piece going off.

At the first shot, the witches looked up, startled. By the second, most of them were on their feet. When he fired a third time, they began to scatter—several, Morris noted, without bothering to put any clothes on.

He turned toward the altar then, and saw the still figure lying in an impossibly large pool of blood. Three seconds later, he was kneeling in the gore, next to Libby Chastain.

Her skin was cold, so cold. But he found a heartbeat. It was slow, but it was still a heartbeat. Morris saw that the blood was coming, although slowly now, from a deeply slashed artery in her leg. He whipped off his belt and used it to tie a hasty tourniquet at the point where Libby's leg joined her groin. He felt briefly creepy about putting his hands there, but then figured that Libby was in no condition to feel outrage at being groped. She was almost certainly unconscious, anyway.

The tourniquet working as well as it was likely to, Morris tried to figure out what to do next. He considered an impromptu blood transfusion, but he had no equipment, and was embarrassed to realize he didn't even know Libby's blood type.

Morris held back a sob. Libby was going to need a miracle to—

Then he blinked rapidly a couple of times. He

happened to know some people who specialized in miracles. *And they were not far away.*

Morris gathered Libby into his arms and tried to regain his feet, slipping on the blood. He finally managed to stand, then gingerly stepped off the altar and clear of the blood pool. Clutching Libby Chastain tightly to him, he began to run.

11:59pm

Pardee was also running—past the trees, through the underbrush on the fringes of Grobius's estate. That woman, the one in black. He knew her from some—

Pardee's right knee exploded in a spray of blood and cartilage and pain. He found himself on his back, looking up at the full moon, before he even knew he was falling.

The woman in black stepped out from behind a tree, a big automatic pistol in her hand. She'd been *ahead* of him, even though he'd had a substantial head start. *She must be in phenomenal condition to—*

"Good evening," she said. "Lovely night for a jog isn't it?"

Pardee said nothing, gritting his teeth against the pain.

"You don't agree?" The woman pretended surprise. "Then you won't mind this." She fired again, and his other kneecap was instantly a bloody ruin. Pardee howled in agony.

"Can't have you running off now, can we?" the woman said. "I mean, we have so much to catch up on."

She stood over him now. "Tell me, do you have an itch anywhere? Someplace you want to scratch?"

Pardee was too busy stifling a scream to answer.

"No? Well that's all right, then." She put a bullet exactly in the spot where his right shoulder joined the arm. He would not be using that arm again anytime soon. Pardee thought he would pass out from the white-hot pain, but even that grace eluded him.

"Last chance to scratch," the woman said, in her melodious voice. She waited a couple of seconds, then fired a .45 slug into his other shoulder, hitting the exact same spot as on his right and likewise shattering the joint.

She watched Pardee writhe and bleed for a while, then nodded, as if satisfied with a job well begun. She put the pistol away, and knelt down next to him.

From somewhere she produced a big knife with a black, partly serrated blade and a textured leather handle. Pardee did not recognize it as a K-Bar, the combat knife that was once issued to U.S. Marines and Navy SEALS.

There was something slightly mad in the woman's face now, but her voice was calm, too calm, when she spoke again, after first placing the point of the blade six inches above Pardee's groin, the ultra-sharp cutting edge facing his chin.

"My name is Hannah Widmark," she said. "I just thought you'd like to know."

Then she put her weight behind the blade, and it began.

Midnight

Walter Grobius still sat, staring at the shape that could be seen within the circle. He had been waiting for it to coalesce into something clearer, better defined, more immediately present. But it never had.

Grobius finally worked up the courage to speak. "I am Walter Grobius, and I bid you welcome."

The shape inside the circle seemed to notice him for the first time. "WHO ARE YOU TO WELCOME ME, LITTLE MAN?" The voice was almost unbelievably deep, and guttural, and loud. It hurt Grobius's ears just to hear it.

"Who am I? I'm the one who sent for you, O great father Satan."

"YOU LIE. IT WAS NOT YOU WHO SENT FOR ME, BUT THAT OTHER WRETCH, WHO CLAIMED TO BE MY FAITHFUL SERVANT. WHERE IS THE TRAITOR? I WOULD CHASTISE HIM. ETERNALLY, FOR A START."

"If you mean Pardee, I'm afraid I don't know. Anyway, Pardee works for me, and—"

"SILENCE, WORM!" Grobius was almost literally knocked over by the force of the voice.

"THE WORTHLESS WRETCH PARDEE PROMISED THAT I SHOULD BE FREE OF MY FETTERS IMPOSED BY THE CREATOR, AND HAVE MY WAY WITH THIS WORLD AND ALL WHO DWELL IN IT, IN RETURN FOR SOME PETTY REWARD."

"No, I'm afraid that's not what I—"

"BE SILENT! NOW THE HOUR IS PASSED, THE CIRCLE WEAKENS, AND MY GLORY WILL NOT BE VISITED UPON THIS LAND—ALL BECAUSE OF ONE INCOMPETENT FOOL. I MUST PREPARE SOME SPECIAL DELIGHT FOR HIM TO ENJOY WHEN HE JOINS ME IN MY KINGDOM—WHICH I NOW PERCEIVE WILL

BE VERY SOON. ALREADY HE SCREAMS AND BEGS FOR MERCY, BUT HE SHALL HAVE NONE IN THIS WORLD, AND MOST ESPECIALLY NONE IN THE NEXT.

"No, sir, I'm afraid you don't understand."

"I UNDERSTAND ALL THAT IS, WAS, AND EVER SHALL BE. I UNDERSTAND THAT THE MOMENT IS NOW PASSED, AND I MUST RETURN TO MY OWN DOMAIN, WHERE THE WORM DIETH NOT, AND THE FIRE IS NOT QUENCHED. BUT I WOULD LEAVE WITH YOU A GIFT BEFORE DEPARTING. DO YOU WISH TO RECEIVE MY GIFT, LITTLE MAN?

"Oh, yes, very much so, that's why I sent for—"

THEN I BID YOU EMBRACE MY LARGESSE. I WILL SEE YOU IN GEHENNA, WORM, AND VERY SHORTLY. MEANWHILE, ENJOY A TASTE OF YOUR ETERNITY."

Pardee's circle was well constructed, and strong. Even Satan was unable to escape it, in his semi-formed state. The books say that a summoned demon cannot harm the summoner or any others present, as long as the circle remains unbroken and they remain outside it.

But the books were not written with the Prince of Darkness himself in mind.

The indistinct shape slowly faded. But in its place appeared a flame, which quickly grew wondrous and vast and terrible—and then, with a roar that could be heard for miles, exploded out of the circle.

Walter Grobius was incinerated before he could fully grasp what was happening to him.

So, too, was everyone and everything within Grobius's compound consumed by that great, unholy fire. Within seconds, nothing remained alive within those walls, no structure stood, not a blade of grass was spared by the flames.

Morris was fifty feet outside the compound when the hellfire raged. It shot out of all the gates briefly, but Morris had run at an angle upon leaving the compound, and so he and Libby escaped the flames, mostly.

Morris did not even look back. He was searching frantically for Eleanor Robb among the group of white witches, all of whom were staring at the inferno with shock on their faces. Ellie saw him, and what he was carrying, and immediately came running forward.

"Libby! Goddess save us! What happened to her?"

"She's lost a lot of blood, an awful lot of blood," Morris said. "Cut in her thigh, here. Deep one." Morris was having a hard time remaining coherent. "Needs blood, lots. Don't know her blood type. More than blood, needs magic."

"Give her to me, please," Ellie said, and took Libby's still form from Morris. She seemed to handle Libby's weight with surprising ease.

Ellie stood holding Libby for a few seconds, her eyes tightly shut. Then she opened them and said, "Sister Elizabeth lives still. And her blood is AB positive."

Morris tried to think. "That's the universal recipient, isn't it? Anybody's blood is good?"

"Exactly right, Quincey. And Sister Louise, who is with us, is a doctor, who never travels without her medical bag."

"I want to donate," Morris said. "Please."

"Of course. But first let's lay Sister Elizabeth down somewhere comfortable. And I want to get the other Sisters working on a healing ritual. We are all exhausted, but the Goddess will give us strength."

They put Libby in one of the Econoline vans, and Sister Louise organized the blood transfusions. There were twenty-two volunteers, including Fenton and Colleen O'Donnell. Ellie Robb also had the Sisters, two at a time, performing healing rituals in the van.

While waiting to see if they would be needed as blood donors, the two FBI agents and Morris talked among themselves.

"What the hell happened in there, Morris?" Fenton said. "It was like an explosion at a goddamn oil refinery, or something."

"I can't say for sure," Morris told him, "but I'm guessing that Satan got sent back home, and wasn't real happy about it. Maybe what we saw was kind of a parting shot."

Colleen was staring at him. "Speaking of which," she said, "that's an interesting-looking burn you've got on the back of your neck."

Morris felt back there. "What bu—ouch! In all the excitement, I never even noticed. How the hell did that get there?"

"Precisely," Colleen said.

Morris looked a question at her.

"Where else have you been exposed to an open flame tonight," she said, "except when you ran out of Grobius's place with Libby?"

"And here I thought it missed me completely," Morris said. "I must be getting slow."

"It's not real bad," Fenton said, peering at Morris's neck. "I've seen worse."

Colleen had an odd expression on her face. "I'm sure you have, Dale. But how many have you seen that were caused by hellfire?"

Morris felt his neck again, gingerly. "Assuming that's what it is, so what?"

Colleen hugged herself, which might have been due to a chill in the air. "I don't know, Quincey. But, I have to say that I find it... troubling."

"Why's that?" Morris asked quietly.

"Because his mark is on you, now."

The three of them were silent after that, until Colleen asked, "What about Hannah?"

"Last I saw, she was chasing down Pardee," Morris said. "I don't know what that was all about, but I'm pretty sure she had some kind of unfinished business with him. I just hope she got it done, before..." He shook his head.

"Didn't get out, huh?" Fenton said.

"I don't see how she could have." Morris's voice was bleak.

"If you didn't actually see her body, be careful about your assumptions," Colleen said. "She's got a knack for survival, our Hannah does"

"What she means is," Fenton said, "that lady's just too damn mean to die."

"Maybe," Morris said. "We'll have to see what the autopsy reports say. It's going to be quite a while before this mess gets sorted out."

Fenton looked past Morris. "Company coming."

Morris turned to see Ellie Robb heading his way.

"Quincey," she said, "I'm sorry—"

"Oh, God damn," Morris said softly. "She's gone, isn't she?"

Ellie looked surprised. "Who, Libby? No, on the

411

contrary—Sister Louise says she's out of danger. I was apologizing because I know you badly wanted to be a blood donor. I forgot to remind Sister Louise, and she got all the blood Libby needed from the Sisters. And, I'm glad to say, the combined healing spell we laid down was very successful."

"Oh." Morris let out a breath he hadn't realized he'd been holding. "Well, I expect I can forgive you for that, Ellie, all things considered. Can I see her?"

"Sister Louise gave her something to help her sleep. Maybe a little later, if you don't mind."

"All right," Morris said. "I reckon there's no hurry, now."

Ellie Robb nodded and started to walk away, but then turned back. "I almost forgot," she said to Morris. "Before she fell asleep, Libby gave me a message for you."

"What'd she say?"

There was an odd-looking smile on Ellie's face. "I'm pretty sure I can render it verbatim." She closed her eyes, and took in a couple of slow, deep breaths. When she spoke again, it was in Libby Chastain's voice. "Thanks for the tourniquet, Tex. I owe you. But if you're ever planning to feel me up like that again, at least take me out to dinner, first."

ABOUT THE AUTHOR

Justin Gustainis is a college professor living in upstate New York. He is the author of the novels *The Hades Project* (2003) and *Black Magic Woman* (2008) as well as a number of short stories. In his misspent youth, Mr. Gustainis was, at various times, a busboy, soldier, speechwriter, and professional bodyguard.

ACKNOWLEDGEMENTS

Christian Dunn, my editor at Solaris Books, made excellent suggestions for revisions and was gracious about the few changes that I did not want to make. Once again, he took my work and made it better, bless him.

I was fortunate to have Lawrence Osborn as my copy editor again. I am both embarrassed by the mistakes I made and grateful that he caught them before the book went to press. In the unlikely event that any errors remain, they are my responsibility alone.

Jim Butcher was generous enough to allow Quincey and Libby to hang out at a certain pub frequented by Chicago's premier wizard-for-hire. Harry is welcome to come on down to Austin and kick back anytime.

Tim Clukey, my colleague, friend, and webmeister, designed and maintains the www.justingustainis. com page, thus giving me a web presence that I can be proud of. You rock, man.

The final draft of *Evil Ways* was completed while I was participating in the 2008 Odyssey Writing Workshop, aka "Ranger School for Writers." The many things I learned there allowed me to revise the manuscript with more insight than I would ever have had otherwise. Jeanne Cavelos, who runs Odyssey, is a goddess. But her associate, Susan Zielinski, is just plain evil.

John Carroll, who has been my friend since dinosaurs walked the earth (or so it sometimes seems) gave me some great ideas that were incorporated into the character of Walter Grobius.

Shelly Becker, Donna Baker, Kathy Baker, René Burl, Deb DeSilva, Kevin Gitlin, Jin Kim, Tammy Rock, and Bobbi Terry (among others), each in his/her own way, helped keep me going through what I will always remember as the Dark Time. Terry Bear hung in there with me, too.

My wife, Patricia Grogan, was the light of my life for more than thirty years. On December 22, 2007, that light was extinguished. This book, everything else I write henceforth, and anything else of worth that I may do, is dedicated to her memory.

SYMPATHY FOR THE DEVIL

Read on for an excerpt from Sympathy for the Devil, *the next Morris and Chastain Supernatural Investigation by Justin Gustainis, coming soon*

Prologue

Hynes Convention Center
Boston, Massachusetts
Halloween Night

His voice, booming though the state-of-the-art sound system, filled the hall and reached out to the people sitting in the cramped seats, as if he were speaking to each one of them individually.

"And so, my friends, even though our efforts have accomplished much, let us not fall victim to the comforting illusion that no battles remain to be fought. The war for the heart and soul of America will go on. Make no mistake about it, a hard and bloody fight it will be, and the victory of virtue is by no means assured."

He paused, looking out at the crowd, the grave expression on his face a testament to the concern he felt for his nation and its future. Then his face, handsome by almost any standard, broke into a reassuring smile.

"But although there is no unassailable guarantee of success in our endeavors, of this much I *am* certain: that with God's help, you and I, all of us who fight for right, will find within ourselves the strength we seek for the struggle!"

The audience erupted into applause and cheers, as they had done four times already. But this time the approbation was both louder and longer. It seemed like it might go on forever.

In the press gallery, *The Boston Globe* looked up from its laptop and said to *The New York Times*, "Knows how to push their buttons, doesn't he?"

"Sure, but that's not hard to do with *this* crowd," *The Times* replied with a shrug. "Throw the animals a little red meat, and they'll jump through all kinds of hoops for you."

The Globe smiled slightly. "Does your editor mind you referring to the devout reactionaries of Believers United as 'animals'?"

"Not as long as I don't do it in print."

The two men resumed typing their stories as the applause from the 5,822 attendees at the Believers United annual convention rolled on like a mighty river. On stage, the man behind the podium was basking in their approval.

A few minutes later, as the speaker launched into his peroration, *The Times* asked, in a bored voice, "Think he'll run?"

"What, for the White House?"

"Uh-huh."

"Shit," *The Globe* said scornfully. "He's running already."

At the reception following the speech, those members of Believers United willing to make a minimum $10,000 tax-deductible contribution to the cause of righteousness were given the opportunity to consume high-cholesterol hors d'oeuvres, wash them down with domestic champagne, and exchange a handshake and a few words with the guest of honor, Senator Howard Stark, whose oratory had so stirred them earlier.

Since the paying guests numbered 108, the funds raised amounted to a tidy sum. By prior agreement, the money would be split down the middle: half into the coffers of Believers United and the rest to the fledgling "Stark for President" Committee, an organization that the senator had carefully refrained from endorsing—so far.

Stark stood roughly in the middle of the short receiving line, a man of average height whose broad shoulders made him look bigger than he really was. Below the carefully styled blond hair, now shot through with gray, the green eyes stared out at the world with the apparent innocence of the country boy on his first visit to the big city – an image that was as carefully cultivated as it was utterly untrue.

Half a million dollars, give or take, for two hours of schmoozing sounds like easy money, but the junior senator from Ohio earned it. He did not resort to the repertory of techniques that every politico learns early on—the bright but meaningless smile, the quick, firm double-pump handshake, the artfully vague words and phrases that might mean anything and hence mean nothing at all. A typical politician would have used all of these, and others, in a situation like this, but Stark was not a typical politician. The support of the Christian Right was going to be vital if he was ever going to use "1600 Pennsylvania Avenue" as a return address, and Stark knew he couldn't afford to go on automatic pilot. Despite the bumpkin image that fundamentalist Christians often have in the media, most of these people at the reception were actually very sharp. If Stark let his eyes glaze over, they would notice, and remember. They were touchy about respect, and, as Stark was soon reminded, passionate about their concerns.

"More than a million babies a year, Senator, butchered in those abortion mills!"

"Now they want to give out condoms and birth control pills—in the *junior* high schools. Can you imagine?"

"Since they've got that Brady law on the books, it's just a matter of time before the storm troopers come knocking on people's doors and confiscating our guns, you just wait and see if they don't!"

"And the man admitted he was a queer, right there in front of the School Board and everything, and they *still* couldn't fire him."

"Have you seen the filth that passes for entertainment on television these days? They ought to drop the name 'cable TV,' and call it what it really is: porno TV!"

"Won't let a kid say the Lord's Prayer in school, but nobody minds if he smokes a marijuana joint outside on the playground. Hell, some of these hippie teachers would probably join him..."

To each guest Stark gave a handshake, a smile, and a few moments of his attention, whether he felt the speaker deserved it or not. Stark was sincere in his opposition to both abortion and increased gun control, but privately unsure about the degree of menace posed to the nation by civil unions for homosexuals, the teaching of evolution in public schools, or the antics of raunchy rock stars.

It went on like that for the full two hours, and not once did Stark let his concentration wander. And so he was understandably relieved when his chief of staff drifted over and said softly in his ear, "We've put in our time, as agreed, and we *do* have that other appointment later. Do you want to get going, or are you having too much fun?"

Without changing his pleasant expression, Stark replied, in a near-whisper, "By all means, let's get out of here, before all this self-righteousness gives me hives."

His chief of staff gave the barest hint of a bow, and a murmured *"Fiat voluntas tua, Domine,"* before turning to address the room in a clear and commanding voice. "Ladies and gentlemen, it was really great of you to invite us here tonight. I know the senator would stay to talk with you all night, if I let him. But somebody's got to be the bad guy and make sure he gets his rest, so that he can have his wits about him when he goes back to running the country tomorrow."

There was good-natured laughter in response, partly at the corny humor, but mostly at the idea that the label "bad guy" could possibly refer to Mary Margaret Doyle, the tall, charming, and beautiful woman who had just paved the way for her boss's departure. And so, after a few final words with Believers United Director Miles Miller, Senator Howard Stark made his exit. As he did so, his chief of staff was at his elbow—a position she had occupied, figuratively, and often literally, since Stark's days as a freshman member of the Ohio legislature.

Mary Margaret Doyle drove with the same quiet competence that she brought to everything she did. It had been quiet in the car for a while but as the headlights picked out a sign reading "Welcome to Rhode Island," Senator Stark said, "Let's hope the media doesn't get wind of this little errand of ours. Laughingstocks don't get elected president in this country. Well, give or take Jimmy Carter."

"The media won't know anything about it," she replied with calm assurance. "Right now you're in your suite at the Copley Plaza, alone, suffering from a bad headache, probably brought on by all the MSG in those awful hors d'oeuvres at the reception. You have given orders that you are not to be disturbed, under any circumstances, before breakfast time tomorrow."

"Great, terrific," he said sarcastically. "So if something major hits the fan overnight, something that we should deal with right away, we won't even find out about it until seven in the morning?"

Mary Margaret sighed. "Woe unto ye, oh ye of little faith," she said. "In the unlikely event that something hits the fan, as you so elegantly put it, one of our staff people, either back at the hotel or in Washington, will hear about it. They have orders to call my cell phone, which is right here." She tapped the black leather bag on the seat next to her, an immense Italian-made thing large enough to serve her as both purse and briefcase. "I have no doubt that our people, properly instructed by phone, would be able to cope with your hypothetical emergency for the ninety minutes or so it would take us to return to Boston. Then we're back in the Copley Plaza through a rear door, up to the eighteenth floor in a service elevator to which I have obtained a key, and back in our respective rooms, in plenty of time for you to save the world."

"You think of everything," Stark said grumpily. "Too bad, while you were at it, you couldn't manage to think up a more convenient time for us to go on this wild goose chase."

"The man said that Halloween night was an excellent time for it. The balance of forces is favorable, or something like that. Besides," she said blandly, "if you really think it's a wild goose chase, then why are you here? Why aren't you back in your room, on the bed with your shoes off, watching boxing on HBO?"

There was silence from the passenger's seat. Finally, Stark said, "If what we've heard is true, if el-Ghaffar can really do what he says he can do, then the implications could be just… staggering."

"The national security implications, you mean." There was a touch of mockery in her voice now.

"Yes, damn it, that's exactly what I mean," Stark said. "What did you think, that I want to use this guy to get rich? Last I looked, the value of assets in the blind trust was something like six and a half mil, not counting the house in Chagrin Falls and a couple of other properties."

"It's just over seven point two million now," she said. "The annual statement arrived last week and has been sitting in your 'In' box. You really should read your mail more often."

"You know, sometimes you can be a real fucking pain, MM."

"So can you, Senator, especially when you use that kind of language, knowing full well that *I don't like it.*"

There was stony silence for the next three-tenths of a mile. Then Stark took in a deep breath, let it out, and said, "I'm sorry, MM. I just can't shake the feeling that this whole thing is going to be a colossal waste of time, and it's got me kind of cranky. But I'm sorry for the way I spoke."

"I'm sorry, too," she said. "I expect I *was* being something of a pain, at that. But let's not fight over this. I mean, you might be right: it could turn out to be a fool's errand. But everything I've been able to find out says there's something to it."

"Conjuring demons," Stark said, shaking his head. "Just like in the fu—uh, frigging movies."

She nodded. "Yes, I know. It sounds like very bad late-night TV—except that it might just possibly be for real. I spent half an hour last month talking with a man who claimed that he had actually seen it done."

"How did he manage that? By peeking in Dr. Faust's window?"

"No, he commissioned it, apparently. He told me that, a couple of years ago, he'd paid a woman in Denver, someone named Victoria Steele, to conjure a demon for him."

"Conjure it to do what?"

"He was a little vague about that part," she said. "Which actually adds to his credibility, when you think about it—very few people want a demon conjured in order to do something benevolent. But he was perfectly willing to talk about the rest, including the fact that the procedure, if that's the word, cost him ten thousand dollars."

Stark whistled briefly. "Witchcraft seems to pay well these days. And no danger of being burned at the stake if you're caught, either."

They continued south on Route 95, which soon brought them to the outskirts of Providence, although they did not take any of the exits leading into Rhode Island's capital city.

"Lovecraft country," Stark said, as if to himself.

Mary Margaret Doyle's brow furrowed. "Excuse me?"

"H.P. Lovecraft. He used to live in Providence."

"Is that someone I should know? He's doesn't work on the Hill, does he?"

Stark gave a bark of laughter. "No, he's been dead a long time. Lovecraft was a writer. Quite well known, in some circles."

"I don't think I've ever come across his work," she said with something like disapproval. Clearly, if she hadn't read Lovecraft, he wasn't worth reading.

"Good to know that there are some gaps even in a Vassar education," Stark said. "My roommate in college got me interested in the guy. Lovecraft wrote a lot of stories, and some novels, back in the Twenties and Thirties. Pulp fiction, I guess you could call it, but well done, nonetheless."

"That's interesting." Clearly, she did not really think so.

"In some ways, yeah." Stark ignored her sarcasm. "Lovecraft wrote a lot of his stories about this race of creatures he called the Great Old Ones."

"Sounds like the Foreign Relations Committee," she said, smiling slightly.

"Lovecraft's guys were even older than some of my

esteemed colleagues," he said. "The Old Ones were supposedly on Earth long before man. They were immensely powerful, almost like gods. Eventually, some savvy humans found a way to control them, to lock them away where they couldn't do us any harm. But in Lovecraft's stories, the damn things keep getting loose."

Mary Margaret Doyle drove on in silence for half a mile or so, then asked her boss, "Is there a moral in there somewhere? Some point you're trying to make, however obliquely?"

"No, I don't think so," Stark said.

"I mean, if you don't want to go through with this, I can take the next exit and turn around. We can stop for coffee somewhere and then head back to Boston. Believe me, I'd understand. I'm a little frightened at the prospect of doing this, myself."

Frightened did it. "No, keep going, damn it," he said gruffly. "We started this, we'll see it through. If this guy turns out to be a fraud, it'll be something we can laugh about later, maybe."

"Maybe," she said softly. "Maybe we will."

They got off Interstate 95 a little south of Warwick. After that, it was all secondary roads through mostly open country, the fields bordered by the low stone walls for which rural Rhode Island is famous. The frost covering the plots of farmland twinkled and sparkled in the moonlight.

There were few road signs to guide them, but Mary Margaret Doyle never hesitated at any intersections or forks in the road. After a while, Stark asked, "I don't mean this the way it sounds, but are you sure you know where you're going?"

"Absolutely," she replied. "El-Ghaffar sent me a map. It was really quite detailed."

"Where is it?"

"I shredded it. After committing it to memory, of course."

"Of course." Stark shook his head slightly.

Finally, a little west of Kingston, Mary Margaret Doyle slowed the car and began peering at the road's right shoulder, as it searching for something. A few moments later, she murmured, "Ah, there we are," and braked again before making a right turn that took the car down a narrow dirt road, tall pine trees lining both sides like sentinels.

"We're almost there," she said.

"Good," Stark replied, and almost sounded as if he meant it.

Another quarter-mile brought them to the clearing, and the house that stood within it. If Stark was expecting Castle Dracula, he was disappointed. The place looked like it might have once been a farmhouse, although what there was to farm in the middle of this forest Stark could not begin to guess. In the abundant light from the full moon, he could see that the building was not quite ramshackle—the outside walls badly needed re-staining, but were all upright nonetheless; the roof appeared to be missing a few shingles, but was still intact; the porch steps groaned when subjected to Stark's weight, but they did not break.

Since Mary Margaret Doyle had been the one to set this meeting up, he let her do the knocking at the weathered front door. It was opened almost immediately, as if someone had been standing behind it, waiting for them to seek admittance.

The man in the doorway smiled. "Miss Doyle, I presume," he said smoothly. "What a pleasure to meet you in person, at last. Please—come in."

He ushered them in with a gesture as economical as it was graceful. They entered what seemed to be a living room, its rugs faded, the furniture old and a little shabby. As their host turned back from closing the door, Mary Margaret Doyle said, "Dr. Hassan el-Ghaffar, I'd like you to meet Senator Howard Stark."

The two shook hands. Since he'd known the man he was going to meet was an Arab, Stark found little that was surprising in the man's appearance. Hassan el-Ghaffar, who looked to be about fifty, was over six feet tall with a build that was slim bordering on skinny. His hair, black with a few touches of gray, was combed straight back from his forehead. The dark complexion bore a few tiny craters that spoke of an early acquaintance with chicken pox, or maybe smallpox. A carefully trimmed goatee covered el-Ghaffar's chin and upper lip. The only incongruity was the pale blue eyes, which are the hallmark of the Berbers of Northern Africa.

"I am delighted you could be here this evening, Senator," el-Ghaffar was saying. "And Miss Doyle, too, of course." The last was said almost as an afterthought, which led Stark to suspect that the Arab had not entirely shaken off his culture's traditional attitudes toward women. Too bad for him, Stark thought. Any man who underestimated Mary Margaret Doyle usually regretted it sooner or later.

"I'm not entirely sure if 'delight' describes my own feelings about this evening, Doctor," Stark said. "I suppose that will depend on what you have to show us."

"Ah, a skeptic!" el-Ghaffar said with enthusiasm that Stark suspected was rehearsed. "I derive great satisfaction from introducing skeptics to the mysteries of the Nether World. It is always interesting to watch them readjust their *Weltanschauung* to the new reality that is revealed to them."

"Readjust their *what*?" Stark was not going to be intimidated by some intellectual's command of ten-dollar words.

"Worldview," Mary Margaret Doyle explained. "Literally, it refers to a comprehensive way of seeing the world, as well as humanity's place within it."

"Well, whether my worldview is due for adjusting remains to be seen, Doctor." Stark said. "But if you're willing to make the attempt, I'm willing to observe."

"Of course, of course," el-Ghaffar said. "I think you will find it an interesting experience. Rather like that enjoyed by those observing the first test of the Manhattan Project, I would think." He gestured toward a door in the living room's far wall. "Come, let us descend."

Stark hoped that the use of *descend* was incidental, and not prophetic.

As el-Ghaffar led them down the creaking basement stairs, Stark said, "It's interesting you should mention the Manhattan Project. I saw a documentary about it last month on the Discovery Channel or someplace. I hadn't realized before then just how much uncertainty there was about the test explosion, out there in New Mexico."

"Really?" el-Ghaffar said politely. "They didn't know what would happen when they set off the bomb?"

"Apparently not. I gather there were serious disagreements among the scientists. Enrico Fermi, I think it was, was betting that the nuclear blast would set the atmosphere on fire and burn up all the planet's oxygen."

"I hope the others were smart enough to take his bet," Mary Margaret Doyle said, stepping gingerly in her two-inch heels.

"Why 'smart'?" Stark asked. "You figure they should have known Fermi was wrong?"

"No," she said. "They should have known that if they lost, they wouldn't have to worry about paying up."

The two men laughed, perhaps a little louder than the witticism deserved.

"Well, you need have no such fears about this little demonstration, Senator," el-Ghaffar said. They had reached the bottom of the stairs now. "This is not the first time I have performed a summoning, and there is no real danger involved, as long as we follow a few elementary safety procedures."

The basement, which consisted of one room, was larger than Stark would have guessed. It might have been designed as a "rec room" by the architect long ago, but it was clear that whatever went on in there now would not be considered "recreation" by anyone—except maybe Johannes Faustus.

There was the pentagram, of course. Stark had done enough reading recently to recognize one when he saw it, and this specimen was hard to miss, since the damn thing was at least ten feet across. The five-pointed star had been drawn on the concrete floor using a liquid that appeared brown in the uncertain light. It was probably paint or some kind of special ink, although Stark kept remembering that blood, whether animal or human, will turn brown when it dries. At each point of the star was a squat red candle, unlit, about eight inches high.

The altar was off to the right, covered with a scarlet cloth upon which a variety of symbols had been drawn in black. Stark thought he recognized a few of them, like the figure eight on its side that was the Greek symbol for infinity, but most of the rest were a mystery. Several appeared to be words written in Arabic, a language that Stark did not read, and which had always looked like incomprehensible squiggles to him.

Atop the altar were a small charcoal brazier, a copper bell, several small ceramic bowls, an old-looking book bound in cracked leather, two candles similar to those surrounding the pentagram, and a long sword with a curved blade. Because of a boyhood fascination with edged weapons, Stark recognized the sword as an Arab implement called a scimitar.

On the floor directly behind the altar was a circle about three feet in diameter, the same color as the pentagram. Ten feet to the left, two more circles were inscribed on the concrete, similar to the one behind the altar, but slightly smaller. It was to these that Hassan el-Ghaffar, led his guests.

"Senator, if you will take your position within

this circle here," he said, gesturing. "And Miss Doyle, inside this one, if you please."

Stark waited for his companion to correct the man's use of "Miss" instead of "Ms.," but Mary Margaret Doyle said nothing. Apparently there were things more important than etiquette on her mind tonight.

Dr. el-Ghaffar stepped back a couple of paces. "Very good," he said. "Now, in a moment I will seal each of your circles." He held up a cautionary hand. "Nothing that will induce claustrophobia, I assure you. But you will each be effectively protected against the demon that I will summon. It will not be able to escape from the confines of the pentagram in any case, but one always takes extra precautions when playing with fire, so to speak." He grinned briefly, the gleaming white teeth an odd contrast with the black goatee and café-au-lait complexion. *If that smile's meant to be reassuring,* Stark thought, *then I think it needs a little work. He's as nervous as a cat in a room full of rocking chairs.*

From a nearby shelf, el-Ghaffar picked up a canvas sack about the size of a ten-pound bag of flour. Bending at the waist, he carefully poured what looked like sand around the perimeter of Stark's circle, then Mary Margaret Doyle's, before repeating the procedure on the larger circle behind the altar. The sand, if that's what it was, appeared to Stark to be shot through with small bits of blue stone. He noticed that el-Ghaffar was careful to create an unbroken circle each time he laid the sand down on the concrete floor.

"Once I start the summoning," el-Ghaffar said,

straightening up, "do not leave your circle for any reason, until the ritual is completed, the demon has been dismissed, and I tell you it is safe. This is vitally important." He looked each of them in the eyes, in turn. "If you disregard my instructions, you will place yourselves in very great hazard."

"What kind of hazard?" Stark demanded. "You just said that this demon that's supposedly going to show up will be trapped inside the pentagram, right? So what does it matter whether I stay inside the circle or walk around the room on my hands, holding a rose between my teeth?"

Stark saw the pupils of el-Ghaffar's eyes suddenly dilate. He guessed that the man was furious, but making a determined effort to control himself.

"I am a cautious man, Senator," el-Ghaffar said. The patience in his voice was clearly forced. "It is true that this work involves some risks, but they are always calculated risks, which means I employ every protection available."

"That's what I don't get," Stark said. "What *are* the risks? What's the worst that could happen if something goes wrong?"

"The worst that could happen?" The Arab shook his head. "Senator, I ask you to believe me when I tell you this: you do not want to know."

"Well, why—"

El-Ghaffar held up his hand, palm out like a traffic cop. "Please! I would enjoy discussing this issue with you at length, but our time grows short. We must be ready to begin by midnight. So let me ask you this: have you seen that famous movie about the shark, *Jaws*?"

A shrug from Stark. "Sure."

"Then I ask you to consider what you would do if you were in the position of the marine biologist in that film, as he was being lowered into the sea in a shark cage. This water, remember, contains an immense Great White shark, to which you would be little more than an appetizer, if it could reach you. Now, you are in the cage, you trust the cage, the manufacturer claims that it is proof against any shark in the world. But, as you are about to be lowered into the water, someone asks you if you would like a tube of shark repellent, just for a little extra protection. Tell me, Senator—would you refuse it?"

The two men stared at each other for several seconds. Then Stark shrugged. "You draw a nice analogy, Doctor, although I'm not sure you've established your premise." He sighed once, then said, "All right, no more questions for now. We'll stay in our circles until you say otherwise. Right, MM?"

Mary Margaret Doyle had been silent throughout this contest of wills. "Of course we shall," she said now, with utter seriousness. "I never contemplated anything else."

Stark looked at her sideways for a moment, but said nothing. El-Ghaffar checked his watch and walked quickly over to the altar, saying, "There is still time, if we hurry."

There was a steamer trunk on the floor about fifteen feet behind the altar. El-Ghaffar opened it, reached in, and brought out a garment of black cloth with red adornments sewn onto it. With a quick, practiced motion, he slipped it over his head and passed his arms through the armholes so that the robe fell into place, its hem exactly one inch above the floor. Stark noticed that the symbols on the robe were the same as those on the altar cloth; only the color scheme was reversed. El-Ghaffar bent over the trunk again and came up with a skullcap in the same scarlet color as the altar cloth. As the Arab carefully positioned the cap atop his head, Stark noticed that it bore the "infinity" symbol in black, exactly in the center.

Hassan el-Ghaffar took his position behind the altar, making sure that both his feet were well within the circle. He opened the ancient-looking book to a page that had been marked with a black ribbon. Looking over at his guests, he said, "I will perform the ceremony in Arabic, since my *grimoire*"—he reverently touched the book—"is written in that language. Also, it is my native tongue and I am least likely to make any mistakes that way. It will be incomprehensible to you, but be patient. You will find things becoming interesting before long."

From the depths of his robe, el-Ghaffar produced an ordinary Zippo lighter and lit the altar's two candles. Then he passed his left hand over them several times, reciting something in a language that Stark assumed was Arabic, although the words themselves meant nothing to him.

El-Ghaffar suddenly stopped speaking, drew in a deep breath through his nostrils, and blew it out forcefully through his mouth.

Seems pretty fucking stupid, blowing out the candles, Stark thought, *after just going through all the trouble of lighting the damn things*.

But the candles were not extinguished by el-Ghaffar's vigorous exhalation. Instead, *something* appeared to flash through the air from the altar candles over to where the pentagram had been drawn in the floor. An instant later, the five candles at the pentagram's points sprouted tiny blossoms of flame and were soon burning brightly.

Stark stared at the newly ignited candles for a second, then, on a hunch, shifted his gaze just in time to catch the glance that the Arab sent his way. *Yeah, I thought so. Wants to see how well the conjuring trick is going over. Well, it's not bad, although I think I saw something as good last year in Vegas. You're going to have to do better than that, buddy-boy, if you want to impress me.*

Nothing very intriguing happened over the next half-hour or so. El-Ghaffar read aloud from what he'd called his *grimoire*, rang the bell from time to time—always for five strokes on each occasion—made mysterious-looking gestures in the air and generally bored Stark half to death.

Then, finally, he lit the brazier.

He first dropped in powders from the ceramic bowls. Stark noticed that each substance was of a different color: first there was blue, followed by green, then brown, then, finally, red. After adding the last ingredient, el-Ghaffar held his hands, palms down, over the brazier, read another few words from the book, then clapped his hands together, hard.

The material in the brazier burst into flame. It burned brightly for a few moments, then subsided to a glow that gave vent to a rather thick, gray smoke.

Stark had been watching the procedure closely. *That's a little better*, he thought. *I didn't see anything drop into the bowl while he was clapping. Of course, some substances will spontaneously combust when you combine them. Or maybe there's a heating element hidden inside that brazier. But it's a pretty good trick, anyway.*

El-Ghaffar's voice was louder now, and had taken on the rhythmic quality of a chant. Among the incomprehensible Arabic words, Stark was starting to hear one that he recognized. He had seen plenty of news footage of various Arab crowds around the world denouncing America as "the great Satan," so the word *Shaitan* was familiar to him. El-Ghaffar was using the word frequently now.

There were no windows or ventilation ducts in the basement, but, even so, the smoke from the brazier was moving now, flowing inexorably toward the pentagram some twenty feet away.

Now you're talking, Stark thought. *I can't figure this trick out at all. Wonder if MM knows how he's doing it?*

He glanced at Mary Margaret Doyle and saw that her expression was serious, verging on grim. Her eyes were narrowed, and a vein in her neck was visibly pulsing in response to the pounding of her heart. Stark decided to save his smartass question for later.

The gray smoke was gathering in the center of the pentagram now, and had grown noticeably thicker. El-Ghaffar's chanting was reduced to one word, and he was saying it over and over, louder and louder: "Sargatanas. Sargatanas. Sargatanas. Sargatanas! Sargatanas! Sargatanas!! SARGATANAS!"

The smoke in the pentagram's center was swirling, congealing, forming and reforming, and finally took on a shape that was vaguely humanoid. Then the gray mist began to dissipate, soon leaving the figure in plain view.

Stark's suspicion that he had been watching a crudely produced magician's illusion disappeared—not unlike the smoke that had been shrouding the pentagram. His skepticism has been replaced by a blend of awe and fear and disgust.

The center of the pentagram was occupied by a rotting corpse. At least, it *should* have been a corpse, except that it was standing, apparently under its own power, and the head was questing back and forth, as if it could see all three of them even though the eye sockets contained nothing but a steady stream of maggots that seemed to be issuing forth from the putrescent skull cavity.

The figure was naked, which gave Stark ample opportunity to observe the precise condition of its decaying flesh, to note the places where the flesh had disappeared completely to reveal white bone matter, and to consider the number and variety of necrophages (beetles, worms, and the maggots, among others) that were finding the unquiet corpse a tasty treat.

The grotesque sight had been present only for a few seconds when its odor hit them like a great polluted tide. It was a smell that the liberators of the Treblinka death camp would have recognized all too well—an amalgam of rot and filth and shit and decay that almost made Stark and Mary Margaret vomit.

Hassan el-Ghaffar appeared displeased, but not especially surprised. "Hearken unto me, disobedient one!" he said sternly, in English now. "Thou wert summoned, as per agreement, and bidden to assume a pleasing form. Do so—now!"

Despite the lack of both lips and tongue, the thing in the pentagram answered, in a voice that was both deep and cultured, rather like James Earl Jones at his most charming. "My form is pleasing to *me*," the voice rumbled.

"Well, it pleases neither me nor my companions," el-Ghaffar said. "Change now, lest I smite thee!" He picked up the long, curved sword from the altar and held the blade an inch or so above one of the candles.

"Peace, peace, I hear and obey. Act not in haste."

For Stark, it was the height of incongruity to hear that voice, so alive and vigorous, coming from something that you might expect to find buried deep in a Mafia-owned landfill.

Then, in an instant, the image of decay and death was gone, replaced by something that was manifestly, defiantly alive. The sculptors who ornamented the Parthenon could not have envisioned a figure of human perfection to rival what now stood in the center of the pentagram. The man stood about six feet, with a cap of tight black curls that matched the eyebrows, which, in turn, perched elegantly above piercing blue eyes. The body was literally perfect—muscular, tight, tanned, and toned, without a scar or blemish. This was not the extreme overdevelopment of a bodybuilder, but rather strength and speed and flexibility brought to the epitome of grace and form usually associates with statues of Ancient Greece's athletes.

And since the man was naked, it was not difficult

to observe that his sexual endowment was entirely consistent with the rest of his physical perfection. Indeed, even as confirmed a heterosexual as Howard Stark found it difficult not to stare at the large, erect penis that protruded from below the flat, muscular stomach.

"Thy form is now much more pleasing to the eye, not to mention the nose," el-Ghaffar said. "Whilst thou art briefly among us, great Sargatanas, I will ask of thee certain simple tasks, well within thy powers to perform." He gestured toward Stark and Mary Margaret Doyle. "These companions of mine would know of thy power, thy wisdom, thy knowledge of this world's affairs, even of those things which certain kings and princes regard as their most closely held secrets. In return, I shall reward thee as promised in our bargain, made freely and duly signed by us both, in mutual obligation."

"*I don't think that will be necessary.*"

The voice was Mary Margaret Doyle's, the first time she had spoken in almost an hour. Both men stared at her in amazement, which quickly turned to shock as—almost casually—she stepped outside the circle.

Stark was mystified. She had appeared to be taking this business seriously from the beginning, whereas Stark's suspicion had evolved into tentative belief only in the last few minutes. *Is she trying to debunk this whole thing? Is el-Ghaffar a fraud, after all? Did she notice something that I've missed?*

If Stark was confused, el-Ghaffar looked stupefied. He gaped, open-mouthed, as Mary Margaret Doyle walked briskly over to the pentagram. The demon trapped inside it seemed to be the only one who did not find her behavior unusual. Instead, he appeared to be watching with great interest.

She approached one of the candles burning at the pentagram's five points, and, with a quick sideways move from her left foot, kicked it over.

This brought Hassan el-Ghaffar out of his shocked silence. "You stupid cow, what are you *doing*?" he screeched. "Put that back where it was, immediately! Quickly, before it goes out! Do it now! *Do you hear me, you fucking cunt*?"

Mary Margaret Doyle turned to look at el-Ghaffar. Instead of the shocked and angry expression that Stark expected to see as a response to the Arab's obscene insults, there was only a wide smile on her face. The smile remained in place as she glanced down to check the tipped-over candle's position, raised her left foot again—and, in one quick motion, stomped the flame into extinction.

What followed, an instant later, was a sudden release of energy that knocked all three of the humans off their feet. There was no sound of detonation, no flying debris, just a force of immense power that burst from the center of the pentagram, and if there was any noise from it at all, it was something that resembled a cry of triumph, although it was a sound that had never issued from any human throat.

El-Ghaffar was the first to regain his feet, although he did so slowly, awkwardly, like a punch-drunk boxer determined to answer the bell for the last round.

Blinking rapidly, he looked toward the pentagram, where the four remaining candles had been reduced to smoking pools of melted wax, and saw that the same fate had befallen the two candles that had been burning atop the altar.

Hassan el-Ghaffar let loose a long groan that combined despair and panic in roughly equal measures, as his befogged brain finally caught up with the dreadful reality that his eyes were showing him.

The center of the pentagram was empty.

Find out what happens next in
SYMPATHY FOR THE DEVIL,
coming soon

"Black Magic Woman is the best manuscript I've ever been asked to read. Keep an eye on Justin Gustainis. You'll be seeing more of him soon."
Jim Butcher

BLACK MAGIC WOMAN
A MORRIS AND CHASTAIN INVESTIGATION
JUSTIN GUSTAINIS

www.solarisbooks.com ISBN: 978-1-84416-541-4

Supernatural investigator Quincey Morris and his partner, white witch Libby Chastain, are called in to help free a desperate family from a deadly curse that appears to date back to the Salem Witch Trials. To release the family from danger they must find the root of the curse, a black witch with a terrible grudge that holds the family in her power.

⊙ SOLARIS DARK FANTASY

NATASHA RHODES

THE LAST ANGEL

A KAYLA STEELE NOVEL

www.solarisbooks.com　UK ISBN: 978-1-84416-646-6　US ISBN: 978-1-84416-577-3

An angel is found murdered on the streets of Sunset Boulevard. To the media gossip mongers, it's the biggest story ever. To the Hunters, an underground monster-fighting hit-squad, it's just another case of "whodunnit". To Kayla Steele, their newest member, it means a last chance to bring her murdered fiancé back from the dead, and to others with a far darker purpose it is the means to destroy the human race.

⊙ SOLARIS DARK FANTASY